D0394085

The Star
of Istanbul

Also by Robert Olen Butler

The Alleys of Eden
Sun Dogs
Countrymen of Bones
On Distant Ground
Wabash
The Deuce
A Good Scent from a Strange Mountain
They Whisper
Tabloid Dreams
The Deep Green Sea
Mr. Spaceman
Fair Warning
Had a Good Time
From Where You Dream: The Process of Writing Fiction
(Janet Burroway, Editor)
Severance
Intercourse
Hell
A Small Hotel
The Hot Country

The Star of Istanbul

A Christopher Marlowe Cobb Thriller

Robert Olen Butler

The Mysterious Press

an imprint of Grove/Atlantic, Inc.
New York

A portion of this book originally appeared in *Narrative* magazine.

Published simultaneously in Canada
Printed in the United States of America

FIRST EDITION

ISBN-13: 978-0-8021-2155-4
The Mysterious Press
an imprint of Grove/Atlantic, Inc.
154 West 14th Street
New York, NY 10011

Distributed by Publsihers Group West

www.groveatlantic.com

13 14 15 16 17   10 9 8 7 6 5 4 3 2 1

For Kelly, my wife.
These words are for her, through her.

Acknowledgments

Thanks to Dr. Wesley Scoles, my physician, my friend, and my go-to Doctor of Mayhem. To Jake Reiss, for the occasional writing space in the Booksmith's back room, for his support of Kit Cobb, and for a certain, splendid personnel decision. And to Lou Boxer, who read every word.

1

I did not expect to find him until we were on board, this Walter Brauer. I knew where he was booked in first class: en suite on A Deck, with my stateroom just around the corner. In the jostle of the crowd at Pier 54, I was content not even to think about him. If he didn't show, that would be Trask's problem. I'd never been late to a war, and here the world was, nine months into the Big One and no one had seen a single Christopher Cobb byline from the action. That was Trask's doing.

No. More precisely, it was my country's doing, so I guess I wasn't as heated up as I know I'm sounding. After my little adventure in Mexico the previous spring, my country had called on me to take some time off and train for the covert work I was happy to be asked to do. But I was also happy to get up on the back of a great greyhound of a steamship and run to the action at last. And I'd still get to be a war correspondent, even as I played this other part as well.

So the quay was jammed and the melting pot was aboil and its ingredients were separating. Thickening at the forward gangway were the third-class kersey caps and head scarves and threadbare motley; aft, the flowered straw hats and derbies and the Sears serge suits of second class; and amidships, the veiled bonnets and the lambskin gloves and the bespoke three-piece sack suits of the first-class swells.

I was traveling with this latter group, and even we were being stopped one by one at the bottom of our gangway stairs, where every parcel, every purse, every box and bag was checked for German bombs. The ship security was tight, and as for the tough Hun talk in the morning papers about it being open season in the North Atlantic on any ship flying a British flag, well, the U-boats had never sunk a vessel doing more than fourteen knots—nor could they—and they'd never dare to sink a passenger ship, especially with Americans on board, for fear it would finally grow Woody Wilson a backbone. I was content to be frisked and stamped and passed along, but it turned out that the strong lavender smell behind me was the pomade slicking down the black, center-parted hair of Walter Brauer, his hat in his hand in calculated deference to the uniformed bull checking us through.

I recognized him from the photos Trask showed me in my last briefing: faintly jowled, densely eyebrowed, wide in the shoulders and short in the legs. The black of his hair was intense—no doubt dyed, as he was pushing fifty—and with the topping of lavender grease he was the very image, it seemed to me, of a petty confidence man working widowed owners of boardinghouses. But in fact Walter Brauer was a German-American who'd some years ago left the U.S. and who'd suddenly shown up in Washington on the sly and was known to Trask and his boys as an agent of the German secret service. What wasn't known was what he was up to, his having stayed in America for not quite two weeks before boarding a steamship to rush back across the North Atlantic. And since it was time for the Chicago *Post-Express* and the U.S. government to jointly send me abroad anyway, the *Federales* thought I might as well get my feet wet following this guy. Maybe even introduce myself as the newsman I was known to be.

All in good time. I stayed just ahead of him through the whole process, with the purser and with the baggage steward, and then I lingered at the foot of the Grand Staircase. I affected an interest in the two electric elevators in the staircase's central well, not trying to enter the just-arrived mahogany car but nodding at the operator and deferring to the handful of women who crowded in. The elevator clanked and ground its way upward and I waited for Brauer, examining the gilded rosettes and medallions on the elevator grillwork as if intending sometime to capture the detail of them in a newspaper story—as indeed I figured I might, to warm up my byline with a "Running the U-Boat Gauntlet" feature story at the other end of our journey.

I saw him in my periphery and I moved away and up the plush, roseate carpet of the staircase. I thought he'd taken casual note of me and it was good to have his first impression be of *him* following *me*. On the A Deck we passed through the first-class writing room and library, held up by Corinthian columns, filled with chairs and writing tables done in eighteenth-century rectilinear simplicity, and cramped into a horseshoe shape by the massive intrusion of the prowside wall, behind which lurked the number two funnel.

I led us along the starboard leg of the horseshoe and out the forward door and into the electric-lit passageway. I passed what I knew to be Brauer's en suite rooms, A23 and A21, and I moved on down the corridor and turned into the transverse passageway. A few steps later, beyond a short, forward-heading corridor from which a stewardess approached with an arm full of towels, I arrived at the door of my own single-room cabin, A12. Still keenly conscious of him, from around the corner, I distantly heard Brauer shutting his door. The steward-ess rustled past me and turned into the portside passageway. A rich, vibrantly modulated woman's voice down the way greeted her: "Ah yes, thank you for these."

"Ma'am," the stewardess said.

The woman's voice said, "Please put them in the suite. I'm bound for the deck."

Her voice lingered in my head for a moment: the voice of an ac-tress, I thought. And then, a little later, my bags unpacked and stowed and my own towel poised before my wet face, I looked at myself in the mirror over the cabin washbasin and I was the one who seemed like an actor. The face before me was no longer mine. I was made up. The water clung to my dense but close-cropped beard, the first beard I'd ever had for more than a few weeks. I'd worn this one for nearly a year. Ever since Mexico. What made me pause here to con-sider myself before a mirror, as if in a scene from a dime novel, was that the bearded one was called by my name, Christopher Marlowe Cobb. It *was* me. And the beardless face beneath, which had always been mine, was now the face of the invented character, from a play that was yet to be written. That face bore a scar on the left cheek: a long, thin scimitar of a scar. For the character, a *Schmiss,* the bragging scar of a German aristocrat from his university days in a fencing club. This one earned by me, however, on a dangerous afternoon in *estado* Coahuila, under the watchful eye of Pancho Villa. The beard of Cobb was consciously put on and could easily be taken off. This other man's scar was permanent.

I dried my face, rubbing hard at it, and I put my shirt and tie and sack coat back on, and I went out of my cabin and took the starboard corridor aft, passing Brauer's suite, not pausing to listen at the door because of a young couple—aflurry with handbags and exclamations of pleasure—entering the other en suite stateroom. I edged by them and then turned into the transverse corridor just before the writing room. I pressed on toward the door ahead of me, and my thought of that door made me realize what had, in addition to Brauer, led me out of my cabin: the woman with the actress voice. If she was bound for our deck, this was the door she would have used.

I stepped out onto the A Deck promenade, and it was largely a strolling and sunning deck, with the railings taken up by lifeboats. More completely so in the three years since the *Titanic* went down: the radial davits had been raised, and stacked beneath each suspended standard lifeboat were an additional three collapsible boats. Even the previously empty railing near the mainmast was blocked by stacks of collapsibles. Indeed, this deck had mostly ship crew moving about. At this point, the passengers seeking a deck instead of a drink likely wanted a railing from which to watch the embarkation.

There was one more deck for the first-class travelers to promenade. I emerged on B Deck. It was more crowded than I'd expected. First class was only half booked in this wartime civilian crossing, but the whole long length of the railing was shoulder to shoulder and there was a throng of others on the promenade as well. I realized the first all-ashore whistle had not yet sounded; the visitors were still on board.

If there'd only been the loose gathering of swells I'd expected, it would have been interesting to stroll along and try to guess which body belonged to the woman's voice I'd heard. But now I focused on casually looking for Brauer. If he was even here. I moved forward on the promenade, keeping close to the deck wall, and ahead was a particularly large grouping of visitors circled up. I recognized newsmen at once. I drew near as an intense flurry of questions arose, with one male voice prevailing. I caught only a few of his words, the end of a question: ". . . a new film?" The reporters fell silent and no doubt all raised their pens, and from the unseen center of this circle came a woman's voice.

It was her.

I slid along the outer edge of the circle of newsmen, looking for a sight line between heads, as she responded with words that sounded offhand and faintly put-upon but nevertheless were ringingly projected, even through the wall of newsmen. Yes, an actress. "I'm going abroad for personal reasons," she said. "No films."

And I found a place to see through three layers of necks and shoulders. Not just an actress. A star. Her face was recognizable from the magazine shelves of any newsdealer in almost any month of the year: Selene Bourgani. She wore a rolling hemp sailor hat as large as a porthole, with Tuscan trim edging the brim, and with her hair hidden in some thick, black, invisible roll beneath it, all of which framed her dusky thin face with its vast, dark eyes, its wide mouth in a perpetual almost-pout, a face everyone on the deck had seen, at some point or other, flickering before them in a movie theater. *The Forest Nymph.* *Sister of the Sea.* *The Girl from Athens.*

When it was clear she had nothing further to say about her upcoming film plans, the voices all rose together again and the reporters' bodies shifted and I lost my view of her. I slid on along the circle, trying to recapture the vision of Selene Bourgani, whose sad and uplifting life story played over and over in the periodical press.

I passed the apex of the journalistic circle, and as I moved back toward the railing and the crowd grew thicker, I glanced away. There, quite near, leaning at the railing with his back to the dock, not looking toward the impromptu press conference but away, down the promenade, with an air of casual indifference, was Walter Brauer. The indifference was another calculated pose, it felt to me. What man would not be interested in a woman the press called one of the world's most beautiful? He was holding a cigarette—rather effetely between the tips of his thumb and forefinger with his other fingers lifted—and he was blowing a plume of smoke toward the bow.

I took all this in while Selene Bourgani denied an interest in the London stage. I looked away from Brauer. I made another step to the side and another and I could see her again, in profile now, her long, straight nose beautifully at odds with the usual standards of beauty of this age. I thought: *I bet her feet are large too and her hands and she is all the more beautiful for defying this world's conventions in these details.* And I was still entranced by her nose, absorbing even the precise curve where its bridge met her brow, a perfect fit, I fancied, for my fingertip, when she said, "I am a film actress."

She'd hardly finished the sentence when one reporter leaped in before another hubbub of questions could begin. "Miss Bourgani," he said, "the world is at war."

He was speaking from somewhere to her left. She turned her face instantly to him—in my general direction as well—and her dark eyes riveted him and his voice snagged as if he were suddenly beginning to choke. He managed to stammer a couple of meaningless vowel sounds and then he fell silent.

The other reporters all laughed. But it was a sympathetic laugh. Hers was a face that could stop a thousand ships.

"Yes?" she said, encouraging him to go on with his question, giving the impression that she'd spoken softly, though I could hear her clearly.

"Miss Bourgani," the reporter began again. "In light of the German threats and this being a British liner, are you afraid to be traveling on the *Lusitania?*"

She turned her face away from the questioner, the turn energized by a sharp, mirthless laugh, the sort of laugh that suggests some little private irony.

Then she fell silent, and everyone in the crowd fell silent with her. She let the silence tick on, consciously playing it, no doubt. Ever the actress, her timing was splendid: she slowly surveyed us until that precise, peak moment when all her listeners had finally Brownie-snapped their bodies and shallowed their breathing to a stop. Only then did she speak. "I am afraid of nothing," she said.

2

I woke somewhere in the dark early hours of what would be our first full day at sea, woke to the sounding of the *Lusitania*'s forward triple-chime whistle. I dozed off, but a few minutes later the whistle sounded once more, a harmonized choir of basso baritones crying out in the night. My mind began to work, and I knew I would remain sleepless for a long while. My initial thinking was pleasantly desirous: I wondered if she was awake in her bed as well, just around the corner, waiting for the whistle to blow again, quaking very faintly from the distant, vibrant working of our turbines. I found myself afraid I would never have a chance to speak to her beyond a passing hello.

I should have been thinking about Walter Brauer. What he was doing. What might have been in his mind on deck yesterday morning. And then I grew afraid that I was ill-suited for the work my country had asked me to do.

I was rushing across the North Atlantic to war, but with an intention I'd never had before. I needed to sort out what I was doing, give myself a pep talk. I was a reporter. A war correspondent. I knew how to look for news, for the truth. It had always been my job to snoop around, and because I knew how to do that well, in Mexico I'd happened upon news of deep importance to Washington. Private importance. So now the process was inverted. Now the snooping would be for Washington and I would just happen upon stories for the *Post-Express*. I wanted to do this. I had seen too much of the savage impulses of men, impulses that we ultimately could not deal with as individuals. I was lucky to be an American. We Americans were also men and could foul things up pretty badly, but our declared ideal was to find a way to make it possible to stop the savagery. To govern without savagery. To live with other governments without savagery. To live with ourselves without savagery. It is what we believe. And so I remained Christopher Cobb, reporter, even as I began to play a more important role in the world. But I was used to finding things out by following the acts of men that are clear to see, out in the open, with their immediate goals readily understandable. This work I was doing now was different.

The *Lusitania*'s whistle sounded again.

Now my mind was all shadow and fog.

For all this thinking, I didn't feel very peppy.

I rose and put on my pants and shoes and overcoat, intending to get some air on deck. I stepped out of my cabin and went to the right and then turned left into the portside corridor. Bourgani's direction, not Brauer's. There were two staterooms en suite along here, but I remembered the deck plan from when I booked my passage. Only the aft suite had its own bath. She would surely be in that one. I approached the door, treading softly. A20 and A22. I stopped. I listened. But all I heard was my heart thudding in my ear like the engine of our ship deep below. This was foolish. I moved on and through the door and out onto the A Deck promenade.

I could barely make out the lifeboat hanging a few paces before me. The ship was wrapped in a gray felt fog. But I stepped away from the door, turned aft, walked into the murk. It was as if the inside of my own head had billowed out to surround me. Inside the fog, I found James P. Trask, the President's man in charge of covert service, talking to me again.

We met a week ago in Washington, at the massive, limestone and terra cotta Raleigh Hotel on Twelfth and Pennsylvania. The after-dinner trade was waning and we began at the mahogany bar but soon carried our Gin Rickeys to a far corner table to speak in private. No one was nearby. High above us, from the center of the roof, a searchlight was lighting up the Washington Monument half a mile to our southwest.

Trask lifted his drink and I did likewise. Each glass held half of the same lime. We touched glasses and took a good swallow. Trask said, "These were invented back in '83 at Shoomaker's, around the corner from all you newspaper boys on Fourteenth. By old Colonel Joe Rickey. He owned the bar but he was also a professional glad-hander and arm-twister. Inventing this, he almost redeemed his whole tribe of lobbyists."

"To Colonel Joe," I said, lifting my glass again.

"Colonel Joe," Trask said. We drank, and he said, "I'd have taken you there but it's still full of reporters."

James Trask was hard to read in any way that he wasn't consciously intending. As befitted his job, I supposed. I was pretty good at reading a man. He delivered this last declaration by angling his square-jawed, man's-man face slightly to the right and drawing out the word "reporters" like slowly pulling a piece of chewing gum off the sole of his shoe. He was clean shaven and—perhaps influenced by my new relationship to my left cheek—I found this a little deceitful in him. Trying too hard to suggest he was transparent.

He was tweaking my nose. I said, "I don't hang around with reporters anymore." Not true, but he knew I was lying and he knew I knew he knew I was lying, and that was the best return-tweak I could manage at the moment.

He smiled. "Don't change your public ways for me," he said. "To the world, you have to be Christopher Cobb."

I did a slow, seemingly thoughtful stroke of my beard, my thumb pressing my right cheek and my fingers descending my left.

Trask knew what I was most conscious of, even before I realized it myself. It was under my hand.

"That was a fortunate little accident down in Mexico," he said, referring to my scar.

I didn't like him reading me. I turned the gesture into an extend-ing of my forefinger, which I lifted and ran from my lower lip to the bottom of my chin, and which I then did once again, as if my intention all along had been simply to smooth my whiskers down. I didn't really expect him to believe it.

"How's your German coming along?" he asked.

"Pretty good."

"You've got an ear for it, I understand."

"I do."

"Are you ready to work?"

"I am."

"I've already informed your paper."

My publisher—that great American mogul, Paul Maccabee Griswold—was an old-style Democrat, the sort who worshipped Grover Cleveland, and he had big political ambitions; he was only too happy to have me play this grand game for his own private political credit.

Trask took an envelope from the inside pocket of his impeccable black suit with the thin, gray stripe, the suit as snuggly, perfectly fit to his boxer's body as the Woolworth Building's glazed terra-cotta. Inside were the photos of Brauer. His jowly face in a formal head and shoulders pose, likely taken for a passport. A snapshot of him standing dressed in academic robes in a grassy courtyard with the arches of a Gothic colonnade behind him.

"Walter Brauer," Trask said. "German. Technically an American citizen. Travels on our passport. But he's been a lecturer at King's College in London for more than a decade. One of the side benefits of our president's pacifism is our present occupation of the German embassy in London. We're looking after their affairs. Playing go-between. Not that my office takes our role as the Swiss too seriously. We've been carefully examining whatever the Huns left behind. I'm happy to say that Prince Lichnowsky and his boys made a rather hasty departure. Though I should point out we're being careful to leave even the prince's cigarettes in their silver case on his desk, exactly as they were last August, in the event the Germans return someday."

"Think they'll fall for that?" I said.

Trask winked at me.

The *Lusitania*'s whistle bellowed me back to the deck. I pulled up my coat collar. I'd not put on a hat and I ran my hand through my hair, which had gone damp from the fog. But the chill was okay with me. I'd spent plenty of time in hot countries these past few years. The whistle faded and then instantly sounded again, as if this were in response to something looming in our path. But what could they possibly see from the helm until it was too late? I could barely see beyond the stretch of my arm. It was all a yellow blur along an invisible deck wall. On the railing side, in a vague, somewhat more coalesced wedge of the universal gray, were an electric light and a lifeboat only a few paces away, but in this fog their identity was nothing more than informed guesswork. I swelled with that kinesthetic burn I'd always felt before the clash of men on a battlefield. The *Titanic* was too much with me.

I needed to focus on my assignment, which was how I managed my war nerves in Nicaragua and Macedonia and Mexico. I stood in the fog and continued drinking with Trask in the bar at the Raleigh.

"He's an agent of the German secret service," he said. But he didn't go on. Instead, he drained the last of his Gin Rickey and then lifted his empty glass to me. "We should have another round of these, don't you think?"

Trask had done this before. Even in our first meeting, he would suddenly decide, in the midst of our conversation, to throw me off balance by making me ask for what I clearly needed to know next. I should have waited him out at the Raleigh, but I wasn't in a mood to play. At least I put it to him in a way he didn't expect.

I said, "What does he lecture about?"

Trask let me see the fleeting dilation of surprise in his eyes. He smiled. "Oriental studies," he said.

"Meaning?"

"He spent his childhood in Jerusalem. His father was in the export business there before he brought the family to Providence."

"So he picked up some languages."

"Arabic. Persian. Turkish."

"He lectures on this."

"And on Islam. He's an expert."

This was the telling thing. The Kaiser had been wooing the Islamic nations since the end of the last century. And in November, three months into the war, in Constantinople, the Turkish Sultan Mehmed V, as Caliph, declared a worldwide *jihad*, a Holy War, on the British Empire and all its allies. The Ottoman Empire embraced Willie, who had been claiming a spiritual affinity with Mohammed for fifteen years.

Trask said, "He's used his expertise to make some friends at their Foreign Office. The Brits have one hundred million Muslims in their empire."

"What's he doing over here?"

"That's the question."

"His family?"

Trask shrugged. "The ones who stayed are dead. He arrived in Washington a week ago. We always watch the Huns on Thomas Circle pretty closely, and Brauer went straight to the embassy. But somehow he slipped out again without us seeing him. We don't know what he did here. But we do know he's booked passage back to Britain. That gives you a week to get ready to sail. You've got a first-class cabin right near his. First of May. The *Lusitania*."

A form loomed suddenly out of the murk, almost upon me, a man, a big man, and I jumped back and to the side, throwing myself against the deck wall, but the man did not lunge for me, he kept striding on past, too fast, given the fog, just a fool with a British accent, throwing a "Sorry, old man" over his shoulder, taking his after-midnight constitutional. Why didn't Trask just expose Brauer to the Brits and let them handle him? Because they were like this guy, rushing in the dark. They had their own agenda. If the world is going to blow up on us, we need to know for ourselves what we're dealing with. And Wilson still wanted to keep us out of the fighting. The way they were all digging in over there, maybe he was right. And maybe I was trained now for this work. I knew how we were supposed to think: figure it out for ourselves, keep to it to ourselves, do what we need to protect ourselves.

My beard was wet. My left cheek beneath was cold except for the curve of the impervious scar tissue. The fog had etched my *Schmiss* into my mind.

And now my eyesight was clearing, as if I were waking from a heavy sleep. The teak deck was rapidly appearing beneath me, before me, stretching forward into the clarifying dark; the lifeboats shaped sharply into themselves all along the way; the electric light glowed nakedly on the deck wall. We were moving faster. I could feel the subtle new vibration beneath my feet. Full ahead.

I was beginning to shiver.

I moved down the promenade to the forward door and I went in. I turned at once into the portside corridor and ran both hands over my beard and through my hair and wiped away the condensing mist on my coat and I moved forward. As I passed Selene Bourgani's door I spoke aloud—louder perhaps than I would have if there actually were someone else in the corridor with me, which there wasn't, but I spoke as if there were—I said, "We're out of the fog now. Any danger is passed."

I felt instantly stupid. I pressed on down the corridor. I thought she might be awake and worried inside. We all remembered the *Titanic*. And we all knew there was a war. For our ship to be bellowing through the night, blindly rushing, this could be a worrisome thing even for a woman who says she is afraid of nothing.

I passed on and I neared the turn of the corridor—I would soon be safely out of sight—but behind me I heard the opening of a cabin door, and I had no choice but to stop, which I did. I would turn. After all, this possibility was also why I'd spoken.

I turned.

She was standing just outside her door, in a beam of electric light from the wall, her hair twisted up high on her head. I took a step toward her, and another. I stopped. She hadn't invited me, but I took this much of a liberty by reflex from the hammer thump of her beauty. Her eyes were as dark as the North Atlantic. She was wearing a crimson kimono with twin golden dragons plunging from her breasts to her knees.

"I'm sorry," I said. "I hope I didn't disturb you."

She looked over her shoulder, as if preparing to sneer: *So where is the person you spoke to?*

But she quickly turned back to me.

How the hell do I know what a woman is about to say? Perhaps she'd looked to make sure we were alone together.

"Any danger is passed," I said, feeling even more stupid saying this a second time.

She nodded. "So I've heard." But her voice was soft-edged. Appreciative.

"All right," I said. "I'll confess. There was no one around. I spoke it aloud in passing in case you were worried."

She nodded again. Faintly. As if in thanks. She was far more subtle in this corridor than she was on the screen.

I grew up backstage in a thousand theaters and watched my mother being a star and I knew how she sized herself for each stage she was on. Since film actresses all seemed to be playing to a vast auditorium, though their faces were ten feet tall—even the great Selene Bourgani— I was surprised she knew how to seem real in this corridor. As for my own face, I had no control at all. It was flushing hot and, I suspected, it was even turning red.

"I wasn't worried," she said.

"No," I said. "Of course not."

"But thank you."

I nodded. Too big a nod, as if I were a hambone of a film actor.

I collected myself and steadied my body and stood there for a long moment, and the moment went on as she stayed motionless where she was, standing in her kimono in her doorway.

Finally she said, in what felt like a whisper but which filled my head, "Good night."

"Good night," I said, and I turned away from Selene, who, according to my childhood Bulfinch, if not the evidence of my own eyes a few moments ago, was the Greek goddess of the moon.

3

After I'd gone to my cabin following our release from the fog, I slept. But I was already awake at the distant sound of six bells being rung on the morning watch—7:00 A.M. by the landlubber time zone we carried along with us. The bell had hardly stopped vibrating when I heard the slip of something under the door. I needed a war; I needed the whisk of rifle rounds past my ears. Here's how I knew: I thought it might be a note from her. It was, instead, an invitation to dine with the captain at his table that evening.

I did not see Brauer again or Selene until the night came and I was dressed in a suitcase-wrinkled monkey suit, packed at Trask's insistence for any secret-agent contingency, the thought of which had made me consider letting my country down to just chase the gunfire. But I packed the tux and now I tied my black tie and squared my shoulders and took the main staircase down three levels to the Saloon Deck. Indeed, I had a saloon ticket to a saloon cabin and I'd spent time very early this morning on the saloon promenade and I was, all in all, a saloon passenger, "saloon" being what the Brits sometimes called first class. But when I walked into the grand dining room, my first wish—a devout one—was that this would somehow suddenly turn into a good old American saloon, with swinging doors and spittoons. I did, however, know how to act this other role I'd been cast in.

I took three steps into the place and stopped. It was swell, all right. The main floor of the dining room, here on D Deck, was decorated in harmony with the writing room and library I'd passed through yesterday, though in a more extravagant way: ivory-colored walls and the straight-lined simplicity of eighteenth-century neoclassicism, with Louis XVI chairs upholstered in rose-colored horsehair and with similarly roseate Brussels carpet runners and with more Corinthian columns, these rising from the oak parquet floor up through the front edge of a large open oval space where the C Deck upper dining room encircled us diners below. The columns rose on to their capital at the base of a floor-high dome, done in ivory-white and gilt and with oil paint-rendered cherubs in tableaux of the four seasons. The dome sat in the center of B Deck, the high-heavenly vault of a three-story floating cathedral of fancyman's food.

The place was full of tuxedoed men and gowned and bejeweled women. They milled murmuringly about, finding their tables, drinking cocktails. I stepped farther in, alert for a center-parted, hennaed head of hair. It didn't take me long to see Brauer. He was at one end of the massive brass-fit veneered mahogany sideboard on the forward center wall. He was alone there, leaning with his back to the sideboard as if it were a bar, but with only a waiter nearby, arranging tumblers on a tray. Brauer held a glass with what looked like a couple of fingers of whiskey—no doubt a good whiskey, in this joint. He did not seem uncomfortable in his solitude. Rather, he seemed quite content to watch the swells milling about before him.

My assignment was too vague: What's he up to? My reporter's instincts had been most famously employed in figuring out the next move of bands of armed men representing governments or organized factions aspiring to become governments. I knew what they were up to from the get-off: destroy the opposing bands of armed men and seize a physical objective on the way to seizing power. I had to slide back to my earlier reporting days to figure out what to do now. I had to think of Brauer as I would a dirty Chicago politician. But with the politician there were plenty of sources to go to. Enemies. Co-conspirators. Facilitators. Victims. And the überobjective of the man I was after was always money, which made certain lines of inquiry pretty clear. With Brauer, on this ship, there was no one to go to but him. And money was unlikely to be the coal in his engine.

So it would just be him and me. I figured my strategy was to treat him like a source for a larger story, somebody who knows something I need to know and doesn't want to give it up, so I don't let him know I want it. I strolled off in his direction.

But I didn't go straight to him. I bellied up to the sideboard as if I expected it to be the bar and he was a couple of paces to my right and I looked around like I was puzzled, like where was the bartender, like where were the taps and the bottles, like what is this useless piece of furniture, anyway. "Huh," I said aloud, and I turned around the way he was turned, and he wasn't looking in my direction. It was like I wasn't even there.

I checked out his drink a bit more closely. Certainly that was a good Scotch. He may have been an expert on Islam but I was thinking he wasn't a convert. His tuxedo looked like it fit him pretty well and he was used to wearing it. Maybe a big cheese academician at King's College who spent all day in his academic robes was used to monkeying up at night to drink with his fellow lecturers in a first-class British saloon where nobody ever raised his voice.

I figured I better stop disliking this guy so actively if I wanted to get something out of him.

"From across the room this sure looked like the bar—and a good one." I said this aloud, keeping my eyes forward, as his were, but keeping my attention on him in my peripheral vision. I'd spoken in half a voice so that I could simply have been a guy avid for a drink talking mostly to myself.

I saw him turn his face in my direction. I waited a beat and then looked at him. He let our eyes meet. "Sorry to bother you," I said, "but I was admiring your whiskey and thinking you got it here."

He looked at his glass as if he were slightly surprised to find it in his hand. "No," he said. "Someone will inquire shortly."

He had a faint wisp of a British accent, like the smell of pipe smoke in a tweed jacket. "Good," I said and I looked away from him.

I thought about his cuffs, which I'd noticed were beginning to fray. Befitting an academic who'd been in London for a decade. I thought: *What's this guy doing in first class?*

I looked his way and he was sipping his drink, still watching the first-class diners gathering in the room, ignoring me.

From above us, in the upper dining room, the ship's salon orchestra struck up a waltz. The group sounded like about six pieces, with a violin and a piano leading the way. They were playing Archibald Joyce's "Songe d'Automne," a lovely, wistful thing made rather sad by its tune being in a minor key. After the first few bars, Brauer's face lifted and turned—ever so slightly—in the direction of the sound, his eyes moving very briefly in that direction and then returning at once to the dining room before him. But his face remained slightly lifted to the tune.

He seemed utterly oblivious of me, so I watched him closely, waiting for him to show his response to the music he was clearly aware of, seeing if, by his nostalgia, perhaps Trask was wrong to be vitally suspicious of our Arabic-speaking spy's American visit, seeing if maybe it was about love or family. But nothing changed in him, not a wrinkle in the brow, not a minute dip of his whiskey hand, not the slightest pause of his eyes in their ongoing desultory tracking of the passing swells.

But then he turned his face to me, slowly, his eyes going straight to mine. At some point he'd begun watching me in his periphery, as I was watching him.

"Sad little waltz," I said, lifting my chin toward the upper dining room.

He did not answer for a moment but kept his eyes fixed on me. They were as black and inanimate as any lump of coal flying at that moment into the ship's boilers. I did not flinch. I kept my own eyes unwaveringly on his, so as to suggest that my staring at him was simply to wait for—even to prompt—his attention.

After a long moment of this, he finally responded, picking up on the waltz of it, not the sadness: "I don't dance," he said.

"I wasn't asking you to," I said, not sarcastically, just drily, figuring he was evidently going to resist any conversation anyway and perhaps my showing a pipe-smoke wisp of aggressive irritation would suggest I'd been just a guy wanting to chat.

He surprised me. He laughed softly at this. As if he appreciated that I'd expressed my irritation with him. "Good," he said.

He looked back to the other diners. But not to dismiss me. Almost at once he said, "They all seemed to know the waltz meant to sit."

So he was indeed new to first class.

"Too bad," I said. "I didn't get my whiskey."

He took the card from his pocket that assigned him a table. He looked off to the left, beyond the nearest Corinthian column. "You nearby?" I asked.

He nodded toward the forward portside corner of the dining room.

Since he seemed determined to say as little as possible, we had an awkward moment as he clearly wanted to move off in that direction and I had him feeling buttonholed. I saw the impulse of his body and he was about to excuse himself in a way that would make it hard for me to stick with him, so I smoothed the way for both of us before he could speak.

"Time to be seated," I said and I took a step forward. We moved off together into the portside main aisle through the dining room.

Brauer said, "And where's your place for dinner?" Was he accepting my acquaintance? Or was this a low-key challenge of my walking along with him? He was hard to read.

"I'm at the captain's table tonight." I said this without hesitation—no feigned humility about it—but I did say it offhandedly. As if I considered it a trifle.

Still, I found myself suddenly a step ahead of Brauer. I stopped and turned back to him.

The announcement had made him pull up, and now he'd fully stopped. "So you are a man of acclaim?" he said.

I offered my hand. "My name is Christopher Cobb."

There was no flicker of recognition in his face. But he did take my hand and shake it. He surprised me with a very solid grip.

"I'm Dr. Walter Brauer," he said.

"I write for a newspaper," I said.

"Ah," he said, letting go of my hand. "Newspapers." The word tasted bad in his mouth, a rancid morsel of food he wanted to spit out but couldn't in public. But this I discerned only in his tone of voice, not his face. He was showing nothing outwardly.

I wished I could simply walk away from this cuff-frayed egghead who scorned popular reading tastes. I couldn't. "I'm strictly a war correspondent," I said, thinking this would mitigate things.

It seemed to.

"I see," he said, and his face did change ever so slightly, with a certain gravity coming over him.

He was an arrogant ass. Fine. I had a little something on him anyway. *Doctor* Brauer indeed. "And you're a man of medicine," I said. "I so admire that."

"Doctor of philosophy," he said, his voice gone weary. As if I should have recognized one "doctor" from another by sight.

I could have given him a disappointed "I see," but I still wanted to find out if I could break through his social walls before I tried anything more extreme to learn about him.

"Just as admirable," I said. "A man of the mind."

I saw what I thought was an incipient smile at this, but before it could emerge, his eyes shifted slightly, and then he overtly looked past me. Whatever he saw induced a clear flicker of outreaching life that I'd not yet perceived in Walter Brauer. But it passed almost at once, and he looked at me again.

I turned to see what he had seen.

So egghead Doctor Brauer was also a man, all right, to have been diverted by this sight, even in the midst of receiving an appropriate compliment for his mind. But he wasn't much of a man, for turning away from this image so quickly.

This was a room of ivory-colored walls and full of women dressed in flounces and loose panel drapes and floating sleeves of silks and chiffons and satins, all in the ivory of our walls or in lilac or in pastel blue or green, a muted space with muted women. And all of it had just been struck by a bolt of black lightning from *la mode moderne*: Selene stood alone, barely inside the doorway, and she was wearing a black velvet gown that held her close even at her legs and the neck was high and sharp-pointed and the sleeves were long and she was edged at hem and wrist and throat with the pale gray of chinchilla fur. The only physical brightness about her—and dazzlingly bright she was—were her hands and her face and her long neck and a flame of a diamond barrette in her upgathered hair.

The band waltzed on, but beneath it the room grew quickly silent as she was noticed, and she did not move and she was noticed by others who told others and then all faces were turned to her and all voices were stilled and I ached to see her hair unfastened and falling upon her shoulders and down upon her breast.

Did her face turn ever so slightly in my direction and did her eyes move to me? I could not say for certain.

4

She did look at me across the captain's table. Most notably in the wine-sipping interval between the *snipe en cocotte* and the quarters of lamb. We sat directly beneath the apex of the dining room dome at a table for ten, a rectangle with four chairs on each long side and the ends curved for two more places, one of which held Captain Turner himself, a small, sailor-muscled man whose very few words were accented straight from the Liverpool docks. She'd been placed by the dining room steward next to a silly ass of a playboy millionaire, Alfred Vanderbilt, primary inheritor of the Cornelius Vanderbilt steamships-and-railroads millions, infamous, a few years back, for having to settle $10 million on a Cuban diplomat for having jazzed his wife, who subsequently divorced the Cuban and then killed herself, alone, in a London hotel. When Selene shot me the look, he was bending to her, whispering something.

The look on her face was too complex for me to understand. It was not *What an ass, rescue me from his company.* But neither was it *I'm being charmed here by this guy, who's in my league and you're not, so stop looking at me like that.* I felt it wasn't about Vanderbilt at all, really. There was a stark resignedness in her look. A look of *I'd lift my hand to you, reach across to you, but there's no use.* She looked at me the way she would if she'd fallen off the ship and was about to sink and she knew I could not save her.

All of this lasted only a few moments. She turned her face to Vanderbilt and instantly she portrayed a laugh, a laugh as false and oversized as any she had ever executed before the cranking of a movie camera.

"You're a writer I should know," a man's voice said from my left.

I was ready to look away from Selene, and beside me was Elbert Hubbard, an eccentric jack-of-all-trades American writer with a pageboy haircut who'd sold forty million copies of a pamphlet brazenly exploiting the story of one of the few American war heroes from McKinley's Cuban affair. So Hubbard could do what? Attack the lack of initiative in office clerks and secretaries and other hirelings in American business.

He knew me, knew my work, was heading to Europe to report on the "mastoid degenerate" Kaiser Wilhelm and his war. As Hubbard talked, I nodded and portrayed attention as falsely as a movie actress, and I prodded my mind to go where it should have been all along: to a table I could not see from across the dining room, to Walter Brauer. The Germans surely did not book him in first class out of a sense of his or any of their agents' high standing in the world. He had business here. Something to do en route. Something that was naturally located in first class.

"Don't you think?" Hubbard said, as if he'd already asked something and I'd ignored him. Which no doubt he just had.

"I rely on your judgment," I said, a line I always found useful in getting phony intellectuals to say quotable things.

He was satisfied and talked on.

The orchestra above us was playing a ragtime piece. I hoped I had not just agreed that the music was degenerate.

Hubbard's pageboy bangs were degenerate.

I also hoped he hadn't asked if I liked his bangs.

I needed to get away. I wanted to observe Brauer at his table, even if it was in passing. Was he dining near someone intentionally? Was he engaged in conversation?

Selene Bourgani was engaged in conversation. Vanderbilt's voice smarmed on in the background. Something, at the moment, about his ninety-horsepower Fiat, how he would drive it to London for a board meeting of the International Horse Show Association.

I leaned toward Hubbard slightly, interrupted him. "Sorry," I said. "I have to visit the washroom."

Hubbard nodded, but his "Of course" was snipped with disappointment. His wife was on his other side and I was a new ear for his socialist-utopian ideas.

I rose, ready to quietly excuse myself to anyone at the table who looked at me. I scanned the faces, passing quickly over Selene and Vanderbilt. Her head was angled toward Vanderbilt's nearby moving lips, her eyes cast into the flower arrangement. The captain lifted his indifferent gaze to me.

"Excuse me, Captain," I said, though as softly as I could and still have him hear me. "I'll be right back."

He nodded.

I began to turn away, but I did glance at Selene once more. Vanderbilt's face was still drawn near hers; he was speaking of a prize high stepper. But she'd lifted her face and was looking at me with that opaque complexity I'd seen earlier.

I nodded.

She nodded in return, I thought, but if I was right, it was the merest possible nod, as if she did not want Vanderbilt to notice.

I moved away toward the portside forward door.

I soon saw Brauer. He sat at a round, corner table, facing in my direction, but he did not see me as I slowed to pass. He was turned and was speaking to the man sitting next to him: a thin-faced, clean-shaven man with a tall, brown but lightly graying, Brilliantined pompadour, nodding at Brauer's words.

I looked away and kept moving. The steward was standing nearby, monitoring three members of the waitstaff who were simultaneously launching themselves from the sideboard with wine bottles for refills.

"Pardon me," I said.

"Yes sir?" he said.

"I have a terrible memory for names, and I want to avoid a social offense. Please remind me of the name of the thin-faced man with the large hair in the corner."

I nodded with careful precision toward the man next to Brauer, and the steward followed my gesture.

He pulled some papers from his inner pocket. "I'm still memorizing names myself," he said. "Let me look, Mr. Cobb."

He'd already memorized mine.

He looked at the table charts. "Ah, yes," he said, pitching his voice low. "That's Mr. Edward Cable."

"Cable," I said. "Of course. I met him in passing but he wanted to speak later. Do you know anything else about him?"

"He's from Boston, Massachusetts. A prominent dealer in rare books."

I began to pat the pockets of my tux. "I need to find that paper I made notes on," I said. "He's on A Deck, I think."

The steward looked at his notes. "B Deck," he said, though discreetly not speaking the number of his stateroom.

But he was accommodating. Like any reporter worth his salt, I would keep pumping till the source dried up. "And the name of the dark-haired man sitting to his left?" I asked.

The steward looked again at his chart. "That's Mr. Walter Brauer of London. An academic, is what I understand."

"Anything else about either of them?"

"No, sir."

"Thanks," I said and I discreetly pulled a half-dollar coin from my pocket and slipped it into his hand.

"Thank you, sir," he said.

I looked back to the round table in the corner.

Brauer was the one listening now. Everyone else at the table was absorbed in other conversations, and these two men were posed in a *tableau vivant* entitled "Private Conversation Conducted in Public." Both of them had leaned their torsos toward each other,

Brauer angling his head still farther in the direction of the other man and casting his face downward, staring at the tabletop as if he were examining a rare book, with Cable likewise moving his head closer to his dinner companion's but focusing on Brauer's ear, putting words there.

The words flowed on and the two faces did not show any emotion during them. Cable stopped speaking and Brauer nodded and the two men straightened. This was not an off-color joke, gleaned from a rare book. Not a critical comment from one man of the mind to another about the vapid conversation going on across the table. This was just about them, and it was serious business.

I pushed through the dining room doors, across the deck's entrance hall with its twin elevators, and down the portside corridor a few paces to the gentlemen's room. I stepped in. I washed my hands at the marble basin. Going through the motions of what I'd publicly said I'd do. And I stood there with my hands dripping for a moment, thinking on the rare book dealer and the lecturer at King's College, how I might befriend them. If Edward Cable was why Brauer was traveling first class on this ship, the loop was closed now, and my getting nearer to them would be difficult.

I dried my hands on one of the stacked hand towels and dropped it into the wicker basket. I stepped from the washroom and strode off down the corridor.

I smelled her perfume even before I saw her. Nothing of flowers. This was the smell of the green things in the world, the unadorned things of a field, of a forest, hay newly mown, and beneath this smell a musky scent, but something faintly sweet as well, lavender perhaps. And in its complex fullness, this was a familiar smell, as a matter of fact, though I did not pause to identify it. I emerged from the corridor and there stood Selene, not moving anywhere, not addressing herself to the elevators, just standing there.

I stopped.

Why had I not smelled this scent upon her earlier? Had she just now refreshed it while waiting for me?

She did look toward me without surprise. But also as if without recognition. Perhaps I'd misread the earlier look, at the dinner table, perhaps I'd imagined a complex yearning there that did not exist. At the beginning of the meal, after our Liverpudlian captain had rung three bells lightly on his wineglass with his salad fork and after most of the table offered him a charmed laugh in return—swells only too happy to embrace the social crudities of a man with power, particularly power over their mortal well-being in the middle of the ocean—he made a cursory introduction of each of us. When he spoke my name and my occupational justification for being at the table, I glanced at Selene and her look was the one I was confronting now: *I can see that some person or other is present here before me.*

So just outside the first-class dining room, Selene Bourgani and I stood alone, looking at each other, and as the moment stretched on and she did not resort to social boilerplate, nor did I, as we did not speak at all but neither did we turn away, the uninflected silence between us began to seem like actual, engaged communication.

But then she said, "I believe the washrooms are in this direction."

Was I wrong about the initial silence? Or was it true and she had not fully realized what was happening? Or had she realized but not trusted that I was feeling the same way and it was up to me to open all this between us?

I'm not the sort of man who could answer such a thing. It was odd enough, under the circumstances, that I was even able to use the part of my brain that could rationally assess her outward signs and could pose these questions. This was my reporter's brain, my reporter's self. I was good at that, but I was very bad at that when I was simply being a man with a woman. A woman who knew something I wanted to know about a story: that was one thing. But not when a woman held some secret upon her body I could read only with mine, a secret I would never tell. In those circumstances, I tended to act first and assess later, if at all.

But Selene had me trying to figure her out. Had me thinking too much.

All right. It was up to me.

I said, "I had to get away from that table for a few minutes."

"What are washrooms for?" she said.

I was ready to think she was here because she wanted us to meet alone. In this last exchange we had both crept closer to each other, close enough to comfortably speak on. Would we banter now? Was that how it was done in her circle? It felt as if we'd begun, but I was hearing something in her voice: the words slid downward at the end of her question. They should have been light; they should have risen up, as if to say: *Here I am; we know how this game is played.* But I heard something else in them, that faintly sad resignedness I'd seen in her eyes at the table: *This is how it's done, but it's not going to work.*

I did not know what to do. So we looked at each other awhile longer. Then she took a step in my direction and said, "Mr. Cobb, isn't it?"

"Christopher," I said.

"Do your friends call you Kit?"

She was the only woman I'd ever met who assumed that.

"My middle name is Marlowe," I said.

She laughed.

"Christopher Marlowe Cobb. Kit then," she said. "May I?"

"Of course," I said.

"You're a famous war correspondent, as I understand it."

"You're a famous film actress," I said, "as I've learned firsthand."

"An actress," she said, softly.

And my mother swirled into my head, draped in ivory himation and chiton but with long black sleeves, playing Medea, perhaps as I first saw her on stage as a child.

I hesitated even to introduce the thought of her to the woman standing before me. But Selene Bourgani was a widely celebrated woman. Though for some reason—perhaps that very celebrity— Selene was making me think like a reporter, what I really wanted to do was put my hands upon her. And so a famous mother could be helpful, given Selene's apparent obliviousness to my own wide demi-celebrity among Chicago cabdrivers and shoe shine boys and shop owners and ballplayers and bowlered-and-bespoken politicians and their equivalents in a hundred syndicated cities, all of whom knew my name pretty well. Maybe film stars didn't read the papers, at least not past the gossip columns.

So I said, "My mother was an actress."

"And Kit Marlowe was her favorite playwright."

"Close to. She was kind enough not to name me William Shakespeare Cobb."

Selene nodded at this, but distractedly, since her brow had furrowed ever so slightly a moment earlier as she began to put my surname with the possibilities; not that my name would necessarily be part of my mother's stage name, though it happened to be. Selene's brow unfurrowed and she narrowed her eyes at me and I knew what she was about to ask.

"Yes," I said. "Her."

"No."

"Yes."

"Isabel Cobb?"

"I am her son."

It was the right thing to tell her, as it turned out.

Selene thumped the back of her right wrist against her forehead and swayed to the side. She provided her own title card: "She swoons," she said.

But instantly she straightened and reached out and touched my forearm. "How foolish of me," she said. "To do a cheap, film-actress emotion at that news. I loved your mother. I wanted to be your mother when I was a girl."

That came out wrong and instantly she heard it. She straightened abruptly as if she'd been startled by an unknown sound.

"Those aren't the feelings I hoped to inspire," I said.

I expected another film-actress gesture. Wide-eyed abashed, perhaps, or flutteringly flirtatious. But a dark something passed over her, leaving her face as I'd seen it across the table: subtle outwardly;

unreadable without knowing the full context of her present life; perhaps numbingly bored, perhaps inexpressibly sad.

Her hand was still on my forearm. She removed it.

She seemed as if she wanted to say something from that darkness. I felt I'd done the wrong thing to try to sneak in a reference to possible feelings between us. It had only made her take her hand from me, after all.

But instead, she managed a smile. I felt her exertion. She said, "Your mother is a very great actress. I wish I'd been able to do what she has done."

"Your films . . ."

She cut me off, which was just as well, as I'd plunged into a comment I did not know how to complete; I had no idea how to intelligently compliment her on her films.

She said, "My films are melodrama at best. And there's always the terrible silence. Not that I ever came close to doing what she did, in the time I spent striving for the stage, even with Shakespeare's words in my mouth."

"Many people love you," I said.

She ignored the comment. "All I have is my life," she said.

By which she seemed to suggest that making films was not part of her life. I thought to ask her if that's what she meant, but I did not. It would sound as if I disagreed. I didn't want to disagree with her about anything at the moment.

"The lamb," she said.

I didn't understand at first. Things had suddenly gotten serious enough that my first thought was that she was segueing into speaking of religion.

But it was simply dinner.

"They're surely serving it by now," she said.

"Ah, the lamb," I said. "Yes."

"Can you give me a moment?" she said.

I didn't understand.

"I am always subject to instant and widespread gossip," she said.

This seemed at first like a non sequitur. My puzzlement must have shown on my face.

"If we walk back into the dining room together," she said. And she waited to see if she needed to explain further.

She did not.

"I understand," I said.

She nodded faintly.

I finished her sentence: "They might think you're my mother."

She laughed at this. A low, sharp bark of a laugh, a laugh I was sure she never unleashed in public. It felt like a sudden kiss.

And she reached out and touched my forearm once more, and then she was gone.

5

The next day was cloudless and windless, and but for the sharp chill in the air, the North Atlantic could have been the Mediterranean in its azure brightness. I roamed the saloon promenades on decks A and B, trying to look casual, watching for Brauer and Cable, and watching for Selene as well. They weren't showing themselves, any of them. I had time to eavesdrop among the other first-class passengers, and I was struck by how many of them were talking about U-boats, worrying about Thursday, when we would enter the War Zone. Midmorning, as I strolled past Lifeboat 11, amidships, on the upper, open A Deck, I turned my ear to a walrus-mustached Brit leaning to his wife—both of them swaddled in blankets on deck chairs—and he was saying, "My dear, we will simply outrun the blighters."

Since this very notion was my own primary source of confidence in our safe passage, the Brit's speaking it led me to reflect on my body's sense of our speed, in my knees and inside my chest and in the press of the air on my face. He led me to remember from B Deck an hour ago, with a clear and open view of the ocean around us, the pace of our passing a great floating tangle of seaweed. And it struck me at last: we were not moving at full speed. No more than twenty knots, I would have guessed, when we should have been doing twenty-five.

I looked up to the smokestacks, which rose seven stories above me. I stepped toward the railing so I could scan them all at once.

The funnels were painted their usual black in the upper quarter, but the orange-mellowed red that normally covered the rest of the stacks down to their base, emblematic of the Cunard Line, was now entirely replaced with dark gray—as if this would make a 787-foot steamship less conspicuous on the face of the sea—and my suspicion about our reduced speed found clear, confirming evidence: the first three funnels were pumping out heavy black billows of smoke, but funnel number four was empty, was coldly silent.

I had a twist in the chest at this. But it loosened instantly. The top speed of a U-boat was fifteen knots—and that was on the surface of the ocean, exposed for all to see. Submerged, our hunter could do about half that. Even if the *Lusitania* were running at twenty knots, we would be an utterly impossible target for a U-boat consciously to hunt down and a nearly impossible target to hit even if we got freakishly unlucky and happened into one's sights, especially if we were executing a standard-procedure zigzag course through the War Zone. When I did my "Running the U-Boat Gauntlet" feature story, I could confirm my instant intuition about what was behind our silent funnel, but on the promenade deck I was certain I already knew. Bucks. Business. Passenger bookings were dwindling because of the war; coal was expensive; one of the four boiler rooms was shut down to save money.

I strolled on. But my three people of interest never appeared, not through the morning, not through the afternoon. At dinner that night, Brauer and Cable were at their corner table, sitting beside each other again, and my hope was that they'd go to the Smoking Room after the last course. But Selene was nowhere to be found in the grand dining room, and when that was finally clear to me, I had a twist in my chest that squeezed harder than the thought of our idle boiler room. I considered leaving the table before the imminent *salambos à la crème*—what the hell was I doing eating something called *salambos à la crème* anyway?—and going to her room and knocking and asking after her well-being, even if only through the closed door. But I didn't. For now I didn't. She wasn't why I was on this ship.

And as the orchestra had waltzed us to our tables last night, on this night they ragtimed us away, but with a piece just right for our gang, "The Operatic Rag," syncopating quotations from Wagner and Bizet and Verdi. I joined the first-classers politely swelling out the forward dining room doors. I kept back a ways in the crowd, letting Brauer and Cable stay ahead of me. The after dinner smokers and socializers were all heading up three levels to A Deck to settle into the Smoking Room, if they were men, or the Lounge and Music Room, if they were women. I went up the stairs behind a cacophony of small talk, a welter of perfume, a rustling din of evening clothes, and at the top of the stairs we men separated from the women and entered our preserve, paneled in Italian walnut and filled with settings of sofas and easy chairs with the simple curves and cabriole legs of the Queen Anne style. Above us, the glass-paneled arch of the top-deck ceiling was darkened by the night.

I hung back at the Smoking Room door and watched Brauer and Cable sit down at one of the arrangements in the center of the room, with four chairs around a small, walnut writing table. The two men sat at right angles to each other, and as the other two chairs remained empty, I moved across the room toward them, making haste when they could not see me, and then arriving in their sight casually, noticing Brauer and affecting a mild and pleasant surprise.

"Dr. Brauer," I said. "Good evening." I looked around the room as if to note how the place was filling up. I looked back to one of the empty chairs. "May I join you?"

Parties of two in a steamship Smoking Room had to expect strangers to end up in their company. Brauer did not hesitate. He nodded me to the empty chair to his right, facing Cable, and I sat.

"Mr. Christopher Cobb," Brauer said to his companion, though in a perfunctory tone, and then he turned to me and said, "Mr. Edward Cable," his voice warming a little.

I reached across and offered my hand to Cable, wondering why they were here, with Brauer uncomfortable and their not being free to speak to each other in the way they surely wished. But perhaps they'd done all the business they needed to do during the day and this was to maintain their cover.

Cable accepted my hand for shaking and he had a gentle grip, the grip of a man used to turning expensive book pages very carefully.

"Mr. Cable," I said.

"Mr. Cobb," he said. And in just those two words his Boston Back Bay accent rolled over me as dramatically as if he were one of my mother's leading men making an entrance, the "Mister" coasting on a schwa to a vanished "r" and the vowel of my name reshaped and drawn out like *awww*-ing at the sight of a Brahmin baby.

The man offered a smile as well, over the shake, a bookman's smile for a serious customer. But he surprised me as we settled back into our chairs. "You are a foreign correspondent," he said.

"Only if the foreigners are killing each other," I said.

He chuckled at this.

I glanced at Brauer, wondering if he'd spoken of me. But Brauer was looking at Cable with a focus that suggested he was surprised at the man's familiarity with my byline.

Cable said, "It's not your writing about battle that has interested me. Your feature work is as good as anything by Richard Harding Davis."

I looked back to Cable, caught his eyes, and searched them for irony. I didn't see any. Too bad this guy was a German spy. I was starting to like him.

He went on, "I remember last year a story you did on a young Mexican woman who wanted to fight for the rebels. Very interesting."

That was a good story, about a special young woman, a feature story in the midst of my little Mexican adventure, and there was nothing in it to cause any suspicion in a German agent. The whiff of danger I was presently smelling was a mistake, was just the ongoing lighting up of pipes and cigars and cigarettes all around the room going to my head. Nevertheless, this cohort of Brauer citing my story from the land that led me to my own secret work: that was a little unsettling. But I was a public person. I had plenty of followers.

"Where do you get a chance to read me so closely?" I asked.

"Boston."

This was possible. "*The Daily Leader,*" I said, which was owned by Griswold and splashed all my words around prominently.

"Just so," said Cable. "You should do a book someday."

"I may do that," I said.

I glanced at Brauer. He'd lit a cigarette and was draping one leg over the other at the knee and turning his body away from Cable. He blew his first drag of smoke into the air and seemed to be carefully striking a pose of indifference.

"I deal in books, mostly rare," Cable said.

I looked back at the Brilliantined man. He was good. He was a mystery.

"What's your final destination?" I asked.

"London."

"Book business?"

"I'm always doing book business."

I turned to Brauer, who was still wrenched away from the conversation. "And Dr. Brauer," I said. "After my little confusion over your honorific, I didn't have a chance to ask. How do you make use of your doctorate?"

There was a very brief moment of utter scorn from Brauer: he turned his eyes to me without turning his body, or even his head. But before I could glance at Cable to see if he was witnessing this attitude, to see how he was reacting, Brauer was uncrossing his leg, squaring his body and face around, and he gave me a straight answer in what sounded like a civil tone. "I'm a lecturer at King's College London."

I grew up backstage in hundreds of theaters across the U.S. and in more than a few other countries and I lived with people who were always in the process of memorizing, stretching their memories all the time, and I loved all the details of things, the names of things, and that carried along to my work as a newsman, remembering and naming and treasuring details, and all of this made me able to do what I was about to do for the arrogant priss who sat before me, who no doubt honored a keen memory as a sign—bogus though it was in and of itself—of intelligence: I said, "*Sancte et Sapienter.*" Which meant, ironically under the circumstances, "With holiness and wisdom." Which was the motto of King's College London, where my mother had a lover for a time while she played Kate in *Shrew* in the West End when I was an impressionable and absorbent thirteen.

Brauer could not hide a tiny backward head flip of surprise.

He couldn't suspect me of being in the same secret business he was, so I figured it was good to keep him from simply dismissing me as a plebian. A little apt Latin seemed to be doing the trick. "So," I said, looking to Cable and back to Brauer, "you boys pals from one side of the Atlantic or the other?"

Brauer's lips disappeared in a thin, hard line.

"Neither," Cable said.

I turned to him.

He shot Brauer a glance, but with a crooked little smile attached. I was looking at both of them as actors. Actors at the Moscow Art Theater under Stanislavsky, doing Chekhov. Working the nuances. Ignoring the balcony. And this smile was interesting. Like they'd talked over their public story about this and Cable had won but Brauer didn't like it and this was the first time they had occasion to say this.

"We've only just met," Cable said.

What I was hearing was either a lie or only a partial truth. They either knew each other already or indeed this was their first meeting, but it was planned and significant. Cable wasn't afraid of my seeing the little smile because he liked his little ironies, liked relishing them, and he couldn't even imagine I'd be on to them.

I took out my pack of Fatimas and offered one across the table, as I said, "Steamships are good for that."

Cable took a cigarette with a nod of the head. I leaned back and realized at once I'd forgotten to offer a match. But before I could, he started patting his pockets and found a box right away. If he had matches in the tux, he also had cigarettes. I didn't let my smile show.

I would've bet that at least half the moneyed swells in first class had that same reflex, to save a few pennies at every chance. I lit my cigarette and shifted to Brauer.

He looked at me while he took a drag, but then he turned his face away and watched his own plume of smoke dissipate in the thickening air. He was still trying to effectively revise his opinion of me as simply a rube.

My next move with Brauer and Cable would have to be covert anyway, so tonight I figured I'd keep playing the nosy rube card till they got wise that something was up.

"Where are you staying in London, Mr. Cable?"

"The Waldorf," he said, without hesitation, one of the poshest places in the city.

"Those must be some pretty rare books," I said. The man wasn't traveling solely on German money. He had family dough as well, I bet.

Cable laughed at this. A full, spontaneous laugh. Not quite what I expected.

I went back to Brauer while his confederate was still keeping the mood light. I said, "The Waldorf's on Aldwych. That's right near your college, isn't it?"

"Purely coincidental," Brauer said. Two things struck me about this. It came out quickly and unemphasized, bearing the timbre of truth, to my ear. He was anxious to stress the casualness of their association. The latter I expected. I'd have to think about the former.

I stayed with Brauer. "It's a nice neighborhood. Do you have rooms nearby?"

Brauer turned his face away, toward Cable. He didn't want to talk about himself. Naturally not. But it was worth my trying.

It all happened quickly, but Brauer's eyes narrowed a bit in looking toward his companion and I got the feeling he was afraid the man was about to answer for him.

Brauer turned back to me and he used his acidic tone to let me know that this meant *no*: "The neighborhood is full of theaters."

"That's bad?" I said. "Prima facie?"

"Of course."

I thought to mention Mother, just to keep provoking him. He took a long drag on his dwindling cigarette and clearly had no more to say about his residence.

But before I could speak, Cable piped up. "He lives near Buckingham Palace."

Brauer shot Cable a look, not quite irritated but not quite satisfied with their coordination.

"So he says," Cable added, with a playful little twirl of the words. I figured he was suddenly aware that his statement seemed to contradict their just having met.

Brauer said, "Merely a small bachelor flat in a building full of them. Not typical Saint James's."

They were an odd sort of vaudeville team, these two, in their public roles. It made me wonder if I'd gotten one or the other or both of them wrong. But Trask had no doubt about Brauer. And these two were fast and seemingly exclusive companions three days into the voyage. Which was why Brauer was here. Trask wanted more from me than Cable's name, but that wasn't going to come in casual conversation.

I wanted to read Brauer's face once more. I'd found in the ward rooms and courthouse corridors of Chicago that the most boldly direct question sometimes actually got an answer, or at least a revealing evasion.

So I turned back to Cable and said, "Rare books must be pretty good money, but Dr. Brauer and I are living way over our heads traveling Cunard Saloon." I came back to Brauer and looked him straight in the eyes. "Forget hod carriers and dirt farmers. Underpaid teachers and newswriters are the ones ripe for the Bolsheviks. I got a whole syndicate footing my bill to the war. How'd you wangle first class, Doc?"

His eyes did not shift away from mine. The pause in him was minute. He said, "It was God's will."

6

This sank the conversation.

Brauer grew even less willing to speak. Cable grew thoughtful. I understood I had to take other measures to learn anything more about these two.

I stubbed my cigarette and excused myself and went out of the Smoking Room at the promenade door.

The night was bright with stars.

I walked forward a ways, in the direction of the entrance door to the stateroom corridor.

I could take the most obvious of the next measures right now. I had a small leather roll of picks, rakes, and miniature torque wrenches and a few weeks of intensive training and rehearsal in their use. I'd pick Brauer's cabin lock and go in.

But I didn't know how long the boys would linger in the Smoking Room. They weren't having a swell experience there so far. I didn't want Brauer walking in on me. Better to wait till the dinner hour tomorrow so I had a substantial and predictable block of time.

A couple approached, leaning into each other and talking low, and they straightened abruptly as they saw me. I passed. They were, I was willing to bet, a shipboard romance just beginning, from their new ardor risking a public show of their feelings but not wanting anyone to actually notice. A little farther along, the canvas cover of Lifeboat 10 was in place but undone at the prow. I listened as I went by. I could hear rustlings inside. Still another couple. They'd been careful to put the tarp back into place, but of course they couldn't refasten it from the inside. These two were young. Each of them traveling with parents or siblings, sharing their staterooms, stealing some privacy.

I liked the nascent romances. Liked it professionally. I thought a good activity tonight would be to go to my Corona Portable Number 3—which was a swell companion who never failed to take me by the fingertips and lead me to my newswriter self—and work on the lead paragraphs of my feature story. Young love blooming, ragtime playing, and the swells of London and New York dolling up as we rushed toward the War Zone.

I reached the aft doorway into the A Deck stateroom corridors. I stopped. Before me in the deck wall were the portholes—rectangular, with iron flower filigrees crowning them—proper windows at sea. I counted them along: one for the first small stateroom and then a gap for the vent and for, I suspected, the en suite bathroom, and then the two windows of the suite. Selene's suite. They were lit. I stepped toward the railing and I could see that the curtains were drawn in both. She was inside. She was awake.

I was grinding a bit now in places on my body I did not want to think about. I'd exchanged words with her. One could even consider that we'd flirted ever so slightly, ever so preliminarily. But what took no consideration at all was that she'd vanished. She'd known where to find me, if she'd been so inclined, but she'd vanished.

I entered at the door and turned down the immediate forward-leading corridor—which, however, led straight past her suite—and I started to stride along, conscious of my first two footfalls, hearing the clear squinch of them on the rubberized floor tiles, wondering if she heard them, and I stopped abruptly, as if to quiet the racket I was making. Not incidentally, however, I was standing now before her door. But I did not knock. I did not make a further sound, except perhaps for a quick intake of air. And perhaps a brief clearing of the throat. Loud enough, I supposed. But I strode on, forgetting to walk softly—I was beyond her suite anyway now—and then I was at the turning of the corridor. I stopped again. Without a plan. Intending— sincerely—simply to take another buck-up-boy big breath or two and then vanish into my stateroom.

And I heard the click of an opening door behind me.

I turned.

Selene was standing just outside her suite, her crimson kimono wrapped around her, her golden dragons plunging down her chest. Her hair was up. Her legs and feet were bare. She saw it was me. She'd suspected it was me. She'd come out because it was me.

I began to walk toward her. She wasn't moving.

I stopped before her.

I'm stupid about women more often than not, but I'm not stupid. I made sure I was standing very close to her. She hadn't budged.

Selene Bourgani was looking up into my eyes, saying nothing. She didn't smell of the forest anymore. She'd found some bed of flowers to lie down in. I didn't feel like trying to name them. She smelled damp. Freshly damp like she'd just come in out of the rain.

I wasn't saying anything either.

I stopped trying to read her eyes, which were on me, which was enough.

Then she said, very softly, "Should I assume by your stopping to clear your throat that we've emerged from the fog?"

And though she was guying me, these words came out of her as if it was the saddest thing in the world. As if she was playing Juliet, as if she was saying "O happy dagger, this is thy sheath."

I firmly pushed that thought away, lest the great Isabel Cobb, whose Juliet I saw a hundred times as a boy, should start filling my head with her voice. *The curtain has fallen, Mother. Go away.*

Selene's hands rose, but not to me. She undid her hair and it tumbled down before me, and as far as my body was concerned, she might as well have just sloughed off the kimono: to see the long, black, cascaded fullness of her hair was to see her naked.

And still another remarkable thing: her eyes were filling with tears.

I didn't know if it was stupid or wise, but I had long before come to the conclusion that you did not ask a woman why she was crying. You didn't stop her from telling you, if she must, but you did not ask.

I did not ask.

But I did care about this. I lifted my hand, though I wasn't sure what to do with it. Before I could lower my hand again, she took it. And she turned and led me into her suite. I closed the door behind me.

I had sense enough to keep my mouth closed as well.

She led me from the parlor of her suite to her bedroom, ivory walled and roseate furnished, with settee and dressing table on one side of the room and two single beds on the other, placed foot to foot, one of which she set me on as she stepped back and squared around to face me. The electric lamps burning in sconces on the walls were made to look like candles and she left them on for me to see. She sloughed off the kimono and now she truly was naked, tumbled hair and lamp-ambered skin and tear-sparkled eyes and all.

Though in Mexico I'd begun to learn that this was one of my stupidities with a woman, I still tended, in these matters, simply to pound and then to sleep. But Selene Bourgani would not let that happen on this night. Soon after we'd begun, she whispered to me, "Please go gentle, Kit. Go slow. All this will end too soon as it is."

And I obeyed her. And she would be right.

7

But for now, after we'd finished, we did not sleep but held each other close on one of the narrow beds, entwined like the two snakes on Hermes' staff. We'd been silent for a long while, so I said, "We're like the two snakes on Hermes' staff." She was Greek, after all. I was trying not to doze off.

We were both lying mostly on our sides, facing each other; her cheek was against my chest; my throat was laid on the curve of her head. She moved her head when I said this, tilting her face upward, and though I could not see her eyes, I sensed she was looking up at me. "Of course," she said. "He was the god of travelers and liars."

I'd bantered with smart women. I grew up the son of a very smart woman who bantered to beat the band. When a smart woman banters, she means at least half of everything she says. At least. My mother schooled me herself as we steamer-trunked from city to city, theater to theater, schooled me by giving me, through all my learning years, a good three thousand books to read and then asking me, all totaled, a good hundred thousand questions about them. I dared not forget a thing. And from what I remembered of the Greek deities, this was a very selective list of Hermes' godly patronage, so I figured Selene thought I was a liar. Or she knew she was. Not that we'd had much of a chance to lie to each other yet.

"God of poets too," I said.

"Are you a poet, Kit Cobb?"

"Nah," I said. "But if they'd been around at the time, he'd've been the god of newspaper writers as well."

"To fit with the liars?" She lifted her face from my chest. I pulled my head back and looked her in the eyes. The electrical filaments of those phony candles were still burning in the room. I was glad. I liked looking at her face, even if she was ragging me. "He was the messenger of the gods," I said. "I'm just a messenger, bringing the news."

She put her head back onto my chest.

"Are you a liar, Selene?"

"Of course," she said. "I'm an actress."

I didn't have an answer for that. We were quiet for a few moments. Then she said, "I'm sorry."

"Because you're an actress?"

"Because I'm a liar."

There was a little catch in her. "I'm sorry," she said. This was about something else.

"That you're an actress?"

"Yes. But your mother . . ."

"It's all right."

"I didn't mean to say . . ."

"That she's a liar too."

"But we do that."

Her head felt heavier on my chest, as if she were pressing in, burrowing, hiding. She grew still. I should've qualified calling my mother a liar. But I felt Selene struggling with something. I kept quiet.

She said, "An actress is trained to be anyone, to do anything." She paused and then, very low, Selene said, "An actress is a fallen woman."

Somewhere outside, distantly on the promenade, in the dark, a woman laughed. Perhaps the lovers from the lifeboat, emerging.

I thought of the newspaper stories of Selene's life, the few things known about her past. She was Greek, the firstborn of a fisherman and his wife on the island of Andros. Shortly before she was born, her father drowned in a storm in the Cavo d'Oro channel. A week later her mother gave birth, and after swaddling her daughter in a basket and placing her on the doorstep of the local monastery, she threw herself off the lighthouse.

From then until she showed up on the doorstep of the Vitagraph Studios in Brooklyn in 1908, things were mysterious in the biography of Selene Bourgani, yielding to reporters, upon questioning, only her classic profile and her most famous quote, "What little I remembered, I have now forgotten." She could indeed have become, in those lost years, a spectacularly fallen woman. Or, more likely, a Greek immigrant girl waiting tables in a Hoboken diner with a boyfriend at the coffee factory. As it was, she was billed by Vitagraph as the Most Mysterious Woman in the World. Of course she was a liar.

She shifted now against me, moved her hand along my side and then onto my back, pressed me closer to her.

"Were you really born on Andros?" I said.

This was the wrong thing to ask. I was continuing to learn. It did not occur to me till that moment: if a woman tells you she is a liar, it doesn't mean she's suddenly interested in telling the truth.

Selene untangled herself from me. Not angrily. Almost wearily. As if the night had ended and she was sorry for that but it was over.

However, she simply sat up and leaned back against the wall. I was happy to find she was disengaging no further. And I was happy to be looking at her naked, ambered breasts tipped in coffee brown, a part of her I had so far failed to concentrate on as I'd intended.

"You've been reading the movie magazines," she said.

"Newspapers," I said.

"All lies." She turned her face to me.

I didn't answer.

"Willful," she added.

"The only kind you can trust," I said.

"Can you get me a cigarette and my wrap?"

"I'm happy to smoke with you, but can't I look at you a little longer?"

"I'm cold," she said.

"All this will end too soon as it is," I said.

She smiled. "Okay. The cigarette will do."

I moved to the other bed where she and I had thrown the pieces of my tux. I found my cigarettes and matches in my coat and turned back to her. I was also still naked and she was looking at me openly. Was this a pleasure for her—I'd never really considered the possibility of this impulse in a woman—or was she just instructing me some more? I took a step toward our bed and the kimono was lying crumpled on the floor. I bent to it, picked it up, straightened. I was facing her and feeling pretty uncomfortable now, to be dangling nakedly before her watchful eye, which is what I figured she intended.

She did not take her eyes off the center of me. And she whispered, "I said the cigarette will do," but in the actress way that filled the room, that would reach the back of the mezzanine. In the way that sounded as if she were lying. I was sorry we'd talked about lies.

But I dropped the kimono at my feet and stepped naked to her and I offered a cigarette, and she lifted her gaze from my body to my eyes, and she took a cigarette and put it between her lips, and I bent to her and I lit it and she sucked deeply on it, keeping her eyes fixed on mine, and then she turned her profile to me as if I'd just asked about the secrets of her life, and she blew a long, thin slip of smoke into the room.

I sat down beside her, putting my back to the wall as well. I lit a cigarette, and we smoked for a few moments, and then she said, "Have you ever killed a man?"

I'd been around a lot of killing in my professional life. And in Mexico last year it had finally become necessary that I do some myself. I'd not been asked this question before, and I found the simple, true answer difficult to speak. It had been necessary. I had done it without pleasure. But I had done it. More than once. My hesitation now was that killing a man was a private act. Even if it was done publicly. It was between him and me. But I would not lie. And to stay silent, as I was now doing, was also an answer, except it implied things about the doing of it and the having done it that were not true.

"Yes," I said.

Selene took a drag on her cigarette. She held the smoke inside her for a long moment. Then she exhaled slowly, filling the air directly before her. "Why?" she said.

I was not getting into this. "It had to be done," I said, hoping this would be sufficient for her.

It seemed to be. She nodded. She said nothing more.

We sat side by side in silence for a long moment, and I realized she was trembling slightly.

I touched her quaking arm. "You're cold."

"I believe I mentioned that before," she said.

"Sorry," I said, and I instantly got up from the bed and picked up her kimono and turned back to her.

She'd risen to her knees, and she took the wrap from me, the cigarette dangling at the corner of her mouth like she was a Chicago street thug. "You stopped looking anyway," she said.

I was surprised to realize that she was right. I didn't know how to explain that. It was the pound-and-sleep in me, I supposed. I didn't know how to explain that either. So I said nothing.

She pulled her kimono around her tightly, her hands crossed on her chest.

I went to the other bed and put on my pants and shirt.

When I returned to her, she was still holding her wrap against her. She did not look up. I understood I was supposed to go.

I picked up the rest of my clothes and threw them over my arm. I stopped before her one last time.

She lifted her face to me. The tears had returned to her eyes. But she said, "It's all right. Thank you for tonight."

I nodded and I left her there on the bed, where she held herself close and said nothing—but at least was not lying—where she was perhaps trying to forget whatever it was that she remembered.

And as I stepped into the empty corridor and closed Selene Bourgani's door, I could not help but wonder who she might be thinking of killing.

8

She remained invisible again the next day. I did not question that all
along she'd intended for me to touch her only once. Did I therefore
think of her as fallen? No. I thought of her as an actress. I roamed
the A Deck promenade in my shirt sleeves in the cold late afternoon
to get my body square with how I was thinking about her.

Brauer and Cable were invisible as well. Brauer's suite had its
PLEASE DO NOT DISTURB sign hanging on the doorknob both
times I checked, midmorning and midafternoon. One stateroom
on B Deck—Cable's, I'd've been willing to bet—also had its sign
on the door. Both men were sick, or hungover. Something.

I dressed for dinner that evening, and I arrived deliberately a few
minutes late. I stepped in through the starboard doors and discreetly
looked across the room and into the corner. The two men had re-
covered and were in their places, just commencing to touch their
wineglasses in a toast.

I backed away and out of the dining room and I went up the Grand
Staircase to A Deck and into the starboard corridor and down to
Brauer's door. I already had my set of lock picks in my pocket.

I stood before the door, and a man and a woman suddenly emerged
from the forward en suite stateroom. They were all decked out for
dinner, and Madame's liveried personal maid trailed behind them, her
mistress ragging her for having buttoned too slowly. The man locked
the door as the maid vanished in the other direction and I slipped

the tools into my pocket. The couple hurried toward me. I knocked on Brauer's door. "Walter?" I said.

The couple passed and I nodded at them. They ignored me. They were late. She was blaming her maid. It occurred to me that Selene seemed not to be traveling with a maid. And that calmed my still niggling unease at our having sex and then her disappearing on me. A woman like her was used to having people around who helped her with every commonplace thing. She obviously wanted to be alone on this trip from the start. I thought: *I should be glad to have gotten what I did from her.*

The tardy couple disappeared around the corner, and the corridor was empty. I withdrew the two implements I needed and bent to the lock. I inserted the shorter, bent end of a torque wrench into the hole and then I slid the pick inside and gently worked it farther and farther along, lifting each tumbler in turn, sensing them with my fingertips, and then I felt the last one lift for me and I turned the wrench and the bolt yielded and I stepped inside Walter Brauer's suite.

I'd noted in Selene's suite which part of the wall to move to and where to put my hand. I found the key in its ceramic mounting and I turned it. All the lights on their sconces flared up brightly through the sitting room.

The place was similar to Selene's in period replication, and, indeed, to most of the rest of the done-up parts of the ship: early neoclassic— sofa, small desk, three-drawer commode, an overstuffed chair and a smoking table—but with a green and yellow motif in place of rose, and with the electric lights on the wall not pretending to be candles.

I focused exclusively on Brauer's things.

In this room, a box of Spanish cigars on the table.

On the desk a couple of books, one on top of the other.

No other signs of habitation. Very neat. The DO NOT DISTURB sign must have gone up after the stewardess cleaned the suite this morning.

I stepped to the desk. I picked up the top book, noting its exact position. Gilt-stamped on the cover was the title—*Germany, France,*

Russia & Islam—and a small German Imperial eagle. This was an English translation of essays written by Heinrich von Treitschke, who was a nineteenth century German historian, an imperialist ideologue and an avid advocate of racial purity. I flipped through the pages and found none of the passages marked, nothing inserted. The essays might speak to Brauer's Germanic politics, and perhaps even to his covert mission. But this would not be an unusual book for any lecturer on Islam at a British university.

I laid it aside. It had been sitting on a slate-colored paperbound copy of the April issue of *The American Journal of Semitic Languages and Literatures*. This was clearly part of Brauer's academic persona. I ruffled through the journal as well, finding nothing, and put both journal and book back on the desktop precisely in their previous position.

The desk had a single drawer. I opened it.

On one side were three yellow Mongol pencils, finely sharpened. In the center was a ten-cent stationer's notebook with pasteboard covers. I thumbed through it, starting from the back, and all the pages flipping by were blank. I arrived at the first page—also blank—and was about to close the cover. But I noticed where the cover joined the pages: a minute, ragged edge ran along the hinge. I looked closely. A couple or three pages had been torn out.

I closed the notebook and put it back where it had lain.

I kneeled before the drawer and looked underneath, as I drew it out as far as I could. Nothing was affixed there.

I stood up and closed the desk drawer.

I went to the commode at the forward wall.

The top drawer held folded shirts and a couple of waistcoats. I gently probed between them and beneath them, making sure the objects did not shift, did not alert Brauer to my having searched. I found nothing. The next drawer had sweaters on one side and, on the other, gloves, four-in-hands, handkerchiefs. I searched it and closed it and opened the bottom drawer. It pulled out slightly heavy on one side, but the surface contents were lightweight and uniformly distributed:

underdrawers and socks and, on the heavy side, a tightly folded black silk dressing gown.

I slipped my hand beneath the gown and felt another book. I lifted away the gown and set it aside, and I picked up a copy of *The Nuttall Encyclopaedia of Universal Information*. Sixteen thousand self-described "terse articles" in seven hundred pages, edited by a Reverend James Wood, published in London. Placed under Brauer's dressing gown in the bottom drawer of the commode, it felt hidden.

I thumbed the densely set, two-columned pages and found no markings, nothing placed in the leaves.

On a personal impulse I turned to a listing under "C." And I read: *Cobb, Isabel, a celebrated American actress, born in St. Louis, Missouri; appeared in London in 1885 and 1897; represented, among other characters, Juliet, Rosalind, Kate, and Lady Macbeth. b. 1859.*

My mother's entry was five lines long. I turned to the entry on "Islam." That major religion, one of Brauer's lecture topics, was dealt with in nine lines, terse to the point of vapidity.

Brauer was intellectually arrogant. He found me and my work beneath him, even as it rated the captain's table, a thing that quite literally stopped him in his tracks in the dining room the other night. He would find *Nuttall* contemptible.

And the reason he was traveling with it was instantly clear to me, thanks to my months with Trask's own lecturers. It was a code book. The exact same volume was in the possession of Brauer's handler, wherever he might be posted; it was no doubt sitting, as well, on a desk in the *Auswärtiges Amt*, Wilhelmstraße 76, Berlin, the German Foreign Office. Perhaps the book was even in the possession of other German secret agents. Some, perhaps, with different cover stories, different useful skills, might even have lain in bed at night in their rented flats in London or Edinburgh or Liverpool or Southampton and browsed the book, might even have hidden the book proudly in plain sight.

Not Brauer. This book tweaked his lifted nose. But he had to use it to decode the instructions he got from the boys in Berlin. They'd telegraph him blocks of numbers referencing page and column and line and word in the book. An unbreakable code, without knowing what the shared book was. Books like this went through various editions; I checked the copyright page. 1909. This would be useful to Trask. We would know the Huns by their *Nuttalls*. Perhaps even read their secret messages.

I put the book back in its place and the dressing gown on top of it. Silk seemed out of character for Brauer. Maybe this was a gift for a woman. You wouldn't think it to talk with him. But you wouldn't think in private he'd suddenly dress like a dude.

I closed the drawer and thought about the process: he'd get a telegram; the telegram consisted of blocks of numbers; he'd follow the numerical instructions to find each word in *Nuttall;* he'd write the words down. Perhaps he'd even received a message on the *Lusitania.* For war security, passengers couldn't send telegrams, but we could receive them.

I looked back to the desk.

I stepped to it and opened the drawer and removed the notebook. Whenever he'd received his last message—on the ship or before he sailed—it was decoded into this notebook. I opened the cover and carefully tore out the top sheet. The paper was pretty thin and the Mongol was a hard No. 2, perhaps requiring enough pressure that it would make an indent on the page below. The tear went cleanly. Its absence would not be noticed. I had hopes.

Then I gave every piece of furniture in the suite the treatment, looking behind and beneath, and with the commode I drew the drawers out as far as possible and checked their undersides as well.

The sitting room had given me all that it could.

I had one more room to go.

I stepped through the darkened bedroom doorway. I have a pretty keen sense of smell, and in the dark, without the distraction of my primary sense, it was even keener. I could not place the faint smell but something was in the air. My first thought: saltwater mildew from the first-class bathroom in the far wall.

I turned the electrical key and the place lit up. I looked toward that far wall. On the left, the door into the bathroom was closed; I myself stood in the mirror directly before me, hanging over the dresser; and on the right, built as a wedged corner piece, was a marble-topped washbasin. Something caught my eye there. I moved the length of the room, aware in my periphery of the two beds arranged foot to foot, as in Selene's suite, but keeping my eyes on what seemed the unusual detail.

Now I stood before the washbasin. And I was right. Two men's straight razors were neatly laid side by side. Two shaving mugs sat behind them. And in one drinking glass, two bone-handled toothbrushes leaned away from each other at the top but angled down to the bottom of the glass where their tips touched.

I knew the smell.

I turned. On one of the beds the covers were stripped open, the sheet exposed.

And all the oddness I'd felt in the Smoking Room, trying to understand Edward Cable as a player in the game of German secret service, was explained. He was simply a bookseller from Boston, sharing a secret, certainly, with Walter Brauer, but not the one I was seeking to understand.

9

After thoroughly searching the bedroom and finding nothing further of interest, I slipped out of Brauer's suite and left him and Cable behind for a couple of hours. I ate à la carte in the Verandah Café and I strolled the promenade and I settled into the still mostly empty Smoking Room, and until the moment I pulled out my cigarettes and lit one up, I thought about other things. About my feature story and about the reporting I would do in the other role I still played—no matter where I went, I'd find stories for Christopher Cobb to cover—and I thought about the Cubs, how I'd miss hearing the scores through the summer, and about the new Chicago Federal League team and their swell new ballpark on Addison. And I thought about Selene, though I tried not to, as I was determined for the rest of the night to keep my thinking just as it would have been before I went to Mexico last year, when I was simply Christopher Cobb, war correspondent.

But when I lit up a cigarette on the end of a couch in the Smoking Room, I let my thoughts turn once more to Brauer. Oddly, he seemed more human to me now. Not so easy to despise. I'd been around a lot of men in tough situations and I knew that these feelings existed in the world. Sometimes men even responded to the stress of battle by reaching out like that. I was ready to think that Brauer wasn't working on board, that he was simply in transit to London, that I'd simply have to follow him to the city and continue to keep track of him there. And I did have the slip of paper in my pocket and a chance to get a little something out of it.

But if the *Lusitania* were merely transportation for him, I still wondered why Brauer was in first class. The cost of his suite would've kept a working-class family of four in a London suburb subsisting for two years. A prohibitive extravagance for his German bosses. An impossible lot of money for a college lecturer. Perhaps Cable had lied. Given their relationship, that would've been possible. Perhaps they hadn't met on board. Maybe they'd planned this rendezvous, and the moneyed Cable had sprung for Brauer's first-class accommodations.

Two Fatimas later, the first influx of post-dinner smokers began to arrive, and among them was Cable. I assumed Brauer was immediately behind him. But he wasn't. At least not right away. Brauer could have stopped in the wash room, but I was picking up something in Cable's manner that suggested he was alone. He drifted in; he looked around as if trying to decide what he would do. If he were expecting Brauer, there would be no doubt: he'd find their accustomed place and claim it before the following surge of diners took away the option. But he was hesitating; he was wondering, it seemed to me, if he should simply leave.

Then he noticed me. He did not brighten, even in a routinely social way. But he registered my familiarity. I nodded. He nodded in return, and he hesitated some more, made a decision. He crossed the room and arrived before me. "Good evening, Mr. Cable," I said.

He nodded again.

"Would you like to join me?" I asked.

"Thanks," he said.

There was a fresh shaving cut on his chin. I thought of his razor lying beside Brauer's. Cable's hand had been a bit unsteady tonight in using it. It was a risky thing, I thought, to keep your face bare.

He looked behind him and backed into the chair that faced the couch. He sat down and went straight for his smokes. As he fumbled with his matches—his hands were still unsteady—a steward appeared and took our drink orders. Two whiskeys. He made his a double.

When the steward was gone and Cable had taken a long, calming drag on his cigarette, I said, "Where's Walter?"

Cable had been watching his smoke and he cut his eyes to me as if I should have known better than to ask about this. That attitude instantly passed. But clearly there'd been some sort of break between the two men.

"Working," Cable said.

"Working?"

"He has a lecture to write."

This sounded fishy. From his pinched tone, it sounded fishy to Cable as well.

I said, "So you two knew each other in London, right?"

"We've only known each other a few days," he said, and he was looking away, talking as much to himself as to me, thinking: *I never really knew this man.* He hadn't been lying about when they met. Now it sounded as if Brauer was through with his bookseller, who no doubt possessed—he did passionately love books, after all—a romantic streak.

I said, "An experienced teacher like him, writing a lecture shouldn't take long."

Cable didn't answer but took a drink of his whiskey. Which was itself an answer to the question I really had intended to ask. Brauer had let Cable know he'd be tied up for the rest of the trip.

I felt a little ruthless now. Cable was just a bookseller. I didn't need to be indirect with him. "Does he have another friend on the ship?" I asked.

Cable looked at me. If my impertinence ended the conversation, it made no difference now. But his face went blank. This was a question he hadn't considered.

I had him talking to himself even as he talked to me, so I pushed it: "Have you seen him with anyone?"

He furrowed a little at this, but he clearly hadn't.

"Did he speak of anyone on board?" I asked.

Cable shook his head no. I was sitting, I realized, with a jilted lover. One who had trusted completely.

I could have pushed harder. But I wasn't all that ruthless after all. And Cable wasn't holding anything back. He hadn't held back from his Walter either, sadly. Once again it was easy to despise Brauer. Which was just as well.

10

So I left Edward Cable with his whiskey and smokes and broken heart, and I sat at the desk in my stateroom with my penknife and a Blaisdell No. 624 self-sharpening pencil and the seemingly blank page from Brauer's notebook. The Blaisdell was a clever thing invented in the last century for big-volume pencil-using offices—beloved by the copydesk at the *Post-Express*—but also, as it happened, perfect for my present task. Its soft, black, graphite lead was wrapped not in cedar but in a narrow, tight band of paper, the new segment of lead being freshly exposed by nicking the next in a long row of indents arranged up the barrel and then unwrapping the paper. This I did several times; in between, I scraped the accessible lead into an ashtray, finely grinding it into a soft, black, graphite powder, with no wood scraps to interfere.

Then I laid out the notebook page and began a process of dipping my fingertip into the black powder and lightly rubbing it all across the surface of the page. The graphite turned the page dark wherever I touched, but the indentations made by Brauer recording the decoded words on the previous page gradually emerged, not fully absorbing my superficial dusting and coming out lighter by comparison.

I did not let myself read the note piecemeal. I concentrated on a uniformity of stroke and the lightest of touches so as not to darken the shallow impressions of his writing. Then I was done. And on the notebook page was this telegram from Brauer's German bosses, decoded from *Nuttall: Deliver to 53 Saint Martin Lane Monday night at 8.*

Maybe it wasn't a person on the *Lusitania* that was of interest to Brauer. Maybe it was a thing. A thing too big to carry with him in his baggage—a thing to deliver—and his traveling first class ensured its being handled more carefully.

I pushed back from the desk and I felt I'd probably done as much as I could do for Trask and for country on this voyage. Brauer seemed to be lying low, even divesting himself now of his forbidden book-man. And the more I let it sit in me, the more I figured I was right, that his mission on the ship was to accompany something, which he would deliver to St. Martin's Lane in London, and which presently was stashed in the cargo hold.

I needed some air.

I was still wearing my evening clothes, though I'd stripped off the tie. The North Atlantic night at twenty knots could be pretty chilly, but I could use some bucking up so I simply rose and stepped out of the room. I turned the corridor that passed Selene's suite on the way to the door onto the promenade.

I had no intention of knocking. Her attitude seemed clear.

But I stopped in front of her door.

I hesitated.

I stepped back and looked closely at the tiny gap at the bottom of the door. A light shown there.

I stepped forward again and I knocked. I immediately leaned near to listen. There was a rustling inside, quite close. She was in her parlor, not her bedroom.

The night was waning, however. I didn't bring my watch, but it was well past ten. I used this to justify saying, "Selene?"

Instantly the handle clicked and the door was opening. But it went only far enough to let her face appear, and one shoulder. A few moments later I would struggle to remember what was covering that shoulder, but for the moment I was focused ardently on her dark-of-the-night eyes, trying to read them in conjunction with the tone of her voice as she said, "Mr. Cobb."

On the surface, this was pretty damn formal for a woman who was stashed in my arms not even twenty-four hours earlier. But the eyes were soft, almost supplicant, almost as supplicant as they were when she and I had begun last night, made more so, oddly enough, by the faux-brittle ironic upturn of her "Cobb."

I was prepared for the door to open fully now, without my even having to utter a word.

But it didn't.

"Miss Bourgani," I finally said, though it sounded flat, a tone prompted by the door remaining mostly closed.

"It's late," she said.

"Forgive me," I said.

"I've not been well," she said.

"My fear of that was why I knocked," I said, a statement that may actually have been as much as thirty-two percent true.

"I probably won't emerge till Queenstown," she said.

"I won't trouble you again," I said, thinking what I found myself not infrequently thinking: *I do not understand women even a little bit.*

"Good night," she said.

"Good night," I said.

Those eyes that twice I'd personally seen fill with tears seemed as if they might yet again. But the door moved and clicked shut before I could be sure.

I should have simply walked away. I'd already reconciled myself to having simply played a one-nighter in a provincial theater with a big guest star. But I didn't walk. I leaned. Toward her door. I had the impulse to listen to her weep.

But there was no weeping from her cabin. Instead, I heard a sharp, low utterance by a man's voice. And she responded in kind. None of the words were clear. But the situation seemed very clear.

I backed away. This suddenly felt terribly familiar. Boyhood familiar. A memory hooked into the same part of my brain as catching frogs and skipping stones and playing mumblety-peg in an empty lot and hitting a rubber ball with a broomstick handle while pretending to be Big Ed Delahanty; or more like falling and flaying both my knees while rounding third base at a manhole cover or spearing the side of my foot with my pocket knife playing Flinch or instantly, drastically regretting throwing a caught frog into a bonfire; or like all of that mixed together, good and bad: me placed outside a closed door in the hallway of some actor's boardinghouse or cheap hotel with my mother letting herself be a woman in a woman's body with a woman's needs but with me being a boy who basically knew what was going on but didn't know nearly as much about it as he wanted and who wanted to expunge from his mind the thought of her doing something like this with a man but who also, deeper in that mind, wanted in some classic way to be the one in her arms. My standing there in a first-class corridor outside Selene's door was drastically different, of course, but similar in just enough ways that I wanted to wipe my hands hard on something and maybe spit, and I turned and strode down the corridor, wondering who the hell this might be inside there with the woman who I myself jazzed just last night. Some dude. Some leading man type. The next actor for her to hold in the next filmed episode of Selene Bourgani's life.

I stepped out onto the promenade.

And I looked to my right. Her two windows. The parlor lit. The bedroom dark.

I had to know one thing. But at least I was above spying in her window.

So I stepped back into the corridor. I turned right—away from her—and moved along the few short steps to the doorway that led into the writing room and library. I stopped. I turned and faced down the corridor toward Selene's suite. I was maybe twenty yards from her door.

I waited. For a few moments I tried to remember what she was wearing, from the little of her shoulder I'd seen. I'd been so instantly and totally riveted by her eyes—I wished I'd looked more carefully into her eyes when we'd been together—that I couldn't even say for sure whether her shoulder was covered in crimson silk. It might have been. I'd never expected a man to be with her, so I just couldn't say.

Then I stopped trying to remember and simply waited. This wasn't jealousy, after all. This was curiosity. This was bemusement. I could just wait. I stepped aside for people who wanted into the writing room and who wanted out. I did that half a dozen times. Maybe more. I waited and I tried to look as if I was expecting to meet someone, and people simply excused themselves to go around me, and I excused myself and let them, and I waited.

And then, with no one else in sight at the time, I heard her door opening. I started to take a step forward, going in slow motion, ready to speed up as the man emerged so that I could seem simply to be coming out of the writing room.

But the man emerged and immediately turned to head forward in the corridor, never noticing me, and it was just as well for a couple of reasons. I'd stopped cold and I was sure I was gaping, and I was glad not to appear suspicious to him. Because it was Walter Brauer.

11

The next time I saw Selene Bourgani, it was nearly ten o'clock on the last night of the last voyage of the R.M.S. *Lusitania*. We were in the War Zone and due to arrive in Queenstown tomorrow afternoon.

I wandered into the back of the large mahogany-paneled first-class Lounge and Music Room, its Georgian easy chairs and settees all turned to face the piano-end of the place and holding all the swells, every sitting space filled and all the standing spaces in the room as well. The traditional last-night talent concert was under way, a benefit for the Seamen's Charities.

I entered as they were laughing and applauding a man in a tux who was catching the last of half a dozen oranges he'd been juggling. I lingered at the back door for a moment, and a young woman, smartly dressed—one of the voyagers doing a bit of volunteer work—sidled up to me with a stack of gold-embossed programs, which were selling for ten cents each. "The Welsh Choir has already sung," she said. "But Selene Bourgani's going to perform soon. Buy a program to remember her? It's for the cause."

I gave her a quarter and told her to keep the change for the cause. I shoved the program in my pocket and began to edge my way around the room, excusing myself, squeezing through the standees, wanting to get closer to the front, more than a little surprised that Selene had emerged for this, but maybe not so surprised, reflecting on it as I moved: this was a public event, an audience, a keeping up of the identity she offered to the world, even as she played some other, quite private role.

I'd already settled into the only conclusion I could about Brauer and Bourgani. She was the contact he'd been intending to make on the Lusitania. She was the person of interest to the German Secret Service, the reason Brauer was traveling in first class. The "delivery" in the coded message almost certainly referred to Selene Bourgani. I'd accepted this as the only possible conclusion. And yet I was baffled as hell.

A man was ragtiming "By the Beautiful Sea" on the Broadwood grand and I found a place against a support pillar near the front where I could see between heads to the performance space. The pianist was followed by a Scottish comedian. I could barely understand the heavily brogued words of his jokes, much less their humor. Some in the audience seemed to catch on—the Scots, no doubt—but most were politely waiting for the next act. I endured this for a time, letting my mind drift to trivial things, and finally I looked around the room.

Edward Cable was sitting in one of the easy chairs in the second row, his arms pulled stiffly to his sides. I sensed this much from his place and his pose and from the manner of the women on either side of him, not to mention from their gender: he was alone, having arrived early to the event, with nothing else to do, pining for his lost companion. The comic tended to raise his voice to a near shout at the climax of each joke. One of those shouts came as I watched Cable. He made the slightest flinch at the volume and did not otherwise move.

Then the comic was done. I looked to the front. A tuxedo bounded up and began talking, but I did not listen. My gaze slid on to the far side of the room. And there stood Selene. She was waiting to go on. Her long, empire-waisted dress was sleeveless, as was her sea-green wrap, and she wore long, black gloves. Her throat and the swell of her chest were bare, as were her arms from her shoulder to the middle of her biceps. I found myself stirred most by the unexpected nakedness of that six inches of arm.

The tuxedo yammered about her fame and beauty, and her face was turned slightly away from the audience but not focused on the speaker either. I wanted her to shift her gaze a bit to her left, toward me. I wanted her to look at me. To see me.

Instead, she closed her eyes for a long few moments. As I'd grown up backstage in countless theaters, I'd often seen actresses do this before going on. But even across this room I sensed something else in her at that moment. She was looking inward. And she was looking ahead. She was about to sing to us and she was reflecting on the secret context. I felt sure of all this.

Her eyes still closed, she lifted her face a little and turned it slightly to the left, as if she had just concluded something in her meditation. And the tuxedo announced her: "The internationally renowned, the incomparably beautiful Miss Selene Bourgani!"

Selene's face descended and she opened her eyes, and she found herself looking straight at me.

The crowd was applauding mightily and a few of the young Brit collegiates were crying "Right ho!" and Selene should have been moving to center stage. But she lingered one beat, and then another, looking at me, though her eyes—at least from across the room—showed me no feeling at all. But the lingering did.

Then she shifted her gaze away and she glided to the place where the juggler and the comic had stood and she turned to the throng and smiled. I expected a radiant, film-actress, outsized smile. But it was not. It was quite small, really, this smile, considering the audience, considering their ardor. And then she gave us her famous profile, as she nodded over her bare shoulder to the pianist.

He played a few bars of introduction and she turned back to us all and she began to sing the first verse.

I knew the song. A couple of years ago, a girl in Chicago and I had a rough-and-tumble, me blowing off steam after covering the Second Balkan War. She owned a cylinder of this song and about played the grooves off it in our couple of months together.

Selene sang it with a deep, dark vibrato:
"I've been worried all day long.
Don't know if I'm right or wrong.
I can't help just what I say.
Your love makes me speak this way."

This much was just as it had been seared into my brain from spin after spin of Mr. Edison's cylinder. But then Selene turned her face to me and she found my eyes and she slowed the song down just a little—the pianist subtly adjusted as he heard this—and I could see her mind working as she improvised and interpolated new words:
"Why, oh why, did I close the door?
You must know I wanted more.
But now I'm crying.
No use denying:
I vanish on the nearing shore."

I can be dense about these things sometimes, but it was me she'd closed the door on, and I had no doubt she intended to disappear from me in England. So when she let go of my eyes and faced the audience and sang the familiar chorus to us all, I had no choice but to think she was still singing to me. Just to me:
"You made me love you.
I didn't want to do it.
I didn't want to do it.
You made me want you,
And all the time you knew it.
I guess you always knew it.
You made me happy sometimes,
You made me glad.
But there were times dear,
You made me feel so sad.
You made me sigh, for
I didn't want to tell you.
I didn't want to tell you.

I want some love that's true.
Yes I do,
Deed I do,
You know I do.
Give me, give me what I cry for.
You know you got the brand of kisses that I'd die for.
You know you made me love you."

And she was done. The crowd was on its feet, applauding and shouting "Brava!" and she closed her eyes again, as she had when she was waiting to go on, as if she were meditating. Briefly. And she bowed. She did not curtsey. She bowed. A long, slow, stiff bow from the waist. The bow of a Prussian officer in a social setting with civilians, feeling uncomfortable, waiting to leave.

She did this once. She bowed only once, and then she looked fleetingly to me, one last time, and she turned away and moved quickly to the far side of the room and disappeared from my sight beyond the crowd.

I followed her progress to the back of the lounge by watching the bodies turning to send their ongoing applause straight to her as she was leaving them.

Then she was gone. And everyone was facing back to the empty space where she had just sung, and they continued to applaud her, even though she had vanished.

12

I stood before her door.

I had approached softly. The corridor itself was very quiet, even though many on the ship were still awake, even now, well past midnight, already a couple of hours advanced into May 7, 1915.

Before the end of the charity concert Captain Turner had stood in the performance space and made a short, clumsy, self-contradictory speech revealing a special telegraph warning from the naval area commander in Queenstown that German U-boats were known to be presently active off the Irish coast, but Turner urged us not to worry, as our ship was too fast and we would have the Royal Navy to protect us but in the meantime don't dare light any cigarettes on deck.

Many of the first-class passengers were now sleeping fully dressed and fitful in the public spaces, on chairs and settees and on pallets on the floors of the Writing Room and the Smoking Room and the Lounge, the Dining Room and the Entrance Hall, even on the landings of the Grand Staircase. Others paced the decks in the dark, wearing their life jackets.

But as I stood in front of Selene's door, there was only silence. I had hesitated for a long while, roaming the promenade decks, wanting to confront her about the man—and the government—she was dealing with, but knowing that now more than ever I needed to play the supporting role of the usable and disposable newspaperman-lover so that I could play the leading role of an American secret agent.

All of which sounded suddenly ridiculous in my head. I was crazy about this woman. I'd soon have to deal with what she was and what she was doing, but I wanted her badly now. I lifted my hand to knock, but before I could, the door swung open and she was a vision in scarlet silk and golden dragons.

She had asked me to come here with her eyes and her song. She knew it was going to be me; I knew she knew it was going to be me; and yet I stood there struck motionless and dumb at the door's abrupt opening.

Now the vision of her was intensified by another opening: her hands moved to the knot of her silk belt and undid it and the belt fell away and her hands rose to her chest and grasped the edges of the wrap and she spread her arms—opening the kimono—and I had to work hard to bolster my dissolving knees.

Since standing up was a struggle for me at the moment, moving forward was out of the question. She did not seem to mind. She sloughed off the kimono and she was utterly naked, instantly, in the open doorway, and she did not move either, though I'm sure she had more of a choice in the matter than I did, and we stood before each other and it was a tribute to her eyes that they were all I was looking at.

She seemed happy to set the rules, as she had our first time. She lifted a hand and touched my lips with her fingertips. Only they were different rules. "Not a word," she said. "And forget the last time. Go rough with me. I think you know how."

This fortified my knees, and I stepped into her cabin and swept her up in my arms and kicked her door shut with my heel. And I did this thing with Selene Bourgani in the War-Zone dark, and though I did it the way I was used to doing it, and though I didn't even have to make myself assume that the woman beneath me wanted it done this way, and though it was all proceeding just fine as far as the bodies involved were concerned, the damnedest thing started going on.

My mind separated itself, my mind went off somewhere quite a ways away and raised a periscope and watched this vessel sailing by in the dark, watched me doing what I wanted with this woman, whose beautiful eyes I could not see, whose beautiful body was simply something to pound inside, whose beauty and public place in the world I was merely turning into a classy version of all the bodies I'd ever pounded inside, and yet all the while, my lurking mind was wondering what was going on with her. She'd wanted me slow and gentle before her meeting with Brauer. She'd wanted me slow and gentle when we were out in the middle of the North Atlantic, when she was still days and nights away from the place where she was going and from the things she would do there. But tonight she wanted it like this. As our arrival grew nearer, was she feeling guilty about what she was going to do? Was she having me punish her for it? Some women wanted to be punished like this.

And then I was done. My body knew it quite well. But with my mind submerged far away, watching, working on its own questions, I missed the moment.

Selene was gasping, was whimpering, she was saying, "More. Keep going. Please." My body had enough left to do that. And I did that. But all I was caring about was what, exactly, Selene Bourgani had gotten herself into, and why, and how I could get her out.

Then she said she was all right. She wasn't. Her body maybe had what it wanted, but I could feel the darkness inside her welling up again and she was not all right. And then we were holding each other close in this outer darkness, on the floor of her parlor in her suite on the *Lusitania,* and now that my body was done, I was fully there beside her again and we neither of us seemed inclined to move. Not to the bed in the other room. Not even to the overstuffed sofa here in her parlor. We lay on the floor and she put her head on my chest and I drew her close.

After a while she shifted her head to my shoulder and immediately laid her hand where her head had been. Upon my heart, I realized. I knew how to grill possible news sources, even by indirection when

I didn't want to put them completely off me. I figured this might be my only chance with Selene. I said, "Are you awake?"

"Yes."

"Are you all right?"

She wasn't going to say no. But her yes was slow and quiet. "Yes," she said.

"I think the Germans could do this," I said.

She was quiet.

"Sink us," I said.

She still said nothing. I didn't like the dark. I wanted to read her face. Was it paining her to confront the perfidy of the men she was working for? Was she like them? I wanted to see her eyes.

"What they did in Belgium when they went in," I said. "In Dinant. Louvain."

She stirred. Her hand came off my chest. Her head lifted from my shoulder, but only for a moment, returning almost at once. And she said, "The world's pretty selective in the massacres it cares about."

She herself applied the word "massacre" to the civilian killings in Belgium. But somehow I heard in her a world-weary justification of the Germans. That's what I wanted her to talk about. If I was to get more from her at this juncture I needed to start with something like: "Which other massacres do you mean?" It needed to sound like an ignorant challenge. I needed to rile her to get her to say things. But I knew what she was talking about. The Brits in India, for example, killing a million locals by exporting their rice in the midst of famine. The Belgians themselves in the Congo, massacring by amputation over failed rubber quotas. I was holding Selene close and I was still a little in her thrall, and contrary to my reporter's instincts, I was reluctant to sound stupid and calloused.

So I improvised in another direction. "Have you ever had a German lover?"

This made her head leave my shoulder and stay away. There was just enough spill of light into the room from beneath the door that I could see her turn her body to face me, prop her head on her hand.

"How did you do that?" she said.

"Do what?"

"Go from massacres to my past lovers?"

"A freely associating mind," I said.

She grunted a little.

"You shouldn't have asked for it rough," I said.

She laughed a little.

I said, "You wanted our last time together to be the last. Then this. Before we quit forever again, I want to know where I'll fit in your memory."

"He wanted to know that too."

"Who?"

"The German. What is it with the smarter men? They all seem to want to know about the ones before."

"The stupid men prefer virgins," I said. "We've got a sense of history."

She was quiet for a moment, and then she asked, "Was your mother happy in love?"

Selene was freely associating now herself. And she wasn't hesitant to get personal. I didn't like the associations squirming to be free in my own head at this question, but at least she made it easier for me to press the only issue I had to work with.

"You'd have to ask her," I said. "I didn't keep track."

I let that sit in her for a moment, and it did, quietly. Then I pressed on. "And your German," I said. "Were you happy with him?"

She wasn't saying.

I got to that question too quick. I backed up. "Who was he?"

"A director."

"Of course," I said.

She fell silent once more. I waited. She wasn't talking.

"Which one?" I asked.

She moved abruptly and I couldn't see how in the dark and I flinched. But her body was suddenly against me again, her head returned to the place on my shoulder where it had been before the talk began. Her hand returned to my heart.

I'd been grasping at straws here. Trying to get her to talk about the Germans. Trying to figure out her connections to them. This seemed just a busted romance. But it was the only card I had to play.

I'm not real smart about women. But I'm smart about reading people, being a pretty good reporter. So after making a certain scale-tipping number of mistakes with women, my reporter skills finally kicked in and taught me a few things. Women, especially ones who have reasons—like jazzing together—to think you've got a romantic future, deep down want to talk about their feelings. So for the first time ever while lying around naked with a female, I said, "You want to talk about it?"

But this wasn't your usual woman.

She lifted her head slightly away from me and said, with an edge in her voice she could use for Lady Macbeth, "I'm a movie star. Movies don't talk. We're in the last reel of our little smut film, so just shut up now and hold me."

Which made me even more interested in her director. I did not believe she was completely at ease with her connection to the German secret service. If they had something on her to coerce her, it might have come from her former lover. I was still thinking about all this when she added, but in the softest of voices, the gentlest of voices, the most natural of voices, a voice beyond the range of her manifest talents as an actress: "Or go the hell away."

There was even the faintest hint of a concluding catch in her voice.

As an agent of the American secret service, there was nothing more I could do now. As a man, I drew her closer and she gave me a kiss on the throat as soft and natural as these last words she'd spoken.

And a knock came at the door.

We both flinched upright.

But she put her hand on my chest, telling me to stop, move no more, make no noise. She clearly wanted to ignore this, whatever it was.

I figured it to be one of two things. A ship official rousing people for some emergency preparation. But there would be more commotion, if that were the case.

The knock came again, a little louder.

Or it could be Brauer.

It was Brauer. His voice outside: "Miss Bourgani."

I felt Selene stiffen.

The knock came again, though. Stupidly, it was more softly. He was second guessing the wisdom of disturbing her in the middle of the night. Which made him continue to try to disturb her, only more quietly.

He even lowered his voice: "Miss Bourgani." He was addressing her formally. I was—in spite of my certainty that there was nothing personal between them—relieved.

He got even stupider. He said her name softly once more and simultaneously tried the latch on the door. Even though it would certainly be locked. And, of course, since it was most recently kicked shut by my heel while I had things on my mind other than securing the door, it was not locked.

The door opened.

A wide shaft of light fell upon Selene and me, sitting naked, side by side, on the parlor floor.

Framed in dark silhouette in the doorway was Walter Brauer.

"Get the hell out," Selene barked.

Walter flustered there. It made him even stupider. "I'm sorry," he said. "I didn't know."

"Get out," she said.

This is how stupid: with us sitting naked before him, he felt compelled to justify his middle of the night interruption. "I wanted to reassure you about the U-boats."

"Mr. Brauer," Selene said sharply.

He blundered on: "They would stop us first, before sinking the ship."

"We hardly know each other," Selene said.

"The passengers would be allowed to disembark."

"I am naked, Mr. Brauer," Selene said.

"I'm sorry," he said.

"So is this gentleman," Selene said.

I knew what was driving Brauer. He was afraid a U-boat attack would upset their plans. This had occurred to him after Turner's speech tonight. The attack could happen at any time, so for the sake of their conspiracy, he had to instruct her in an alternate plan, even if that meant doing it in the middle of the night.

"I'm sorry," he said again.

"Get out." Without a single "s" in either word I'm not sure how Selene made that sound like a hiss. But she did.

Brauer was finally getting the hint.

He was starting to close the door. Not fast enough.

"Out!" Selene cried.

And the silhouette vanished; the door clicked shut; the room went dark.

Selene and I sat there for a long moment not moving.

I wanted to say, "Who the hell was that?" It was the best question to ask to perhaps elicit an unguarded response.

But for maximum effect, it had to be asked instantly. I'd already waited too long.

Which was for the best anyway: she might have seen Brauer and me speaking together; he might have mentioned me to her, as an unusually snoopy newsman she should take care to avoid. I didn't want her to catch me in a lie, pretending not to know him.

I said, "That was Walter Brauer, wasn't it?"

Though I could not see her in the dark, I could sense her face turn to me.

Perhaps she didn't know I'd encountered him. This could be just as useful, her abruptly realizing I knew him. I could even hint I knew *about* him.

I waited. She waited. Then she said, "Yes."

"How do you know him?" I asked.

She called my bluff before I could get it started. "How do you?" she said.

I still wanted to seem to both of them to be an ignorant third party. No verifiable lies. Nothing suspicious. "I met him around," I said. "Had a drink and a smoke with him and a bookseller friend of his a few nights ago."

She did not reply to this. But along all the places where our arms and thighs were touching, I felt a faint loosening of tension in her.

"And you?" I said.

"Something similar," she said.

"Really?" I meant this rhetorically, but I heard it sound like a challenge. It was already spoken, so I went ahead with the rest of it, even as I felt her tensing again. "He seemed awfully forward in the middle of the night," I said.

She snorted. It was that female, dismissive "men" snort that is recognizable even in the pitch black.

I was relieved. She was taking it as jealousy.

"The night's over, Mr. Cobb," she said.

I couldn't dispute that. But I didn't move.

"Time for you to go," she said, though once again the softness of her tone surprised me.

I rose. I gathered my clothes from the floor, my eyes finally adjusting a little to the dark, with the help of the crack of corridor light beneath the door.

As I put on the first thing, my shirt, I heard her move away toward the bedroom. Without a word.

Later, after I slipped on my shoes and after I kneeled to them and tied them and rose, after I'd finished with dressing, I hesitated, thinking to go to the bedroom door, to say something to her.

But I didn't. A darkness like hers was spreading into my mind, like the darkness in the eyes after taking a blow to the head.

I moved toward the corridor door.

And then there was a rushing from behind me.

I turned.

I think part of me would not have been surprised if she were rushing to me with a knife that she'd plunge into my chest. But neither was I surprised when she leapt into my arms, still naked, hooking her legs around me, and she kissed me hard on the lips.

Nor was I surprised, when I tried to move into the room with her, that she just as rapidly disentangled from me and dismounted and backed away into the darkness, saying, "I'm sorry. That was good-bye. We're done now, Kit Cobb."

13

And the *Lusitania* steamed into its last sunrise. And we all steamed with it. I slept only a little after leaving Selene. I rose and I wrote some and I packed my things and I ate lunch, with the ship orchestra playing "The Blue Danube," and I went down to the Purser's Bureau in the Entrance Hall on B Deck and I retrieved the constant hidden companion of every foreign excursion of my war correspondent career: my money belt, with a stash of gold coins and with reporter credentials and a passport protected inside, for hot countries and cold, for wet countries and dry, for mountain battlefields and city back alleys.

Then I returned to my cabin and I opened my shirt and I strapped the belt around me and I fastened my clothes around it as if I were about to mount a horse and ride into actual danger, and I chuckled. I don't chuckle. But I affected a tough-guy ironic chuckle, like a bad actor doing a melodrama hero. Like I was such a well-equipped tough guy who thrived on danger but here I was, trapped in a chuckle-worthy lesser world that booksellers and pamphlet writers and sons of tycoons and mothers with their toddlers inhabited. Here I was, simply about to go through customs in Queenstown, Ireland, and board a train for London, England, with a secret mission to sneak around and think about what college lecturers and film actresses might be up to, having lately been used up and kicked out the door by a beautiful woman. This latter probably was the main thing that prompted the phony chuckle.

And even while I was going through this little fit of pique, like an actor in a repertory company peeved by the no-account role he'd been given to play, a U-boat captain was watching us do fifteen substandard knots in a goddamn straight line directly toward him and wondering just how lucky he was going to get.

Pretty goddamnn lucky, as it would soon turn out.

I stepped onto the promenade and the sky was clear and the sun was high and I felt how slow we were going right away. I walked aft, and the portside was full of people crammed at the brief stretches of open railing between lifeboats. The coast of Ireland was distantly visible out there. Some people were murmuring reassuring things about that. Others, who knew ships and their speed and their bearing, were muttering about our vulnerability. And even the ones who were made hopeful by the sight of land were unsettled by the absence of Turner's promised Royal Navy. We were alone.

I knew the muttering was right. I had a pretty refined nose for the whiff of war, but it was attuned to land forces, clashing armed men, so I was willing, in all fairness, to temper my instinctive assessment of officers out here on the ocean, even civilian ones, in spite of the fact that Captain Turner, from my two encounters with him and from this present sailing strategy, seemed to me a classic example of military hierarchy: a guy who was mediocre and competent at some lower level but who had inevitably been promoted to a rank and responsibility where he was finally stupid and incompetent. But that conclusion was more from my mind than my gut, and I liked to rely on my gut in combat zones. So I took on the enlisted man's attitude. I put my mind off the forces I could not control. Somebody else was guiding this ship.

I had my own present jitters, but they were professional and personal, and the sight of Ireland held no appeal for me, so I turned and hustled forward, passing beneath the portside Bridge Wing, casting, as I did, a quick glance up toward where Turner was bungling along. I followed the curve of open passageway beneath the Main Bridge and arrived at the starboard side, where there weren't so many passengers, and I slowed down and I thought to step to the rail just forward of Lifeboat 1. The vast, indigo sea lay out there with the sunlight scattered brightly upon it, and it struck me that Turner might have once been a brilliant guy, a potential genius of an officer in any self-respecting, land-based army, but he had been driven to stupidity and incompetence by staring too long at vast indigo seas with sunlight scattered brightly upon them.

So I kept walking. I'd gather a few last quotes for my sea-voyage-through-a-war-zone feature story and yes, maybe take a peek at the Irish coast to work in a few pretty landscape details. I passed Lifeboat 3 and 5 and 9 and passed Lifeboat 11, beneath the high-towering number-three funnel, and then it seemed that a great iron door slammed shut behind me and the deck beneath my feet quaked and I stopped and I knew instantly what it was. I turned and from beneath the starboard Bridge Wing a plume of water was rising and dark scraps of the hull and smoke from 350 pounds of TNT and hexanite—a U-boat had just plugged us—and I reflexively sucked in the still-pristine air around me and my breath caught and I hardly let go of the breath, I hardly began to lift my face to the rise of torpedo-spew when a second sound began. A quick-gathering massive thunder-roll of sound slammed against me and the deck bucked—and I knew—I knew it was the half dozen forward boilers ripping us open—and I staggered back and the plume that had begun from the torpedo-strike bloated instantly, rising and thrusting and scrabbling upward suddenly full of steam and coal and cinder and wood and iron and it rose above the funnels, as high as a Chicago skyscraper, and it expanded and it seemed it would cover me, and I turned and sprinted aft two strides and a third, but I wanted to see, I wanted to be able to write this moment accurately and I had to see, so I stopped now.

I turned and shoulders were bumping me, people were scrambling past, and down the way at about Lifeboat 5 the steaming rain was beginning to fall, the black metal hail of boiler and hull, and as it came down I lowered my eyes and a man in morning clothes was vanishing there and the clang and clatter of it all filled the air and yet

I could also hear the heavy exhalation of human breath rushing past me and Lifeboat 5 was splintering and tumbling beneath the crashing and thudding fragments of the *Lusitania*. And yes. Yes, I could see now the soundless fall of body parts from belowdecks, a torso, a leg, a head. And the falling and the tumbling and the raining went on for a time, and a time more, and it seemed a long time, but it was a short time, and then there was silence.

For a breath-snagged moment, there was silence.

A seagull cried out above me.

And then more silence.

Except now the great metal groaning of the ship. The deep, vast grinding of metal.

And a distant heavy rushing of water into the gash of our forward starboard hull.

Suddenly I was light in the feet and in the leg and in the shoulders as the bow of our ship plunged to the right and the whole starboard length of the ship began to fall over with it.

My chest seized as I expected to fly beyond the railing and into the sea. I threw my arms out, danced like a boxer, to try to balance.

And the ship's plunge ceased as abruptly as it began.

I was still on deck, still on my feet.

We listed maybe fifteen degrees starboard and downward but we were stable at that angle for the moment and we were plowing forward.

Even as the wordless cries of fear began all around and the first of the lying sons of bitches who wore Cunard uniforms called out from somewhere behind me that we were just fine, that we couldn't sink, this much was clear to me right away: because of the deep inner engine room source of the second blast and because of the pitch of the deck and the angle of our bow into the sea, the *Lusitania* was going to sink, and pretty goddamn quickly.

And a thing came into me, and it was not a thought; it came from nowhere near my mind but rather from my skin, from my blood, from my bones: I was filled with Selene. I was filled with her and

I was apart from her and I had to lay my hands upon her now and carry her away from this sinking ship.

I loaded and locked a battlefield focus: there were others around me, many others, and we all shared our mortality and our peril, but as with an infantryman in a company across a field of fire from a bunker and a gun, the assault on which was the single and utter purpose of his life, all the other people around me blurred into the background, became immediate only when they were directly involved in my mission.

I strode forward and already people were rushing out of the Main Staircase doors to the Boat Deck and I was thinking to enter at the point closest to Selene's suite. But as I veered to the rail and around the bodies flowing onto the promenade I could see up ahead. All the rubble from below and the remains of Lifeboat 5 lay blocking the doorway I wished to enter. Lay, as well, outside Brauer's windows.

I wondered for a moment about him, about what skills he might have to save himself. I knew the further trouble we were all in. From our list to starboard, the lifeboats on this side of the ship had swung out on their davits to the farthest extent of their snubbing chains and would be brutally difficult to launch, especially as our momentum would carry us for miles yet, sucking in the sea, and on the portside the lifeboats would be pinned against the hull and be even harder to launch.

I had to go in through the doors to the Main Staircase. And I had to stop thinking. There were two sets of double doors, double but narrow, fine for elegant comings and goings but this was the Boat Deck and everyone from the Lounge and the Writing Room were already jammed here, and the Main Staircase was no doubt filling with the upsurge of people from the lower decks who were mobbing up behind, and everyone was pressing hard, trying to get to the lifeboats.

I didn't want to cross the current of that mob inside to get to the forward-leading corridor, so I danced through the dispersing flow of bodies out here on the promenade and then planted myself on the far side of the jamb on the forward set of double doors, beside the desperate outrush of bodies. I took a breath—like preparing to leap from a trench on the front—and I turned my shoulder forward and I concentrated on the seam between jamb and emerging body and I inserted my shoulder there, braced my legs, pressed forward to lever myself inside, and a man's shoulder met mine hard and he was coming from above me by the angle of our list and he drove me back around.

And I did it again, this time with a woman emerging, all seal coat and honeysuckle scent, and she was coming out straight and I wedged at the seam and turned her sideways just enough, putting my hands onto her arms so she would not fall, and she continued on out as I slid across her and around the door frame, and I was in a tiny vestibule and the slow thick flow of bodies pressed me against the side wall and I edged inward and then to another door jamb and to a small man in a rain slicker who I turned sideways and he was all right and sidling away and I levered my way inside and the crowd surged from behind and I was slammed hard into the wall, but it was only a short few sideways-driving steps more and I curled to the right around the corner, and I was free of the mob.

The doors to the Writing Room and Library were before me. I stepped to them and through them and the list made it hard to sprint but I moved as fast as I could, skirting tipped chairs and scattered books, and now half a dozen bodies were lurching toward me, strapped into their life jackets, heading away from their blocked door onto the Boat Deck, and I jinked between and around them. I passed through the forward doors of the Writing Room and into the starboard forward-leading corridor, and as I did, I finally was struck by the brightness of the space I'd just left. The room's portholes, which were square and large as proper windows, were filled with the afternoon sun, which meant the outside porthole covers were open. The quick sinking would escalate even faster without a chance to execute porthole discipline across the ship.

Now the false assurance of the dimness of the cabin corridor warned me of a different imminent danger. The electric lights blinked off and everything went black and they flickered back on. The crossway to the portside was just ahead and I stepped to the intersection and two more bodies bumped into me and then veered past, heading aft, ignoring our collision, a woman weeping heavily and a man murmuring "It's all right" and "It's all right, my darling."

I stood at this juncture—before me was Brauer's suite and beyond was my own stateroom—and I took a quick inventory. My money belt was strapped to me. I patted the pockets of my sack coat and felt, deep in an inside pocket, my leather-pouched set of lock picks. I gave one brief thought to the things still in my cabin. Only my Corona Portable Number 3 and the words I'd written on it these past few days gave me a twist of serious regret, but this was, in fact, a meaningless exercise. There was no time. It was impossible now to do anything except turn and press on, which I did, my legs suddenly heavy from the incline, as heavy as in a bad dream.

As if they'd been trapped belowdecks and finally found the staircase, a couple of fears scrambled up into my chest and then into my head: *She's probably already gone. And you have no plan even if you find her.*

But I knew this from the wars I'd covered: thinking is how you die. You react. And either you do things right or you don't. But nobody can think fast enough to live.

A few steps more and I turned into the portside forward-running corridor and then I was at her door and I pounded on it.

From outside, from the portside promenade, I heard men suddenly cry out together, men in some heavy, physical, coordinated task, and then a scraping and a scuffling and then shouts and a clanking and creaking and suddenly very nearby a massive clang of struck iron and a crack of wood and the corridor quaked beneath my feet and many voices were screaming, and I could picture in my head the whole quick terrible sequence: some crewmen tried to launch a lifeboat against the list of the ship, tried to push it out together and away and the men working the falls failed to let the ropes out in their split second of opportunity and the lifeboat swung back on board on its davits and crushed the crew and threw the passengers against the deck wall.

Selene could have been out there.

She might have just this moment died.

I was crazy. Why was I knocking? I tried Selene's door and it was locked.

This was good. She wouldn't rush out in these circumstances and then lock her door behind her. She was inside.

"Selene!" I cried. And again: "Selene!" I backed away to kick the door in. It would be up the incline and I struggled to secure my footing—the opposite corridor wall was too far away to brace myself—and I planted my foot on the floor as best I could, straining into the rubberized tiles, and I kicked hard just below the door lock.

A little give. But it was still locked. I kicked again and stumbled forward. The cries went on from the deck. The electric lights flickered and went out. And stayed out. The generator was dead. My throat clamped shut.

I couldn't see the door. It was before me but I needed to aim well to kick this thing open. But around a corner about fifty feet aft was the door to the promenade. Its porthole spilled a little light that seeped just far enough into the corridor that it let my eyes begin to adjust.

I set myself once more and kicked, and I set and kicked again and the door popped open and instantly banged back shut. But the lock was breached. I stepped forward and pushed through into Selene's suite.

I flinched at the light.

The door slammed behind me.

The portholes were lace-curtained but unshuttered, letting the day pour in.

Shadows flashed there at the windows. A jumble of sharp voices and moaning. Clanking of chains. I made them blur away from me.

I turned.

The sofa. The chair. The whole parlor. Empty. Selene was gone.

But there was one more room.

I stepped quickly across the floor and into the bedroom.

And I saw her.

She was lying on her back on the farther of the two foot-to-foot beds. She was dressed in shirtwaist and skirt and flat shoes. Her hands were crossed on her chest. She was very still.

I thought of goddamn Juliet and plunged forward, sat down beside her.

She stirred.

I put my hands behind her shoulders and pulled her up, pulled her against my chest. She was warm. She was moving. I put my mouth against her ear. "Selene," I said.

And her hands fell upon my back, pressed me against her.

We held each other and we did not speak and I grew stupid once again. I figured it was me she'd been waiting for, figured she'd been lying here waiting in the midst of mortal chaos because she needed me to arrive before she could think to be saved.

But she was simply clinging to me.

"We need to go now," I said.

She pulled away a little and looked me in the eyes, her face half in dark shadow, half in the light from the porthole, that half flickering with the shadows of the chaos outside.

"It's too much for me," she said.

"I'll help you," I said.

She shook her head faintly, and I could see her mouth make a thin, asymmetrical smile, an ironic smile, and though it was a leap, I didn't think I was stupid about this: I felt pretty sure that what was "too much" for her was more than just finding a way to save herself from drowning; she was choosing whether or not to live, whether lying back down on this bed and dying was the only way for her to refuse to work for the Germans.

What did they have on her?

An irony was dawning on me as well: to talk her into escaping with me would be to preserve her for the Germans' plan.

I embraced the irony. I said, "You have so much to live for."

She put her hand on my chest. It wasn't clear to me if it was a gesture of connection or a gentle *Go away.*

"Let's do this together," I said.

Her ironic smile again.

Voices outside the window.

She turned her face sharply in that direction.

I was locked in to Selene and I'd missed the words out there. A woman's voice. Something about a child. I knew how little time we all had now, before the *Lusitania* went down. I was pretty sure the lifeboats were mostly useless. The children could not be saved.

"I can save you," I said to Selene.

She looked back to me as sharply as if I'd cried out from beyond the porthole. The irony was gone from her face.

She believed me. I wasn't sure I believed myself. But we'd try this together.

"Okay," she said.

We both leapt up from the bed.

"Life jackets," I said and I was ahead of her, striding into the parlor and to the tall wardrobe in the forward corner. I opened it and the upper shelf was jammed tight with two G. M. Boddy life jackets. They would not yield to a moderate grasp. I yanked them hard and they tumbled out.

I knew the design from a steamer in the Gulf. They were full of kapok in a strong drill casing, and if you put it on right, you'd float for days no matter what the seas. I worked quickly at the three knots to open one and Selene watched and she started on the knots on a second jacket before I'd finished. She was committed to this. Good.

We slipped them on, one big Falstaffian pad on our chest, five others around and behind us, one of them high between our shoulder blades to keep our heads above water no matter what. We tied each other in.

I took her hand and we went through the door and into the darkness of the corridor.

We turned right, toward the portal onto the Boat Deck.

It was our nearest way out. And it was worth taking a moment to see if the portside was indeed impossible: if my fear was wrong, then we'd be mad to contend with the upswell of bodies from belowdecks in the starboard exit doors.

We staggered along for a few steps, finding where to center ourselves in our bodies, balancing low in the legs, and we turned into the short portal corridor. My hand and Selene's hand found each other without a thought driving them, without a glance from either of us. We held tight and moved to the portal.

I turned the handle and heaved the door open and we stepped out. A few yards aft, a lifeboat filled the deck, pressed against the wall. Battlefields had taught me to see and not to see splashes of blood and bodies splayed and crushed and others laid out writhing, and I looked back to Selene. She was seeing clearly what I did not. Her vast dark eyes were looking beyond me and they were wide with the carnage and with a thought I could read: it was better for her just to go back to her cabin and lie down and cross her arms on her chest.

And so she was letting go of my hand and she was recoiling backward toward the door and I knew from the rushing and crying around me and the angle of the deck beneath our feet and the lifeboats pinned against our hull that we should get away from the portside, and I reached out and grabbed her at the wrist before she could vanish and I dragged her forward and I cried "Look only at me" and I pulled her behind me for my first step forward and another—we would head for the starboard side, but not by the exit doors—and then I didn't have to pull, and her wrist in my trailing hand twisted, but only so her own hand could grasp me in return, and she was with me, our hands holding at the wrists and I pushed hard through the narrow spaces between bodies, staggering at times as the angle to starboard tried to throw us down, but the angle forward helped us rush and we hugged the deck wall using it when we could, bracing our passage with our free hands or even at times with our feet, Selene slipping now sideways, and we got her up, clambering at each other with our hands, and we made our way forward, and in my functioning consciousness were only her hand and mine and the series of physical objectives I would set, one by one, to focus our rush. The Bridge Wing first, floating before us, and we stumble-rushed along and it neared and we swerved out from a staircase to the bridge and now we were passing beneath the wing and immediately ahead was the curving turn of the deck wall at the forward crossover passageway, and I knew we had to take that carefully, we dared not lose our footing in the turn, for there would be nothing on the other side to stop our tumble and I didn't know the state of things down that slope, and so I pulled us up sharply, in the shadow of the Bridge Wing.

I turned us and we pressed back there against the wall. Just to my right the corner began its curve forward. Selene intertwined her fingers in mine and squeezed tight. Briefly. And then her hand went slack.

I turned my face to her. Selene Bourgani's famous profile was before me, her head laid back as if she'd returned to her cabin bed. Her eyes were shut.

"Don't give up," I said. I could barely hear myself.

I realized there was a great din all around me of voices and chains and steam and footfalls and distress whistle and groaning hull metal and sobs and I blocked it all out once more and I leaned nearer to Selene and I cried out loudly, "Selene!"

Her face turned to me and her eyes opened.

"Stay with me," I cried.

She stared at me blankly for a long moment. I was afraid she was losing her will. I thought to shake her, even to slap her across the cheek. This mood would kill her. Would kill us both.

But she stirred. She nodded to me: *Yes.*

"I need to check," I cried, motioning over my shoulder to the corner of the deck wall. "Then we move."

She nodded again.

I let go of her hand and turned and laid my chest against the wall and I worked my way left, carefully, along the curve, feeling the pull grow stronger on me, feeling it in my chest, and I pressed harder into the wall, stretched my neck to the left, waiting to see what I needed to see, hoping the sight would come before I was grabbed off my feet and thrown forward.

And then I could see, and I strained my legs to stop.

I stopped.

This is what I saw: the deck fell sharply toward the water, and beyond the foremast the water was foaming in a sharp, slashing angle across the forecastle, with starboard railing and capstans and hatches and windlass already vanished utterly beneath the sea and, with them, the far end of the passageway to the starboard side.

I pulled away, pressed my back against the deck wall, edged around the curve, thrashing in my head to visualize a way out for us, with the portside promenade a death trap and the forward passage to the starboard promenade blocked and the inside starboard portals clogged with chaos.

I was off the curve once more and I turned my face to Selene.

She was gone.

I pushed away from the wall, scrambled upright.

I looked up the incline of the Boat Deck.

Bodies jumbled there, black-uniformed crewmen pulling at people in the nearest lifeboat, dragging them out—and this was why I could not let myself see too much—and therefore think too much—I was immobilized now trying to understand the incongruity of the crew unloading the unlaunched lifeboat—but they were acting on orders based on the desperate reality that the rivet heads and flanges down the side of the hull would rip the boat open in its dragging descent, even as these men no doubt proclaimed the lie—since there was no official Cunard alternative—that the ship was unsinkable.

I had to stop trying to figure things out with my head. I was losing any sense of what to *do*. I had to trust my body simply to act now.

And I found my body sparking with undirected energy to find Selene.

She was not visible.

And then she was.

I saw her white shirtwaist and dark skirt against the sky, emerging at the portside railing from beyond the wide, upright column of the Bridge Wing. She was moving up the deck, slowly, looking out to sea, as if she were taking some fresh air after lunch.

I knew a way.

I scrambled up the deck toward Selene. She did not move as I came near, and I stepped to the railing beside her. She seemed not even to notice.

We clung to the rail and watched the wide, bright, sun-flecked sea together for a few moments, as if the deck was deserted and I was ready to offer her a cigarette and later we might even work up to a kiss.

Then I slipped my arm around her waist.

And to my relief, she laid her head against the point of my shoulder.

I angled my head toward hers.

In spite of our appearance at the rail and my sharp focus on her, I was fully aware of the welter all around us. I bent to her, brought my mouth close to her ear so I could speak loudly enough to be heard but still sound tender, like an actor wooing an actress and projecting the performance to the back of the mezzanine. "Selene."

She lifted her head away from my shoulder.

"I want to hold you close to me once again," I said.

She lifted her chin just a bit.

"In this lifetime," I said.

She nodded.

She turned her face and looked up into my eyes.

We could delay no longer.

I took her hand.

"We have to go over," I said, flipping my head a little toward the top of the ship.

And we turned and we cut across the deck to the stairway and we were going up and the stairs were empty—groups in panic follow the obvious paths, stack up at exit doors, refuse to act against their conditioned response—and we were climbing fast and we emerged onto the rubber-matted flooring outside the wheelhouse. The windows were a few steps forward of us and I couldn't see inside and I was glad for that, glad to miss an image of the quiet chaos in there. We turned aft.

And a junior officer stepped from the bridge doorway, directly into our path. He lifted a meatpacker's hand, giving us his palm.

We stopped. Though I didn't want to do it because I was afraid Selene would run again, I knew I had to let go of her hand.

I gave it a squeeze and released it.

"Forbidden," he shouted. "Go back."

A pistol was wedged into his belt on his right hip. He was under orders to protect the bridge with deadly force.

"We're just going through," I said.

His palm was coming down and it was angling toward his hip.

I took a quick step forward as his hand neared the pistol and my right fist was closed tight already and I stepped once more, planted my leading foot, my left foot, out ahead, and I stopped and he grasped the pistol and I set myself and the barrel was coming free and I drove my fist forward—an overhand right—shifting my sight to his face, seeing only his deep-clefted chin, and I was pivoting my whole body from the hips and pushing off on my back foot and driving through and I caught him square in a boxer's sweet aiming spot, right on the point of his chin, and there was a crack that I could hear above the siren roar and there was the clean, hard yielding and the release and the flying away. He landed hard and bounced and settled, and the rube's jaw was glass: his head lolled to the side and his eyes rolled back and closed.

I turned to find Selene.

She was standing beside me, a step behind.

She was staring at the unconscious man.

And she surprised me. On her face was a keen, narrow-eyed, steely focus.

Something had shifted in her. It let me move on to what was next. "Can you swim?" I said.

Her hands moved to her waist and she unfastened her skirt and it fell to her feet like a punched-out sailor. She stepped from it and stood there in black stockings, white drawers to the knees, and the boun-teously phony bosom of her life jacket. "Yes, I can swim," she said.

And I did not have to hold her hand.

I turned and Selene and I stepped past the unconscious junior officer, and before us was a waist-high wall, and bellied up to it just beyond was the fat body and great gaping black maw of a cowl ventilator, as tall as the bridge. No doorway through to the Hurricane Deck. But there was a passable space between the vent and the Bridge.

"Over," I said to Selene, and I stepped aside. She went to the wall and put her hands on it and I grabbed her waist in my hands and lifted and she went over and I followed and she let me pass her as we went around the ventilator.

We crossed straight over to the starboard side and began to work our way up the incline of the deck, which made moving forward heavy-legged and hard, but we held tight to the railing, resisting the sideways incline of the ship, which would make falling down to the Boat Deck and then into the sea light-chested and easy.

I watched below as we moved, assessing the situation, seeking an opening for us. The deck seethed with passengers, and I was struck by two surpassingly sad things. One was this: hundreds of people were dithering and flustering and drifting and huddling about in faux calm, but there were dozens of different currents and directions, moving forward, moving aft, lurching to the rail's edge, clinging to the deck wall; worse than the sadness of the few wild retreats I'd seen of men on a battlefield, where at least their direction was clear, this was a vast shifting image of hopelessness, seen from above as if by a powerless or an indifferent god. And the second sad thing was all the bare heads, all the bare heads of men and women and children whose world was a world of hats and caps and scarves, of heads covered beneath the sky, and now all these people had been lifted desperately from the bareheaded safety of belowdecks or they had already stripped themselves of their coverings as they faced a plunge into the sea.

And the sea was very near to their deck now.

I watched a lifeboat amidships, pulled out by the list to the farthest extent of its snubbing chains, the boat almost full with huddling bodies, and a woman was poised at deck's edge—she still in fur-trimmed coat and hat and veil and without a life jacket—and men's hands in the boat reached out beseeching her to try to jump across the six or eight feet of empty space to them. She leaned forward and then back and then shuffled her feet and wobbled and tried to work herself up to the leap, while at the running blocks at each corner of the boat gap in the railing, crewmen pulled hard at the falls, the man forward visibly quaking from the strain of keeping the bow up high in order to level the boat with the sea instead of the deck.

The woman couldn't bring herself to jump and she broke away and retreated into the paralyzed crowd and a shout grew up and three others of those waiting behind—two of them men—surged forward to make the leap and a skinny young man in shirtsleeves and suspenders lunged in front of the others and planted his foot and left the deck just as the quaking forward crewman slipped at his feet and his legs buckled and the bow of the lifeboat dipped abruptly and the skinny young man tried to stop and he twisted and he fell disappearing into the gap and a great cry rose up in the lifeboat as it dipped farther and farther down at the front and the forty or so people inside tumbled out in a great flailing of arms and legs and the aft crewman fell now too and all the ropes were loosed and the lifeboat and all its passengers vanished from view.

I'd seen enough. I turned to Selene and she let go of the railing and she began to back away, her eyes wide.

I stepped to her, put my hands on her shoulders, stopped her. I did not have to shake her. She grew calm at once beneath my hands. Her eyes relaxed and they focused on me and then narrowed once more in the resolve I'd seen on the bridge.

"We have to go into the water now," I said. "As quickly as we can, as easily as we can."

She nodded.

I said, "Our jackets will help us. We swim as far away from the ship as possible. After that, there will be plenty of things afloat to cling to."

She nodded again.

All this seemed feasible to me. If it was, if we ended up safely in the water, I still worried about the ship capsizing on us. But I didn't say so. I worried about the great sucking vortex at the ship's last vanishing. But I didn't say so.

I said, "Let's go. We'll use the rail, but try not to look down. Just follow me."

She nodded a last time and I turned and I led us back to the railing and we headed aft, passing from the shadow of funnel number one, and I was still trying to visualize if we needed to leave the Hurricane Deck. We'd have to be patient if we stayed. We'd have to wait for the very last moment for the sea to come to us. But with the bow filling, the ship could suddenly rear up from the stern to sink.

We left the rail to go around another cowl vent, which was no longer taking in fresh air but spewing thick black smoke from belowdecks, and beyond it we cut back to the railing and I leaned out and looked ahead for a way down to the Boat Deck. About fifty yards farther on, past funnel number two, was a staircase.

Suddenly the ship began to quake beneath our feet and a great metallic groan filled the air coming from all around us and I stopped and turned and I cried "Hold on to me!" and Selene put her arms around my waist and I gripped the railing hard with both hands and the *Lusitania* shook and it grabbed the breath out of me as it lurched toward the sea and I braced my hips against the railing and a many-voiced human cry came from below us and Selene held me tight and we stopped, we did not capsize but we stopped, and the cry below ceased abruptly and I looked and bodies were still careening and flying against the Boat Deck railing and over and gone but we'd stopped for now and the angle toward the sea was worse but it felt as if the angle forward had abated a little—just a little—we could still move, we still could move.

"Not much farther," I cried. "Careful placing your feet."

Selene knew to take her arms off me and we both clutched the railing and we moved aft as quickly as we could, pulling with our arms as much as driving forward with our legs, placing our feet carefully with each step so they would not slide from under us, and we approached funnel number two and its shadow fell upon us and I heard Selene gasp and she stopped and I looked behind me and she was staring upward and I followed her gaze and the top section of the listing funnel was directly over our heads.

"Just watch me," I cried.

She lowered her face and I turned and we moved on.

And we were at the staircase and it was opposite the Marconi shack—its wireless antennae rising from its roof to join the long, taut telegraph lines strung from foremast to mainmast—and the door was gaping open and inside an operator sat in a bolt-secured chair, hunched over his key, tapping furiously away. I wanted to step to him and grab him by the arm and pull him away. The ship was lost; whoever was going to hear us had heard us already. But this was one of those guys you find in times like this who'll die doing what he signed up to do. As I led Selene down the stairs I thought: *If I live, I'll put this man—and what he was—in the story I'll write.*

And we were on the Boat Deck.

I looked to the left and staggered back, throwing my arm across Selene, startled as if I'd turned an alleyway corner into the chest of a hulking stranger. The sea had claimed the deck almost up to my feet.

Which was fine. We didn't need to seek the right place to enter. It was waiting for us.

The slash of sea before us foamed at its claiming edge.

I turned us aft.

Astern, those who had no life jackets and those who had them but could not muster the nerve to use them were clambering at the last two lifeboats, which were swinging wildly at the end of their snubbing chains.

"Here," I said.

I took Selene by the hand and we moved toward the railing a few paces aft.

A little farther along, a man in a union suit was meticulously folding his pants, with his overcoat and his coat and his shirt already carefully stacked at his feet.

Somewhere a woman was sobbing.

The bridge siren abruptly stopped.

I let go of Selene's hand and we were at the railing.

"Up," I said and she climbed the railing and swung her legs over and she balanced a moment there and I came up beside her and I took her hand in mine once more and I looked at the sea and it was full of bodies alive and dead and it was full of planking from wrecked lifeboats and I looked down, and the drop was less than ten feet but a deck chair spun directly below us and I felt Selene's body as it started to move outward and I cried "Hold" and she tried, she gently braked her body, and the deck chair bumped the hull and it spun and Selene was starting to rebound backward, was starting to fall backward and I slipped my arm around her and kicked hard with my heels against the bottom rail and we flew a little away from the hull and we had only water below us and we fell and the cold grabbed me by the feet and rushed up my legs as I took my arm from around Selene's waist and I sucked in a deep breath and the water rushed up my abdomen and my chest and I flinched my eyes closed and my face flashed sharp cold, the cold raked through me and the sea was heavy upon me and now I was no mind at all, I was only my body I was only the memories of my muscles and I was the sinking and I was the slowing and I was the stopping. And I was the gathering of arm and flattening of hand and coiling of leg and then I was the stroking upward and I could feel my chest rising ahead of me rising as if on its own—the life jacket lifting me—and the pressure of the sea fell away from the top of my head and from my forehead and my eyes and my cheeks and all my face and now my shoulders and I was in the air.

I gasped in the air and I opened my eyes, and swinging to my face as if to kiss me hello was a sweet woman's face, her large eyes closed, the lids smooth and white, the face was very white and angled to kiss me, angled too far sideways, and I was no mind at all, I was only my body before her, and my body assumed she was Selene, and she was dead, I knew, this woman approaching me, and I clutched tight in the chest, but then I knew it was not Selene, and then bumping my face was a coldness beyond the coldness of the sea, a terrible coldness bumped a last kiss upon my cheek, a good-bye kiss sliding across my mouth and she moved away, she could not linger and she was gone and she was a stranger and she was dead, and I heard myself gasping, gasping for breath in the cold sea but gasping for the mistake my body had made and gasping to know if Selene had come up from the place where I had just been, and my arms knew to turn me, and a few yards away Selene Bourgani's famous profile floated as if she were beheaded and I gasped again and then her shoulders appeared and her arms, and she was thrashing and turning, and her face swung around to me and we moved toward each other, this stroke, and this one, and we watched as each other's living eyes grew nearer.

And we touched hands and we were in a dark shadow and we knew not to look above us, we knew not to consider the *Lusitania* about to fall upon us, and we turned side by side away from the ship.

And we swam.

14

So Selene Bourgani and I shared a deck chair when the *Lusitania* went down, having swum out far enough that the last whipping of the loosed Marconi wires just missed tangling us, though it dragged many others under, right before our eyes. We clung to the floating chair and we lifted our faces to the ship.

The stern rose from the water, and the massive starboard white propellers showed themselves, still spinning slowly, glinting brightly in the sun, and the *Lusitania* diminished before us for a long few moments like a knife blade disappearing into a chest, and then it stopped, as if it had struck bone, and it no longer evoked a blade, as its keel simply settled downward and it was gone.

And there was no vortex. That thing it struck: it occurred to me how shallow the sea was here, within ten miles of shore, not even four hundred feet deep. The ship struck her bow to the ocean floor before she was fully under, and so when she vanished, all that was left was for the air within to blow. And it did, a last upswelling dome of white, and then the sea lifted beneath us and we were glad to be holding this chair and we rose and we fell and all around was a low, ongoing wordless cry.

We could not listen. We could not watch. We hung on to the chair, just to keep us from drifting separately, and we looked each other in the eyes. The ones who made it off the ship in one piece and yet would die on this day—and there would be many—were those without life jackets or those without any emotional reserves, the ones for whom this was such an enormous thing that they went "Ah to hell with it" and gave up the ghost. But the ghosts still cried out all around us till the bodies they came from sank or floated away.

And Selene and I just looked at each other and murmured to each other. Little things.

"Are you cold?" I would say.

"Oh, not anymore. I'm numb now," she would say.

"The sea is very calm," I would say.

"The sun is warm on my face," she would say.

And when a particularly terrible human sound would wash over us and I could see in her eyes that she heard, I would say, "Don't listen."

And she would say, "I can't hear anything but my heart." And perhaps she would add, "Or is that yours?"

We would say these things, or things very much like them, over and over again. We didn't mind the repetition.

And then at last I said, "Sing to me."

And she did. Softly. "You made me love you. I didn't want to do it. I didn't want to do it."

And so we floated. And later some crewmen got to a collapsible lifeboat that had drifted off right-side up, and they were able to raise and lash the steel-framed canvas sides, and the men began to pick the living from the vast sargasso of bodies, and they found us.

And before sunset Selene and I were on the deck of a fishing smack, huddled in blankets and drinking tea, quiet now together—we found that all we could be together for now was quiet—and by dark we were in Queenstown.

15

The city's white row houses, lit by gas light and torches, were stitched into the side of the abrupt-rising hills by cobbled streets. The fishing boat put in at the Cunard wharf and the forty or so of us hobbled onto land. We all ached terribly after the exertion of having saved our lives in the sea and then having huddled for some hours cramped on that tiny boat deck.

We found ourselves on a cut-stone wharf that was crowded with the swaddled dead. Selene, still wearing the boat captain's bright yellow slicker and sou'wester and smelling of mackerel, clung to me as we picked our way through, noticing the small bundles, which were the children, noticing the ones with faces framed in the open folds, noticing one bundle in particular: two faces bound in one blanket, jaundiced by the lamplight, mother and child, pressed together as if for a photographic portrait but having waited so long for the flash, they'd fallen into a deep sleep. Selene gasped and clung harder to me, and we angled our faces to each other, focused once again only on the two of us, until we entered the large open hall of the customshouse.

The place was dim, unprepared for night landings, and it was crowded with living bodies—hundreds of us now—and some of us were bumping about near the door in the first confusion of arrival. The familiar tones and cadences of the voices of low-level officialdom were directing us, as if we'd just left a steamship and were going off to retrieve our luggage and queue up for the customs boys to search for the booze and the tobacco and the silver plate and the books and the sheet music. And, to be honest, the faintly patronizing, coolly efficient voices were reassuring now, turning the horror into the routine, as much as that was possible with the background of moaning and coughing and whispering and with the quaking and the trembling and with the travelers being damp and bareheaded and with many of them clad only in their wetly clinging underwear and some showing flesh, too much flesh. We looked at these exposed bodies only out of the corners of our eyes, even as dry, dark-uniformed bodies emerged in the dim light to throw blankets over the nakedness.

And Selene and I leaned into each other.

The official voices propelled us into roped-off lines, the wounded who needed immediate help being sent to triage at the far end of the hall, the rest of us guided to the long, alphabetically sectioned wall where our luggage would have been placed but which now led to tables where they gave us coffee and then passed us on to queue and wait for a Cunard official sitting behind a large ledger book. We all waited to approach the book one at a time, Selene waiting before me, clutching hard at my arm, keeping me close. I thought this was because she still needed to rely on me.

Then the man at the table was looking our way.

"Next," he said.

Selene let go of my arm and turned her face to me and I was surprised at what was there: a hard mouth, pressed thin, but eyes gone wide and gentle, and her head tilted a little. She was about to reenter the world as Selene Bourgani. She'd twice already tried to end our connection to each other. Now it was as if all that we'd done together these past hours—searching the sinking ship for escape and then entering the sea and clinging to life there amidst the dead and dying and then rising together into safety and landing once more on the shore—as if all that was just one more night of lovemaking and this thing between us could not last.

She'd been clutching my arm, keeping me close, because she knew it was time for me to go.

Realizing all this, I also realized I'd missed an opportunity. I'd tried not to intrude upon the silence we kept with each other since we'd been lifted from the sea. Perhaps if I'd pressed her to speak of Brauer, to speak of what it was she was intending to do, she would have told me what it was my job to learn.

But it had never occurred to me. The silence had been inside me as well.

And now she said, "Thank you."

And I knew she would break away from me.

All I could do was nod.

She turned and moved to the desk.

I could not hear, but the man in the Cunard uniform sitting behind the ledger spoke, and then Selene spoke, and the man jumped up and gave a little bow.

A film fan, no doubt.

She said more to him, and he bowed again. He would grant her a special favor. He motioned to the ledger.

She drew her forefinger down the right-hand, half-filled page. Then she did the same to the left-hand page. Then she turned to the previous two-page spread.

I knew the name she sought.

Halfway down on the right, her hand stopped. She lifted it away and she straightened up.

She nodded to the official, and he sat back down.

She signed her name.

They spoke a few words more.

I was right about her. When she was finished, she did not look back to me but moved off at once, searching the crowd.

I approached the desk, the ledger, the Selene Bourgani fan in the Cunard uniform.

And after I'd signed my name and nationality—my pen-stroke going suddenly heavy, assertive, from a complex surge of feeling at writing *United States of America*—after then taking an abrupt, retained, chest-lifted breath at being an American upon this day, I turned and she was gone.

Before I could take a step away, the Cunard man, craning his neck to confirm his upside-down reading, said, "Mr. Cobb is it?"

I turned back. "Yes?"

"Would you be so kind as to wait behind my table? Someone has come to collect you."

"Miss Bourgani was with me, as you saw."

"Yes."

"I was supposed to meet her . . . Did they assign her a place to sleep?"

"Most of the first-class passengers are going to the Queen's Hotel."

"I'll be back in a few moments," I said.

The Cunard man stiffened; he was responsible for me waiting. Before he could protest, I said, "I won't be long," and I moved off.

I watched for her yellow slicker to flash in the crowd, but my goal was the streetside doors. I did not see her among the bandages and slings and blankets—the half-naked bodies were disappearing into blankets—and now the doors were in sight and I saw the yellow there amidst a dark brace of Cunard ducks and I swung wide in my approach to them, ready to let her go.

I saw her from behind. She was speaking to a guy with a clipboard, and then she moved off through the doors.

I followed, brushing aside the Cunards' importunings. She'd pushed through already, and I stopped and looked through the glass. She turned her face to the far left and then swept her gaze slowly toward the harbor street, where the merchants on the far side—milliner and ironmonger, draper and men's clothier, sellers of fish and poultry and cakes—all were lit up inside, as the whole town had awakened to the rescue; and then her face kept moving right, across a square and to another long row of wider buildings—the Queen's Hotel included—and above them, up the hill, an arch-supported roadway climbing to a Gothic-spired cathedral. I thought that Selene's eyes would come to rest upon her hotel. But she did not pause, she scanned on, and then she abruptly stopped. Her face drew very slightly forward. She was checking her perception.

And from that direction a figure was moving now, coming out of the shadows, wrapped and hooded in a blanket. Selene straightened and waited, and the figure stopped before her, and she was speaking, and the blanket came down off the head. It was Walter Brauer.

16

That she was seeking Brauer did not surprise me. Whatever hesitation about him she'd had in response to the torpedoing of the *Lusitania* was overcome by her rescue. And whatever had been the allure of her rescuer, that was overcome by the renewal of her mission for the Germans, no matter what those transient reservations might have been. What did surprise me was that Brauer had figured out how to save his own skin. Perhaps luck had played a part. But I knew I'd better not underestimate his resourcefulness or his toughness, bookman-fancying King's College lecturer though he be.

Selene, in response to something Brauer said, lifted her chin a little to gesture over his right shoulder. He looked in that direction—at the Queen's Hotel—and I knew enough for tonight, given that someone was seeking me out. I needed to attend to that.

So I backed away from the door, turned, and made my way through the hall to the ledger table. As I approached and passed beside him, the Cunard man taking names gave me a relieved glance.

I stood behind him, as he'd asked, and almost at once a serious weariness shuddered through me. I bucked myself up and even did a long-habitual bucking-up gesture: I shot my cuffs. Except over the past few hours my cuffs had apparently decided to permanently shoot themselves. I considered my body down to my squishing brogues, surprised that I'd left them on. I'd gone into the water in a gentle-man's blue serge suit and I now stood in a schoolboy's blue serge suit, my adolescent wrists and ankles protruding like cowlicks from cuffs and pant legs.

"Mister Cobb?" a man's voice said.

"Master Cobb," I said, lifting one outgrown sleeve as I looked at the speaker. He had a round face and most everything about it was the color of wheat spike before a harvest, skin and hair and eyebrows that wheat-field yellow, and in the midst were unblinking pale eyes, their color hard to identify in the shadows of the customshall but they were pale, unflinching; he was a fleshy, wheaty man wearing a three-piece suit of his own money-crop color but a shade or two darker, baked for a while.

He flashed a willful little smile and he nodded at my right wrist. "We'll take care of that."

He offered a doughy hand doing one of those I'll-hesitate-a-second-and-muscle-up-my-squeeze-to-equal-yours kind of shakes; I had the feeling I could squeeze harder than he could, though I also had an inkling this guy could surprise me. He said, in a flat plains accent common to a large number of *Post-Express* readers, "I'm James Metcalf. United States embassy in London."

He paused now and lowered his voice a bit, turning it into a covert elbow nudge in the ribs. "We have a mutual friend in Washington."

"The other James," I said. James Polk Trask.

Metcalf doled out one more of those little smiles. "He's the one."

Then the smile vanished at once and his manner changed abruptly to the studied gravity of an embassy Guy. "I'm glad to see you've made it."

"I am too," I said.

And Metcalf took charge, which was fine with me. So I found myself in the well of a two-wheel jaunting car pulled by a sixteen-hand mule, a bundle of new clothes beside me and two bespoke suits being done up overnight. We were bone-rattling our cobblestoned way up the hill behind the wharves, bound for the Admiralty House that sat above the city, where an Admiral Lewis Bayly ran the British Fleet in the North Atlantic and where I'd get some decent food and a bed but I shouldn't expect a drink.

"Sorry, old man," Metcalf said. "The admiral's a teetotaler and so is everyone else, as long as they're under his roof."

I grunted. I hadn't the time or focus or opportunity to think about a drink so far, but this struck me instantly as bad news.

But Metcalf removed a flask from his inside coat pocket and handed it across to me. There was a pretty good whiskey inside and I took a couple of bolts of it as he watched in silence. That was enough of the whiskey for tonight. In spite of the past eight or ten hours, I wasn't interested in getting drunk and I handed the flask back to him.

"Thanks," I said.

He offered me a cigarette. A Capstan Navy Cut in a flat tin.

I took one and he did too and he lit them for us and I blew the smoke out to sea, which lay below me now, sucked up into this harbor, all sparkly calm from the harbor lights and acting like it never could hurt a soul.

"They call this Spy Hill," Metcalf said.

"Imagine that," I said.

"From back when it meant just a place to watch the ships."

"I bet it's become that again."

"Back when you didn't count and classify the warships and telegraph Berlin."

Metcalf was clearly the guy I was supposed to report to. I looked toward the driver sitting above us.

"Later," Metcalf said.

"I figured," I said.

And then we were at Admiralty House, which was a massive, boxy, neoclassic Adam-style building built into a sharp upslope, with three stories at the back and a fourth, half-underground basement story that showed its windowed facade only at the front. Inside, the place was as sparse and grim as the admiral himself, whose junior officer years were crusted on his face and who gave me a curt smile with his handshake, the kind of smile that would, in other circumstances, seem dismissive but between men sharing a war passed for comradely.

And then at last—after a too-brief period of be-stupored happiness lying in a great porcelain tub of hot water and after donning my new cotton pajama suit and silk dressing gown and after a lamb chop in the Admiralty kitchen and a pot of strong coffee—at last, shortly before midnight on the day the *Lusitania* was sunk by a German U-boat in the North Atlantic, I sat high on the widow's walk of the Admiralty House smoking British cigarettes with James Metcalf of the U.S. embassy.

The admiral had departed from our company soon after the handshake, but in the few parting words he'd referred to Metcalf as "Gentleman Jim." So as Metcalf and I took our first drag of our second cigarette together, Queenstown now simply stacks and hedgerows of rooftops and a scattering of harbor-front lights below us, I said, "'Gentleman Jim,' is it? From the boxer?" Meaning the former heavyweight champion Gentleman Jim Corbett.

"Do you have a taste for irony, Mr. Cobb?"

"Kit. From the playwright," I said.

"Kit," he said.

"Sure," I said. "I like a good irony."

"Yes, from the boxer, thanks to the ambassador and his fondness for the prizefights. But I am among the least violent of men."

"A gentleman," I said.

"An irony within an irony," he said.

We concentrated on smoking for a little while. Or I did, at least. The tobacco was smoothing a few of the day's jagged edges in my head. I took a deep drag and let it go with a long exhalation, and I did that once more. Metcalf simply watched me as he let his own cigarette smolder between fore and middle fingers, suspended near his face with his elbow on the arm of his chair.

Like a real gentleman.

After the second long pull on my Captsan, I said, "So what are we authorized to say to each other?"

"Whatever you would say to your stateside James."

I nodded, but for now I quietly took another drag on the cigarette.

"At this point," Metcalf said, "it might merely be moot, but were you able to learn anything about our man Walter Brauer?"

"The most recent thing I learned is that it's not moot," I said.

Metcalf straightened a bit in his chair. He seemed suddenly to become aware of his cigarette. He flicked the long ash and took a drag. "So he's alive?"

"He is."

"What were the earlier things?"

"His business is with Miss Selene Bourgani."

This brought Metcalf forward in his chair. "The film actress?"

"That's right."

"Are you sure?"

I told him the events on the ship. Many of them. I told him about finding out the connection between Bourgani and Brauer after suspecting an American bookseller. I told him about *Nuttall* and the coded message and the planned delivery of something—likely the actress—to the address on St. Martin's Lane on Monday night. I told him about Brauer's personal interest in the seller of books, the necessary secrecy of it being a potential point of leverage with the man.

I told Metcalf nothing of my own personal interest in Selene. Or of hers in me. Like I was a real gentleman. I also kept the anonymous German film director to myself for now; it was too vague anyway, and I didn't want to have to explain how I came to know about him.

I told my story and then I said, "She's in the Queen's Hotel."

"And Brauer?"

"I don't know where he's staying. But from the look of them on the ship, if we know where she is, we'll soon find him."

Metcalf rose from his chair. "I'll wire our man in Washington for instructions."

"And Bourgani?"

"We'll see what our instructions are. But in the meantime I've got a local here who can keep an eye on her."

I stood up as well. "I need a couple of things right away. For my public self. The war correspondent."

"Of course," Metcalf said. "You've happened upon a story, it seems."

"It happened upon me," I said.

17

For the following two hours, in an office papered in war maps, I banged at a clumsy old Imperial Model A with a curved keyboard and a downstrike type bar. My body wanted badly to collapse after the events of what was now the previous day, but a pot of coffee kept me afloat like a kapok-filled life jacket, and I wrote a hell of a front-page, king-beat, firsthand, exclusive story about the sinking of the *Lusitania*. The Admiralty's Marconi man even transmitted it for me to the *Post-Express* at what was fifteen minutes past nine in the evening, Chicago time. We'd miss the morning bulldog edition, which had to be leading with the worst possible hobo mulligan of a *Lusitania* story, full of wire bits and speculations and anti-German fulminations, but this one would be way ahead of the other stories, the real stories, even with Trask needing to sign off on it, per his agreement with Griswold.

I had a copy sent directly to Trask in Washington as well. And I just gave all of them straight facts and some war correspondent derring-do. I was that kind of reporter anyway, believing the inevitable anti-German fulminations should be printed on the editorial page, not on the news pages. And as of a day before yesterday, Germany was still happy to let American reporters into Berlin to hear their side of things. Trask had always expected me to end up in *der Vaterland*, and if I stayed objective about this murderous sucker punch they'd delivered, it might make things go easier for me. The facts spoke for themselves anyway.

Among the facts, however, were none about the film actress I saved along with myself. That was her story to tell, if she was of a mind to.

And then I finally got to bed in an upper-floor officer guest room. I did a lot of heavy-legged, slant-decked, wave-lapped running in my dreams, and I woke in a sweat before dawn. I got up and walked around and around the room, happy to have an even-keeled floor and dry feet. But what was floating and moaning in my head in my waking state was a thing I'd done and totally forgotten about till now: coldcocking that junior officer on the bridge of the *Lusitania*. Did he wake up in time to save himself? Did he wake up in time and with a clear enough head? Did he die because of me? If he did, that was too bad. But I'd necessarily figured at that moment, given what he was trying to insist on, that it was either him or me. No. It was either him or me and Selene. I did what I had to do. He shouldn't have been blindly enforcing a wrongheaded order in a stupidly literal way at a time like that. He should have let us pass on by.

I slept some more and woke to James Metcalf making an ungentlemanly door-banging entrance into my room. He had a large, leather Gladstone bag and a couple of tailored suits and big plans for me. He pointed out that the bright light outside was being provided by a well-risen sun.

"How well, exactly?" I asked.

"Nearly ten o'clock well," he said.

I was sitting now on the side of the bed and had found the floor with my feet, a simple act that I realized was registering in me as a great relief.

Metcalf set down my new bag and laid out my two new suits on the bed next to me. He said, "You need to dress quickly. We have to get you to Kingstown by this evening. Which means by automobile."

"What's in Kingstown?"

"Bourgani and Brauer. They rented the hotel owner's auto and hired a driver and took off an hour ago. They're crossing the channel tonight to catch the train to London from Holyhead at one-thirty tomorrow morning."

"And so am I."

"And so are you."

"They still want to make that Monday delivery."

"So it seems."

"Did you hear from Trask?"

"He said to keep doing what you're doing, at least for now. Follow and observe. Our boys are looking into the film star, and we may know more about her by the time you get to London. You're at the Waldorf. We don't know where Bourgani will be. Follow and observe. But we've got the address of Brauer's flat."

Metcalf pulled an envelope from his inside coat pocket and handed it to me. "What we know is in here. If things happen quickly, just go to the embassy and identify yourself and ask for Smith. If Smith's out, the front desk is secure. You can leave a message in a sealed envelope. I'll be in London about twenty-four hours after you. I've given you some new documents as well. I presume yours are damp."

I nodded. "But I saved the government's gold."

"Good man," Metcalf said. "Some pounds sterling in there to see you through, however. We can assess your further needs in London."

"I can tell you the biggest one right now," I said.

I paused and puffed a heavy breath and squared my shoulders to make sure he knew I was serious.

"Yes?"

"I've lost two of these in the past twelve months on your behalf."

I paused again.

"You've got my full attention," Metcalf said.

"A Corona model number three portable typewriter," I said.

"Right," Metcalf said. "Which reminds me. Trask also thinks the news story is fine as is. Thinks you'd write pretty fair novels, but just make sure they're not about spies."

And so I spent the next eight hours in a Vauxhall-D staff car, with a blessedly laconic sublieutenant driver, heading north to Kingstown, sometimes creeping behind cattle on dirtways and sometimes running at sixty miles an hour on straight tarmacadams. For the first hour or so

I had trouble telling my brain to shut the hell up, and I found myself thinking about Woodrow Wilson and his own odd brain, how unlike a commander in chief he was, how he invaded Mexico last spring to kick out a tin-pot dictator he didn't like and to protect American oil interests but then immediately hunkered down in Vera Cruz and went no farther. How he'd been avidly talking neutrality in Europe and then expedited the ongoing sale and shipment of American arms to Britain. I figured I could see the consistency of all that: the big-business wing of the Democratic party holding sway. But there had to be at least a hundred American dead on the *Lusitania*. I wondered if he'd pull the trigger now.

Probably not. It made better business sense to sell American arms to Europe than to sell them to ourselves and use them. I wanted to doze off at that thought, but I slid on to the Germans torpedoing the ship with their own agents on board. Did that cast any doubt on Brauer and Bourgani? It was unlikely that those who knew about the agents would think to coordinate with the German navy. The U-boat captains were lone wolves; they didn't raise their periscopes and then worry about who booked passage on a major British steamship that had suddenly, miraculously appeared in their sights. And with the Knockmealdown Mountains of County Waterford rising out against the horizon, all this thinking I was doing finally blurred into the fatigue of my North Atlantic adventure and I slept.

And then at last I was in Kingstown. The RMS *Leinster,* a two-funnel Irish mail packet, was at anchor and blowing its all-ashore whistle, and I boarded, not catching any sight of Brauer and Bour-gani. I found myself in a private cabin, with double berth beds on one wall and a train compartment bench seat on the other and not enough space between to do a six-whiskey stagger. What I knew, from Metcalf's information, was that the cabin next to mine held Selene Bourgani, and somewhere on the other side of the ship a similar cabin contained Walter Brauer. What Metcalf didn't know was that we all were directly over the engine room, and as we hammered our way into the Irish Channel, the cabin and our bodies quickly merged into one quaking entity, making it impossible to distinguish the vibration of the floor from the vibration of the metal frame of the berths from the vibration of our stomachs and our teeth and our brainpans.

I tried for a long while to sleep, but I found myself staring at the wall, beyond which, I was given to believe, lay Selene Bourgani, who was as remote to me now as one of those made-up women mugging their emotions on a moving picture screen.

At last I got up and dressed and went out of my cabin. I turned away from her door and made my way down the corridor to the Cabin Deck entrance hall. I went up the staircase to the Boat Deck and directly into the large, aft wooden-bench lounge for passengers making the five-hour trip without a cabin.

The space could hold maybe four hundred travelers. A hundred or so were scattered, sleeping, throughout the lounge. But I turned to step out onto the deck, and in the three rows of benches nearest the exit doors were a dozen sleeping passengers. They seemed to be together but not together, near to each other but not touching. Men and women; some sleeping, some awake; a few smoking, no one talking. But something seemed to bind them together. I drew near, and then I knew. I quickly scanned back into the lounge to see if the City of Dublin Steam Packet Company had given a certain overt departing instruction. It hadn't. This little eddy of travelers was singular in this: all but two of them were wearing their life jackets. And I knew at once where they'd come from. Indeed, as I passed them by, I looked more closely at their life jackets, one after another, and all the jackets were the same. A word was stamped on the bosom, in a Bodoni bold font, like a *Post-Express* headline: LUSITANIA.

I hurried on through the doors and out onto the deck and it was utterly dark out here. The portholes were all closed and the running lights were off, and though the ship was shrouded in a mist thick enough to be called a fog, we were sounding no warning, we were making no sound at all, and we were pounding along at better than twenty knots. Of course the U-boats were in the Irish Channel as well. And I was struck by a thought I didn't remember ever having on any official battlefield, where, no matter how extensive the field of operations, everyone knew there were places behind the lines or across the sea where things were peaceful, things were safe. On the deck of the Irish mail packet *Leinster* I thought: *All the world is plunging forward in darkness now, and nowhere is safe.*

18

Over the next few hours of fitful sleep and brain-rattled thought, I decided that for now it would be best to keep as much away from the sight of Selene and Brauer as I could. I knew where Brauer lived. I could wait to follow him whenever I wanted. I knew where both of them would be tomorrow night. And if Selene wasn't there—if Brauer's coded message was an instruction to deliver something or someone else—then he was more centrally important than the film star anyway. And there were a few things I needed to do before that appointed time in St. Martin's Lane.

So I hid out and hung back on the *Leinster* and then again on the London train, waiting till the conductor found me lingering in the sleeping car vestibule in Euston Station and he said, "You need to move on along to your destination, sir. We're off now to the switching yard." I picked up my bags and stepped down to the platform, and up ahead the flock of reporters had already descended to pick the brains of the several dozen *Lusitania* survivors, who were identifiable by their dazed looks, occasional bandages, and ill-fitting clothes. I was glad for my Queenstown special privileges, as they included a deceptively well-fitted suit and crisp-brimmed trilby, and I plowed through with hardly a glance from anyone.

The Waldorf still had a reservation for me, though I was a day late. The desk clerk, with a paste-brush mustache on his stiff upper lip, drew himself up proudly to explain that the hotel checked with the Cunard Line through the night and as recently as an hour ago before canceling yesterday's no-shows. He was happy to announce that the hotel would have a room for anyone confirmed by Cunard, whenever they might arrive.

This was good but the hotel gave me the willies and I suspected it would do the same for any of the other confirmees. The Waldorf's Portland stone facade was all eighteenth century Frenchy neoclassicism, as was every stick of furniture and every lamp and every bit of trim in its lobby and its Palm Court. I did not doubt the rooms would carry on the style. In other words, we who survived the *Lusitania* would be checking into its immobilized doppelgänger, as if we'd in fact all drowned on Friday and this was a meticulously bespoke purgatory.

The clerk slid my key across the desktop. "One other thing, Mr. Cobb," he said, and he turned a bit aside and bent beneath the front desk.

He emerged with what I instantly recognized as the leather and wood carrying case of a Corona Number 3.

Purgatory is heaven if you can write about it and hang your byline on it. The rest of the day was clear before me.

"From a Mr. Metcalf," the clerk said.

"Thanks." I put the key in my pocket and picked up the typewriter by the case handle. But just as I was about to move away, I finally remembered something about the Waldorf. Something that had niggled at me ever since Metcalf told me where I'd stay. Now it suddenly struck me.

"Pardon me," I said to the clerk.

"Yessir?"

"I want to check on a friend of mine who was scheduled to come in."

"What's the name?"

"Edward Cable," I said.

The guy's mustache seemed wired to his column-running forefinger, shifting restlessly from side to side as he scanned his reservation book. But then both finger and mustache stopped abruptly.

He looked up at me. "I'm sorry," he said, his voice pitched very low. "Mr. Cable's reservation was canceled this morning by the Cunard Line."

There was no reason for this to surprise me. He'd have no skills to save himself. Cable had become a mere footnote to this whole affair anyway. And I had long since developed the battlefield skill of taking the death of even somebody you were chummy with—nascent pals with, even—pretty much in stoic stride. But for the first two or three steps I took away from the front desk at the Waldorf, it was all I could do to keep from buckling at the knees.

19

I did hammer some words from my new Corona 3 through the day, the faux Louis XVI furniture of my room vanishing from my mind, even as the *Lusitania* filled my foolscap. I was out in the street by five in the afternoon and walking the half mile east along the Strand, St. Paul's dome the distant reckoning point. I entered the much narrower Fleet Street, with some of the big papers located along here and most all of the rest of London journalism headquartered on the side streets sloping down toward the river. I turned into Whitefriars, which was narrower still, the sky above me strung thick with telegraph wires, and I went in at a fine old sixteenth-century building, which may have watched Sam Johnson pass by. This was the office of the London *Daily Transcript,* the English-language flagship of Griswold's international *Post-Express* syndicate.

None of the dailies in London did a Sunday edition, as odd as that might have sounded to a Chicagoan, but only the working class read the news in Britain on the Sabbath and the advertisers could sell only so many tinned sardines and corn plasters. So the lobby of the *Transcript* was barely starting to warm back up after a few extra hours of quiet. But I made a stir. I said my name and the young man in the glass reception cage in the lobby jumped up. He'd read some of my stuff over the years, I supposed, loving the war stories, seeing as he was a young man.

I was soon on the top floor with Reginald Bryce, the editor of the *Daily Transcript*, leaping up from his desk in much the same manner as his boy on the ground floor.

"Mr. Cobb, it's a superb and coincidental pleasure," he said, offering a handshake with enough firmness to qualify for a Chicago street corner meeting between a couple of old Rough Rider buddies.

"Our men at the *Post-Express* like your work a lot," I said.

"A fine honor. A fine honor indeed."

"The coincidence?" I asked.

"Your story will rule majestically over our front page tomorrow morning," he said. "And an excellent thing too, since that was contingent, of course, upon your surviving the Huns' vile attack."

"It was vile, wasn't it," I said.

"If there's anything we can do for you."

"Thanks," I said, and of course that was why I was standing before him. "Do you have somebody on staff who knows the motion picture business?"

I ended up three floors down, personally delivered by Reginald Bryce to the small but windowed office of Gwendolyn Bryce, the big man's very own wisp of a searingly green-eyed daughter, a pioneer of British motion picture journalism. She did not jump up from her desk but stayed framed against her twilight gray window. Her handshake was just about as firm as her old man's.

I sat. The old man left. Gwendolyn, having only repeated my name in greeting so far, instantly said, "Do you know the fate of Selene Bourgani? She was on the ship with you."

This girl was all reporter. She and her kind would probably have to get the vote first, just for appearance's sake, but I got the feeling she could replace her dad one day.

"She's alive," I said.

"Superb," she said, flipping open a shorthand notebook on her desktop and taking up a pencil. "How do you know?"

"I saw her in Queenstown. As we were being processed."

Gwendolyn made a few quick, thin-line Gregg notes, and she would continue to write whenever I spoke, though her eyes always remained on mine. "Do you know how she survived?"

I hesitated only a moment. I didn't intend to write about Selene. "You'll not attribute this to me," I said.

"Of course," she said.

"You understand I'll be giving you a scoop," I said.

Her eyes did not flicker. "I do," she said, with an ellipsis of reportorial negotiation at the end.

"I'd like some information from you, as well, unattributed."

"I'll do what I can," she said. "I would very much like to know all there is to know about the fate of one of the great stars of motion pictures."

"I understand she went into the water quite near the last moment," I said. "In a life jacket. She is a very good swimmer and got clear of the ship. She was picked up by a fishing smack and ended up in the customshouse at Queenstown wearing the fishing captain's yellow slicker and his sou'wester. She is presently in London, as of early this morning, but I don't know where."

Gwendolyn's shorthanding raced at more than a hundred words a minute, nearly as fast as I spoke, and her eyes went from a jaded "what-have-you-got-for-me" to a giddy "oh-my-stars."

I stopped speaking. Her hand stopped writing a few moments later.

She asked, rather breathlessly, "Any other details, Mr. Cobb?"

I said, "From beneath her sou'wester, tendrils of her black hair clung to the back of her long, white neck."

Gwendolyn's bosom rose with a sharp intake of air and caught and her eyes went almost dreamy, as if she were crazy about me and I'd just told her I loved her and had taken her into my arms.

I smiled at her. "You are made for reporting, aren't you," I said.

She let go of her breath and wrote her Gregg symbols with exaggerated slowness as she unfurled—just as slowly—a very sweet smile. "I have not buttered your toast in this conversation, Mr. Cobb, but

I do know your reputation and it seems well earned. Thank you for these details. They are golden."

"I know you'll put them to good use."

"And what can I do for you?"

Part of me wished mightily to say "Let me take you away for a drink when your paper goes to bed." But I didn't. I couldn't.

"Details in return, Miss Bryce."

She put her pencil down.

I said, "Who is Selene Bourgani's German-director lover?"

Her head did a very faint snap at this. Not the question she expected. I let her know I could read her mind: "Not a war correspondent's sort of question, I am well aware. But it was you on the *Transcript*'s staff I came to see, after all."

She smiled again, a quick, sly one. "I'm sure, nevertheless, you'll put my details to good use."

"I will."

She said, "No longer her lover, I would guess, since she's been in the United States making movies for the past two years while he's been in Germany turning into the Kaiser's personal documentarian."

My own breath caught at that. But I kept quiet.

"Kurt Fehrenbach," Gwendolyn said. "He came out of Max Reinhardt's troupe and did a film called *Der Lilim*. Very interesting. Propelling our infant art form into precocious adolescence. A work of expressionism about a modern-day daughter of Lilith. Played by Miss Bourgani. Do you know about succubi, Mr. Cobb?"

"They are quite passionate women who keep late hours," I said.

I had already passed up a chance to flirt with Gwendolyn Bryce—rightly—but here I was doing it again, though quite archly, expecting her not even to pick up on it. But for the very reason I wanted to flirt, she picked up on it.

"I am all work, Mr. Cobb," she said, though with a glint about her that made her declaration ironic, which was, no doubt, her own style of flirting.

This had to end.

"So they broke up," I said.

"She came home. He went to Berlin."

"What's her real story?"

"The gaps? Nobody has found out. She stays mysterious, which is how she wants it. And she's good at it. You want to know about Theda Bara? Born in Egypt to an Arab sheikh? Stuff and nonsense. She's from Cincinnati, Ohio, and her father was a tailor. Lillian Gish, the gorgeous child? She was nineteen, not sixteen, when Griffith started her off, which is just as well because he started her off in more ways than one. But Selene Bourgani? Her romantic, humble beginnings on the island of Andros of course have no records to confirm them, and who knows where to look next."

"So what you know about her is that no one knows anything."

"We do know about Herr Fehrenbach. What happens on and around movie sets are things a reporter can work on. So there are some other names, if you'd like the list."

"I wouldn't," I said, and I tried to sound cynically bored about that. I tried not to stir around in my chair. Both these things were difficult. One might have expected my squirminess to lead me to reconsider making that offer to Gwendolyn Bryce: *You put your newspaper to bed and I'll put you to bed.* But even if I tried, I couldn't have done that now. The image of the damp wisps of hair clinging to Selene's neck had been tormentingly revived by the thought of her other men. And the lock I most wanted to pick later tonight was on St. Martin's Lane.

20

I would've had more luck with the editor's daughter.

At 2 A.M. on Monday morning, my leather roll of entry tools tucked in an inside pocket, I moved briskly along St. Martin's Lane, the crowds of diners and theatergoers that nightly jammed this narrow, electric-lit street mostly dissipated, and the shops darkened. The numbers were descending and I passed a pub at the corner of New Street, number 58, and then a narrow alley of bow-windowed houses, still lit by gas, and only a few more steps ahead was number 53, and from the storefront I reckoned it to be, a piss-yellow light was dribbling into the street. I stopped. I crossed to the other side. Almost directly opposite the meeting site was the opening to Cecil Court. I stepped around the darkened pub at the corner and then edged back to lurk and watch.

Number 53 split the ground floor of a four-story brick building with number 52, a Friends Meeting House, the Quakers narrowly on the right, behind a pair of double doors, and the Germans sporting a wide storefront window to the left of their oaken door with a three-tier glass transom. They were Metzger & Strauss, Booksellers. The locus of German agents in London was a bookshop sharing a wall with a bunch of pacifists.

The light was coming from the back of the bookshop, through an inner door, and from a nearer spot of light—a desk lamp, I supposed—in the midst of the massive shadows of bookshelves. I could see no figures. But this was hardly the time for breaking and entering. Too bad. I would have liked a private preview of the evening's meeting spot. I'd have to do it another way in a few hours, after they were open, not so private but still a preview. And that meant deciding about who I would become—who I would portray—a decision that had lately been looming anyway.

I slipped away south on St. Martin's Lane, striding quickly, and I passed before The Duke of York's Theatre, its neoclassic columns a trifling echo of the portico columns of St. Martin-in-the-Fields, just down at the end of the lane. Mother played a trifling comedy at the Duke of York's in a short run after *Taming of the Shrew,* when I had my adolescent London adventure with her.

The ironies of the last few minutes multiplied and I fairly trotted back to the hotel, where I slept fitfully and woke to find, in my morning paper over my eggs and bacon and marmalade in the Palm Court, a Christopher Cobb byline pinned beneath a trumpet blare of a double-deck headline:

LUSITANIA HORROR
Eyewitness Account

Reginald Bryce, true to his word. I held my breath as I scanned the front page of the *Daily Transcript* and its jump-page spread, and I saw only stock photos of the *Lusitania* and of a German U-boat and a cartoon of the Kaiser thigh-deep in the ocean with blood dripping from his hands. I let go of the breath when I found no stock photos of me.

I needed now to consider a disguise for my book browsing this morning; this gave me more options. I put my paper down and picked up my coffee to think. Across the sunken floor—bright beneath the glass roof—between the potted palms, near the piano at the far side, sat a man who'd caught my eye when he'd come in a few minutes ago. He was a thin man in a gray tweed suit with a beard and Brilliantine-assaulted hair made to lie flat on either side of a center part. It was the beard that caught me now. He had a newspaper before him—not the *Transcript*—slightly raised but not enough to shield his face. He glanced up very briefly, directly at me from across the way, and I looked off abruptly. His beard wouldn't change by his realizing I was studying him, but my impulse was to observe unobserved. I glanced back at him and he was reading.

His beard was full but moderately so, trimmed square beneath his chin. It was a beard that registered strongly as one but didn't draw attention to itself. If I were to do a beard that wasn't my own, that would be the one. But the principle I'd learned—not just from Trask's boys but from my years hanging around theaters—was that simpler is better. The less you change of yourself to resemble someone else, the more comfortable you'll be in your role.

No one at 53 St. Martin's Lane knew what I looked like. I could be anyone. I could be German. Outwardly I was ready.

21

Two hours later I figured the shop at 53 St. Martin's Lane would be open and I went out of my hotel room, thinking about the challenge before me and closing my door even as the PLEASE DO NOT DISTURB sign flapped at my hip. The door clicked shut and I took a step away and saw the girl with her cleaning cart down the corridor. I stopped and turned back. But the sign had caught its lower edge in the doorway and was angled directly at me, telling me not to disturb the room. Perhaps my readiness to pick locks had made me more sensitive about people entering my own space. I accepted the sign's advice and went on. I'd always wondered why you'd make a bed you were going to unmake a few hours later anyway.

And at number 53 there was another sign asking for no disturbances, a hand-written one propped in the corner of the window near the door: CLOSED TODAY. I'd seen no troubles on my walk west from the hotel. After all, the Admiralty and the main government offices were only just south of where I was standing, and St. James Park and Buckingham Palace were a little farther west of that. This neighborhood was the haunt of the upper class. But one of the prime page-2, *Lusitania*-related stories in the *Transcript* this morning had been an account of the widespread anti-German rioting in the slums. Mobs had been roaming through the East End looting shops run by Germans. In another part of town, not so far away, the Metzger

& Strauss, Booksellers sign would have been a billboard for a brick through the window. On the day of the "delivery," these boys wanted to play it cautious.

I drew closer to the window and tented my eyes from the sunlight. A desk sat facing the street in a front reception space, and at the desk sat a broad-shouldered, beardless man with upstanding bristled hair. The writing lamp beside him was off. He was reading loose pages on the desktop and I rapped on the window with one knuckle. Just loud enough to be heard. A confidential rap.

The man looked up at me.

I touched my chest and opened that hand toward him: I wished to come in.

He pointed at the hand-written sign.

I said, loud enough to be heard through the window, but barely. No louder. "*Bitte,*" I said. I put my head and tongue and lips into my German impression. Like an actor. But not simply to do an accent. I would speak only German now for these Germans. "Please may I come in," I said.

The man behind the desk straightened.

His cover identity was a bookshop keeper. German perhaps even in that, at least until lately. His deeper identity was quite ardently German. I was perhaps a countryman, in dangerous times. He rose.

He motioned me toward the door as he himself moved to it.

I stepped there and I waited and the lock clicked at the handle and I listened to the welcoming sound of tumblers falling into place. I could have picked that thing easily last night.

The door opened.

The man was maybe sixty and his face was wide and craggy, a face more suited for making book than selling books.

"Thank you, my dearest sir," I said. *Mein liebster Herr.* I laid it on thick.

He did not soften. That face probably was incapable of softening. But he stood aside and let me in.

"I have lived in this country for some few years now," I said, "and I did not trust these people before. Today it is much worse. It is very dangerous." This declaration was not as much to explain my insistence on entering as it was to explain a possible trace of an accent in my German, something I'd worked hard to expunge but still worried about a little.

The man grunted.

He'd let me in. But I needed a reason to hang around.

"I'm sorry to come at this late hour," I said. "But on this night I felt the strong need to read in my own language. I have nothing in my flat but English words."

"Look then," he said. Though the statement was terse, his tone was almost comradely.

"This part of the city seems quiet still," I said.

"We must all of us be careful," the man said.

I was lifted by the pronoun.

He waved generally at the shelves. "The books in our language," he said, "are found in each subject."

"Thank you," I said. And then, "Do I have the honor of speaking to Mr. Metzger or Mr. Strauss?"

"Metzger," he said.

I waited only a moment, expecting him to ask me my name, and I had decided to be Herr Vogel, a private nod toward a former comrade. But he did not ask.

He crossed to his desk and sat down.

Arrogant goddamn Hun.

I moved to the aisle along the wall that separated Metzger and Strauss from the Quakers. I faced the high shelves, hung with a ladder on a rail, stretching toward the back of the shop. The place buzzed faintly from the silence and was redolent of the vanilla and turf smells of old books.

I moved along, touching them, seeming to read their titles intently, pulling one now and then from its place to thumb the pages. I was seeing nothing. I was vaguely aware that I was in a section devoted to volumes on history. But I was most keenly aware of the twisting iron staircase to a basement that I was approaching, and the open door to a back room, an office, beyond that.

I was here on a long shot. I was not happy with the present need simply to sneak and snoop. If I was going to do that, at least I wanted to do it in the Germans' lair. I had it in my head that there might be a place inside 53 St. Martin's Lane to hide away, to be present at the evening meeting. A stupid thought. There seemed no way to secret myself in such a place even if I found one. Perhaps if I could somehow transmit an anonymous threat, or news of an East End mob coming to this neighborhood, I could induce them to leave the place for a while. But I was not thinking clearly: in that case, they would also move the site of the meeting.

But here I was. At least I could see what there was to see.

I looked toward the front of the shop.

Metzger and I were out of each other's sight from the near-ceiling-high cases of books. I turned to the office and moved toward the open door quietly but quickly.

Before me I could see the bentwood back of a chair facing into the room and then the whole chair and the end of a refectory table, and then, on the back wall, to the right of the storage room door, the edge of a steel gray hulk of a thing I thought I recognized. I reached the office door and stopped just this side of it. The hulking thing revealed itself now as what I'd expected: a safe with a spinning combination lock. To the right of it was another open door, into a darkened rear storage room, wooden boxes of books dimly visible, stacked inside. More stupidity: I could not see the far third of the refectory table, much less the rest of the room, but I stepped inside.

And someone was there, sitting at the other end of the table. If Metzger had the face of a bookie, this guy was his debt collector. He was my age and a big guy, and by the broken and mended face of him, a brawler for all of his spawn-of-Attila life. He was coring an apple with a staghorn hunting knife. He looked up sharply at me and put the apple down.

And even as the fruit hit the tabletop, a great dog jaw of a hand landed on my shoulder and dug in.

The debt collector was rising, though rather slowly, it seemed to me, almost in leisure, like this was no kind of surprise, and the knife was rising with him. And without hearing its approach, without feeling the slightest stir of air, I was suddenly aware of the wide, craggy face from the front of the store—rather like the sea might feel the tidal pull of the moon from behind the clouds—and very near my left ear, Metzger said, "Now what would make you think to come here, Mr. Cobb?"

22

These two were very confident. The guy with the knife paused where he stood and drew his free hand across his chest to wipe off the apple juice. Metzger was breathing in my ear and waiting for me to come up with an answer to his mostly rhetorical question. Granted, I myself should have been hesitating, as surprised as I was at his identifying me. But when I signed on with Trask and the boys in Washington to do these secret things for my country, I resolved in tight spots to strike first and reason later. And though time did seem to be going rather slowly, given the sudden intensity of the situation—like being thrown from a horse and seeming to fly through the air in a downright dawdle—in fact, it took only the briefest of instants for me to decide between Metzger's balls and his instep, choosing the latter, on his right foot, being that I was right-footed and a pretty damn good stomper and this was a more direct and immediate act than lifting my leg and trying to kick blindly behind me into his crotch.

So: up and down and my nice new Queenstown brogue crunched hard and deep and pulverizingly into the top of this guy's foot and his dog-bite hand flew off me toward the pain, and the knife man went wide in his eyes and I was spinning to my left now, around Metzger, who was screaming in a German I hadn't studied, and I was behind him and he was listing to the side and making an effort to turn with me but I put my hands behind his shoulders and shoved him into the office just as the guy with the knife was arriving and they both went sprawling, the bentwood chair clattering against the wall, but I'd done all I'd needed to for now and so I hustled down the aisle, betting I could find a copy or two of a 1909 *Nuttall* on the shelves if I had the time, and I was out the door, and though there was a pretty good flow of midmorning pedestrian traffic and maybe, therefore, a bobby or two around, it was nevertheless not out of the question that the guy with the knife would hide the thing somewhere on his person and vault over old man Metzger and come after me. So I plunged straight on across St. Martin's Lane, dodging a honking taxi, and I rushed into Cecil Court at not quite a run but a pretty quick almost-jog, dodging around and behind every little gaggle of passersby, trying to stay out of the sight lines behind me, and finally, seeing no coppers and having a relatively free fifty yards ahead, I all-out ran till I turned sharp into Charing Cross Road.

And as I beat it south down this busy street, I had the time and focus to wonder what the hell had just happened. When I'd feared a photo in the morning paper, it was simply one of those overwrought precautionary worries I'd consciously taken on in my new role, for to my knowledge there had never been a photo taken of me with my post-Mexico beard. And this beard—along with closer cut hair and a dustup scar or two—was a transformative thing. I'd even had an office girl at the *Post-Express,* who was sweet on me, look twice when I presented my bewhiskered self to her, close up, on my own home turf. There were only two people who could have tipped off the boys at number 53 about the nosy journalist who got very close to their special delivery package: Walter Brauer and the package herself, Selene Bourgani. And it was unlikely to have been Brauer on his own. For him to have risked speaking about me—his German bosses would likely blame him for any breach of security from a fellow American—he had to have gotten at least some confirmation from Selene that I'd survived the *Lusitania.* And probably more. I felt pretty certain Brauer had not seen me on his own after our rescue. I was more certain of that than I was of Selene not betraying me.

This notion slowed me drastically, made me veer away from the street, made me stop and put out a hand and lean against a honey-colored facade of Bath Stone. This emotionalism about Selene Bourgani had to stop now. She'd been two brief interludes of jazz. Done with. She was nothing now. She was dangerous now, the object of my work now.

I lowered my hand and straightened. I looked over my shoulder at the building that had been holding me up. The Garrick. Another theater. Of course. I walked on.

And fifteen minutes later I was in the corridor leading to my room at the Waldorf Hotel and I was thinking it would do me well to focus on the danger at hand. Danger it was. I was known to the Germans in London, known as a suspicious person at the beginning of this day, known as worse now.

I approached my door, took out my key, put it in the lock.

Something was wrong.

I couldn't place it at first.

Then I realized: my PLEASE DO NOT DISTURB sign was hanging straight and loose from the doorknob. I'd left it caught in the door.

I'd already made a rattle with my key. But I slipped it straight out and I took a step backward and I looked quickly both ways along the corridor. It was empty.

If someone were inside, they'd be standing much like me, perhaps in the center of the room. Perhaps we were facing each other now.

I thought it could have been the maid. But the sign said not to enter. The Waldorf would be strict about that with its employees.

I looked both ways again.

I needed a weapon. I'd had a pistol in my bags on the *Lusitania*. The damn war correspondent in me had kept that item off my priority replacement list. A little irony: I'd always gone to shooting wars armed only with my Corona. This sneak and snoop stuff was a different matter.

It was time to decide: walk away—even perhaps making sure my departure was audible and then waiting and watching at the end of the corridor—or go in.

This was easy.

I stepped forward and put the key in the lock and pushed the door open hard and spun back, away from the door, and I pressed against the wall beside it.

I heard not the tiniest stirring inside.

I took a deep breath and looked around the jamb.

No one was visible inside.

I stepped in and backed the door closed, noting the possible hiding places.

The door to the bathroom was open—as I'd left it—and no one was there.

Across the room was the massive mahogany Louis XVI wardrobe. A man could hide in the space behind the tall central doors.

The other possibility was beneath the bed. But the wardrobe was the only place he could effectively use a pistol upon discovery. I figured I could handle anything else. So I moved quietly to the desk and brought the chair to the wardrobe and set it on its back legs and leaned it against the doors beneath the brass handles, standing away to the side as I did so.

Then I moved to the bed and knelt and looked beneath. No one was there.

I stood, and the wardrobe was silent, and I thought of what an intruder might have learned from the room.

Nothing here suggested an identity other than war correspondent. The incriminating documents were inside the money belt strapped around my waist beneath my clothes. But I needed to know if someone had been looking. It felt likely, though my first surge of readiness for physical struggle was receding.

This let me slow down, let me realize that I smelled a faint trace of something. Vanishing perhaps even as I smelled it. Something vaguely familiar. I grasped at it as it dissipated, or as I became accustomed to it. Smells could be like that, even odd ones, even bad ones; they could be there and then vanish from your nose even though someone else just arriving would notice it anew.

This was what? Something of alcohol, ether even, a little resiny, none of these and all of these and something else and my nose just quit on me with this scent.

I tried to place it, but it was gone.

Okay. What else?

A car honked distantly somewhere down Aldwych. The clock ticked on the nightstand.

I turned back to the wardrobe. He was too quiet to actually be there. But if he was indeed hiding this quietly, he was too much a coward and probably unarmed.

I set the chair aside, and I yanked open the doors.

Before me were my clothes and my stashed Gladstone bag. Just that.

Was anyone here at all? A punctilious maid could simply have freed the sign on my door in passing.

I looked more closely at the objects in the closet. I was always pretty careful in how I put things away, and I felt certain the bag had been clasped when I left this morning. It wasn't now. But I couldn't be sure.

I closed the wardrobe and moved to the desk.

I liked to square the edges of the foolscap I'd written on. This I did with something like a compulsion. For my own sake, but also, of course, for this very purpose, to detect a prying eye. The eight pages of the follow-up *Lusitania* story I'd been writing were carefully stacked beside the Corona, the bottom of the pages even with the bottom of the machine, as they should have been. But I looked more closely. The paper edges were squared up, all right. Someone was careful. But the stack had not been tapped on the tabletop until even and then gently fingertip squared. There was a minutely visible layering of the pages at the bottom edge. Someone certainly had been here.

Neither Brauer nor Selene knew I would be at the Waldorf. I myself didn't know until Saturday morning, well after the last time I saw either of them.

Something else was wrong and I didn't know what.

The Germans had their own mystery to figure out. How did Cobb know to go to the bookstore? Brauer would swear up and down that the coded message had safely been destroyed.

We none us would get very far in our figuring.

I had a few hours till their meeting with Selene.

In the meantime, I needed to find myself another hotel.

23

I stepped from the Waldorf with my bags and put them down and took a careful inventory of all the men and automobiles in the vicinity. I hailed a taxi—one of the ubiquitous French-made Unic Landaulettes—and instructed the driver to just weave around the streets off the Strand till I told him to do otherwise.

I kept a watch on anyone who might be following till I was confident there was no one, and then I directed my driver to the Arundel Hotel, not far away, on the Embankment. It was a Tudor-style building faced with red brick, with rooms about my age, which was okay. Not done in Louis XVI, the furniture sliding all the way up to the rule of Victoria, particularly to the styles of that recent era that drew on dark, heavy Tudor carving, all of which was absolutely *not* sinkably neoclassical, so I actually felt I'd improved on my lodgings.

As soon as I'd unpacked, I stood before the mirror hanging over my washbasin and I confronted my face, which was now recognizable to my adversaries. When I looked at men's faces, tried to assess them as men, the first thing I often noticed was whether they'd been seriously struck by some other guy. I'd been struck. There were some old fighting scuffs here and there. But I'd been lucky never to have my nose rearranged. It was still on the straight and narrow, my nose. And my eyes were pretty clear. Dark as Chicago street tar but clear and steady. Over the left one was a white wisp of a scar the length of the last joint on my thumb, from a bit of tumbling shrapnel in my first real war, in Nicaragua, and mighty lucky I was for it to have just grazed on past.

As I took stock of my own mug, the principle of disguise that was running in my head was *Keep it simple.* Still, the change needed to be striking. If I was to learn anything else in London, I'd have to risk being seen, at least from afar, by people who knew me.

The beard was clearly the thing to change. I kept it pretty tightly cropped, but it definitely registered to the eye. So the beard I'd taken a shine to at breakfast wouldn't work; it wouldn't be enough. Especially from a distance, I'd pretty much be the same man. This one had to go.

I stropped my new razor—bought this morning, and I was glad it was at its sharpest—and I lathered up heavily and I shaved. I did my right cheek first, the easy one, the one I'd always known. Then I did my left cheek, carefully working my way down and up and around until all that remained, traced vividly white by the last of the lather, was the thing that prompted the beard in the first place.

I bent to the basin and rinsed away the heavily stubble-freighted shaving cream from the sink and I silently thanked the Arundel, as it had hot running water even at this hour. I soaked a hand towel in water as hot as I could stand it and wrapped my face from the eyes down. I soaked up the warmth and rubbed both cheeks clean and brought the towel down.

I was prepared for this, but it had been months since I'd faced this man, and I admit my breath clamped tight shut, from chest to throat.

I confronted my familiar, hairless face, but on one cheek was that long Turkish scimitar of a scar, a thing that I knew was there but saw now with a shock, like visiting a childhood memory I'd previously thought was pleasant and now realized had been full of pain.

But this hadn't been child's play, the crossing of swords with another German out to do no good.

And this benefit had come from it: the thing looked exactly like a German collegiate dueling scar. Intentionally so, as a matter of fact. And it was real, my own personal *Schmiss.*

The riots in the East End suggested the danger of assuming this identity in London. But I had a solution for that.

I used the room telephone to call for a bellhop to run an errand to a nearby chemist shop and I soon had a roll of gauze and a cloth arm sling, and he was a good boy, this cockney bellhop, as he had to go to another shop to find me the fritz-handled cane I'd asked for, with a hardwood shaft and an iron tip. He also brought a jar of cold cream and a bottle of alcohol and a bottle of spirit gum, which I knew from my theater days would be easier than straight collodion to put the dressing on my cheek and to take it off.

I stood once again before the mirror, having cut some thick squares of gauze to cover the scar. With the cane and the arm sling I would look like the sort of man who was beginning to appear in the streets of London: a wounded soldier, bad enough off to be mustered out. That would be conveyed with the limp and the arm.

I opened the bottle of spirit gum.

And instantly I understood that trace of a smell in my room at the Waldorf. Spirit gum. Of course. It had been a decade since I'd used it. That last time was to affix a stage mustache and muttonchops. The smell in the room was spirit gum.

I could not imagine why.

Someone himself in disguise. With fake facial hair.

Again: why? The Germans could send any mug to search a room. Any mug with his own mug that he could show in public.

I had no answer for now, but I knew I was not as lucky as that hypothetical mug; I could not show my actual self.

I brushed the spirit gum onto my face and applied the gauze. I changed into my second suit of clothes, a blue serge. I put my left arm into a sling and hobbled out on my cane into the street. I stepped into a taxi—using an upper-class British accent—and I made for the address Metcalf gave me for Brauer. He had a bachelor flat at number 70 Jermyn Street, between St. James Square and Green Park. I had the taxi driver drop me half a block east of Brauer's building, an odd-looking, seven-floor corner affair with both a gable and a turret sitting pretty much side by side.

I got out of the taxi as quickly as I could in keeping with my new disability and I paid the driver. As I was about to walk away, he called me back to him, "Gov'nor," he said, and I turned. He pulled off his cap and nodded at my arm. "Thank you for your service," he said.

"We'll kick their bloody asses," I said, maintaining my upper-crusty accent. This made his head snap in surprise, and then he lifted his face and laughed.

Which was a good exit line for a good performance and I hobbled off on my cane before he could say any more. Only then did I realize that by cursing with him like a pal—sincerely so, Chicago-style—I'd given him a better feeling about the swells of this country than the swells deserved.

I moved along west, and the taxi went past me with the driver giving me a respectful nod, which I ignored in order to start bringing him back to the class reality of his bloody country.

I crossed Jermyn Street to the north side at Brauer's corner, with Bury Street dead ending there. A couple of doors farther west was a pub, Hotspur, opposite the entrance to these bachelor flats, which had an engraved sign on the lintel: MARLBOROUGH CHAMBERS.

I entered the bar and sat at a table at the front window. It was still early and slow in the place. I figured I might be here a long time. The delivery wasn't till eight tonight, about a half hour after sunset. But I didn't know where Selene was and probably didn't know where the meeting would be, now that I'd compromised the shop. So Brauer was my only link, and I was a little nervous that he might've gone out this morning and would stay out. I had to keep his door under surveillance for as much of the day as I could.

I nursed Black and Tans for hours, keeping to myself, ignoring the day drunks, and then the light was waning and then it was getting on toward half past seven o'clock and the darkness was washing over the building facades and I was seriously worried Brauer wasn't in his bachelor flat at all but off somewhere and I'd completely lose the thread.

And then finally there he was, stepping out of the Marlborough Chambers and looking up and down the street. I guessed for a taxicab. I was glad he didn't find one. If he'd caught an isolated taxi passing by, I'd have been hard pressed to get one to follow him. But he turned west and walked off.

I put some cash down and got up quick, belying the bum leg, if any of the guys at the bar were watching. But I was out the door and done with the pub and dotting the pavement with my cane in a quick trot as long as Brauer wasn't looking my way.

Staying always on the opposite side of the street, I followed him along Jermyn and then north on St. James. He never once paused or looked back, never considering he might be followed. The next corner was Piccadilly, and as soon as he reached it, he stopped and looked to his left. For a taxi, I again presumed.

I crossed St. James, trusting my disguise now, and I passed him by, my face averted, dragging my right leg. A newer model Unic, with its headlamps flanking its radiator, was a hundred yards ahead, coming this way slow enough to be scouting a fare. I stepped to the curb and into the street, giving a quick glance in Brauer's direction. He was partway into the street himself, his hand raised, focused on the same taxi.

I turned my back in his direction, lifted my hand discreetly but clearly for the taxi, and it stopped. I stepped into the glass-partitioned tonneau, and I took up the speaking tube and told the cabbie simply to drive on. When we were clear of Brauer, I looked out the rear window. His back was to me, his attention up the street. I told the driver to pull over and wait. Brauer soon caught a massive Panhard Levassor, which would be easy to spot in traffic. He passed us and we followed.

Brauer took us to the Savoy.

It was arguably the best hotel in London. Certainly it was the most elegantly out of place in this ubiquitously begrimed city, thick with coal smoke and acrid fog. The Savoy was faced with pale pink terra-cotta and it had a bright green tiled roof. The river side was open and unfettered; Monet had painted the Battersea Bridge and the Houses of Parliament from an upper room. But the Strand approach was down a short street they'd created a decade ago between existing buildings, and the hotel entrance was dim beneath a covered court, lit in the gathering dark of twilight with gas lamps.

Brauer kept his Panhard waiting while he hustled inside. I kept my Unic, engaging the driver, a quiet old man with a crumpled face and an upcountry accent. I had him for the next few hours if need be, and I started his employ by having him turn us around in the short approach street to face the Strand, and we backed up far enough for me to watch the main hotel doors from the taxi rear window.

I mostly kept my mind in suspension for the task at hand. But waiting for Selene to make her entrance was difficult for me, since I expected never to touch her again. I even thought for a few moments about spirit gum. It was a classic smell of the theater. And just that tenuous association with acting gave me a brief, ridiculous thought that it had been Selene in my room. Of course it had not.

Then she appeared. Selene was a dark slash against the glow of gas, wearing a form-fitting ankle-length black coat and a black turban hat with a veil. Brauer was a lapdog trailing pantingly along as she glided from the hotel door and into the taxi. Brauer scrambled in behind, and the Panhard rolled away, disappearing briefly from view and then emerging from the covered court and gliding past us and into the Strand.

We followed.

I suddenly realized where they were heading when we turned from Bedford into the short and narrow New Street. A few moments later the Panhard made the left into St. Martin's Lane. I knew number 53 was just around that corner. The Germans hadn't changed their plans. Brauer was taking Selene to the bookstore.

I took up the speaking tube and told my driver to turn in the opposite direction onto St. Martin's and stop at once by the curb, on the right-hand side.

The night was dense now with the overcast dark. The streetlights were electric and we were parked not much more than fifty yards from number 53. We sat just past and across the street from another West End theater. The New Theatre. Its facade lights were bright but I was masked in the deep shadow of the tonneau, and I watched through the back window as Selene and Brauer stepped from their taxi and crossed quickly into Metzger & Strauss, Booksellers. The Panhard pulled away and went off down St. Martin's toward Trafalgar Square.

I withdrew my watch, and it said 7:56. As I held the gold-filled Elgin, all the newly acquired objects of my life suddenly lapped at me like the North Atlantic at my ankles. I became keenly conscious that the two people who'd just flashed before me in the dark shared that whole event, and so, as I pressed my post-sinking timepiece back into the watch pocket of my post-sinking pants, an odd little complicated tremor passed through me.

Another taxicab turned out of New Street and rolled to a stop at number 53. I shook off this upswell of trapped air from the vanished *Lusitania*. I waited for the taxi passenger to emerge. Another principal player perhaps, not associated with the shop. The streetlight was six or eight yards farther along St. Martin's; Selene and Brauer had appeared mostly as silhouettes. I watched closely as the taxi door opened.

A man emerged. A slim man, informally dressed in a sack suit, with a soft brimmed hat turned down slightly in front and back, and in a brief flash of dark cameo I could see a sharp-featured profile and a moderate beard. And then he was gone. His cab departed and the street was quiet save for the shuffling past of barhoppers and restaurant diners, the theatergoers already settled in their seats.

I had time now to wonder: given the events of the morning, why had the Germans not moved the venue for their meeting? Perhaps I'd drastically overreacted. Perhaps this morning they'd never suspected me of anything other than being a snoopy newsman. Perhaps that squeeze on the shoulder would have been the worst of it.

But surely they'd felt the danger of my somehow knowing about the bookshop.

And then I went cold. They kept the meeting here to bring me back to them. The guy with the knife and maybe some others were already outside the shop, hanging around the neighborhood, waiting for me to show up so they could finish the work they'd wished to complete this morning.

I withdrew farther into the shadows of the backseat.

24

I scanned all the passersby, all the lingerers, every man within sight of the taxi. Only two that I could see seemed suspicious. But I was relying on the shadows around me in the tonneau, and there were plenty of shadows on St. Martin's Lane to hide the Huns.

One of the men I didn't like the looks of was just across the street, in the far left lobby doorway of the theater. He was a burly man in a three-piece tweed without a hat, smoking a cigarette. This one was the right physical type. He was nearby, and he had the best chance to be checking me out as well. He was hatless, which made me notice him as out of place. That should have made me less suspicious of him, the men watching for me not wanting to make themselves noticeable. But the Germans were smart, and hatless in front of a theater would be smart.

So I watched carefully as he finished his cigarette. He dropped the butt and stubbed it out with the toe of his shoe. If he lingered on, if he lit another, that would make him a real suspect. But instead he turned and opened the door and went in. I could see him through the windows, crossing the lobby. The curtain had gone up a few minutes ago. He was the director. Or the playwright. Calming his nerves.

The other guy was farther up and also across the street. I turned my eyes to him. He was still there. He was mostly just a dark shape, but clearly a big guy. He was standing a couple of closed shop doors this side of Cecil Court. Even as I watched, he eased back into the deeper darkness of the doorway behind him.

I would've put two bucks on the nose that this one was a Hun.

I figured I could sit here in the shadows and wait it out and follow someone at the end of the meeting. I wasn't getting inside the shop anyway. This taxi might have seemed a bit suspicious after a while, but the Kaiser's boys couldn't clearly see who was inside, and what glimpses of me they might get didn't square with my known appearance. They sure weren't going to try to drag a vague someone out of the back of an automobile on the streets of London on spec.

So what was my frame of mind, that I should have almost immediately climbed out of the taxi? I'd never reported on the battles in other people's wars where I didn't push as close to the field of fire as I could. Now that I was actually, officially—if secretly—involved in the action against the enemies and potential enemies of my own country, I'd been turned into a goddamn lurker. A sneak. A second-story man with lock picks in his pocket and theatrical disguises. I was once again reduced to watching others do the real stuff, much as I'd always done, only without the bylines. Those few seconds of a fracas in the bookshop were the best of my official secret service career so far. Sitting any longer in the shadows in the taxi, watching from the wings still again while the real actors performed in this play—and not even being able to hear their lines—those would be just about the worst moments of that career. So I figured the least I could do was get out of the taxi and drag my bum leg past the shop. I might see a thing or two inside. I might even pay a visit to the guy in the doorway across the street.

As soon as I was on the sidewalk I decided that since he was pretty much on my path to the bookstore, I wouldn't wait; I'd drag my bum leg right past that guy in the shadows.

I took on my wounded veteran bit part and labored across the street and past the theater, and I focused on the doorway up ahead where I knew he was watching. Let him check me out. Let him decide I was a nobody so that when I crossed over to the bookstore and looked in the window, it would take him some extra time to get suspicious. Or just let him go at me right away. That thought quickened me. Made me want to drop my role and simply deal with him. But I didn't. Instead, for the moment at least, I relaxed into the role, made the limp look real. But I prepared for action. I angled out to approach along the farthest edge of the sidewalk. I kept my eyes on the doorway.

He stepped forward a little. A thin slice of him appeared, not quite lit by the electric light across the street but at least suggested by variations of darkness, from hat brim to forehead and nose to shirt front and legs and shoes. Perhaps the sound of my approach—the step and the scrape of me—had brought him out. His face turned toward me but I could see no features.

I stepped and scraped, stepped and scraped along, and his face was turning as I approached, following me. I'd been inside the dark stretch of street long enough that my eyes had adjusted and I was close now and at last I could see the wide, broken face. It was indeed a Hun; it was the Hun with the staghorn knife who'd tried to rush me at the bookshop.

"Evenin' Gov'nor," I said, sliding down the social scale to make me chattier with a stranger in a doorway.

The Hun didn't speak. He glanced down at the drag of my foot. I came even with him and I saw his right hand move inside his coat. A reflex he'd no doubt have even if he were ready to believe I was a local and not the man he was looking for. I trusted the differences in my appearance, especially in the dark, given the brevity of our previous encounter. But I took another step and would soon have my back to him and so I had to make sure.

I stopped. I turned to face him. "Got a fag?" I asked.

He kept his gaze full upon me, though I couldn't read his eyes in the dark. His hand remained inside his coat, on the handle of the knife, I felt certain. He said nothing.

"Cigarette," I said, putting my two fingers to my mouth to mime smoking. And I tightened my own hand on the T-shape of the fritz handle of the cane, splitting my fingers firmly around the shaft.

He still wasn't saying anything. I thought he might not speak English. Or if he did, he'd have a clear German accent, and if he believed my wounded-British-war-vet disguise, he'd know there could be trouble. He kept hold of his knife inside his coat.

"You a bloomin' mute, ducky?" I said.

He motioned me off with his free hand, a measly little flick of the wrist, like I was a fly on his nose.

I didn't move.

"Go away," he said in a ponderous German accent.

Perhaps I should have let things be. He didn't recognize me. But that was temporary. I wanted to cross this street and see what I could see inside the shop, and I knew I wanted to do even more than that, knew somehow I had to get inside, get closer to what was going on; I knew I had to run more risks now to properly play this role I'd taken on, and I was finally absorbing the reality of the *Lusitania,* the reality that the Germans were becoming the mortal enemy of my country whether formal war had been declared or not, and this man before me intended to find me and kill me and I'd be compelled to have this out with him very shortly anyway. I needed to make a peremptory strike against my enemy.

"With that accent," I said, "you're the one who should move away."

I said this in my own voice. He straightened, looking hard at me in the darkness.

"That's right," I said, ripping my left arm out of the cloth sling. I figured it was only fair that he knew who I was and what was at stake in the fight to come. "I'm Cobb," I said.

His knife hand started to move and I had an easier path. My right hand was trigger-ready and I drew up the cane as the knife was coming out and I grabbed the shaft of the cane with my left hand as well, gripping it hard halfway down like a rifle and this was the basic bayonet move. I took a forward step to leverage the thrust of the cane aimed now for the middle of his forehead even as the knife blade glinted as it came free, even in the darkness catching the tiniest fragment of light, but I had to focus on the target and my arms were rushing and my torso powered forward behind this strike and his head was moving off center, he was quick and trying to dodge away but the metal tip of the cane caught him just at the curve of his right temple and his head jerked at the blow but I couldn't drive through, the hit didn't feel solid, and yet his knife hand did jerk away from the striking arc he'd begun, and I was pulling the cane back quick to strike again but his head was hard and the blow had glanced and he grabbed the shaft of my cane with his left hand even as he reeled, as he stumbled deeper into the doorway, and so I couldn't simply pound him unconscious and I was happy now to play the chess game, sacrificing the cane for both my hands to be free to use on his knife arm, so I let go of the cane handle and it flopped away in his wrenching grip and both his hands were suddenly occupied, which also gave that knife an extra beat of distraction. I grabbed his right wrist in both my hands just as he was beginning a new thrust and in these moments when it was two arms straining against one I twisted the knife sharply from its rush and forced it inward, toward the center of his own chest because he would not stop coming for me, the Germans wanted me dead, and he was strong and his left hand clapped over mine at his wrist and it was both his arms and both mine, both his hands and both mine, and the knife stopped its plunge and we strained hard and we came to a quaking suspension and the knife quivered only a few inches before his chest and he was backed against the door and it was all darkness around us in this tiny place, in this upright casket which echoed with our heavy grunting, and the knife quaked and I strained against this terrible force beneath my hands, squeezed all my body into that knot of hands and he was braced against the door but I was leaning a little downward and my left leg was pressed hard against his right leg and I figured I might have the tiniest fragment of a second to divide my energy, and the leaning would help and our hands trembled and our arms trembled and I took a quick breath and I began to lift my trailing leg and I felt his hands gain strength and felt my own begin to yield, but only for the briefest moment as I flexed my right leg and thrust it hard forward into his crotch and he grunted and I felt the strength in him waver and instantly I redirected my own energy to the knife even as I was falling into him and I drove the blade forward and into his chest.

I let go and leaped back at once. The blade had gone in deep, I knew. I wanted no part of him now. I straightened upright and from inside the shadows before me came a tightly squeezed cry, remarkably low, remarkably soft, compressed as intensely as our fists had been moments ago, and I felt a sharp pain at my ankle and I jumped back a little. He'd kicked me. But it had not been a conscious blow. The Hun's feet were shuffling hard, from the pain and the panic and from something like the reflex of a dog struck down by an automobile in the street and lying on its side with its legs still moving as if it could run away from this thing that had happened, run from the pain. It was like that with the Hun: his feet ran and ran and he went nowhere; he could not escape what was happening in the center of his chest. And then the feet stopped running, and they slid a ways toward me as his legs went slack, and the sounds from the shadows stopped, and everything stopped, and he was dead.

25

I looked left and right. No one was near. This had all happened quickly. He seemed not to have any confederates out here or they likely would have been arriving. I could see the Hun in the deep shadows. He was sitting upright with his back against the door, his head angled to the side. I looked down at his legs. They were stretched onto the sidewalk. I kneeled beside them. I caught his legs at the backs of the knees and raised them so they were out of the way, so that he was in a hunched sitting position in the doorway. He was a drunk sleeping one off. He was bothering nobody. There were plenty of drunks and beggars sitting in the darkened doorways of London. Until an actual bobby came along and decided to poke him, he'd be ignored. I would have a little time.

I picked up the sling from the sidewalk and stuffed it in my pocket. I reached into the darkness beside the dead man and retrieved my cane.

I crossed the street and stood before the window of the booksellers Metzger and Strauss.

The shop was dark and seemingly empty. I moved to the front door. A shade was drawn but I put my eye to the very edge of the pane of glass, and in the narrow gap I could see along the main corridor to the rear of the shop. The stairwell was dark; the office door was closed but its bottom was edged in electric light.

My only question now was how to get in. My lock picks were in my inside pocket. I racked my memory for a crucial detail: was there a bell on the door? I'd gone through only this morning but I could not bring that one sense detail back. I was very good at noticing things and I cursed myself softly at this little slip. I didn't know if there was a bell. But I had to assume there was. Many shops had bells and no shop in London had a more acute need to be alerted if someone entered than Metzger & Strauss. I did not know how to deal with a doorbell from the outside, especially if it was wired to ring in the back of the shop.

I'd been along this block of St. Martin's twice. A detail I *did* remember was a null observation: I saw no passageway back to the courtyard or whatever sat behind these buildings. The whole four-street cincture was likely the same, a monolithic frontage of shops. The way to the rear of these storefronts was through one of them. So I stepped one doorway south, to the Friends Meeting House.

Through the double glass-paned doors there was only darkness. I picked the lock.

I closed the door quietly behind me but left it unlocked. I turned. Only darkness lay before me and I walked into it, the potted plants and wall-hugging furniture of the reception area fading at once from my sight. I lit a match and held it up.

I found the door into the Meeting Room immediately before me. I simply had to keep heading straight to the rear of the building. I opened the door and stepped in as my match flickered out.

But a light remained.

I could see the dim forms of bench seats in rows facing the far platform, where a dozen wooden chairs were lined up. Upon one of the chairs burned a candle. It gave me enough light to find my way to the center aisle and I went down, and as I moved, I saw, in the penumbra of the candle glow, the door out the back of this sanctuary, leading in the direction I wanted. Focused as I was on this, I pulled up with a start at the hunched back and bowed head of a man on the aisle seat of the second row. I was nearly upon him and he'd heard my approach, and now that I'd stopped, he straightened up, but he did not turn.

He wore a stand collar and a dark coat; his head was bare and his hair was white. He spoke without looking at me. "Are you a friend of the truth?" he asked.

I understood this to be a thing some Quakers called each other. But it was also a fundamental question of philosophy and intent. So I said, "Yes."

"We must not fight," he said. "The world must not fight. The Lord put that on my heart and I am glad to have said it aloud in your presence."

I had to move by him now.

With this man, in this room—and the feeling would pass, I knew—but at that moment, I felt suddenly heavy-limbed, felt suddenly empty in the place in my own body where the knife had plunged into the Hun. I felt remorseful. Remorseful at lying to this man, letting him think I was a fellow Quaker, remorseful at what I had just done in the street. I'd killed before, in the past year. Killed, as tonight, in self-defense: after all, I'd let the Hun draw his knife first. But as I stepped even with the old man, and he lifted his face to me, I felt remorseful at how much easier it was to kill than it had been only a year ago, remorseful at how quickly all this remorse would pass.

And the old man looked at me, the candlelight flickering in his dark eyes. He would never lift his hand against anyone. He would sit alone in this place of quiet, and he would meditate with God about how we all should never lift a hand against anyone. And he would be dead wrong about that, as far as the practical world of governments and of modern weapons and of the vast, institutionalized wickedness of humankind was concerned. But he was also right.

"I'm sorry," I said.

He nodded at me. And he turned his face away and he bowed his head and I beat it out the back door.

26

The courtyard was very dark and it stank of garbage and waste and it rustled with rats. My remorse was gone and I shuffled my feet not to trip on unseen things, and then I was at the rear door of Metzger & Strauss.

The window I'd passed and the window in the door were painted black.

I expected that trying to pick the lock in the impenetrable dark of this doorway within this courtyard surrounded by these multistoried buildings on this moonless London night would be a tricky business, but I was getting used to my job, and once I found the opening of the keyway with my fingertip and got my pick and torque wrench inside, it was good doing this in the dark. The darkness made it entirely about the feel of things unseen in the keyway, and that was how it should have been anyway. And when the last pin yielded and I felt the shear line go clear and I was ready to rotate the plug, I paused. I focused on being quiet. I eased the plug around and opened the door with the meekest of clicks.

And I froze.

Voices and light.

But not in this room, I quickly realized. And the voices murmured on without a hitch even now, even after the sound of my entry. They were distant, from another room.

Which is what I should have expected. This was the back room I was entering. I'd seen through to it in the rear wall of the bookshop office this morning. I realized that door must still be open.

This was dangerous but it was also an opportunity.

I stepped inside.

Across the rear storage room was the open door to the office, and framed brightly there in modernist composition was a center cut of the refectory table and Brauer's brown tweedy back overlaid with the curves of a bentwood chair. No eyes were visible.

I closed the door softly behind me. I turned and waited where I was standing for a moment. The voices were pretty low and I couldn't pick up the words clearly. The floor was stacked on both sides of me with boxes in irregular rows, and I ducked down and circled behind them to the left, out of sight of the door, moving along the nearest row.

I gave a brief thought to the contents of these boxes. Books. This was an ongoing plausible bookstore, after all. But what else could be delivered here as if they were books? If the Germans wanted to mount a sabotage campaign in England, the explosives could well pass through here. But that was not my business tonight.

I was treading softly now in a severe crouch behind the chest-high row of boxes nearest the office.

As I drew near the open door, I was concentrating fully on being quiet and not yet trying to render the murmuring into words.

But an abrupt silence caught my attention.

I froze again.

Had they heard me?

I'd move no more if I hadn't already given myself away.

But now a man's voice spoke in German: "You are all right? You are making sounds again." The voice was soft-edged in timbre but hard-edged in tone.

Another man answered, also in German, "I will be all right when he is dead." German can transform a voice, and I'd heard his only briefly in English, but from the context I figured this was Metzger, attending the meeting with his broken foot and not taking it real well. I was certainly on the other side of the wall from my meditating Quaker: I had a sharp little twist of pleasure at the present state of Metzger's murderous pal in the doorway across the street.

"You expect word on that shortly?" the first man said.

"If he is what we think he is," Metzger said, "he'll come and we'll have him."

"Can we get on with this?" a third person said. I went rigidly silent inside once more, though I'd expected to hear this voice. It was Selene.

"Of course," a man said in English. This was the first German speaker, I surmised. His overtly impatient tone with Metzger and his stepping in as the commander of the agenda to reassure Selene suggested he was the one in charge. Perhaps Herr Strauss? "Herr Metzger," he said, with an intonation as if prompting him to do a prearranged thing.

In the brief silence that followed, I heard a rustling of papers, perhaps pulled from a pocket and pushed across the tabletop.

Metzger said in English, "Herr Brauer, if you would be so kind as to keep the envelope with your name upon it and hand the other to the lady."

"Of course," Brauer said.

Metzger said, "They canceled the daylight passage. I've rebooked you on the boat train to Flushing, night after tomorrow. You'll cross over to German territory at Baarle. Everything you need is in the envelopes."

"My apologies to Herr Brauer," Selene said, "but is the escort necessary?"

Metzger said, "Constantinople is a long way."

"But it's by your vaunted Baghdad Express, yes?"

Metzger began clumsily to explain. "Most of the way but . . ."

The man I figured to be Strauss cut him off. "We have arranged all of this so far, Miss Bourgani. Please trust us further. Herr Brauer will handle what remains to be done in *Istanbul*."

He stressed the Turks' preferred name for the city, no doubt shooting Metzger a critical look. Their kaiser was the self-avowed brother to Islam. Istanbul, not Constantinople. This was an important detail.

I made this quick assessment while the sound of the man's voice buzzed in my head like subtext. Until this moment I'd heard him speak fewer than half a dozen words in English. Now he sounded familiar.

"The Pasha's people and ours must meet to arrange the first contact."

I strained at placing the voice but felt blocked in some odd, undefinable way.

New sounds now: an opening of a door—the door from the front of the shop—and a slight scraping of chairs.

The man I took to be Strauss said, "Herr Strauss. These are Miss Selene Bourgani and Herr Brauer, whom I think you've met."

The actual Strauss had a voice raspy from a lifetime of heavy smoking. His manner was old-school courtly. "Miss Bourgani," he said in British-inflected English. "I am enchanted. Your face fills the dreams of millions."

"Herr Strauss," Selene said.

Strauss said, "We deeply appreciate your assistance in this most delicate of tasks."

She did not reply in words and I longed to watch all the physical nuances of the characters in this scene. I particularly longed to see the face of the man I'd mistaken for Strauss, the man whose voice still echoed in my head. Where had I heard it?

I assessed the shadows around me, wondered if I dared to lift my head above the boxes.

Metzger said in German, "Any sign outside?"

"I only looked for a moment, getting out of the taxi," Strauss said, also in German. "I didn't see Karl. But that's the point, yes?"

Metzger grunted.

I shrank back deeper into the darkness and began to rise a bit from my crouch to look.

"Can we speak in English, gentlemen?" Selene said.

The familiar man replied, "I'm very sorry, Miss Bourgani. It's rude of us." His English was perfect. And his accent was American, though without any regional hint at all. Whatever "standard American speech" was, this was it. Meticulously learned.

The bright, angled slice of the office appeared before me: Brauer, seen from behind but also now from the side, sitting upright, blocking the view to the far end of the table, though I couldn't say for sure I would've seen that far even if he wasn't there.

"Sometimes we have peripheral matters to discuss and we speak in German by reflex," the man went on.

"Is there more?" Selene said and I saw a movement just to the right of Brauer: Selene's black-sheathed shoulder rolled into my view and then out again.

The man with the soft-timbred familiar voice ignored her. "*Bitte,*" he said. Then he quickly repeated in English, "Please." And a gray-tweed-clad wrist, a delicate-fingered hand appeared in the air beyond Brauer, from the end of the table, gesturing toward an invisible chair. "Sit for a time, Mr. Strauss."

A chair scraped.

The wrist and hand vanished.

"It will only be for a *brief* time, Miss Bourgani," the invisible man said.

I crept back farther, leaned to my left, trying to catch a glimpse of him. Though the angle improved, the visible slice of the doorway shrank as well. I could see Selene's shoulder; I could see that she had not raised the veil on her hat. She was sitting there shrouded before these men. Given the familiar man's impulsive leveraging of his empowered status—making Strauss sit—it must have been nagging the hell out of him that Selene wouldn't show her face clearly to him.

"Perhaps if we can have a little drink together before we go," he said. "We humbly request this gesture of friendly feelings, dear lady."

I thought: *This guy is good. He'll lift her veil yet.*

He did not wait for her reply. He said, "Mr. Brauer. If you'd be so kind as to pour the wine."

Brauer twisted his body in the direction of the man. This had taken him by surprise. He was being put in his place as well. He might have thought he was a high-toned university intellectual, but in this room he was the office girl being sent for coffee.

He straightened and began to push his chair back.

I quickened at this. I leaned just a little more to my left. He was about to reveal his boss.

The chair screaked on the floor, the noise consciously made worse, I suspected, by Walter daring to express his displeasure.

He rose and stepped to his left, and he was gone from my sight.

And there, at the end of the table, was the man with the square-trimmed beard who'd been reading his newspaper across the Palm Court this morning.

27

Almost at once his face swung in my direction. I ducked below the bookcase. I'd made no sound. He was probably turning to Selene.

His face was a blur now in my head from this quick glance, and there was very little that was new. The beard again dominated my impression of him. His eyebrows were bushy; that was something I'd not noticed across the Palm Court. His plastered hair with that center part was vaguely brown. But I still needed a clear and steady look at him from close up.

His attention did indeed go to Selene. He was talking trivially to her about the wine. A nice German wine.

He'd been watching me this morning. That much was clear. There were other things to consider about this man, though I felt further away than ever from recognizing his voice. I might have been wrong about that. But I had to shut down my mind for now. I was still lurking a few feet from my own little den of German spies and I needed to listen.

Playing up that soft-edged quality in his voice, Squarebeard prattled on about how they discovered the beauties of late harvest grapes in the Rheingau. "What seemed to be too old, what seemed to be rotten, turned out to be the sweetest and finest of all," he said, and I could imagine him leaning to her, touching her wrist lightly, putting the mash on Selene Bourgani.

Then for a time there were only clinking sounds and bits of conversation about everyone getting a nice glass of late-harvest Riesling, and then a silence fell over the table.

I wanted to rise up once again to look into the room. But either Brauer was back in his chair and I'd see nothing or I'd be directly in Squarebeard's line of sight and it would be too dangerous. I stayed where I was.

"So then," Squarebeard said. "It is time for us soon to go, but first a toast. To Miss Bourgani and to international understanding that will help bring about a quickly achieved but eternal peace in the world."

A beat of silence during which, no doubt, Squarebeard repressed the gagging reflex from his tripewurst of a toast, poor man. Surely he didn't fool Selene; he could have simply toasted to the crushing victory of Germany over all her enemies and to the establishment of a vast new Germanic Empire and saved himself this discomfort. Then the glasses clinked and Metzger and Strauss, in unison, murmured *"Zum Wohl."*

A longer silence fell upon the room as they drank, broken only by Metzger praising the pleasing sweetness of the wine and by a desultory murmuring of agreement.

This thing would soon end.

I had to decide what to do. They'd leave in several taxis, as they'd come. Who might linger? I'd heard some useful things but nothing of the details of what Selene was expected to do in Istanbul. I could wait for whoever remained possibly to reiterate informally some of what I'd missed.

But Squarebeard might clear out quickly and he was the one—the obvious leader of the group—I was most interested in.

He didn't give them much drinking time. Suddenly a chair scooted and it must have been his. He said, "So we must go now."

Glasses clinked down to the table.

Chairs began to move.

Shoes began to scuff and shuffle.

I backed away and circled around the side of the rows of boxes and I reached the rear wall. I crouched low again and moved toward the door as quickly as I could without audible footfalls.

Before I stood in full—though shadowed—sight of the office, I peeked from my crouch a last time. The bright frame of the doorway for the moment showed only a center slice of the refectory table, and then a body moved into frame, the large, laboring body of Metzger, bracing himself with his hand on the tabletop, hobbling in severe pain on his broken foot.

He was heading for the front of the shop, to show his visitors out. I did not have time to wait till the office was clear. I rose slowly and then took a brisk step to the door, eased it open, and went out into the night, carefully closing the door behind me.

My passage was in darkness now but I moved as fast as I dared. Along the back of the shop to the Friends Meeting House. Through the Quakers' back rooms. I paused only before I entered the Meeting Room.

It was dark. The candle was out. The old man was gone. Matches lit my way past the empty benches and through another door, and before me, in the windows of the front entrance, was the street, almost bright by contrast, with its taint of electric light.

The handle did not yield to my turn. Of course. The old man had locked up on his way out. I turned the bolt key and I opened the door slowly, quietly. Voices were coming from nearby to the right. My German spies scattered from under their rock.

I took a step back and pulled the sling from my pocket and reset my left arm in it. I tapped my cane to the floor. I touched the gauze on my cheek to make sure it was there. I could cross the street. But I was still hungry for any scrap of information. For a closer look at Squarebeard. For a glimpse of Selene. I had to be bold now and trust my disguise. I would pass before their very eyes. I figured at the very worst there'd be a delay for them to realize who I was. I could handle any of them in a scrap and could simply outrun them if need be.

They'd soon know I'd been around anyway when the dead body in the doorway made his appearance in their little drama.

I took a quick initial look in their direction before stepping out. It would help if they didn't realize I'd entered the scene from just next door.

Squarebeard was disappearing into a taxi.

"Damn," I said, almost aloud. Almost.

The others were distracted.

It was too late for the boss man, but I stepped out quickly, dragging my putative bad leg—overacting terribly—and the taxi containing Squarebeard slipped past me, his shadowed face flashing by in the tonneau.

He did not look my way.

Ahead were agitated voices. Hushed, not rendering themselves into words, but the contentious intensity was clear.

Selene and Brauer had moved a ways down the street, toward the corner, and they were face to face at the edge of the sidewalk, Brauer with his back to me. He raised his left arm, signaling for a taxi.

I limped slowly their way.

Selene's voice rose, lost its hush: "Mr. Brauer, the next taxi is yours or it is mine. You will not escort me. Is that clear?"

I was passing the front window of the bookstore. In my periphery I saw shadows moving behind the front desk lamplight.

Brauer's voice rose to match hers. "I am following my orders."

Selene said, "You will take me to my final destination but not to my hotel."

I slowed to keep as much of the conversation before me as I could, lowering my face and turning a little to the right, showing my bandaged cheek, which would arrest any brief glance.

Brauer said. "I will fetch Herr Metzger. He will tell you."

"You go do that," she said.

"Taxi," Brauer cried.

I glanced their way. Brauer had taken a step into the street. An earlier model Unic, a 1908 12/14, tall and sputtery, with a foreshortened tonneau, approached. Selene turned to watch the taxi.

And then a whistle cried sharply from across the street—the garbled, trilling sound of a bobby, like two differently pitched whistles blowing at the same time, not quite blending but not quite separating themselves. The cop blew three short, sharp times in a row, a call for other bobbies in the area.

My handiwork had been discovered.

Brauer jerked his head in the direction of the sound. Selene didn't look at all but stepped forward and flung open the back door of the taxi and vanished inside, and before Brauer could turn back, she'd slammed the door.

I realized I had to follow her. She certainly didn't think Brauer was putting the mash on her and this wasn't about proving her independence. She had somewhere to go.

I wanted to sprint away back to my own taxi, but that could draw the attention of the bobby, and so I walked briskly instead.

I glanced into her tonneau and Selene was giving her driver instructions.

I pushed on more quickly.

My driver was alert. He'd turned his Unic around to face this way, so he could watch for me, and he started up now, even as another taxi cut me off, turning from New Street into St. Martin's.

I heard Brauer cry, "Taxi!"

I figured he was going to follow her as well.

I glanced back and I caught a glimpse of her old Unic puttering off as Brauer's taxi, a British Napier Landaulet, slid into its place. The Napier's cloth rear top was down, but Bauer opened the door into the forward hard cabin and he began to climb in.

I took the last few strides to my Unic and leaped into the back. I grabbed the speaking tube and told my man to follow the taxi in front of us, which was following the taxi I was primarily interested in, and he said "Yessir" as if he actually knew what I wanted, and we were all off.

28

We went south on St. Martin's and then swung east into the Strand and almost at once were passing the massive, rusticated stone, Edwardian-Baroque Cecil Hotel. The Savoy was next door. Maybe I was wrong about Selene.

But the driver hailed me on the speaking tube and said, "The taxi of interest has turned in. Would tha like me to stop?"

"What's the taxi just ahead doing?"

"He has gone by but is stopping now."

"Turn in," I said, "and park like you did earlier, facing the Strand."

And we did. I leaned forward to watch for the '08 Unic to emerge from the covered front court. It came out almost at once. Too quick to have dropped Selene and gotten a new fare. She played this smart but assumed Brauer would have gone off at once when he saw her turn in at her hotel. And sure enough, as the taxi puttered past, I caught a brief glimpse of her turban hat and veil in silhouette.

I told my man to follow. Selene's taxi turned right, onto the Strand, and I told him to pause long enough to see if the other taxi was going to follow as well.

Brauer did. He was as suspicious as I was, and he was going to check this out.

We three wagon-trained along the Strand, passing the neoclassical facade of Somerset House, which was full of the quotidian, no-spies-necessary government—taxes and probate and the records of birth and death and marriage—and then, in exactly the same architectural style, the Strand campus of Brauer's own King's College drifted past.

I settled back in my seat and stopped watching the city for now. We trekked on into Fleet Street. I wondered how far east Selene would go.

I turned my thoughts back to Squarebeard. A voice heard briefly or distantly or long ago sticks in your head, it seemed to me, not just from the sound of it but from the circumstance, the location, the face of the speaker when you hear it. I tried one last time to recognize Squarebeard's voice, but since I'd seen his face, none of this was coming together. He used his voice well. My hands flexed at his softly sneaky masher-pitch about late-harvest grapes. That voice was familiar but perhaps because it sounded similar to somebody from my own past. Probably some actor I'd met along the circuit with my mother. Someone, after all this time, I would never be able to identify. Nor did I need to.

And I thought of Selene's mission. To spy for the Germans, apparently. In Istanbul. On the Turks? They were Germany's ally, but I only had to look at my own mission—sneaking into Britain's war—to find that possibility plausible. In the old Chinese military axiom that you kept your friends close and your enemies closer, you had two challenges. Keeping the enemy closer was the obvious one. But you still might have to work hard and secretly to keep those friends close. The military best interests of a Turk-invoked international jihad would not necessarily fit with the Germans' best interests.

As of two weeks ago the Turks had begun fighting on their own Eastern Front. The Brits and French had landed on the Gallipoli peninsula with the intention of taking Istanbul and opening a supply route into the Black Sea for the Russians. Hell, everyone figured the Triple Entente had already agreed to let Constantinople turn into Tsargrad. This was a particularly important time for the Huns to get the inside scoop on what their ally was planning to do and how.

But there was another possibility. Squarebeard mentioned an approach to a pasha, a member of the Turkish ruling elite. Maybe Selene's real work would be for the Turks themselves. Perhaps the Germans were providing Selene for an Ottoman mission. What would the Turks want that they'd need a female Greek-American film star to do the job? For that matter, of what particular use would such a woman be to the Germans? What covert skills did she possess to make her uniquely useful?

Only one answer came to mind. But my feelings were too raw about Selene Bourgani to go any further with that.

So I closed the throttle and let my thoughts sputter out. I found myself looking sightlessly at the passing street. I turned my face to the forward windows of the taxi, and looming before us was the massively becolumned Great West Door of the Christopher Wrenassainced St. Paul's Cathedral.

We veered to the right and around the cathedral and still we followed Brauer and Selene. Down Cannon Street we went and past its eponymous train station and soon we were approaching the castle within a castle within a castle of the Tower of London, the spaced, rising stacks of ancient stone seeming to fill the dark of the night ahead. This too we circled, and immediately we were skirting the northern edge of the St. Katharine Docks, the ships invisible behind the high brick facades of the warehouses joined in a long unbroken row.

Then we angled up onto St. George Street and the only hint of the vast London Docks lying beyond the immediate rows of commercial buildings was the proliferation among the storefronts of ship chandlers, with their windows hung in deck lights and signal lanterns and with their barrels of tar and pitch and rosin huddling dimly inside. And, as well, the clothiers' windows were showing peacoats and slickers instead of sack suits and frocks.

And now we turned off St. George into a street of brick warehouses on both sides, which loomed six stories above us in canyon cliff face, and the darkness of the night deepened around us. New Gravel Lane. This was on the way to nowhere. And when we got free of the warehouses and into a run of sack makers and rope merchants and pubs, I expected what soon came: my driver hailed me over the speaking tube and said, "They will be stopping up ahead."

I leaned forward to the front tonneau window, and I could see before us Brauer's taxi pulling abruptly to the curb.

"Go on," I told my driver.

We passed Brauer and fifty yards farther along we approached Selene's Unic, which had stopped before a pub on a corner.

"Take the right turn," I said to my driver.

He did. Onto Coleman Street. He knew to go slow. I let him roll twenty or so yards farther and I told him to pull over.

I removed the arm sling, which had been hanging loose for the ride, and put it on the seat. I considered the cane but left it behind as well. I stripped off my jacket and plucked off my hat and I jumped out of the taxi on the driver's side and stepped forward to him.

He looked at me. Ready to do whatever I needed. "You're a good man," I said. "I'd take you to battle with me any day of the week."

He nodded at me once, and his mouth tightened and pursed ever so slightly. The smile of a man with the qualities I was appreciating at that moment.

"Can I borrow your cap?" I said.

He was wearing the perfect thing: a good, well cared for but well traveled, working-class cloth cap with a soft, flat one-piece crown.

He did not hesitate. He grabbed it off and handed it to me.

I gave him the same nod and the same smile he'd lately given me.

I put his cap on my head—it was a pretty good fit—and I walked back toward the corner, no longer lame and arm-slung, ready to rely on my workingman's cap and a shirt that was new but unchanged since Queenstown and a beardless face dominated by an already London-dingy bandage. And rely on my showing up in a place that no one would expect me to be. It was worth the risk.

I approached the Block & Tackle, Spirit Merchant, which had a large bright window looking onto Coleman Street, with the brick facade above it painted: WALKERS WARRINGTON AND BURTON ALES.

I slowed and looked in at the window. Selene was standing before a table. I shrank back a bit, as she was looking in my direction. She had lifted her veil and she could have seen me watching her if she'd only shifted her eyes. She was just beyond the right shoulder of a man whose back was to me. He was standing in front of a chair pushed away from the table, apparently having just risen for her. He was holding himself stiffly upright.

It was clear she'd come to see this guy.

Her eyes stayed fixed on him. For all her screen-actress largeness, I had to look closely to read her. Which was part of what I read, of course. Her face was as stiff in its inexpressiveness as the man's posture.

I dared not watch from this angle any longer.

I moved along the sidewalk, heading for the front door, keeping my eyes on these two all the while.

Her hands were clasped before her. She was still wearing that clinging, black, high-fashion dress with the chinchilla wrists. She seemed more than ever to be dressed for a state of mourning, though from all I knew, she was merely dressed for a state of film-star vamp-ish mystery.

Her face was vanishing as I moved, and his face was emerging. I was in no one's line of sight so I stopped to study him, even as these two seemed to be studying each other. His face gave me a dark undertow of a thought about what this stiff and untouching and, from what I could see, silent confrontation might be about. He was a good-looking guy but in an odd mix of ways: exaggerated features of a sort, a prominent nose, large eyes, a wide mouth, but for their size somehow delicate still, and his skin was dusky but not quite swarthy-masculine, a Mediterranean or Slavic, cut by some whiter blood. His dark hair was starting to streak with gray and his face was starting to jowl up a bit around the chin. A leading man type gone a little to seed. He wore a three-piece suit and he looked comfortable in it, though he was broad in the shoulders and the suit was cheap and she had come to him, after all, in a scruffy bar on the docks, clearly his turf. And the thing that ran in me from the way they looked at each other—knowing but estranged, wanting to touch but not wanting to touch—was that this was still another man that the vamp Selene Bourgani had taken to bed for a while and then booted out the door.

And this made me think again how she likely would conduct her espionage work in Istanbul. The logic of her doing it that way. The ease of it, for her.

So I kept on jittering around on the sidewalk outside the bar, compulsively trying to read this guy's face, trying to imagine where the hell she met him, trying to throw a brick and scare off that nasty little rutting street tom of a Manx who was presently trying to claw his way out of the center of my chest.

The guy's lips moved now, but not a lot, and he motioned to the chair across the table from him, and they both sat.

I slipped away, went around the corner, pulling my cap low over my eyes, glancing up the street on this side to Brauer's taxi, which was still sitting there, beyond Selene's, which was also still sitting there. At least she expected to leave this guy's company tonight. Which didn't mean anything, really, about what they might do in the meantime, somewhere nearby in private, if they could warm this present chill between them.

Not that any of this mattered to me.

Not that I actually could rely on anything I was thinking on this subject, stupid as I could be about women. I realized I'd better be grateful the Germans hadn't targeted me with this woman.

I stopped for a moment at the front door of the pub, and I lit a cigarette so I could casually glance across the street.

Brauer was there. Also jittering around, under an electric lamppost, smoking his own cigarette, no doubt trying to decide if and when he should come closer and take a look. He was probably not in a position—nor did he have reasons—to distrust her, but he was feeling very uneasy, with her being his responsibility and wildly out of control.

She was sitting with her back to the door. I stepped in.

The guy she was with could have looked up and noticed me, but he didn't. They were leaning a bit toward each other now, across the table, and they were talking.

I was standing still and I didn't want to make my interest in these two obvious, so I looked around and found that the dozen or so men scattered about were, most of them, looking at me. They all had an off-the-same-boat look, all from a crew hired from the same bunch of locals somewhere, maybe in Tangier or Port Said, with a dark intensity of face and features. Maybe they had the same origins as the guy with Selene, though without the mix of some other peoples in them.

I was starting to think the bar did indeed have an ethnic core to it. At that point, I just didn't know what it was.

I myself clearly wasn't part of the core. The dark sets of eyes in the bar were still lingering on me. I nodded at a few. I was just a guy from a ship in his going-ashore clothes out to get a drink.

After I'd openly acknowledged enough of these stares, these guys all finally looked away.

To the right was a long, stand-up bar with a wall of bottles and a wide central mirror. I moved past Selene and her man. She was speaking low. It wasn't English. The words I heard were often throaty, sometimes almost Greek, sometimes almost a Semitic language. It was neither, I felt certain. Well, maybe Greek. That was Selene's movie-magazine story, after all. Maybe everyone in this bar was Greek. But I'd known a few Greeks along the way, covering Chicago First Ward politics. And this didn't quite sound Greek to me.

The man was listening intently, one hand now on the tabletop. He'd be reaching across soon to give her wrist a pat or her elbow a squeeze.

I moved a couple of small steps past them, planning a sight line by way of the mirror. I bellied up to the zinc bar and hunched over, anchoring my elbows. I turned my head a little to the right and there they were in reflection. I could see her face. I could see the side of his head. He hadn't reached out to her yet, though that hand was still lying on the tabletop. She'd finished talking. Over my shoulder I could pick out his voice, a richly deep voice, those throaty sounds floating across to me, strings of *h*'s tracking after consonants.

"Drink?" Another voice, with the same throatiness in its accented English.

I straightened.

The bartender was one of the boys from the core. Dark in skin and hair and eyes. A commanding nose.

I had to keep my voice low. Few words. I motioned toward the taps. "Burton," I said.

The bartender nodded but didn't go.

He let his eyes travel down me, from my face to the center of my chest and onward, quite deliberately, till they stopped, and he angled his head a little. "You okay?" he said.

I looked.

There was a splash of blood on my white shirt, around my lower abdomen, just above the belt line. From my work in St. Martin's Lane. I'd been carrying the Hun's blood around on me ever since.

29

I flipped some fingers at the bottom of the bandage on my left cheek. The gesture led me to put on a light Italian accent for my English, still keeping the volume low, all to further mask me from Selene's nearby ear.

"They make the bandages not so good anymore," I said.

At once I figured this was a mistake. Although they still hadn't entered the war, the Italians were part of the Triple Alliance.

But the barman looked me in the eye and gave me a nod—a guy's nod, like he knew about fights with sharp objects—and he stepped away to draw me an ale.

Selene and her older man were still trading low words in their mystery language, and my eyes briefly followed the bartender. But I stopped at the cleared space around the cash box beneath the mirror.

Attached to the wall, low, just over the tin box, was an image of a flag, not much larger than a postcard. It was divided into three equal vertical stripes: red, green, blue. This wasn't Greek. It wasn't any flag I recognized.

I glanced into the mirror.

Selene was the one who was making the move. Her hand was groping out over the table now, falling upon the man's wrist. He put his own hand over hers and they talked on in the language, I suspected, of red, green, and blue. I looked at the beer that was just now landing in front of me. It was pale.

I took a drink.

Too much hops, as far as I was concerned.

I had blood on my shirt and a beer I didn't like in front of me. I was obviously out of place in this bar in the presence of a woman who I didn't want to recognize me, and I wasn't understanding anything she and her man were saying anyway.

It was time to wait outside.

I didn't want to cause a stir on my departure, however, so I downed the bitter Burton ale in three swallows, wiped my mouth, put some money on the bar, and eased away. I passed the now intertwined hands, and I gave the man one last, reflexive glance. He had a long straight nose and my mind photographed it and I briefly registered her own famous profile as I went by, but I did not let my mind linger on her, and Selene and her man were behind me and I approached the door. I lowered my face for Brauer and went out the door and around the corner and up to my taxi.

I stopped by the driver's side of the vehicle and he was sitting there behind the wheel, not off having a quick beer in another pub, not even lounging in the street, but behind the wheel. A good man. He turned his face to me as I approached and I took his cap off my head and fitted it on his. He let me.

"Thanks," I said. "Turn us around and bring us close to the corner."

He nodded.

Only when I was climbing into the tonneau, when he thought I wasn't looking, did he adjust his cap to suit him.

And we waited.

Perhaps fifteen minutes went by and I held myself in suspension.

I didn't want to, but finally I looked again in my mind at Selene's profile. I didn't want to, but something was nagging at me, something from my eyes, not my reason.

Then it struck me: her man's thin, straight nose, the precise curve where bridge and brow met, the angle of the forehead. I'd registered this same profile in person more than a week ago. And it was Selene. From the first time I saw her in person, as she was suffering the questions of the reporters on the deck of the *Lusitania*. This was familial similarity. This was her father.

And as if on cue, he came around the corner.

He was striding briskly. He and his daughter had been in a preexisting state of estrangement in their first moments together in the pub. A long and hard estrangement, for them to have been separated by an ocean and then to have taken up with each other like that from the start, looking like wounded old lovers. And yet they came to entwine their hands. They came to some reconciliation. But now she was off to Istanbul—had she told him where she was going, what she was doing?—and so this was a hard parting for him. He was striding away from her firmly, as a man would, to control his feelings and maintain his manhood.

This assessment ran quickly in me as I shrank into the shadows of the tonneau and he passed by across the street. I slid to the streetside door, was ready to follow him, but as my hand went to the handle, he turned in at a doorway to a three-story brick tenement fifty yards or so down Coleman.

I opened the door and stepped out.

I moved into the middle of the street and looked for a number on the building. Over the lintel, a dingy 22.

I watched the facade, looking every few moments to the corner of New Gravel.

Soon a light came on in a second-floor window. I noted its position. I stepped back to the taxi and told my driver to be ready for the resumption of our little parade.

I entered the tonneau and leaned forward to watch out the front window.

The '08 Unic rolled into view from before the pub and crossed our line of sight, heading south on New Gravel Lane. A few moments later, Brauer's Napier passed by in pursuit. We followed.

I was aware at once that something was going on. Not with our three-character melodrama. Out to the east. In the sky. I thought it was lightning. I didn't think any further about that, as I was preoccupied with the first clues of an alternate biography for Vitagraph's Most Mysterious Woman in the World. But we didn't drive very far before the lightning yielded a clap of distant thunder. But it seemed to be thunder only if you'd already distractedly assumed you'd seen lightning. Part of me instantly recognized the punch-thump of an exploding shell. My taxi stopped abruptly, and a few moments later my driver leaned across the front seat to try to see something in the eastern sky.

I slid across and looked. Three narrow columns of white light were separately, restlessly sweeping the sky. Searchlights.

The speaking tube jingled and I took it up. "Zeppelins, sir," my driver said. "Raiding the East India Docks, I'd say. The two taxis have stopped before us and will not be entering the Wapping High Street—nor will aught else—till this be finished."

I thanked him and looked again at the sky. The searchlights still had not found the airships, but they were drawing nearer each other.

I stepped out of the taxi on the left side, into the street.

The near warehouses were low and scattered, south of the Shadwell Basin, and then there was a clear view across the meander of the Thames and into the distant light flecks of Dog Island, which held the West India, Millwall, and South Docks. The stars were blotted out, but the ceiling was pretty high, plenty high enough for the German dirigibles to drop their bombs. At the distant edge of my view—at the East India Docks, as my man had reckoned—a column of flame had flared up.

Now the tip of one searchlight, nearer in, was suddenly clipped downward and clotted at the end by a bright tubular object. The air defense boys had found a Zeppelin. The other two searchlights whisked to that vicinity as well, one of them quickly finding a second airship, which closely trailed the first, and the third light rushed on behind, to continue the search.

As interested as I was in the air assault, I lowered my face and looked to the south. A mere fifty yards ahead, against the darkness, Selene Bourgani had stepped from her taxi and become an even more deeply dark shape, immobile, elegantly erect, facing the raid. I tried to see her figure there in the night by the reality of what she was planning to do. In this moment she was a sentinel for the German airships, a monument to their assault on the Fatherland's enemy. I still had trouble getting this to make sense. I may have discovered her own living father, but she was still the Most Mysterious Woman in the World. What was she doing with these people?

And another dark shape passed before me, this side of Selene. Brauer had also stepped from his taxi, his face lifting to the eastern sky.

I looked too.

The searchlights had all converged on the two Zeppelins and I could hear the distant report of three- and four-inch guns, the far off rattle of machine guns. The Brits were using what they had—utterly unsuited for firing upward at airships—to stop what now began: a flash of quick-climbing, flaring light beneath the Zeppelins, and a fragment of a moment later the brittle thump of a bomb, and then the flare and thump again, and again. We were near enough to all this that with each bomb we instinctively braced ourselves for a frontal blow from the concussion, but instead a blow surprised us from behind: a quick aggression of air that rushed against us and then onward to fill the vacuum created by the updraft of explosives from above.

And their salvos spent, the Zeppelins came toward us, the lights tracking them, the great glistening white hulls drifting to us and above us as if we were on the floor of the sea and these were the dead and bloated bodies of sunken ships, this one above me now the *Lusitania* itself, torpedoed and glowing in its ghostly afterlife and come to reclaim those who had escaped, to take the three of us away with it.

But that impression flared brightly in my head and vanished instantly.

This was, in fact, the fiercely deployed German war machine passing overhead. And I was well aware that the man and woman standing near me in the dark were in its service.

30

Istanbul was not where I had expected to end up when the secret service boys finally let me take a crack at this war. They hadn't either. And deep into that eventful Monday in London, after I'd made sure Selene returned to her hotel and I was heading back to the Arundel, I finally took time to wonder if, in fact, that's where they would have me go. For all I knew, they already had some other sneak-and-snoop Johnnie in Istanbul, someone who'd get the chance to take his own crack at Selene Bourgani. But either way, him or me, Metcalf was arriving tomorrow and the German team was leaving the next day, and I needed him and his minions to work on a few things right away. Even if it wasn't for my benefit.

So I asked my man and his taxi to stay with me for a while longer, at which he gave me a slow nod yes and a touch to the brim of his cap even before we'd talked about money.

I dashed up to my room and was happy to actually put some words together on my Corona, banging out a report and a list of queries for Metcalf, covering everything from Selene's German movie director-lover to the man I strongly suspected was her father, from the flag on the bar wall to the smell of spirit gum, from a square beard at the head of a table to a dead Hun in a doorway. And I told him that if I was going forward, I needed a pistol. And—a thing I almost forgot—I let him know I'd changed hotels.

Then I was off again through the night, back along the Strand, past Charing Cross just south of Metzger & Strauss, Booksellers, across the street from which there'd been a bit of an incident earlier this evening. And the Strand turned into the Mall and the Mall led us to the front gates of Buckingham Palace and we circled good King George V, perhaps just as he was having his man adjust the shoulders of his pajamas.

We ended up on the southwest side of the palace gardens, in Westminster, at Number 4 Grosvenor Gardens, at the north end of a long, attached block of grand Second Empire town houses, five stories high with slate pavilion roofs and tall mansards. The houses were three bays wide and each had the same front porch—there were a dozen or more such, arrayed down the street—with squared granite columns holding up garlands of stone flowers.

Somewhere between my hotel and these stone flowers, I'd also given a brief thought to my killing a man tonight. To my *having* to kill a man. This thought came shortly after we'd circled Buckingham Palace and I had actually given a few moments of brain time to the King's pajamas. Ironically. But still. I'd killed a guy tonight and I hadn't really expected to, given all the little pitter-pat of sneaking and snooping that my recent secret service work had entailed. Now I'd found it necessary to act more like a soldier in the field than a spy. But maybe I didn't understand the spy stuff yet. Or maybe I was supposed to have finessed that confrontation somehow. But I couldn't see how. And I'd done this before, killed a man. And even as I was thinking this, as we'd rolled to a stop in front of the embassy and I took in the architectural details as I always did, I knew that I was about to forget the dead Hun, pretty much for good.

Which made me pause on the sidewalk before the embassy of the United States of America and silently pledge the blood of an enemy—and the ease with which I'd shed it—to the defense of my country. However subtle the circumstances or untraditional the battlefield.

I rang the bell at the timber double door and it opened to a U.S. Marine in his dress blues. I told him I was Christopher Marlowe Cobb in search of Mr. Smith. Which suddenly sounded like a phony name to me. But after asking me politely to wait and closing the door in my face, it took only a few moments for him to return and invite me in.

I stepped into a marble foyer hung with an American flag and a framed Woodrow Wilson. The marine joined a similarly attired comrade—they were both sergeants—and they stood at parade rest, flanking the main staircase. In the center of the foyer was a large oaken desk with a telephone receiver prominent at the sitter's right hand, the sitter being an apparent civilian in a dark blue sack suit, with the jacket buttoned up tight—even here late at night—and with the same close-cropped hair as the soldiers.

He nodded me to a wingback chair on the wall.

I sat, and soon there was a clattering of feet coming down the staircase. And then Smith.

He strode across the marble floor as I rose and he gave me his hand firmly. "Smith," he said. "Ben."

He was about fifty, with a shock of gray hair, a comfortable vision, like a Chicago City Hall reporter on deadline, his jacket somewhere else, his shirt sleeves rolled up to his elbows, his tie askew. He was working late, and I wondered if he looked the same when Metcalf was around, who I had a feeling didn't approve of his boys looking like Chicago City Hall reporters. I liked Smith for his casualness around the embassy, even more so if the boss wouldn't approve but he was doing it anyway, after hours.

"Cobb," I said. "Kit."

"We got a little worried about you," he said. "I dropped round to check on you at the Waldorf this evening."

"It's all in here," I said, handing over the sealed envelope.

He nodded at my bandaged left cheek. He knew about the *Schmiss* beneath: "Set to unveil your sordid past at Heidelberg, are you?" he said.

"Things happened."

"You want to go up?" Smith gave a slight toss of his head toward the staircase behind him.

I hesitated. I was feeling a little weary, having lately escaped a sinking ship and snuck around pretty seriously and killed a man wielding a knife.

Before I could answer, Smith said, "You probably have a story you don't want to tell twice."

"I wrote the highlights," I said, nodding at the envelope in his hand.

"Got it," he said. He cupped my elbow and turned me toward the front door, stepping up instantly beside me and putting an avuncular arm around my shoulder. We moved toward the night. "Hold down the fort, boys," he said raising his voice to pitch the comment to the marines covering our retreat.

We pushed through the eight-paneled doors and stepped out onto the porch, and we stopped in its deep shadow.

He offered me a cigarette and we lit up and blew some smoke into the sooty London night air.

My loyal taxi was sitting at the near curb, a couple of automobile lengths north, at which, after our second, silent puff, Smith nodded. "Is that yours?" he said.

"Yes. Good man. Been with me through a lot tonight."

Smith grunted. Then he asked a question about a thing I kept forgetting and he'd apparently waited for us to be alone to ask. He nodded toward my shirt, down near the belt line. The blood. I'd forgotten it again. "Is that yours?" he asked.

"Nope."

He grunted again and took another drag on his Fatima. He said, "Metcalf's somewhere out in the Irish Sea about now, but I'm to wire him at Holyhead if I hear from you."

"Sounds like serious worry."

"Of course."

"Like you expected me to be dead."

"That's always our expectation."

"You from Chicago?" I asked, trying to compliment him on his straight talk, though I realized he might not know what I was referring to.

But maybe he did. "You from Cleveland?" he answered, which was a curve ball that dropped in for a strike.

"Nope," I said.

"Nope," he said. "But thanks for thinking I might be."

"I'll give you the key to the city sometime," I said.

"First you got to dine with the boss," he said.

"Okay."

"Good pudding for you, Kit Cobb."

"Yeah?"

"He likes swank food. Carlton Hotel at six. Escoffier's joint."

"I'll think of it as a last meal," I said.

31

The next day I had a fine morning and afternoon at the Arundel doing what I tried to convince myself I still primarily did. I wrote newspaper stories. I finally finished a follow-up feature about life after having a steamship sunk out from under you. I curved and faded and even plausibly made up some of that one, seeing as my life after the sinking had some atypical and secret elements to it. Which was okay, since second-day, stretch-it-out-no-matter-what-it-takes stories after very big ones often were full of curves and fadeaways and lies, and it was just something you lived with as a reporter and you figured the Joes on the street who read you didn't give a damn about that anyway, if the story was good. And I also wrote a pretty damn fine authentic eyewitness story about a Zeppelin raid on London. I got those telegraphed off and had a good hot bath, seeing as the blood of the Hun had seeped on through the shirt and also colored Kit Cobb. Though a little water cleared me of that deed just fine.

When I got out of the tub there was a knock on the door. I wrapped a towel around me and I went to the door, but I didn't open it at once.

"Yes?" I said.

"Bellhop, Mr. Cobb. I have a parcel for you." It was a thin, reedy voice, almost adolescent, and I remembered the bellhop on duty tonight looking very young.

I opened the door.

It was the bellhop.

And inside the parcel was a tuxedo and a note from Metcalf. *Wear this. But watch your cigarette ash. It's a rental.*

So I got duded up in my monkey suit and went out in a taxicab to the Carlton Hotel, which seemed just like the place for Metcalf, since it was cut out of the same *pâte pâtisserie* as his embassy, with French Second Empire pavilion roofs and high mansards, and with a green slate dome foamed up on top to boot.

Metcalf was waiting in the vestibule inside the front doors on Pall Mall.

He brightened at the sight of me coming through, the fleshy wheatiness of him now a harmonious part of his decor, draped bespokenly as it was in the black and white of his tux.

He stepped to me and offered his hand, greeting me in full moniker, though he sounded devoid of irony, almost admiring: "Christopher Marlowe Cobb."

I shook the hand. "Gentleman Jim Metcalf," I said, also without irony.

He laughed. "My element, here," he said. "I have good food for you."

"And some information?" I said, a little regretful at once for pushing the business when he wanted to push the eats.

He took it in stride, the smile never faltering. "Of course," he said. "In due time."

He led me into an inner quadrangle that suddenly made London—given the central lobby experience at the Waldorf as well—seem to be as enchanted with palm trees as Mexico City. Here was another Palm Court, covered over in a glass roof and full of trees and green-cane easy chairs.

We brisked through and then up a wide marble staircase and into a clotted-cream-colored restaurant with garlands of gold leaves on the ceiling and cut-glass chandeliers wired for a softly glowing electricity. Beneath us was a densely soft claret carpet upon which a man in tails glided soundlessly to us and bowed stiffly at the waist. "Mr. Metcalf," he said. "Right this way."

And so we ended up in a secluded far corner of the culinary home of the Cy Young of chefs, Georges Auguste Escoffier, whose eminence I already knew even before Metcalf dropped his voice into a reverential hush and made the case for him in somewhat different terms, Metcalf being a guy who knew his food. I took only some of this in—though the food itself would shortly make me pay more attention—but for now I had my mission heavy on my mind.

Metcalf stopped talking abruptly and smiled up at the waiter who had just arrived, not with a menu—I learned that we were in Maestro Escoffier's hands, for seventeen courses—but with *Caviar Oeufs de Pluvier*—caviar arranged spillingly from the eggs of a plover as if the fertility of a bird was expressing the fertility of a fish. I was intrigued by all this but took the occasion of Metcalf's silence to say, "Am I going to follow them?"

Meaning Brauer and Bourgani.

He well knew who I meant, but he ignored me and nodded a thank you to the waiter and he leaned forward over his plate. I thought at first that he was saying a silent grace, but his nostrils were flaring, delicately but purposefully, and I understood Metcalf to be—for all his gentlemanliness and professionalism—a sensualist and not a religionist. He said, without looking up from the eggs upon eggs, "Didn't you tell Mr. Smith that you intended to treat this like a last meal?"

"I did."

"I myself have come to treat every meal that way," Metcalf said, and he turned his face to me now for the first time since I'd breached the protocol of the *repas du connaisseur*. He smiled a complex little smile, part of which was "What a pleasant but stupid child" and part of which, I suspected, was "Given the job you've signed up for, you better be serious about the last-meal stuff."

But I answered his words: "Even with your desk job?"

This caught him a bit off guard. The smile disappeared. But nothing unpleasant took its place. He shrugged and said, "One can get hit by a taxi on a London street."

Okay, I thought. I was in this whole thing with Metcalf, however he wanted to play it. He knew what I needed. So I broke off our conversation and I leaned over my caviar and flared my nostrils to the saltwater low-tide smell of animal fertility.

And we were silent when we were eating and consciously made only small talk when we weren't, going through a *Consommé aux Pommes d'Amour,* the "apples of love" in this case turning out to be a very different view of a damn sweet Illinois tomato; and egg-shaped dumplings of Rouen duck ground up and whipped up with egg whites and with spit from a swift's nest, a thing I was happy not to have known about as I ate it; and a dish that wedded crayfish and a hot pepper cream, which would have gone over pretty well in my birth city of New Orleans; and a course of baby chicken roughed up by ground pepper; and a frogs' legs course, with lowly frogs not sounding quite up to this kind of treatment, so Escoffier renamed these creatures *nymphes,* which was an unsettling leap of imagination, as these naked legs were arrayed on our square plates flushed pink with paprika. I figured that guy Freud would have a field day with the maestro's dreams.

Then we had a dish before us, in silver timbales, that would lead Metcalf to speak more fully. We leaned toward it together, as had become our custom, and he said, "*Croûtons* of bread crumbs fried in butter. Black truffles in a reduced demi-glace. And cocks' kidneys. No hens. Only cocks. They're hot, as you can feel on your face and in your nose. You eat a cock's kidney when it is hot. Begin."

I did.

And, as was *his* custom, he kept his eyes shut as he chewed. But this time, after he was finished chewing, he kept his eyes closed for a few moments more, saying, "You've done good work."

"Eating cocks' kidneys?"

"That too," he said.

"What's next?"

"It's not where we expected you to end up."

"At least the war's arrived," I said. "There's Gallipoli."

"There's Gallipoli," he said.

"How's that going?"

Metcalf wagged his head. "The English bungled it. Caught the Turks unprepared at the Dardanelles, but when it was time to move from the sea assault to the land, the Brits couldn't get their troops in for a month. They let the Germans and Turks wire the beaches, deploy their men, arm the forts, even build supply roads, for Christ's sake. It's going to be long and bloody out there."

"So am I going?"

"You're going."

"As?"

"Well, that depends on how it unfolds."

"I take it you've got a German whipped up for me as a possibility," I said. "I don't expect any more unfolding between now and tomorrow night."

"Smith will bring you a packet after dinner," Metcalf said. "We're preparing you for a number of possibilities. Nice thing about having control of the German embassy. We're a fine little document factory."

"You understand about my shaving."

"I do."

"Sorry it limits us."

"The gauze helps with that," Metcalf said, studying my left cheek. I'd freshened the bandage. He said, "An American journalist is still more or less persona grata from here to Constantinople."

I was tempted to pointedly correct Metcalf on the name of the city, in the way Squarebeard had corrected Metzger, but I let it pass.

And Metcalf continued: "You could stay bandaged as Christopher Cobb till you grew your beard back."

"I could."

"On the other hand, at least among the core group of Huns in this matter, Kit Cobb is known to be a dangerous man."

"And the two principals tomorrow night both know me by sight."

"Even with a *Schmiss*," Metcalf said, agreeing.

"Dangerous, huh?"

Metcalf lifted an eyebrow. *Of course,* he said, without saying it. I said, "You understand . . ."

He stopped me with a wave of his hand. "Of course I understand. I'm glad you have the knack."

"Knack?" I wasn't getting sanctimonious on him. It just struck me as an odd choice of a word.

"To effectively save your own life."

"*That* knack," I said, letting go of the qualm.

"It's gotten a workout the last few days," he said.

"Which reminds me," I said. "You got my pistol?"

"Smith."

"And Wesson?"

"Ben Smith."

"After dinner?" I said.

"After dinner," he said. "A Mauser, by the way. A small but effective Mauser."

"I've had them pointed at me."

Metcalf nodded and he sipped at the wine that Escoffier's sommelier had paired with the last few courses, an eight-year-old white from the Loire Valley. I was a pretty good drinker, but I was a bit overwhelmed with information already, getting it and seeking it, what with the task ahead of me and the things I didn't know about that, and with what I was learning about this very odd but ravishingly assertive food, and so the subtleties of the wine were entering into and then instantly vanishing from my head. The wines were good. This one was white and dry. For the seasoned drinker in me, that was enough for this night.

And we did not resume our talk until a *Samis de Faisan* landed before me and I took it all in and kept it: a pheasant twice cooked but still pretty near to gamey raw, surrounded by a muddy-rich sauce based on what the folks in New Orleans would call *roux*, this roux happening to be an intense one, with the essence of salt belly of pork rolling around on my tongue in the company of the bird.

Metcalf opened his eyes after swimming for a while in those muddy, pheasant-strewn waters, and he tapped his lips with his napkin. Almost daintily. A good roux and pretty-close-to-nature bird meat properly required a stronger gesture, a more assertive mouth wipe than that, it seemed to me. But that was a nuance of this kind of dining that maybe the swells hadn't considered.

I wasn't one to criticize or advise a gourmet in his own realm, however, so I simply waited for Metcalf to be satisfied with the state of his lips, and then I said, "The guy I'm calling 'Squarebeard.' Ring any bells?"

Metcalf straightened and widened his eyes, as if he was coming out of a reverie. He looked at me and focused. "You never saw him close up?"

"No."

"That was a good medium-range description, though."

"He could be any number of people, you're saying."

"No one who rings a bell."

I reached for the glass of white.

Metcalf said, "This thing you smelled in your room."

"Spirit gum."

"Yes. Actors use it for *what*?"

Of course. Beards.

I didn't answer but we looked at each other for a moment.

"He was around the hotel that morning," I said, following what I took to be Metcalf's train of thought. Squarebeard could have been the guy who was in my room.

"It's possible," he said.

"That we don't know *what* this guy looks like," I said, finishing his thought.

"Possible," he said.

"You boys tracking any German agents who like to make up?"

"This has only recently occurred to me," Metcalf said. "We'll put our heads together and see who comes to mind."

"But if Squarebeard does do disguises," I said, "and if he's good at it, it's to make sure he *never* comes to mind in a situation like this."

"You'll soon be fifteen hundred miles away. We'll try to figure him out while you're gone."

"Did you figure out the guy I take to be Bourgani's father?"

"You sure you got the room right?"

"It's position in relation to the street. Yes. Absolutely."

"It was empty," Metcalf said. "Seemingly uninhabited. Clean as a whistle. Which, in that tenement, in that part of town, is suspicious in and of itself."

"The flag behind the bar?"

"We're working on it. It's not a country we can identify."

"There are countries out there our State Department doesn't know about?"

Metcalf shot me what appeared to be that pleasant-but-stupid-child smile again. "Okay," he said. "We know it's not a country. Not a current one."

"Hey," I said. "It's a big world. You guy's could've missed one."

Metcalf chuckled. An indulge-a-pleasant-but-stupid-child chuckle. He'd gotten touchy all of a sudden. He said, "Have you asked yourself how Metzger knew you on sight? Even with you portraying an expatriate German?"

"I've asked."

"And?"

"Brauer."

"Well, did you give him some cause to be suspicious that didn't show up in your report?"

"No."

"So let's say he mentions your casual shipboard encounter to the boys at the shop. That wouldn't be enough for them to go straight to strong-arming you."

I didn't say a thing.

I'd given the impression in my report that I'd only seen and identified Selene from afar, nodded at her across the captain's table, and covertly observed her get-togethers with Brauer. Only that.

Yes, it could have been Selene who made a point of me to the boys at the shop.

Or it still could have been Brauer. Yes, him. He did walk in on Selene and me. I was jazzing the Huns' prize spy and then I showed up at their secret headquarters. Sure they'd strong-arm me.

I still didn't say anything to Metcalf and he'd taken to sipping his lately refilled wine.

I sipped mine, and I consciously kept my face as placid as Metcalf's in spite of an abrupt, retrospective worry: for the Germans, there was still the matter of my knowing about the bookshop. I was worried now for Selene. But there'd been no indication from the meeting I'd heard that they thought she'd compromised them. There was no reason for Brauer to have told her about the bookshop while onboard the ship. If anything, it was Brauer who had some explaining to do. Yet they clearly still trusted him as well. So that detail was a mystery for the Huns. Discounting a severe coincidence, the only possible explanation for my showing up at the bookstore was my being in the same racket they were.

Then Metcalf and I had before us a flaky, golden pie crust the size and shape of a custard cup, sealed at top and bottom and rim.

He and I leaned and sniffed and, to my surprise, Metcalf started talking even as he began to cut into his fat little pie. Normally he'd talk first and then eat in meditative silence. This time, I realized, I was supposed to listen beneath his words. "There's something exotic inside," he said. "And it's all very simple."

I started to cut as well, and a warm rush of deep-forest, deep-shadow, dug-deep earth smell rose up and into me.

"Truffles," Metcalf said, lifting a bite before him. "Rare and beautiful. You dig one up; you strip away the earth from it and lay it out bare; you give it some brandy; you put it under the covers; you heat it up; you eat it."

He put truffle and crust into his mouth. He closed his eyes and kept them closed.

I looked away from him. I cut myself a good bite of *Truffes Sous La Cendre* and put it in my mouth, the sweet coating of crust dissolving

ROBERT OLEN BUTLER

away, and I closed my eyes and I held the warm fold of a truffle on my tongue, tasting a secret thing, hidden long from view, put now inside me and held.

I knew what Metcalf was actually saying.

I chewed the truffle gently and let it go down inside me and I looked over at Metcalf, his eyes closed, his mouth at rest, perhaps holding his own truffle in there still.

"Of course," I said. "You take it and you eat it."

"Be careful of women in this job," he said, without opening his eyes, without changing the angle of his head.

"Yes," I said.

"Inadvertently, of course, but did you let on somehow about your true identity? When you were *with* her?" He leaned just enough on the "with" to be discreet but clear about what he meant.

The secondary lesson in this was to trust your intuition about situations. Which is what he was doing right now, about Selene and me. I was already pretty good at that, but it was worth the reminder.

"Of course not," I said. "She was jazzed by a famous newspaper-man. Strictly that."

"You figure Brauer knew about it?"

"Yes."

"There you are," he said.

"There I am," I said.

He opened his eyes but directed them to his *truffes.*

I thought he'd warn me about leaving important issues out of my reports.

But he didn't. I liked him for that. We simply fell silent again.

And we ate until we had new wineglasses and, in them, a decade-old cabernet from Château La Tour Carnet.

"Now you'll see something," Metcalf said.

He was not speaking about the wine, though the first few sips were very good, but about the small, porcelain ramekin that arrived for each of us shortly thereafter.

Within, a tiny bird lay on its back, plucked and missing its legs but, I would later learn, in no other way altered, its having been trapped and fattened on millet and figs and drowned in Armagnac—literally drowned to death in French brandy—and then simply salted and peppered and baked in an oven complete with bones and blood and organs. I had barely taken my first look at it when our waiter appeared and handed me a large, embroidered white napkin.

He gave another to Metcalf, who said, "This, my friend, is an ortolan bunting. Considered by many to be the heart and perhaps even the very soul of French cuisine. As for our own souls, we each place a napkin over our head, hiding our face. It is true that this confines and enhances the aromas. But it is also true that we thus hide our faces from God, as we devour this innocent songbird, the human soul, of course, being not without its flaws. The Big Man's eye is on the sparrow. It is also on the ortolan bunting. You may bite off the head and set it aside if you wish. There is no shame in that. But you eat everything else. Put it in your mouth whole, and after the first celestial rush of its fat, you chew. Very slowly."

And with this he vanished beneath his napkin.

Was I going too far for Metcalf?

I put the napkin on my head and it dropped before my face.

I picked the bird up in my two hands. Though it weighed less than a pair of kid gloves, it was so clearly a *body*, I held it with both hands and did not let its head fall back. Though I knew I had to bite that off.

Metcalf was faintly moaning nearby. From the fat, no doubt.

This whole meal. What was this meal? Not a last meal. And surely, it now occurred to me, not a meal at the U.S. government's expense. Metcalf must have his own money, I thought. A lot of it. He dined here often. He brought me with him. But he was also the man guiding me on behalf of my country.

A crackling sound began nearby. Faint and slow. He was beginning to chew his songbird, this Gentleman Jim.

I lifted the ortolan, inclining my head forward to make way beneath the napkin. I was glad God could not see. Nor anyone else.

I brought the bird to my face and I opened my mouth and my teeth found the bird's neck and I bit through, the bones yielding easily and the head was free on my tongue and I quickly reached in and removed it and I placed it back into the dish.

I shuddered.

I've had some wretched food in my life. I've shared food with soldiers at war. Ragtag units badly provisioned in hot countries. I've eaten field slumgum, maggoty meat heated in big pots with dirty water and weed roots. But that was from necessity. That was as respite from gunfire. And I had never shuddered.

I shuddered from this songbird's head.

And from its body, which I now laid on my tongue.

It was tiny, fitting in my mouth as if custom-made for eating, soft there but still structured—I was aware of the whole structure of bones within—and it had settled there only a moment and I had only just closed on it, very gently, when the warm rush of the bird's body fat—the savor at once rich and delicate—filled my mouth and rolled down my throat.

I did not moan but I understood Metcalf's exclamation.

Then I began to chew, the bones cracking softly, the taste turning from delicate and reminiscent of hazelnuts to gamey now—bird blood and organ meat, though still in a low key, scaled down to the size of this small singing creature—and even the tiny gamey surges of its lungs and heart carried a hint of the Armagnac, like honey and plum.

And it went on and on, the full chewing of this bird. I eventually grew impatient, but I had a mouth full of tiny bone shards and they were beginning to abrade my mouth and it was as if God found me after all, beneath my embroidered napkin, and His judgment was upon me.

But at last the bird was gone.

I took the napkin from my face.

I looked at Metcalf. He was still covered.

I drank my cabernet. Too fast. Trying to wash the bird from my mouth. Another lesson perhaps. Something about a sensual thing that's intense and delicious but goes on too long and then goes bad.

My glass was empty and I turned back to Metcalf and I started. He was unmasked and looking at me.

As soon as he knew he had my full attention, he leaned a little in my direction, as if I'd just been delivered to him on a plate. And he said very softly, "You may have to act again as you did last night."

I knew what he was talking about. But I had the odd reflex to play dumb.

"How so?" I said.

He looked at me steadily and did not reply and I knew what was behind his eyes: *I know you know what I'm talking about. Don't play this game.*

"The knack," I offered.

"That's the act I was referring to," he said. "But perhaps a different context."

Now I really didn't know what he meant.

"Preemptively," he said.

In my report to him I hadn't written of the killing of the Hun in detail. There was already a preemptive taint to what I'd done, which I did not mention. As I chewed slowly on that, I stayed quiet. Metcalf thought I was being dense.

He leaned closer. He spoke even more softly.

"I'm thinking at the moment of Brauer," he said. "You might find it necessary to kill him."

I spoke with equal softness. "Gentleman Jim," I said. "I thought you were among the least violent of men."

"I am," he said. "But I have absolutely no qualms about advising men of a different temperament."

I said, "Knowing what's necessary when the threat isn't imminent. That's a different knack."

"For the good of our country," Metcalf said, as if that clarified things.

I could have called him on that. But I didn't. He seemed to read my eyes or, perhaps, to hear how he'd sounded. He said, "You should trust us and the work we give you. The good of your mission is the good of the country."

"I understand," I said. And I suppose I did. I had the sanction to kill.

And when I'd spoken these two words, something apparently shifted in my mouth, from between my teeth, and I felt a small, sharp pain in my cheek.

I turned my head away from Metcalf and reached into my mouth with forefinger and thumb, and I extracted a sliver of songbird bone.

32

The meal lingered on till past midnight.

When I was at last released from the tuxedo and ready to have a final night's sleep in a good bed before heading off to an unknown number of nights' sleep in unknown circumstances, I lay down in my bed at the Arundel and almost at once a knock came at my door. Three quick, firm raps.

I rose and moved quietly across the room, and as I did, my mind finally began to work properly and I anticipated what this was, the mention of it seeming to have been a very long time ago, with all that food in between. But I did not touch the doorknob; I turned my head to listen; and as if I'd been observed the whole time, a voice outside immediately said, "Cobb. It's Smith."

I opened the door.

He had his suit jacket on, but his tie was askew. I was willing to bet his shirt sleeves were rolled up under there as well.

He held a kit bag and an oversized, cabin-top leather valise.

"Come in," I said.

He passed by me. "Sorry to disturb you in your union suit," he said.

"It's one in the morning," I said, closing the door.

"The boss wanted this done before dawn."

Smith was at the bedside. He closed the covers and laid the two bags on top.

"The boss has one hell of an expense account," I said.

Smith turned to me and he shot me a sly little smile. "I told you it was good pudding."

"I'm thinking the government didn't pick up that tab."

"He's got serious family money, our Mr. Metcalf. As I understand it. He's a bit secretive."

"As we might expect."

"As we might expect," Smith said, turning his back on me, though he went on with his point. "He dines at the Carlton once a week. Often alone. Usually alone. You got his attention."

"Did he give you the same treatment?"

"Nope." Smith turned around holding a Mauser pocket pistol in his hand, sideways so I could see its lines, pointed toward the ceiling. "This is yours, I believe," he said.

I extended my right hand and he put the pistol in it.

The last time I saw one of these it was coming out from inside a suit coat with the intent to kill me. I'd seen a similar one with a similar intent not too long before that. This little thing had begun to get my goat. I was happy to make its friendly acquaintance at last.

It rested easy and light in my hand, hardly more than a pound.

"Thirty-two caliber," Smith said. "Magazine's in, but empty. Shells in the bag."

I wanted him to stop talking. This pistol and I were getting to know each other. I turned away from him and lifted the Mauser and settled the front post of its barrel in the rear V-sight, with the head of a rose in the wallpaper as the target. All through last year's little adventure in Mexico, I'd carried a Colt 1911. A fine but large weapon that was now at the bottom of the North Atlantic, a loss that only just now fully struck me. Too bad. But this covert, diminutive Mauser, with a .32-caliber kick, seemed just fine too. Like going to a lighter bat to get around on a Walter Johnson fastball. Very nice.

I lowered my arm.

I looked at Smith, who was looking at me with an expression that seemed part respect, part fear, and part distaste.

Maybe I was wrong. Maybe that was too much for a look and I was just under the spell of Escoffier putting a bunch of crazy things together onto a single plate. Or maybe I was just feeling all those things about myself.

"What is it?" I asked Smith.

"There's no *it*," he said. "Just watching a guy who knows what he's doing."

"I hope," I said.

"You got a tux for me?"

"In the wardrobe."

"I'll trade you for the three-piece wool suit in the kit bag," he said, and he crossed to the wardrobe and pulled out the tux.

"What's special about the suit?" I said.

"Berlin tailor. So in a pinch you don't have to explain a British label."

"This German with a tailor in Berlin. He's got a name?"

"I didn't look. It's on documents in the portfolio. Including a diplomatic passport." Smith was crossing back to the bed. "I'll take the kit bag. You keep the valise. You've got a lot of stuff in there. Some alternate selves. Whatever doesn't fit with who you are should go into the false bottom in the valise. The least whiff of your being a spy and any of the countries you'll be passing through would walk you into the nearby woods and shoot you."

"I get it," I said.

"One thing you don't need to hide. The ticket for your cabin on the *Mecklenburg* tomorrow night, heading for Vlissingen. The Brits call it 'Flushing.' You take a train from Charing Cross to Folkestone."

I was going in through still-neutral Holland, my corridor to Germany.

Smith laid the German suit on the bed, and now he was pulling out more candy-store treats from the kit bag: a belt holster and a couple of boxes of .32 caliber bullets.

Smith stuffed the tuxedo into the kit bag, closed it, and turned and stepped to me, offering his hand. I went to tuck the Mauser in at my waist, to free my right hand to shake with him, but I found this didn't work.

"You need trousers for that," Smith said.

"Right," I said, shifting the pistol to my left hand and beginning to shake Smith's hand good-bye.

"Don't get me wrong," Smith said, keeping the handshake going, "Mr. Metcalf is no dilettante. He knows his job. And he says you do too. Good luck out there."

Metcalf's declaration of my competence took me by surprise and I said nothing in return but finished the shake with Smith. As soon as our hands separated, he slipped past me and headed for the door.

But he stopped abruptly and turned back. "I almost forgot," he said.

He dug something out of his inner coat pocket and handed it to me. "Telegram from your boys in Chicago."

I took it with a thank you and he was gone.

I opened the cable and it was from Clyde Fetter, my editor in chief at the *Post-Express*. He wrote: *Lusitania escape story a killer. Excuse the expression. Follow up solid. Loved the airships. Regular Joes on State Street and beyond agree. You are still the king of the king beat. Keep throwing strikes. Clyde*

Which was a good thing.

Nevertheless I tried to give my attention right back to the Mauser. My skill with it seemed more important to me for the foreseeable future. I loaded its magazine and tucked it into the nightstand drawer.

But when I'd returned to bed and the room was dark, I didn't fall asleep for a time. I found myself thinking hard about the Christopher Cobb that I still tried to believe was me, tried even to believe was the *primary* me: Christopher Cobb, the newsman. And so I thought of dessert this evening at the Carlton Hotel.

Metcalf and I had eaten songbird together and had spoken openly of my license to kill. There was nothing more to say except to speak of the food and to eat dishes built around foie gras and asparagus and sea oysters and on and on in voluptuous silence. But with the imminent arrival of dessert, Metcalf roused himself from the culinary trance he'd put us both in to praise Escoffier's brilliant young assistant pastry cook.

He said, "You'd never know to look at him. A thin little wisp of an Indochinese man you'd expect to find pulling a jinrikisha somewhere out there in the French Far East. Or throwing a bomb for a gang of anarchists in the Balkans. But you'd be wrong. This guy is a native genius. The maestro plucked him off the cleaning brigade. He caught him routinely putting aside half-eaten food to give to the poor. But the maestro saw something in him and made him an offer: give up your ideas of revolution and learn to make pastry. Which he did. And his work is about to arrive."

And it did, on a black plate. *Pleine Lune Sur Indochine*. In the center was a large, white glutinous globe. The full moon over Indochina. On its face was a drizzling of pomegranate juice. There was blood on this moon. Which was, in fact, a sticky-rice cake filled with fruit, both fresh and dried, and with nuts, but dominated by the flavors of mango and brandy and a citrusy flavor, but not a citrus I knew, as if the fruit grew in the ground instead of in the air. Lemongrass, Metcalf told me. And it was very good indeed, the handiwork of this apparent jinrikisha runner.

And I met him in Escoffier's kitchen, where the Carlton's once-a-week Gentleman Jim Metcalf and I were invited after dinner, and I was introduced to Georges Auguste Escoffier himself—a tiny man, dressed not like a chef but like a diplomat or a banker, in a frock coat and striped pants—and to the young genius of a pastry chef, who wore the traditional kitchen whites and a tall *toque blanche* and whose name—I finally heard it properly from his own lips—was Nguyễn Tất Thành. I was introduced as Christopher Cobb, the famous American newspaper foreign correspondent. This made Mr. Thành's eyes widen.

And at his first opportunity, while Escoffier and Metcalf ardently talked truffles, Mr. Thành drew me aside, beneath a hanging row of gleaming copper pots, where we quickly found a common language—an outsider's passable French. He spoke to me rapidly, softly.

He said, "I was in your country three years ago. In New York City and then in Boston. I admire what your Declaration of Independence says, though I looked for its fruits in your streets and in your government. I'm sorry. I looked with very little success. But your press. Your newspapers. Your magazines. I have seen them speak openly about the evils of your society and about the evils abroad in the world. I urge you, Monsieur Cobb, to turn your skills of . . . what is your English word? *Muckraking.* Please I implore you to turn your skills toward the evils of empire. Empire driven by business. This present war is about empire, and empire is about rich people getting richer, exploiting the people that they rule by imperial force. And please . . ."

"Cobb." This was Metcalf's voice. "I want you to hear this."

I kept my eyes on Thành. "Please," he repeated. "Begin with the Vietnamese people."

Metcalf said, "It's what I was telling you about black and white."

He was referring, I assumed, to truffles.

But I was having trouble drawing my eyes away from the unblinking eyes before me, eyes as black as the heavens surrounding a moon touched with blood.

Thành said, "You are a man who seeks the truth. You can give the news of this to the world."

I turned away from him now, this Indochinese, this Vietnamese.

But in my hotel bed, on the night before Christopher Cobb, the American secret agent, was to put out to sea once more in pursuit of German secret agents, it was not so easy to let that little man go.

33

And it was, indeed, Christopher Cobb the newsman who boarded the SS *Mecklenburg* just before midnight. In his passport photo he had a close-cropped beard. In the flesh, he was clean shaven with a fresh bandage on his left cheek, but people do shave, and they do injure themselves, particularly escaping from a torpedoed ship. If you were to look inside his suit coat, you'd find the label of Eisner und Söhne, but Cobb was a famous, world-traveling American journalist and he could plausibly have gone to a German tailor in his travels. The Dutch were unlikely to take him into the woods and shoot him over a thing like that.

Cobb or not, I had to stay out of sight of the firm of Brauer und Bourgani. This was going to be an ongoing challenge all the way to Istanbul. In the Gladstone bag I had some spirit gum of my own and some items of facial disguise I'd purchased at a theatrical supply house in London on my writing day; I was going to have to be resourceful. And somewhere near the Belgian border, I was going to have to turn into someone else.

For that, I had choices in the valise. Choices and a wily surprise from Metcalf. When I'd risen this morning I'd opened Metcalf's leather valise. First out, wrapped in a leather band, was a bundle of letters-of-passage and credentials, using photographs of me clean shaven, with my naked *Schmiss*. These would transform me into Jacob Wilhelm von Traube, with diplomatic passport and with alternate credentials making me either a press attaché or a military attaché, as it might suit the situation.

The next thing out of the valise was an American passport. It had a photograph of me in my close-cropped beard. But I was not Christopher Cobb. I was Walter Brauer. Metcalf without qualms. Metcalf advising. Not ordering, of course, this Gentleman Jim, but subtly advising a man with a certain knack to consider what might be good for his country.

Subtly until I found the hidden flaps on the edges of the lid to the false bottom. I lifted the lid away to expose the recess beneath.

And there lay a weapon the like of which I'd handled and learned to shoot in my training late last year.

A secret service special. A pistol crafted by the outside-Washington boys from a .22 calibre, single-shot, bolt-action, 1902 model Winchester rifle. It had a severely sawed-off barrel, trued up very nicely; the two original open sights and a folding peep sight; and a stock of black walnut replacing the Winchester's varnished gumwood, curving down into a swell pistol grip. It fired a .22 Long rifle cartridge with real punch and tight-cluster precision. What turned it from a tough kid's target pistol into a serious weapon for America's on-the-sly warfare was the threaded coupling driven tight into the end of the barrel and the thing that screwed onto it: the black metal tube lying next to the pistol in the bottom of the valise. A Maxim Silencer. With the aid of the box of .22 Long heavies, specially made by the Maxim Silent Firearms Company, that lay next to it, this tough guy could plug a man between the eyes from a hundred yards and not make a whisper of a sound. Not just silent in the report; the Maxim's special round even took away the whipcrack of a bullet in the air. Not to mention the device cut recoil to almost nothing. It was too bad you had to reload after each shot, but only single-shot weapons gave up their gases completely to the silencer's mechanism. Not a big price to pay for that big benefit.

All of which I admired at the sight of Metcalf's little surprise.

Admired too much. Admired so much—which was the point, of course—that I got itchy to use it.

And I understood Metcalf's message clearly: this was how I was supposed to kill Brauer in his ship cabin without raising an alarm.

But I simply put the Brauer passport, along with Herr Traube's, into the recess, as well as my own disguise items; I fit the lid back on top, and I packed the bag.

Metcalf still stopped short of giving me a direct order. It was my choice how I managed my identity on the way to Istanbul. And I chose at least to begin my journey as the Christopher Cobb I'd always been. The war correspondent. I'd ignore, for now, that I was carrying another kind of war in the bottom of my bag.

34

The *Mecklenburg* was a medium-sized ship, not quite half the length of the *Lusitania,* not spacious but not cramped, so I hung back on the pier, in the shadows of the terminal building, watching the first-class gangway till Bourgani in black led Brauer in tweeds up the first-class gangway.

I followed.

I once again knew the cabin numbers for the two people of interest to me. Metcalf had his sources at the British ticket agents, no doubt through his English counterparts.

My cabin was the portside equivalent of Selene's on the starboard side, both of us at the aft end of the inner passageway. My windows looked out on the promenade, as did hers. Brauer's cabin was just forward of Selene's.

We were under way by half past midnight and I lay down on my bunk, intending to sleep, my Berlin jacket and waistcoat hung on the back of a chair, the pants folded on top. Whenever I knew I'd have trouble sleeping, I'd get very neat with my clothes. And I was right. I simply listened to the distant, forced-draft fans feeding air to the turbines and felt the vibration of the ship, prominent in the *Mecklenburg* but not terribly unpleasant. I hoped it would jiggle me to sleep. But still I didn't sleep, even after we'd cleared the Thames and revved up to twenty-two knots for the long, dark run across the North Sea.

I finally gave up. I was restless in the way this job tended to make me restless. Following and snooping: I wasn't very suited for that. So I dressed in all but my tie and went out of my room. Brauer and Bourgani weren't going anywhere. And it was wise, when I knew where they were, to just stay completely out of their sight. So I headed forward along the corridor.

And I began to smell something.

There was just a whiff of it. It slid into me and then out again and I concentrated and there it was again. Maybe my recent stint in Escoffier's joint had heightened my sense of smell, made me oversensitive in an often faintly fetid world. This had a whiff of way-too-fancy cookery. No. Not fancy food. Old food, rotten food. No. Not that but with a little taint of that maybe. But something more, something vaguely familiar, which made me interested.

I reached the first-class reception area, between the cabins and the smoking room. I stepped across to the smoker, and the place was empty but for a couple of gents in a far corner with their cigars diminished to butts and starting to doze. The air was permanently thick with the scent of old tobacco, and this other smell was hiding here. Masked now. I could still pick it up if I concentrated.

The nearly empty smoking room reminded me of something I'd noticed waiting for Selene and Brauer to board: the ship was only sparsely booked. I stepped back out into the reception hall and looked across to the staircase leading to the second-class deck below. I moved to it.

The smell I'd been following wafted more clearly up the steps. I entered the smell, descended into it, and it began to identify itself: sweat and grime and female smells; urinal smells and sick child smells and unchanged-clothes smells; long-on-the-road and living-in-communal-tent smells. I stopped on the landing. I didn't need to go farther. I knew this smell from the wars I'd covered. It was the smell of refugees. Nine months into the war, going east from England, the *Mecklenburg* and its sister ships carried rarefied travelers in the direction of the war. Going west, the ships still occasionally carried a sanctioned mass of those who'd fled the Germans from Antwerp and Flanders, from Liège and Luxemburg, and who were still trying to find a final refuge.

I ascended the steps again.

The most recent westward passage of the *Mecklenburg* must have been a passage of the dispossessed. It would take some time at sea to exorcise the scent of these ghosts.

I needed air myself.

I turned toward the starboard side.

I was fully conscious that I did so. I would look carefully before entering the promenade. Surely Selene and Brauer were sleeping. It felt as if everyone was sleeping on this ship but me. It was all right simply to walk past her window, I thought.

I opened the door onto the deck.

I eased out, looking aft.

The promenade was empty. The windows in the last two cabins were lit. Selene's and Brauer's.

All the other windows were dark.

I should have stepped back in.

But it was time to snoop.

I crept aft.

And up ahead I began to hear their voices.

They were muffled. The windows were closed. But I heard them. Shouting.

I quickened my step.

They would be distracted. I would crouch beneath their windows and listen.

A few more steps; the voices were becoming clearer; then they abruptly stopped.

I strode on, expecting them to resume. The silence persisted.

And then I heard a muffled pop.

It was small caliber. But it was a gun.

I bolted the final few yards. The bastard had shot Selene. He'd confronted her about the bar near the London Docks. He'd discovered something. He'd shot her.

The first window now. No caution. I looked in. Brauer's cabin. The electric light was burning. But it was empty. Of course. He'd sought her out in her own cabin to confront her.

The next window. I stepped to it.

Inside, Selene Bourgani was standing in the center of the floor, back to the door, but with her face angled downward. She held the pistol in her hand waist high, pointed slightly upward and slightly to her right. A small black purse was open in her other hand. I could well imagine she had not moved anything but her face in the few moments since she'd shot Walter Brauer.

He was lying on the floor on his back, and he wasn't moving either. She must have plugged him straight in the heart.

35

Selene lifted her face and looked me in the eyes. If this were the movie version of what she'd done, I would have expected her to act out a major emotion. Choose one: shock, horror, fear, rage, guilt, relief. Choose a couple of those. And they would have been bigger than life. But she showed none of that. Her beautiful face—and it was very beautiful indeed, for her having just shot a man—merely subtly acknowledged me, showed that she knew me. Was that the faintest nod she had just given me? The title card might well have read: *Oh, it's you. Are you off to Holland as well?*

I left the window. I entered at the aft portal and approached her door. I knocked. I expected to have to knock a few times. I was only just now getting my brain to start to work. I was afraid that the cabin doors would begin opening down the way, that people would be right behind me when I finally got her to open up.

But apparently no one was stirring. And many of the cabins were empty. I knocked again. More softly.

The door opened.

"Come in, Mr. Cobb," she said.

I did.

She closed the door behind me.

I took a step toward Brauer's body.

He was wearing his coat but he had no waistcoat, and his white shirt had a tight, red, silver-half-dollar-sized circle just beneath the sternum.

"I believe you know Mr. Brauer," Selene said.

Only now—with me seeing Selene's handiwork from her point of view and hearing her voice immediately behind me, and with the smell of hot metal and gunpowder lingering in the room like the smell of recent sex—did it occur to me that she'd just killed one man who she thought was helping her and that she had before her another man who she figured was out to stop her and was a killer himself. And she had a pistol in her hand.

"I do know him," I said. "Can't say I like him very much."

I was relieved that Selene slid up beside me.

We both were looking down at Walter Brauer.

In my periphery I could see the pistol still in her hand.

I glanced at it.

Her gun hand was not quite as composed as the rest of her. It was holding the weapon as if it expected Brauer to suddenly spring up and it would have to finish the job. And maybe it was starting to tremble a very little bit, this hand.

The pistol was a Colt 1908 Vest Pocket model. I liked a small and unobtrusive pistol, if you knew how to apply it. I was carrying one myself on this trip, though it was—stupidly—packed in my bag in my cabin. That snub-barreled Colt, though, looked excessively small and I glanced at the more or less instantly dead man and it struck me that Selene knew how to apply her tiny pistol excessively well. And I suddenly thought I might not yet be out of the woods.

She was continuing to study Brauer and I turned back to him too.

So I took as a premise, for the sake of argument, that she wouldn't use that pistol on me, at least for now. What then? What was my next move? She'd just shot a guy to death. He was clearly unarmed.

She interrupted my train of thought.

"He tried to rape me," she said.

Okay. She was offering an explanation, so I figured she probably wasn't going to shoot me, at least not right away. But I knew Mr. Brauer better than she realized, so I also knew she was lying. She wasn't his type.

Not that this was a point to argue with her.

The quick and simple question was: If my government wants to stop this woman's secret mission, why not just turn her over to the authorities for shooting an unarmed man?

This was all going through me not as reasoning, however, but as a crackle of emotion. These were the issues but I could smell that complicated lavender and hay and musk thing she put on herself and I could visualize the naked parts of her where she would touch on that scent with her fingertip. And I felt Metcalf's hot little mandate slide down my throat like birdsong fat: my government not only sanctioned me to kill; this was the guy they wanted dead. I thought: *How do I blow the whistle on a dame I'm still crazy about for doing my own dirty work?*

So I looked at her. That profile. Her father's profile. And I said, "Can I help?"

She turned her face to me.

She looked at me with take-me-in-your-arms eyes. Which I figured looked pretty much the same as can-you-get-rid-of-this-dead-body eyes.

She nodded yes. I can help.

I kneeled beside Brauer and I bent near, into his own lavender smell, cheap and strong, from the pomade on his slicked-down hair. I placed two fingers in the hollow beside his windpipe. He was still warm, but I moved my fingertips around, pressing and waiting, pressing and waiting, and I felt nothing stirring. He was dead. Given the placement of her shot, I wasn't surprised.

I pulled back a bit and looked at his shirt, where the bullet went in. The silver-half-dollar bloodstain had blossomed into a ragged-petaled red boutonniere. And on these petals was a dark dusting of soot and gunpowder. She'd been pretty close for the kill.

In helping her now, the blood was my concern. There wasn't much here at the entry point. If the entry angle had been a little upward, from below—and from the way I'd first seen Selene through the window, that was likely—then the wound would be a flap of skin that had mostly closed back up. If I was wrong about the angle, the entry spot might still pretty much seal up, but it's what happened after entry that I was concerned about: a tumbling bullet, splintering bone into shrapnel, maybe even exiting the body at the back. It was what he was lying in that was my present worry.

I didn't want to move him too drastically until I understood the situation. So I ran a hand behind his right shoulder, along the rough tweed of his coat, and I lifted at his spine between his shoulder blades. I leaned over him and reached around and more or less hugged him—which made me uneasy for more reasons than one— and I ran my right hand downward, gingerly, expecting perhaps to feel blood.

There was nothing.

I laid him back down.

She was lucky or she was good. Good was what I was afraid of.

I was acutely aware of her presence behind me, standing over me. But I was useful to her for now.

Perhaps she'd moved her little bag before her as they argued, waist high; perhaps she'd feigned tears and sought a hankie and pulled her little Colt. Brauer had been standing close to her. She simply drew the pistol and kept it there at her waist and maybe took a step nearer and angled the barrel upward and shot him beneath the sternum and toward the heart. No bones in the way. Nothing to make the bullet tumble. It went straight through a ventricle but did not exit the body.

He was bleeding all right. But it was all going into his lungs, and when those were full it would flow over into the cavity of his gut.

"Neat job," I said.

Which was a bit of unnecessary bravado on my part.

But she simply grunted. A short, sharp exhalation of a sound rather like the sound she made, over and over, during the rough-stuff pounding she'd asked for in our last encounter on the *Lusitania*.

Which reminded me of another moment that night. She'd asked if I'd ever killed a man. Was she planning this all along?

That was a matter to consider later.

Brauer was about to leave us, so I began to go through his pockets. I did not look at her but I could feel Selene watching me carefully.

A fountain pen in an inner coat pocket. I could keep it there, but I wanted to make sure she knew I wasn't hiding anything—in case I wanted to hide something—so I held the pen in the air in the direction of her previous grunt. The pen disappeared from my hand.

A handkerchief in his breast pocket. I offered it. She took it.

His cabin key. My hand found it in a side pocket of his coat and I had a fraction of a second to decide what to do. She would no doubt like to check out his things on her own. She would know the key was on him if the door was locked, so I wouldn't accomplish anything by palming it and hiding it. Besides, I had my lock picks. It was best to make her think I was being open with her. All this went through me in a flash.

I pulled the key from his pocket and held it up.

There was a brief pause. She knew what it was; she was taken aback at my offering it. Good.

It vanished from my hand.

I eased him over just enough, first one side and then the other, to pat down his rear pants pockets. They were empty.

I leaned over him and pressed my left hand into his left front pocket. Empty.

The right pocket, immediately in front of me, was easier. I slid my right hand inside, at the angle he would.

And something was here. A piece of paper. Folded.

No figuring necessary. Instantly I palmed it.

I drew my hand from the pocket and I sat back on my haunches. "Is there a hand towel at your basin?" I said.

"Yes," she said.

"Get it."

I waited, not watching her move, keeping my eyes on Brauer, keeping the hand with the palmed note hanging limply at my side. She would be watching me, even as she did what I asked.

The towel dangled down in front of my face.

I didn't look up at her.

I said, "Keep it. Watch his mouth when I pick him up. There might be some blood."

"All right," she said. She stepped beside me, on my right.

"Other side," I said. "Be ready when his head falls to the side."

As she circled me to my left, I moved around on my knees to place myself at a right angle to Brauer's body. I also slipped the palmed piece of paper into my right-hand coat pocket.

I crossed Brauer's legs at the ankles and his hands at his waist.

"I'll need you to open doors," I said. "Cabin door. Door to the promenade. Look through them first to make sure no one is around."

I put my left arm behind Brauer's shoulders and strained him upward. Dead weight. Bad leverage from my knees. My arm began to slide upward and I forced it down, into the center of his shoulder blades, and his torso was coming up.

His head lolled to the right.

Selene's hands and the towel rushed to it, and I shifted my attention to his knees. I put my right arm beneath them and he felt steady in my grasp and I strained hard in a dead lift, sliding him up my thighs far enough to raise my right leg beneath him and place that foot flat on the floor, and I set him on my right leg.

"Door," I said.

I had leverage at last and I used my arms but also my right leg, rising up from the knee, and both my feet were on the floor and it was simple now. I was standing with Walter Brauer in my arms.

I looked at Selene for the first time since I'd answered her eyes: *Yes, I can get rid of this dead body.* She was at the door, opening it, her head bare and her hair rolled up high, the long line of her body dressed once again in form-clinging black. Maybe this was the occasion she'd been outfitting herself for since Monday night.

The cabin door was open and she leaned outside. She looked both ways and drew back in and pressed against the wall, clearing a path for me.

"It's okay," she said.

I stepped to her with Brauer and motioned with my head for her to come inside the room.

She slipped past me. I turned sideways and squeezed through the door with Walter, rolling him flatter against me, chest to chest, for a moment, scraping through the jamb.

I was standing now in the center of the corridor and feeling very exposed. I looked in both directions.

Still empty.

The door clicked behind me and I followed Selene to the end of the corridor and we turned left into the vestibule. She opened the portal to the promenade and stepped outside. Framed darkly in the doorway, she spoke from there. "We are alone," she said.

I moved forward and squeezed through and I was abruptly buffeted by the wind of our twenty-two knot run. The deck quaked under my feet and the urgency of all this rushed suddenly upon me.

I crossed the promenade quickly—one step and another and another—and I was at the railing. I set my feet squarely beneath me and I lifted Brauer higher, up to the top rail, and I rested him on it for a moment, my arms dilating with ease at the release of his weight, happy now just to balance him there.

We were on the first-class promenade. Below was another promenade on the second-class deck.

"Selene," I said.

She came at once to my side. "Yes?"

"Lean out to see if there's anyone at the railing beneath us."

She put her hand on her hair as if she were keeping a hat from flying off in the wind. She bent over the railing and looked down.

She straightened again. She stuffed the bloodstained towel into Brauer's jacket. Smart. If she tried to throw it away on its own, it could fly back onto the deck below.

"Get rid of him," she said.

I moved my arms from beneath Brauer and quickly put my hands on him, one at the shoulder and one at the hip, and I pushed hard.

He leapt out and then away to our left as if caught in the wind, and I leaned forward, watched him falling rearward toward the face of the sea, his arms flaring open, and he splashed into our wake and lifted on a wave, and the *Mecklenburg* rushed on, leaving Walter Brauer in the darkness behind us.

36

So we straightened at the railing and turned our backs to it and stood there a moment looking like a couple who'd simply had a nice meal in the dining saloon and now had come out for a breath of air, a long-married couple who could stand beside each other on the deck of a ship on a night that was full of bright stars—I happened to notice this as I'd turned away from the sea—and not say a thing and not quite touch and seem entirely comfortable with that. As if everything important had already been said long ago.

Then we left the promenade—it would have been hard to say which of us initiated this; perhaps we'd both done it at the same moment, spontaneously—and I held the deck door open for Selene and I followed her to her cabin and she held that door open for me. I stepped in and stopped in the center of her floor and she closed the door and crossed past me. We still had that air of taking each other for granted after long familiarity.

She sat on a woven-reed bergère chair that faced the bed and I sat on the edge of the bed directly opposite her, and now the language of our bodies said that we intended to have a conversation on a topic we both anticipated. But in fact we remained silent for a long while.

I imagined that she was trying to figure out how much to lie to me and what sort of lies might be convincing and, indeed, if it made any difference if she were convincing or not.

But it did matter, of course. She needed to be very convincing. She'd just killed the Germans' agent who was playing an integral part in their larger plan; this was all improvised; they hadn't sent her out here to do that. She'd just torpedoed her own steamship and here I was again apparently ready to help her swim away. I'd already saved her sweet stern once tonight.

I had my own personal figuring out to do. My own calibrating of lies. Certainly I knew a great many things she did not realize I knew and I had to decide what to continue to keep to myself, what to let out to her, what to lie about. Now that I'd dumped Brauer I was committed to keeping her mission going for my own benefit.

So we sat.

The ship's turbines hummed. The room swayed. Both rather distantly, however.

And we sat. And there was a moment when she looked carefully at the bandage on my left cheek.

I wondered if she was trying to place it, if she'd had some brief, peripheral glimpse of it in the bar.

But she studied it only briefly and I saw nothing behind her eyes. She was good at masking things, but I figured I'd see at least a little something in her if she realized I'd followed her to the rendezvous with her father.

And we sat.

And I had time to wonder what had happened to her pistol. It was no longer visible. She had no pockets. My eyes moved to the smoking table beside her chair. In its center lay a small, black, snakeskin bag with a silver frame. I'd already hypothesized its use. She must have discreetly taken that with her to the promenade deck and put the pistol away.

I moved my eyes back to her and she was watching me closely.

Somebody needed to speak.

But we both stayed silent a few moments more.

Finally she said, "Thank you."

"Don't mention it."

She hesitated. As if what would follow were spontaneous. But she had a plan now. She said, "You killed a man."

Another neat shot, her ambiguity. She could be talking about our conversation on the *Lusitania;* when she asked if I'd ever killed, I said yes. Or she could be talking about the Hun on St. Martin's Lane. She could even be talking about me taking the fall for Brauer. I had more apparent reason to kill him than she did. She was letting me choose how to take this. Which would suggest a direction for her lies.

"So did you," I said.

"He was trying to rape me," she said, as if I'd believed it the first time.

"I've never killed a man who wasn't trying to kill me," I said.

"Then we are both innocent souls," she said.

I gave that a moment of silence.

Then I said, "That's something I haven't seen yet in the filmic art."

I expected to have to explain the comment. But without a hesitation she said, "Irony?"

Which was one of the reasons I was still enchanted with her, this quick, telling thrust of her mind. And, under the present circumstances, one of the reasons I was more than a little afraid of her.

"Irony," I said.

She smiled. Like here we were communicating so effectively.

I smiled the same smile. I said, "Tell me what you think the present irony is."

This she did hesitate about. I was letting *her* choose.

But after a few moments, she decided to smile again, a small, sweet—and yes, ironic—smile. She said, "That we should be innocent, though we have killed."

If we had actually decided, as it was beginning to seem, that we would banter now instead of getting down to serious lies and revelations, I would have contradicted her by saying, *No, the irony is that you say we are innocent souls when we are not.*

But I wasn't ready to banter.

"The irony," I said, "is that Walter Brauer was a homosexual."

What flickered in her face may have been the first spontaneous expression of off screen emotion I'd ever seen in her. No simple label for it existed; she couldn't make it larger than life if she tried.

But she'd be back in full control of herself any moment now. I pressed my advantage. "So why did you really kill him?"

"Who are you?" she said.

"Who are you?"

"Did you kill that man on St. Martin's Lane Monday night?"

"You mean the guy they would've sent after you when they found out you murdered Brauer?"

She flickered again. But only very briefly. "Murder? What makes you think you know anything about it?"

"That's how they'd see it."

"Or anything about them?"

"So then why did you really kill him?"

"Who are you?" she said.

I stood up and took a step in her direction.

She flinched backward in her chair. Another real emotion from Selene Bourgani.

I was surprised to feel a quick, throat-clutching pulse of regret at her fear of me. Though I knew a little fear would be useful.

I gave her a small, sweet, ironic smile.

I lifted my hand and she flinched again, minutely, with her eyes. But without looking directly at it, I reached to her left and picked up her purse. I did not let go of her eyes, where her own sense of irony had now returned. No more flinching. I did not look at the object in my hands as I opened it. I felt the pistol where I'd expected to find it and I took it out. I closed the purse and dropped it in the direction of the smoking table.

And still we did not let go of our gaze. She didn't even glance at the pistol. She knew what I'd done.

I put the pistol in my inner coat pocket. I let my lapel go and my coat closed. The pistol thumped me softly and then lay heavily against my heart.

I said, "I'm the guy who has helped you out in a big way three times now."

She said, "The third being the man in St. Martin's Lane?"

"Who would have come after you," I said.

The irony dissipated in her eyes.

"They've got others to send," she said, very softly.

I sat down on the edge of the bed once more.

I asked it a third time: "Why'd you kill him?"

"He doubted my allegiance to the German cause."

"With reason?"

"With reason."

"Who has your allegiance?"

"Nobody," she said. "Me. I have my own allegiance."

"But they thought it was with them."

"That was in my own best interest."

"To work for the Germans and make them think you wanted to."

She said nothing.

"Why was all that in your best interest?"

"Look," she said. "Just because you chose to help me out a few times and have now taken away my only means of self-defense, doesn't mean I'm ready to tell you all my secrets. They're personal. Not political. Personal. And I'm keeping them personal."

"All right," I said. "So I'll just walk through that door and leave it at that. You can figure out on your own what to do next. Do you think Selene Bourgani can actually hide in this world? They'd find you."

I started to rise.

"Wait," she said.

I sat.

But we returned to silence.

I didn't let it go on. I said, "I'm not going to wait long enough for you to think of a new set of lies."

She shifted her pretty butt on the woven reed seat.

I decided to help her out. "Did your boy Kurt know something about you?"

She let out a long, slow breath, her shoulders and her chest visibly sinking. She said, very, very softly, "I should be more careful who I sleep with."

"Actresses and directors," I said. "That's an old story." I didn't need to say this. But Mama and a few of her guys came to mind. And it was time to seem sympathetic with Selene anyway.

She said, "Actresses and handsome newsmen on doomed steamships."

I shrugged.

And she said, "Especially when he's not just a newsman."

The sympathy was a mistake. I needed to press the attack.

But she spoke first: "So where's *your* allegiance?"

"To my country," I said.

She smiled very faintly. That flicker of irony again. "From what I could gather over the past few days," she said, "you've got your own troubles waiting for you up ahead."

"I can manage mine alone. You can't."

"What do you want?" she said.

"For starters the truth."

She nodded faintly. She waited. She said, "And what do I get?"

"What do you want?"

"As you said."

"Help."

"Yes."

"I can help you," I said. "I can't help the Germans."

"And what will you want after the starters?" she said.

"That depends on what the truth is."

"I want more too."

I shrugged again. Like I was ready to walk out of the cabin and let her handle her own problems.

She said, "Only if the truth makes it worth your while."

"What more do you want?"

"The truth," she said. "For starters."

We both fell silent for a moment.

I said, "It was a hell of a lot easier for us to agree to have sex."

She drew that big breath back in; her shoulders and chest rose. "Sex is always easier than the truth," she said.

I nodded. I wasn't quite sure why. Maybe at the probable truth of that. Maybe just to act as if this was now some sort of intellectual discussion, as if I weren't ready to take the easy path, right then and there. A tendril had fallen from the thick, up-pinned coil of her hair and down her neck, kindled in the electric light. Her smell in the room seemed more of the musk now than the hay and there was no longer anything in it of flowers. Sex is easier than patriotism as well.

But I bucked myself up the way I did when my job was to face a field of fire with soldiers who were making news. I said, "What were you planning to do for the Germans in Istanbul?"

She pushed the tendril of hair back off her neck. As if she'd known it was there all along and now that it had failed at its appointed task she was dismissing it. She said, "You may have missed your journalistic calling, Mr. Cobb. Your movie-gossip reportage was correct. I had some private times with Kurt Fehrenbach. Actresses and directors."

She actually paused now to tuck that bit of hair back up into the rest of it on the top of her head.

I waited.

"The movie ended and all of that did too," she said. "Though we've remained friendly."

"Remaining friendly is always easier than the truth," I said.

"But harder than the sex," she said.

I thought: *Which is why I'm glad I have your pistol.*

"So Kurt went on to become the darling of the Kaiser," she said. "His personal filmmaker. And a hobnobber with important people on the Emperor's staff as well."

She paused. She turned her face to her bag and reached for it. But her hand stopped, hung in the air.

"Did you forget I have your little friend?" I said.

She withdrew her hand and looked at me. Her brow furrowed ever so slightly, as if I'd just hurt her feelings.

"I forgot I have no cigarettes," she said.

I reached into my outside right coat pocket. Next to the piece of paper from Brauer's pants I found my Fatimas. I withdrew the pack and I stood and stepped across the space between us.

She lifted her face to me. It was one of those looks from one of those positions that made you want to take a woman into your arms. Instead, I tapped the closed half of the top of the pack on my forefinger. One cigarette emerged from the open half. I moved the pack near her.

Her face, waist high, was still upturned. She smiled at me. Then she lowered her face and looked at the extended cigarette. I expected her to lift her hand to take it.

She didn't. She leaned forward and put her lips around the cigarette and pulled it from the pack with her mouth.

I did not move. I probably could not have moved if I'd wanted to.

But she was waiting for a light.

I dipped into my left-hand coat pocket and drew out a box of matches. I lit one. I brought it toward her face. She touched my hand and guided the flame to the end of her cigarette.

She leaned back, inhaled long and deeply, turned her profile to me, and blew the smoke toward the window through which, not long ago, I'd seen her standing over the man she'd just killed.

I waited for her face to come back to me. For a long moment it did not. She kept her eyes on the window. Perhaps she was thinking of that same moment.

She seemed a long way from answering my question, truthfully or otherwise, and the smoke of easy sex was in the air between us. I could see through it, but that didn't make the more difficult thing any less difficult.

What did help, in this particular moment, was the sharp nip of pain on my fingertips. The match was still burning.

I waved the flame away and tossed the match on the floor. Right where she'd planted Brauer, as a matter of fact.

I stepped back to the bed and sat down.

She turned her face. She looked faintly disappointed once again. But not for long. We were still working on the new rules of the game between us.

She said, "Who would you say is currently the most important man in the Ottoman Empire?"

She still seemed to be far from the answers I wanted. But I was willing to play along with her for now.

The answer to her question was easy. Eight years ago a mixed bag of nationalists, secularists, pluralists, and various other haters of the despot "Crimson Sultan" Abdul Hamid II got together and hatched the Young Turk Revolution, which overthrew the Sultan and tried to reinvent the Empire. Three of the Young Turks achieved pasha status and became a ruling triumvirate, but one of them was clearly running the country from the position of minister of war, and he also happened to be the primary instigator of the Ottoman alliance with Germany.

"Enver Pasha," I said.

Selene nodded. "Enver Pasha. And it turns out movies are all the rage in Istanbul and he's my biggest fan. Biggest as in most intense, or so I'm told. One of the biggest in the world-leader category as well. Maybe old Wilhelm is a fan too and has him beat in that department. Who knows about Woodrow Wilson."

"From the way he conducts his foreign policy," I said, "I don't think you're Wilson's type."

"Be that as it may," she said. "Enver somehow conveyed his intense regard for me to the Kaiser who told Kurt who conferred with a bigwig at the Foreign Office who had his minions find me, and they had the right documents and I received some impressive telegrams from all the impressive people in that daisy chain of impressive people and they all wanted me to . . ."

At this point, though she had been rolling out this tale with absolute aplomb and wry worldliness, she abruptly broke off. The crack in her voice didn't seem scaled for a theater audience. Indeed, it seemed like something she wanted to suppress. All right: perhaps wanted to *portray* as something she wanted to suppress. But I was prepared to keep both possibilities on the table.

She straightened and looked away and composed herself, and she said, "They want me to do certain things. The fundamental one being to spy on him."

She stopped talking.

I said nothing.

There was this odd sense of plummeting in me, in my chest, in my limbs. An image of the man flashed into my head. It was vague, really, derived from the grainy news photos I'd barely glanced at over the past few years. But it was clear enough to accelerate the plummet: he was merely a thin-framed swarthy little man with black, uptwirled, Kaiser mustaches, downright dudish-looking, as a matter of fact. *To hell with this,* I thought, *I already figured this was her primary skill as a spy.*

I almost said something stupid. About Turkish men still having their personal harems. About Enver maybe making room for her.

I didn't. I was glad I didn't.

But she seemed to read it in me. Or maybe even in herself. She abruptly shrugged and turned her face away and said, "You know, maybe you *should* just walk out the door. I'll deal with the consequences."

That wasn't what I wanted.

"I'm already in pretty deep with you," I said.

She gave me her face, her eyes, once more.

"How was it all supposed to happen?" I said.

"We were going to the Pera Palace Hotel. Walter Brauer was going to meet someone. I'd wait. That's all I know."

I didn't say anything.

She said, "Except then Brauer would deliver the goods."

This line was delivered cold. Okay. She was going back to the frame of mind that was letting her do these certain things she was supposed to do but which were so much against her inner nature. It seemed to me now—and I was relieved at the feeling—that Selene Bourgani was overwriting her little scene, was overplaying her little part.

"Clearly this is difficult for you," I said, trying to keep the irony out of my voice.

"Yes," she said. She was ready to sniffle.

"So we're back to truth time," I said. "Not that I'm in *so* deep that I don't still need the straight dope, if you want me to hang around and help you."

Her face did not change in the slightest.

I made sure mine didn't either as I tried to focus on what I needed to know. I'd been a bit too eager to show off my knowledge when I'd dropped Kurt Fehrenbach into the conversation. I was an idiot showing off for a woman. I missed a logical step. I jumped in with her director-boyfriend after she asserted her allegiance only to herself and not to the Germans. Old Kurt might indeed have something on her that was the leverage to make her work with the German secret service, but the issue at hand had been why she killed Brauer. Fehrenbach's scoop on her couldn't be the same as Brauer's. Fehrenbach used his to make her a spy; it already had to be okay with Berlin. Brauer's lowdown could have been worth her killing him only if it put her in serious danger with the Huns.

I said, "I need to understand two things. If the Germans want you to seduce Enver Pasha and work him for what he knows and they don't, why did you agree? And why did you kill an unarmed Walter Brauer? Those two answers need to make sense to me together."

Again, nothing going on in the face before me. Outwardly. The spinning of her brain's turbines, however, was pretty much drowning out the ship's at that moment.

"I'll give you an answer," she said. "But a little truthful clarification from you first."

I presented the blank face and the silence, which I'd been learning from her.

She didn't care. "You think I'm a German spy," she said. "And you're an American spy. Correct?"

This much was obvious. "Correct," I said.

"Your people know some things about Brauer and about me and no doubt about Metzger and Strauss, as well. Correct?"

"And about the guy with the phony beard," I said.

There was a little loosening in her. "So you think it was phony too," she said.

"Who was he?"

"The boss."

"Any name?"

"They called him Herr Buchmann."

"The 'bookman.' Phony beard, phony name probably."

"Aren't they clever?" She let the irony ooze thickly this time.

He was known to the Brits, I thought. Or making sure he never would be known to them.

I put this out of my mind. It was my own fault, bringing Square-beard up at this point, helping her slide away from straight answers.

"My questions remain," I said.

She waved off my prodding. "So isn't that all we need to know? We both of us are playing the same role. You happen to be doing it for the American government. Willingly, I presume. I did hear you pledge allegiance a few minutes ago, didn't I?"

I nodded.

"And I pledged disallegiance to Germany. I may be out for my-self, but your country is mine too. And don't ask that damn 'why' again. America's fine but it's in second place with me. Do you really need to know what my old boyfriend has on me and why I'd shoot Walter Brauer to death and why I'd have sex with a small-sized, waxy-mustached, garlicky Turk with three wives and a Napoleon obsession? Maybe I didn't like Walter's tie. Maybe I'm a sucker of a slut for guys with garlicky breath, especially if they're running a whole empire. Maybe I'd have sex with Enver Pasha for free but in addition the Huns are paying me big, in real, imperial gold. What difference does it make? Why should you help me out? Because whatever the Germans want to learn on the sly from Enver Pasha, you and your boys would like to know as well. Let me work for you both. All you sons of bitches. Why don't you and I agree to that right now and stop all the idiot questions and then have some easy sex to seal the deal?"

This, for the moment, seemed reasonable.

37

This time the question of gentle or rough didn't even come up. This deal was sealed in hot wax. I pounded and she pounded and the only disagreement between us was when she declared, with her words broken into eight distinct phrases from our ongoing activity: "If you finish . . . now . . . or even soon . . . Kit Cobb . . . I will get . . . my pistol . . . from your coat . . . and kill you."

I heeded her warning. Selene Bourgani and I extended things to her satisfaction, though my own personal problem with extending this sort of thing cropped up: my body kept on, but my mind drifted off. At first, not entirely, as the departure point was a surge of jealousy at Enver Goddamn Pasha. With the thought of what a man like him was mysteriously able to command from a woman like Selene Bourgani, I began, indeed, to despise Enver Pasha, despise him perhaps not with the depth but surely, I fancied at that moment, with the intensity felt by even the Greeks and the Armenians. Of course not with their intensity either, but yes, my mind had wandered as far as the massacres of both those peoples in recent years, and I thought how these Young Turks were no better than the Crimson Sultan in this regard, given what had already been reported of their actions against the Greeks in Smyrna last summer and Thrace the summer before, and against the Armenians in Adana soon after these new boys came to power, six years ago, those actions being the wholesale slaughter of every Greek and Armenian in sight—man, woman, and child. Which gave me a thought that got drowned out by screaming.

This was from Selene beneath me, though it was not—I was happy to realize—a scream of rebuke. I was still working out okay for her. Maybe, indeed, my thoughts of politics and massacres were helpful in that regard. She was finishing up and would soon let me do likewise. And then she stopped screaming and her own mind apparently wandered off and I was happy to finally put my stamp in the sealing wax and blow it till it cooled.

Afterward, as we lay wrapped tightly together on the narrow bed, the thought that slid into me a few minutes ago returned. And when we rather gently untangled and sat side by side with our backs against the wall smoking Fatimas, I said, "Your Greeks have a real beef with your garlicky Turk."

She finished blowing a plume of smoke before her as if she hadn't heard. But then she turned her face to me. "*My* Greeks?"

"Your life story."

"I think I told you once already that was all lies."

"I figured you might have lied about some of the lies."

She nodded faintly. "I could do that," she said. "But I didn't."

She looked away again and took another drag on her cigarette.

I made my voice go quite soft. Actually it wasn't so willful as that. I did know that if I wanted an answer, I needed to be soft. I'd often used the trick with news sources. But at that moment I did indeed feel a little surge of gentleness about Selene and her phony public life and her raging private dramas and desires. I said, "What *is* your story?"

"I'm American."

"By birth?"

"Not quite."

"And your parents?"

She watched the smoke she'd just blown in a long, thin ribbon till it dissipated into the cabin air. When it was gone, she said, "Cypriot."

"Greek-Cypriot or Turk-?"

"Both. I come from far back, intermingled. We didn't take a side in that fight."

All this came easily from her. Which didn't mean any of it was necessarily true. But there was even less reason to believe the overt publicity tales about her.

"So the island was Cyprus, not Andros," I said.

She exhaled softly, without smoke. "Part of me comes from Andros, I guess. My first lover was a Greek and he took me to Andros for the deed. I was fifteen. He was forty-five. I had a certain look about me and a certain willingness and a certain freedom to act. He owned ships. I was fond of Andros. I was fond of him. He was like the leaves of the olive trees on the mountains there. Silver laid upon green."

We both fell silent for a long while. Both of us smoking. This thing about her first lover: it was maybe the only thing she'd ever said to me that had instantly felt true.

Then she broke the silence. "How will you save me, Kit Cobb?"

I took a long drag on my cigarette and began my own moment of contemplating the smoke I was blowing. But she interrupted.

"I was glad to stop your damn questions," she said. "Glad to do what we just did. But we have to face facts now. My usefulness to the United States of America won't last long when the Germans and Turks find out about Brauer. I'm afraid the best you can do is shield me long enough so I can get on a train or a ship or a donkey cart and try to vanish."

All that was delivered with a flat, steady tone. This was a tough dame, even without a pistol in her hand.

I said, "Did you have any sense that Brauer would remain in Istanbul as your contact?"

"No. I got the impression he'd be coming back to London."

"Did you hear anything to give you the impression he was personally known in Istanbul?"

"I think he'd studied there some years ago. But I didn't pick up on anything else, one way or the other."

This was a chance we'd have to take, I thought. Obviously Metcalf figured Brauer was unknown by sight in Istanbul or he wouldn't have urged me to kill the man and take his place. Not that Metcalf would hesitate to take a chance—even a big one—on my behalf, seeing as he was advising a man of a different temperament from himself.

"I can play Brauer," I said.

She turned her head to me sharply. "You can pull that off?"

"I can."

"Good," she said, with an intensity that struck me as odd. Maybe it was relief. Maybe she suddenly felt her place on a train or ship or donkey cart was enssured. That made sense. But there was something in her at that moment I wished I could get her to talk about.

"I know this has been scary for you," I said.

She shot me a look that confirmed my gut feeling. This intensity wasn't about a release of fear. It was something else.

She was on her feet and moving to her clothes.

She bent to them and I tried to memorize the flash of her body. Each time always felt like the last time with Selene Bourgani.

"Selene," I said.

She turned to me, pressing her dress to her chest.

At least she did turn.

"I know you're not afraid," I said.

I could see her mind working for a moment, trying to figure me out. Then she said, "I know you're not either."

38

She dressed.

I dressed.

The deal sealed, we were all business now.

"We need to search his cabin," I said.

"I have the key," she said.

"I know," I said. "I gave it to you."

"I knew it was in his pockets somewhere," she said. "You couldn't have actually fooled me, now could you."

"I didn't need to fool you," I said.

"You hadn't yet taken the precaution of stealing my pistol," she said.

"You needed me," I said.

"I still do," she said.

All business.

I reached into the pocket of my jacket and removed her Colt. "I think we'll be all right for the trip," I said. "But you never know."

I opened my palm to her, with the pistol lying in the center.

She looked at it. She looked at me. "I'm grateful," she said. And she took the pistol. "That's the truth," she said.

"I believe you," I said.

Selene stepped to the smoking table and picked up her bag. She put the pistol inside. And when her hand came out, she had the key to Brauer's cabin. She handed it to me.

"Let's see what we can find," she said.

And we were standing in the center of Brauer's cabin, an exact replica of hers.

We looked around for a moment before starting to dig.

His waistcoat on the back of a chair. A large suitcase under the window.

"Was he really a homosexual?" Selene said.

"Yes."

"How do you know?"

"I knew."

"He didn't try to strike up with you, did he?"

"No. He had a rendezvous on the ship."

"That other man he was with?"

"Yes."

"I only saw them across the dining room."

"Not sure if it was prearranged," I said. "It could've been casual."

"So Walter had depths," Selene said. "Poor man. His friend apparently didn't survive."

"I didn't see him in Queenstown."

"Walter seemed a bit dazed. How does a man like that mourn? I'd think perhaps more readily. More like a woman?"

Walter's love life was no longer relevant. He was dead, after all. Maybe Selene's little surge of interest was an aftermath of her killing him. I wondered if he was her first.

I crossed the room to his suitcase, picked it up—it was heavy, still packed—and I laid it on the bed. I undid the straps and opened the lid. It was neatly packed with clothes.

I doubted that the things I was looking for would be in here if there was an alternative. He'd keep those closer. "Was this the only bag he was carrying?" I said.

"Here it is," Selene said.

I turned to her.

She was at the narrow wardrobe beyond the foot of the bed. The door was open and she was bent inside. She straightened and carried a morocco valise toward me. I moved the suitcase toward the head of the bed and she placed the valise at the foot.

It opened from the top.

She stepped to the side, let me do this, though with a keenly watchful eye.

I dipped in.

A fitted toilet case. I checked inside. It held only the usual items, including the straight razor that first told me about him and the late Edward Cable. I put the case on the bed above the valise, starting a stack with a reflex impulse to note the layers and the arrangement for repacking. As if to prevent Brauer from later realizing his bag had been searched. But he was dead.

A folded dressing gown. These were things he wanted in his own hands if his suitcase went astray. I removed the dressing gown and it struck me: black silk. This and everything else Brauer was carrying was new. But he'd had a black silk dressing gown on the *Lusitania*. He'd replaced it exactly. I found myself not liking this task. Old Walter was getting to be too real to me, watching him make very personal decisions.

And a union suit. Really too personal. I felt like his mortician, learning way too much about him in order to put him finally to rest. Toothpowder. Hair brush. Other things that hardly registered. And then near the bottom, a book. He did not replace his Heinrich von Treitschke. But he was reading *Deutsche Schriften* by a similar German ideologue: the Orientalist, biblical scholar, and anti-Semite Paul de Lagarde. Walter was keeping up with his early-childhood first language. That was good to know and a very useful thing when I portrayed him. I couldn't fake Turkish. But I could do German.

I put the Lagarde on the bed, and next from the dim depths of the bag came another book. It gave me a pleasing jolt. This one he did replace exactly: *The Nuttall Encyclopaedia of Universal Information*. The 1909 edition, I had no doubt. I did not let myself show any interest in it, immediately putting it on the bed next to the *Deutsche Schriften*.

I glanced at Selene, who was craning her neck to read the book titles. "Not my personal choice of train reading," I said.

Selene grunted but left off looking at the books.

The last object at the bottom of the bag was a long sealskin wallet. I removed it. I opened the wallet and drew out a sheaf of documents.

I sorted through them with Selene watching closely. His tickets to Istanbul, arriving on the sixteenth. And tickets back to London for the twenty-second. His passport. I was glad to see that it was like my bogus one: American, not British. Letters of passage and recommendation to officials along the way. I'd examine them more carefully later.

"These are what I need," I said.

I replaced the papers in the wallet and put the wallet into my right inside coat pocket.

She did not protest.

I repacked the valise but I left the two books on the bed. It was the *Nuttall*, of course, that I truly wanted. I just didn't want to draw attention to it.

Then Selene and I rummaged through Walter Brauer's clothes in the suitcase, both of us feeling very uncomfortable, betokened by our bated silence and the quick agreement that there was nothing here.

I stuffed the clothes back in the suitcase and closed the lid. I glanced at Selene. She was leafing through the Lagarde.

I let her. I began to buckle the straps on the suitcase.

"Did you mean to leave these out?" she said.

I looked at her.

She was thumbing the *Nuttall.*

"Yes," I said.

"Why?"

"I'm preparing for my role of Walter Brauer," I said.

"Did your mama teach you to prepare like that?" I couldn't tell whether this was skeptical of me or sarcastic about her. It would not have been my mother's assumed method of preparing for an acting role. She was a larger-than-life actress of the old school, or had been when she rose to her young-leading-lady stardom, though a few of the things I'd seen her do as she moved into middle age were smaller, more intensely real. Moscow-Art-Theaterish, even.

"She had big-paying audiences in a big space, not a Hun with a gun standing in front of her," I said.

Selene closed the *Nuttall,* reached down and picked up the Lagarde again, stacked the two books together, and handed them to me.

"Your props," she said.

I said, "Is there anything else you want to look at in here?"

"No."

"Then would you carry these for me?"

I handed the books back to her.

She furrowed her brow in puzzlement.

"I need both hands," I said. "Why leave any questions behind? If you'll hold doors and check for insomniacs on the promenade, let's complete Walter's disembarkation."

The brow unfurrowed with a small, sweet head tilt of respect.

"Of course," she said.

I moved Brauer's bags off the bed, opened the covers and disarranged them, and punched a head dent in the pillow. I picked up the bags and followed Selene to the door. She switched off the lights and we left Brauer's cabin and dropped Walter's bags in the sea.

And then we stood in front of Selene's cabin door as if we'd been on a dinner date and the delicate question was just arising of whether or not we would kiss good night.

Her eyes, though, narrowed a little, like a cat showing it trusted you, and they mellowed and went suppliant and then flitted wide and willed themselves to be quite calm and rational. A whole run of feelings had come and gone inside her, and at the end of it, she said nothing at all. She simply handed me Brauer's books, turned and opened her door, and disappeared.

39

I locked my cabin door. I took only one step into the room before stopping and removing Brauer's folded piece of paper from my pocket. I could see now that it was familiar canary-manila telegraph paper. I unfolded it. Typed in blue, by a Morkrum telegram printer, were 19 groupings of numbers, eight in each.

Nuttall.

The cable was recorded at Western Union, Folkestone. The recipient was Walter Brauer, care of the Zeeland Steamship Company. The sending identifier: Wilhelmstraße 76, Berlin. Which was the address of *Auswärtiges Amt.* The German Foreign Office.

I tossed Lagarde onto the bed and sat in the woven cane chair. I pulled the smoking table in front of me like a desk. I put *Nuttall* in the center and laid out the telegram beneath it.

This was a very recent development or Berlin would have contacted him more reliably before he left London. The first number was 00620403. There would have to be four factors: page, column, line, and word. I looked at the last full *Nuttall* page. Number 699. The maximum number of digits was three. This made sense, since the first group began with two zeros, to let this discretely read as page number 6. I turned to it. There were two columns, expressible by a single digit. I counted the number of lines. Seventy-six. Expressible in two digits. And I saw a couple of lines with ten words. Two digits.

Eight digits all together, which squared with the number groupings I was looking at. I could read the code.

And one at a time the words emerged, which I wrote in the space above their corresponding numbers.

change
plan

I was right about the structure of the coded words.

meet
Pasha
man
pass
word
Gutenberg

I paused and briefly considered the odd phrase "Pasha man," but of course *Nuttall* simply did not have a possessive form of *pasha*. I would be meeting the Pasha's man, his aide de camp, his assistant.

And the next word: 49321301. *Pera*

Palace
own
room

He would come to me at the hotel. We'd refer to Gutenberg. Another *buchmann*.

sometime
upon
16th

That was the day of our arrival.

Only four words to go and I paused briefly. The type in *Nuttall* was small and the electric light was dim and counting the lines and the words was hard going well past midnight.

The next word: 43514204.

This took me to the entry on Thomas Middleton, a contemporary of Marlowe and Shakespeare. The first column on the page, forty-second line, the fourth word was the middle word of the title of one of his tragedies: *Women Beware Women*.

Beware

I was still inclined to hear this note as being addressed to Walter Brauer. I had to hear it the way it must be played: they were talking to *me*. Brauer's dangers were my dangers.

The next word was 15123101: page 151, column 2, line 31, the first word.

And I was looking at my mother's entry in *The Nuttall Encyclopaedia of Universal Information*.

Cobb

Beware Cobb. I felt an icy grinding in me at this. Not because they perceived me as a threat. But because the German spymaster had found my mother in this book and used her. It was as if he'd put his hands upon her.

I pushed on. I had to beware of *me*. Okay.

Two more words.

where

And the last word was page 487, column 1, line 64, word 3.

unknown

Perhaps it was the slight relief I had at this head scratching in Berlin over my whereabouts, but the location of that word in *Nuttall* made me laugh out loud. A poem from a Victorian English poet named Coventry Patmore: "The Unknown Eros."

Beware of Cobb, for he was now Brauer, of unknown eros.

I did feel better about one doubt that had begun to creep into me, concerning a secret that Selene was still withholding. What did Brauer say to her to provoke her to kill him? It had to be seriously threatening. I had begun to worry, as I'd decoded this message, that what he confronted her about had come from this telegram. And if it had, then she was already compromised in Istanbul. But it hadn't.

Perhaps Brauer's handlers were indeed doing what Smith and Metcalf were doing for me, trying to figure out what the man in the bar was all about. Brauer pretty clearly had not gone inside on that night. He might have returned yesterday, but that tight little group in there would stonewall a man like Brauer. My guys still hadn't dug up anything; Brauer's couldn't have either.

Walter must have come to her tonight and tried to bluff her into revealing something; maybe he threatened her. The bar in the East End was a very touchy subject for Selene. But if that's what the argument was about, the question remained, even more critically: why was this such a threat to her in Istanbul that she'd lose her head and kill him?

We had some travel ahead of us.

I figured I might find some leverage with her along the way to learn more.

40

And so a certain Walter Brauer, resident of London but traveling on an American passport and approved in documents from the highest official levels in the German Foreign Office, and Selene Bourgani, also an American traveling with her own weighty German endorsements, entered Holland at Vlissingen. This was the one place we kept our German credentials to ourselves. Then we boarded a train shortly after dawn, and when we were under way, we stood before each other once again, in front of her compartment, and once again we did not speak until it seemed she would simply vanish behind her door. But at last she said, "How far to Berlin?"

"Twelve hours," I said.

"I need to sleep," she said.

"The German frontier is four," I said.

"Till then," she said.

And our credentials—in the smoke-filled, coal-gritty, body-warmed and body-scented wooden customs hall in Bentheim on the German frontier—drew instant heel clicking and bows from the Kaiser-mustached official.

Which led to lunch on the train, on clean linen and with the rolling outwash plain of northern Germany whisking past. Selene and I did not speak much.

At some point I said, low, "Things went well at the border."

She turned her face to the window. I watched her eyes catching something outside and sliding away with it, catching another thing and sliding, scanning the landscape quickly, over and over, restless eyes even as everything else about her was utterly motionless. I thought: *It's all right for now; I won't speak to her; she's preparing herself for what awaits us at the end of our journey.*

But suddenly her eyes stopped moving, though they did not turn to me. The afternoon was cloudy and the window gave us back our images if we cared to look, and I imagined she was focused now on herself there, the ghost of her face floating motionless upon the flashing landscape. She said, very softly, "After Berlin . . ." And she stopped.

I lowered my voice to match hers. "Yes?"

"I don't want to be alone," she said.

I had the impulse to reach across the table and take her hand. But I did not. I said, "All right."

In Berlin we changed trains. We walked together on the platform beneath the vast, steel-trussed vault of the train shed at Friedrichstraße Station. As we approached the first-class coaches, Selene slipped her arm inside mine.

And so, as the train still sat in the station, with the scuffle of feet through the coach passageway, with the hiss of steam and the gabble of voices outside the window, with my bags stowed and my tie straightened, when a sharp, clear rap came to my sleeping compartment door, I crossed the floor a little breathlessly and slid the door open expecting Selene.

A thick-necked man in civilian gray filled the doorway, gray also in eyes and in thickly upstanding hair and in walrus mustache. I took an instinctive step backward. Again, my pistol was in a bag.

But I was Brauer.

Indeed, the man asked, "Herr Brauer?"

"*Jawohl,*" I said, my mind shifting to this language that needed to be part of my reflex self now.

He said, "Welcome, if briefly, to Berlin." His German was clipped and precise and emotionless.

"Thank you," I said. "Come in."

He did, closing the door behind him.

I had no idea who he was. I was having a delayed surge of gratitude that he had no idea who I was either. I was beginning to rely on Brauer's not being recognizable. But was I supposed to expect this guy?

The large gray man was before me again, offering a hand, which I took. "I am Kaspar Horst," he said, "from the Foreign Ministry. I wish I had some schnapps for us to drink, but the train will soon depart and I have to leave you to do your work."

"Please," I said, motioning him to the bench seat along one wall. We sat beside each other.

"She is nearby?" he asked.

"The next compartment," I said.

He lowered his voice drastically. "She is stable, this woman?"

"Sufficient for our purpose," I said.

"Good." He glanced at my left cheek. I had to repress the impulse of my hand to leap there, to make sure the bandage was in place. As long as I was Brauer, the *Schmiss* made me a liar. "You are hurt?" Horst asked.

I said, "You are aware, surely, that I had to save my own life on the *Lusitania,* when our efficient U-boat corps sank it?"

"*Ach so,*" he said, flaring his hands. "Who could have anticipated that? That would have been very bad. Very sadly ironic."

"We were lucky to escape," I said.

"The Wolf will follow you," Horst said.

He paused and I worked to keep calm. He'd changed the subject abruptly. And *Der Wolf* was somebody he clearly expected me to know. I wondered if it was a reference to me, to Christopher Cobb.

The moment of silence was probably not long but it seemed at the time to go on and on. Then Horst said, "He is afraid this man Cobb will cause more trouble."

I nodded. "Even in Istanbul?"

"That's his fear. The Wolf will come to you soon."

"Good," I said. *Bad,* I thought. *Very bad.*

He rose. This was why Kaspar Horst had been sent to me at the Friedrichstraße Station. To alert me to *Der Wolf* coming to help. Shit.

I rose with him. "I have return tickets . . ."

"He'll find you first," Horst said. "Needless to say, you will take any future direction straight from him."

Horst offered his hand. I shook it. "Thank you for the help," I said, using my anxiety to play grateful enthusiasm. The lie of good acting.

"The Emperor is counting on all of us," he said.

41

This was the vaunted Berlin-to-Baghdad Express, the great umbilical of Germany's nascent Asian empire, though it still had big gaps beyond Aleppo and we ourselves would have to leave it in Budapest and head for the Romanian coast and a steamship down the Black Sea to avoid Servia. But immediately before us were twenty hours to Budapest, and Selene and I spent most of it on her narrow bed, even after there was not a drop of anything left in either of us to give or to receive or to exude, and yet we stayed in that bed and we smoked and we slept and, now and then, we tried some more with our bodies, tried to give and to take, and we were fine when that didn't go much of anywhere, laughing at it even, like an old couple who had sweet intentions and patience with each other because of some good, larger feeling they shared, but we said very little, not like lovers at all in many ways, not like that old couple either, in this respect, though we should have been intensely curious about each other—I should have been about her, professionally at least—but sealed as we were in a room in a coach on a train that surged and slowed and stopped and surged and slowed and surged again, its whistle as distant and as mournfully vowel rich as the cry of a rutting cat, we put away any questions or issues that came from outside this shuttered window, this shuttered door.

We did dress, twice, once to eat another meal in the dining car with the landscape dark outside, and once scrambling into our clothes when the passport officials boarded the train at Teschen, on the Hungarian frontier, and they knocked on our door only to quickly click their heels and bow their way back out again in response to our German documents, two youngish men with immaculate Hungarian officer uniforms and large mustaches. Selene and I both noticed them exchanging a knowing little smile over these two lovers as they slid our door closed, which we laughed about much harder than it warranted, which revived our bodies a bit for one more tumbling and soft pounding before a good six hours of deep sleep wrapped in each other's arms.

And then we were in Budapest.

And immediately before us were twenty-four hours to the Romanian port city of Constanţa.

We did not have to say more than a dozen words between us for us to decide that I would go to my own cabin now and close the door and we would not see each other again until we arrived on the shore of the Black Sea.

Which was what we did, across the Hungarian plains and over the pine-quilted Carpathian Mountains and all along the wheat and corn fields of Romania, a landscape that could easily have been Illinois except for the water-buffalo-powered plows.

And then we were on the SS *Dacia,* a 3,200-ton mail steamer of the Romanian State Railways doing the Black Sea run to Istanbul with 120 first-class cabins and two special cabins built to accommodate the women of a Turkish harem.

And we ended up once again in each other's arms, this time in my cabin. In the first hour we made love, and it felt as if it was the last time Selene and I would ever make love, though that had become a routine feeling for me, an inevitable part of the act: from our almost tender commencing kiss, to her threat on my life if I didn't keep going, to her final scream, to the cigarette afterward, to a voice in my head going *I bet this is the last.*

But on the *Dacia,* upon the Black Sea, there was a new coda to our jazz suite: we segued immediately into a close embrace burrowed deep beneath the sheet and blanket. And Selene wept.

Wept and trembled.

Silently for a while, and then she said, "I'm afraid."

"It's all right," I said.

"This is the only time you'll ever hear me say that," she said.

"It's natural."

"I won't *feel* it again either," she said.

"You can."

The ship pitched a little and she flinched.

"Is it about the ship?" I said.

"Partly."

I said, "This is the first ship you and I have been on that's not threatened by submarines."

"Maybe that's why I'm free to be afraid."

I could understand this. Some of the best soldiers I knew felt their fear after the battle, not during it.

"That comes with being able to loosen your hold on your courage," I said.

She held me more tightly.

Partly the ship, she'd said. I understood this as well. I myself was starting to feel a rat-toothed gnawing in my chest, in my throat.

Der Wolf was on his way. I was to meet someone at the Pera Palace who expected me to be Walter Brauer and therefore expected me to be an expert on Islam and to speak Turkish, skills Metcalf had failed to include in my leather portfolio. Just for a starter.

The sun had set outside our cabin window. When it rose again we would arrive in Istanbul and the curtain would go up on our final act.

42

We came down the Bosporus, which was narrow enough to look like a river and which, therefore, for a boy who knew rivers mostly by knowing the muddy Mississippi, looked shockingly blue. And Istanbul appeared on its hills as a bit of a shock as well. It mounted from the blue water draped with a good deal of tree-dense green, its stitching of Western buildings white in the lately risen sun and its profusion of mosque domes and minarets a pleasant geometric spangling in the broad sweep of the city.

As we drew near, though, previously overlooked swaths of brown in the tableau were clearer and more pervasive. These were the intense runs of dingy wooden houses along what we would soon learn were the city's winding, labyrinthine streets, narrow and filthy and foul, fully purged only by the periodical burning down of whole neighborhoods of these houses, which would spring back up, instantly dingy and combustible once more.

And as we eased up to the quay at Galata, the minarets now seemed to me as profuse in Istanbul as smokestacks in Pittsburgh. And as definitive: they were the big business of this place. I took all this in—the impressions of this approach and arrival and mooring—while standing next to Selene at the railing of the *Dacia*, and just as I was beginning to revise my own first-vision impressions of this town, I felt her shudder. I wished she'd shuddered at the thought of Enver

Pasha, but I guessed this city on top of all that was what finally got to her. At least to a shuddering extent.

When Selene and I stepped off the disembarkation launch into the Place Karakeuï, we discovered a man in full chauffeur livery standing beside a 1908 model Unic taxi, holding a sign for the Pera Palace. And so we found ourselves sitting shoulder to shoulder in the tonneau of the same model taxi that carried Selene before me to the London Docks. I did not speak to her of this little irony.

By my reckoning we had an option to go straight up the hill from the Galata Bridge, but we turned west and followed one of the limited number of main streets—though the Unic still bounced and groaned and swayed severely on the cobbles—and then we climbed the hill the back way to the European enclave of Pera, avoiding the twisted, narrow, rubble-cluttered streets for the sake of the hotel's well-to-do Western guests. We passed through the shadow of the 14th century Galata Tower, which rose fifteen stories from the hillside, once a military structure but now a fire-watch station, with a high, Gothic gallery of round arches and on top of that a stack of three, diminishing flat-roofed cupolas.

Then we turned into the street the locals called Meşrutiyet Caddesi, but known within Pera itself as the Rue des Petits-Champs. The street cars were electric, the shops were elegant and mostly French, the cafés had tables on the sidewalk, and all the storefronts already had their awnings unfurled against the day's sun, vast, rippling, white-cloth hangings looking like the backsides of Berber tents. The local men in business suits were indistinguishable in style from the men on Chicago's State Street except they each wore a red fez.

And in the midst of all this, there was a rolling of metal wheels and the crackle of electricity bearing a reminder of the war: a tram passed us full of the vacant faces and bandage-swaddled arms and foreheads of wounded men being transferred, Turks up from Gallipoli.

I pressed toward the window to watch them pass and then looked forward to an abrupt contrast. Up ahead was the Pera Palace, the extreme version of this whole mission's neoclassical motif, the style seeming more aridly aloof after seeing the boys from the battlefield. The hotel looked like a mostly unaltered stone box, registering on the eye about like a Jack Daniel's shipping crate, but without the juice.

Just before it, we turned into a narrow, cobbled side street, traversing the short side of the hotel, and then turned again and stopped before the main entrance.

Selene and I stepped down from the cab, and a couple of young fezes in long, brass-buttoned, pigeon-gray uniforms rushed forward to deal with our bags. I put a hand lightly under Selene's elbow to guide her the few paces across the sidewalk. But I caught a movement in my periphery to the right and I looked that way as a German officer, who had just stepped from a taxi behind us, took a stride in our direction.

Selene looked too and we paused for the man, who gave us a quick, dismissive glance, easily accepting that he should go before us. His uniform was the German *feldgrau*—field gray, but with tones of green to blend into a battlefield—and his shoulder boards each had two pips. A full colonel. He also wore a *Pickelhaube,* the ridiculous, black, polished-leather spiked helmet that sat up over the ears protecting very little except the feelings of inadequacy of the officer beneath it. Did I feel Selene tense up a bit beside me? These were her guys. These were the guys I had to deal with.

The tin-pot Hun did a sharp right face in front of us and a guy was coming out of the hotel with the same beefy face but wearing a three-piece tweed suit and a matching Alpine hat. The man in the suit stiffened and paused and shot a crisp salute at the uniform, who saluted in return. The one disappeared into the hotel and the other turned to his right, heading up the Rue des Petits-Champs. The colonel was returning from a night on duty or a high-level early staff meeting, perhaps at the German embassy just up the street. The lesser officer in mufti was off duty. The Huns were dressing down to civies to keep a low public profile. Which meant privately they were working hard to control the Turkish government.

Selene and I followed the colonel into the marble entrance foyer and we checked in at the front desk, which was off to one side. I half expected further instructions to be waiting for me, but there was nothing. We went up the short staircase at the back of the foyer and stepped into the vast central space that lifted your chest like a cathedral or a major mosque. This was the grand Kubbeli Salon, with six domes floating fifty feet overhead, though secular domes, profusions of circular glass panes—the Western quarter's architectural nod to the religious big business down the hill and across the Bosporus on the Golden Triangle of Stamboul. At the north end of the space were double doors. We passed through them and stood before a mahogany electric elevator car whose portal was an abrupt departure from all the neoclassicism: its cast-iron gate was an open-web facade of violent art nouveau curves.

The door clanged behind us. The operator opened the circuit, and we rose, the tops of the six domes soon appearing below us, becoming the faux floor of an atrium rimmed by four levels of rooms, the passageways balustraded by more art nouveau iron. We arrived at the top and we stood before her room, mine just a little farther along.

Our journey from London was finally over. We were now left with the need simply to wait—helplessly to wait—for the Pasha's people, whoever they might be, to contact us.

And though I suspected it never seriously entered either of our minds to wait together, Selene felt obliged to apologize, which was a surprising thing to me, a tender, almost sentimental gesture on her part, it seemed: "I'm sorry," she said. "I need to be alone now."

"I understand," I said. "But you're not facing all this alone. I'm still with you."

This animated her eyes, very briefly, very subtly—I could not even say how it was I knew that she'd come alive behind them—and she turned from me without a touch and she opened her door and disappeared.

I stood there quietly, not walking away to my own room, not even turning, not moving in the slightest. I remained like this for a long while, long enough for the elevator to hum and jangle its way down to the ground floor and then come all the way up again. I heard the elevator door open at the center of the atrium, and that made me turn, as I expected it to be the gold-buttoned boys with our luggage. But it was the German colonel.

I straightened, my limbs surging with restrained energy: a reflex of preparation for a possible danger. Foolish, under the circumstances, though it more plausibly occurred to me, as he walked the thirty yards or so along the passageway toward me, that he might be my contact. He did not have to be a Turk, after all, my contact for this initial meeting. Indeed, I was hoping the approaching officer was the one. We'd speak German. I could be very convincing in German. A Turk would expect the Islam scholar from Britain to speak Turkish. I still didn't have a plan to finesse that.

The colonel neared. His eyes held fast on the straight line to his room, which obviously was beyond me. And since I was close to Selene's door, I was just outside of that immediate line of sight. He seemed not even to recognize my presence.

He passed.

I turned to watch him.

He went a couple of doors up the passageway and stopped and unlocked his room—still not looking my way—and he entered. The door clicked shut.

I knew to expect a large contingent of German staff officers at the Pera Palace.

Keep your friends close and your enemies closer.

I went to my room, which was two doors beyond the colonel's, near the end of the hall.

Inside, the room was harmoniously eclectic: an Uşak rug of Persian palmettes and olive vines in gold and pale red; Byzantine medallioned brocade drapes; more nouveau cast iron in the headboard; and, yes, even a bit of Louis XVI neoclassicism in a mahogany wardrobe.

I parted the drapes, opened the French windows behind them, and stepped onto a balcony. The benign feeling I'd had at first seeing the city from a distance returned, this time from above: the wooden houses showing their red tile roofs; the high, tight, almost military stands of cypress; the Bosporus slashing blue across the middle distance; and the domes and minarets catching the morning sun in Stamboul across the way.

I leaned heavily against my balcony and turned my face south and west. A hundred and thirty miles away, the estimates made it fifty thousand dead—Turk, Brit, French—and plenty more mutilated, like the boys on the tram.

And thinking about the carnage made me jump a little when a heavy rap came from inside the room.

The door.

I turned, moved through the French windows, crossed the densely soft rug, not thinking, ready to be Brauer if I could. I would insist on German with a Turk. *Deutschland über Allah.*

But as I approached the door, I noticed something lying on the carpet before it. An envelope had been slipped through the crack.

I bent to it. Picked it up.

Whoever it was didn't seem to be hanging around.

I opened the door and stepped out.

The passageway was empty in all directions.

I stepped back into the room and closed the door.

I opened the envelope. The note was handwritten in English: *Turn left outside hotel, immediate right. Third cross street is Çatmali Mektep. Coffeehouse with yellow dog.*

This didn't sound like the Germans. But if it was Metcalf's man in Istanbul and he knew to leave a message for me in Walter Brauer's room, then they'd watched me arrive at the hotel. And they were expecting me to have killed him.

43

I stashed my bags and threaded the holster onto my belt so the pistol rode in the small of my back. I'd asked for a left-handed holster, though I was right-handed, so I could draw from back there. I'd gotten the idea to hide a weapon in this place before—a hunting knife, in Mexico—to good effect. This would be the place for my Mauser in Istanbul. I figured I'd more likely have to draw with stealth than with speed.

The passageway was clear and I went five levels down the heavily carpeted staircase and into the Kubbeli, where I walked casually, keeping an eye on anyone keeping an eye on me. I was okay.

The immediate right turn at the corner of the hotel led me along the western edge of the public gardens, where the Judas trees were blooming in pale purple. The fronting shops mostly catered to foreigners, but the block before Çatmali Mektep seemed to be blending back toward the Turks, though well-to-do ones. The hattery had fezes in the window. A barber in white was working on a man in a suit, but in a chair on the sidewalk. The coffeehouse was indeed a house, not the working-class java fiends' usual set up of a raggedy divan and a few chairs under a wooden lean-to. But the yellow dog was mangy and indolent, one of the rare survivors of Istanbul's canine holocaust the previous year, when tens of thousands of feral dogs, for which the city was infamous, had been rounded up and dumped on an island in the Sea of Marmara to starve. This yellow mutt had been wise to endear himself at an establishment for influential Turks.

The Turks didn't drink liquor, by their religion. They were pretty seriously committed to that, most of them. But they made up for it by more or less constantly drinking coffee; Allah apparently disapproved of altering yourself into fuzzy fumbliness with booze but was quite tolerant of you sparking up your engines with caffeine. Some of the coffeehouses were worth State Street, like the one I'd just stepped into, but a divan under wooden planks wasn't the lowest-class incarnation either. That would be the undercapitalized joint sprung up in any bit of shade under a tree or beside a wall or even improvised with a couple of chairs out in the middle of one of the common, rubbled, bare-earth plots between Istanbul buildings. Coffee and tobacco and endless talk: these were the left and right ventricles of Turkish life. For the men, of course. The women were mostly invisible behind the window latticework in the wooden houses. I wondered what their preferred vice was.

The air before me was laced with two strong smells, the distinct bite of the Turkish coffee and the smell of the *tunbeki,* the water-pipe tobacco, the exhalations from which were befogging the air already, though it was barely two hours after sunrise.

I knew the etiquette. There were more than a dozen men in fezes, sitting in twos and threes on couches and tables. As I entered, the conversations all stopped and all eyes moved to me. I recalled that movement of eyes at the London Docks. But this was a different thing altogether. There might have been a freethinker or two amongst these men, but most of them were Muslims; Ottomans, no less, so they were Muslims who had a long history not unlike Christian history—namely, marching into countries where a bunch of folks thought differently than you about life and God and you ground your righteous heel into their throats. I was an infidel. But not inside here. In this house—and on the most threadbare couch in the most desolate, rubble-strewn vacant lot—coffee and tobacco were the common sacraments of the whole human race.

So to each man in the room individually I gave a *Merhabah*—saying the word and softly thumping my heart with my fist—and each man did the same to me. And revved by coffee and smoothed by tobacco and huddled together within these walls in fellowship and endless talk, these boys truly meant it: *I offer my heart to you as a friend, sharing, as one, these basic pleasures of life.*

One of these men, the owner of the coffeehouse with the yellow dog, turned from the bar along the back wall, with its cauldron of live coals and its line of small, long-handled, curve-spouted pots. He stepped away from his coffeemaking and approached me. We did one more *Merhabah*, one more thump to the chest, and the man said, "Mr. Cobb?"

"Yes."

"Follow me, please."

He led me to a door at the back and into a narrow hallway, dim and full of the smells of the front of the place, but not the current versions. These smells long ago had been brewed and smoked into the very walls and floor of the place. A fresher smell of tobacco, though, came from the last of several open doorways along the hall, the others giving onto dark rooms, this one lit with an electric bulb hanging from the ceiling.

As soon as I stepped into the doorway I sensed the Turk behind me slide away and vanish.

The man before me was no doubt my American embassy contact, but at first glance he seemed in some ways to be of a different sort. He was sitting crosslegged in his stocking feet on a divan at the back wall, his suitcoat folded beside him, a red fez sitting on top of it, the long coil of the leather tube of a water pipe in his mouth and a cloud of smoke around his head. The head itself was topped with a dense bed of feed-corn-yellow curls.

His tie, however, was still firmly knotted at his throat, and the eyes that lifted from the vase at the bottom of the water pipe on the tabletop before him were the instantly engaged and fixedly focused eyes I'd seen before in the boys doing this kind of work.

That fixedness: somehow it felt cynical, ruthless even. I'd seen the look in the eyes of certain lifelong Chicago ward politicians when you peeked behind their public demeanor by getting them on the verge of drunk, or by getting them mad in front of other people they didn't want to show that side of themselves to. I was thinking now in retrospect that I'd seen this look in Trask and Metcalf both. Maybe even Smith. Maybe I had it too, that look. Maybe it was also the look of a good news reporter.

This guy gave me that look but then raised his hand as if to say *Hold your horses for a moment.* And those cynical eyes closed to savor the smoke of the coarse, strong Persian weed.

"Ah," he said, his eyes still closed. "*Tunbeki.*" Which was the weed. I could imagine him dining with Metcalf at the Carlton and the two of them filling the dining room with their moans of pleasure.

The eyes opened and resumed their stare as if the divine *tunbeki* had utterly failed in its high purpose of soothing the spirit of the body it filled.

The man put the pipe aside, unfurled his legs, and rose.

I stepped to him.

We shook hands. "You're Cobb."

"Yes."

"I'm Ralph Hansen. Cultural attaché, American embassy."

As we shook—his was firm—I said, "Culture, is it?"

"Didn't you notice my fez?"

"The locals out front are still wearing theirs."

"I'm off duty."

And he started to refurl himself on the divan. "I waited on the coffee till you arrived," he said. Settled now, he patted the seat. "Join me."

I took off my coat and folded it and took off my shoes and sat cross-legged beside him. He passed the pipe to me. I took a drag of the *tunbeki*, and it went straight to the brain, acting smooth but working to unsettle things. I passed the pipe back to him.

He took a very big drag, and the owner appeared in the doorway with a brass tray and jingling cups and glasses. He set them on the low table before us. Two of each of these: a three-finger coffee cup on a saucer with a dark brew crowding the top and a glass of water, boiled pure.

We sipped the water for a while first, which was the Turks' way. Then we drank the coffee by lifting cup and saucer both. Hansen sipped the water quietly and the coffee noisily. I wasn't sure if that was the Turks or just Hansen, so I stayed quiet on both. The coffee itself was sludgy and heavy but not as bitter as it looked; pretty good, actually, though eventually the very finely ground beans floated up with each sip and there was no alternative—the Turk would wish none—to drinking the grinds down with the coffee.

We did this in silence for a few moments, and then Hansen said, "Any contact?"

"How did you know?"

He slid his eyes to me. However much he seemed to be under the influence of the Turks' coffee and tobacco, these eyes seemed professionally acute. "Know?" he said.

"That Brauer is dead."

He pursed his lips. "You waltzed into town with the star of the show."

Of course they were watching. From the quay onward.

"Just curious," Hansen said. "Was there a fuss on the *Mecklenburg* a few days ago?"

"I disposed of the body and its bags," I said.

Hansen whistled softly through his teeth. "Good man," he said.

"That was *all* I took care of," I said. "The disposal."

He set his coffee down. It was the only sign that he was intrigued. When his eyes came back to me, they had not changed.

I set my coffee beside his.

And I told him all the things he needed to know about the passage to Istanbul. Everything but the extent of my relationship with Selene.

He kept his eyes on me for every word.

And when I finished, he looked at me a few moments more and then he nodded, as if we spoke different languages and somebody in his head had been translating all this time and was a sentence or two behind.

"Where did Mr. Trask come up with you, Christopher Cobb," Hansen said, more statement than question.

"It just happened."

"Well, I admire your instinct to keep this thing going with her. It won't be easy."

I almost said, *All right, then I'll just walk away now.* It had to be in his mind. But for whatever reason—the woman, the sport of it, taking this job for my country seriously—I didn't want to do that.

He said, "I wouldn't trust her gratitude."

"I don't."

For once, something was happening behind his eyes that he wasn't comfortable with. I figured I knew what it was. This question was overdue. I waited to see how he'd ask it.

"Tell me, Kit," he said. "Do you have a *personal* hold on her?"

"I do," I said.

"Good man," he said.

"But I don't trust it," I said.

"Of course not," he said. And then: "I'll wire Mr. Trask, but I would expect us to be very interested in what comes of this."

"The critical thing," I said, "is for me to plausibly remain Walter Brauer until he heads back to England. If he disappears on the return, it won't compromise Bourgani."

"Who are you most worried about?"

"Anyone who knows Brauer by sight. And anyone who expects him to speak Turkish."

"And anyone who knows *you*."

"Of course," I said. "But at least my public reputation is mostly through a byline. I haven't turned into Richard Harding Davis."

"Him I'd recognize," Hansen said.

Davis, a good writer and middling reporter, had consciously made himself a celebrity, even letting his pretty-boy face become the male equivalent of the Gibson Girl. I'd had my own mug in maybe half a dozen photos in magazines over the past few years. But field shots, always with a big-brimmed hat of one local sort or another. Hard to see me; harder to remember me. At least that was my hope.

"And then there's *Der Wolf,*" Hansen said.

"I saved him for the climax of my list of worries. You know him?"

"I've heard of him."

"Yes? Out here?"

"He's been mentioned by our counterparts in some bad business in several parts of the world."

"What do you know about him?"

"Nothing. *They* know nothing. The Brits. The French. The Russians."

"Not what he looks like?"

"Nothing," Hansen said. "But the deeper in we get, allying ourselves to the Brits, the more interested we are on our own account. And if he's after you . . ."

Hansen completed his sentence with a shrug.

I said, "If he's coming after Cobb, you figure he's got to have some way to recognize me."

Hansen nodded again, very faintly. "Maybe so," he said. "Did Brauer have a beard?"

"No."

"As far as your contacts here know, he could've grown one. You could put one on like their man Buchmann."

"Did Metcalf come up with anything on *him* yet?"

"Or you can simply dispose of The Wolf," he said, with a sly little slow-unfurling smile that made me uneasy. I figured every goddamn American embassy that had guys like this knew me now as a man with a knack.

"Buchmann," I said, reminding him of my question.

"We don't seem to have anything," Hansen said.

And a thought thumped into my head. "He was in disguise," I said.

"Evidently."

"But he seemed important, by the way he was treated, the way he spoke."

Hansen raised his eyebrows. He knew where I was going.

I said, "And you and the French and the Brits and the Russians are all scratching your heads because you can't learn anything about *Der Wolf.*"

"I get it," he said.

"And what I did in London was a direct affront to him. He'd handle this himself."

"I get it," Hansen repeated, at about half the volume.

We looked at each other.

Hansen nodded. "Like I said. Simply dispose of the big bad wolf." This had a quite different tone in its reiteration. Somber.

We sat silently for a moment. The cloud had vanished from the vase of the water pipe. The coffee was cold.

For all my figuring, I was very uneasy about the next few days. Even the next few hours. Between the boys in Washington and a couple of major embassies, my mission right now was pretty much to wing my way forward on my own to see what might possibly develop and wait for a bad guy they didn't know bedbugs about to show up in disguise to kill me and see if I can kill him first.

"We're just gonna improvise this thing, aren't we," I said.

"That's the business sometimes," Hansen said.

He let me sit with that for another moment.

And the next logical thought came upon me. If it was just about me, I'd've been willing to continue improvising. But I figured I owed Selene Bourgani something more: "Maybe the way forward has to be improvised," I said. "But if I don't pull this off, if somebody realizes I'm not Brauer before I get out of Istanbul, what's our plan of retreat?"

"If you can last through the week and start the trip back to London as Brauer, we'd give you a quiet exit somewhere along the line."

"And if this thing blows up?"

"You can't just run to the embassy. I hope you understand."

"I get it. That's what I *can't* do."

He waved off the next sentence.

But he did not give me an immediate answer. His thinking on the subject led him to lean forward, pick up his coffee, register its coldness, put it down.

I figured I better make things clear before he arrived at an answer. I said, "If I can get the woman out, I will."

He registered what I said, but again he didn't answer at once. I wondered if he had the authority to accede to me on the spot.

He did. He said, "The embassy has a guardship moored down the hill, at Tophane. The gunboat *Scorpion*. Starting tomorrow, each night from dark to dawn, I'll have a man in a launch waiting at the foot of Tophane Iskelesi Caddesi at the west end of the dry docks. Tell him Ralph sent you."

"Thanks."

"Make it as clean as you can."

"I should get back to my room."

"There was one bit of information from London," he said. "The flag in the bar at the London Docks."

At which point our coffee man appeared in the doorway.

Hansen waved him away, though gently. And he did it with a few sentences of explanation in what sounded like fluent Turkish. I realized I'd been underestimating another of these secret service boys. I had to stop doing that.

He turned back to me.

He smiled again, as if he knew I'd just reassessed him. He said, "The flag was the brainchild of a priest thirty years ago. Red, green, and blue were colors of God's rainbow for Noah, and for the people who once upon a time had their own country with Mount Ararat sitting in the middle of it."

I knew where he was heading with this.

He said, "And now it's the rallying flag of their twentieth-century nationalists . . ."

"The Armenians," I said.

44

I hustled back toward the hotel. The *Nuttall* message said first contact would be "sometime" today. Brauer would have stayed put. I
had enough problems being convincing as Brauer; I didn't want one
more. But that concern set my pace, not my preoccupation. The street
was a blur to me, registering only enough to navigate it, because of
Armenia. I knew some of the history. The old Turks had treated the
Armenians brutally. And the Young Turks orchestrated a couple of
nasty slaughters themselves. If the bar in London was a meeting place
for Armenians, then almost certainly the mystery language spoken
there by Selene and the man I took to be her father was Armenian.
Cyprus was another lie. For her to have fed me a second consecutive
lie about her origins meant she thought the truth would be a problem
between us, even with me being in the midst of covering up her killing of an unarmed man. And that problem was clear now. She was
heading off to be Enver Pasha's mistress for reasons she still would
not fully reveal. I could see why her being Armenian would deepen
that mystery. And she didn't even know that I'd watched her meet
her father in a London bar that catered to Armenian nationalists.

I could have speculated about all this. But I preferred to ask.

I hustled even more quickly off the hotel elevator and along the
passageway.

I stood before her door.

I knocked.

There was no sound inside. I did not volunteer that it was me. She had no reason to think I knew more than I'd known when I left her earlier this morning. But neither did she have any further wish to speak to me. I wanted her to open the door without expecting me. No sound was coming from within.

I knocked again.

Nothing.

I put my ear to the door. I still heard no sound.

I knocked again.

As the silence persisted, I began to think she'd gone out. She had her own agenda, of course.

I moved away to my own room. I went in and pulled my packet of lock-picking tools from my bag. In the passageway again I made sure I was alone, even looking over the iron balustrade into the atrium. The elevator was out of sight and the chains and gears were silent.

I returned to Selene's door and bent to the lock and did my work. The tumblers fell into place and I turned the knob and pushed.

The door opened a few inches and abruptly resisted. A slide-chain lock was securely in its groove. Selene was inside the room.

She was not visible and so neither was I. I took a quiet half step farther to the side just in case.

Even as I did, her voice floated out to me. "Please," she said. "No service."

She took me for the maid with a pass key.

I pulled the door to.

I figured I would let this be, for now. She would either stonewall me further or lie some more. It would be better for the time being for me simply to be watchful of her. The problem of who would knock on *my* door and what might then need to be done could make this Armenian question moot anyway.

Moments later I slid my own chain lock into its metal groove. I took off my jacket and tie. The jacket smelled strongly of *tunbeki*. I thought to work on a news story. The Zeppelins already having yielded some actual hard news, I hadn't yet figured out what other printable stories I might glean from my secret life of the past week. I could curbstone a good feature with the best of them, and it was in my mind to do so. But then I abruptly recognized this as an old reflex that was dangerously wrongheaded under the circumstances. The typewriter and the story coming out of it would be hard to explain to my Enver contact.

So instead I pulled Lagarde's *Deutsche Schriften* from my bag, opened the drapes to the morning light from my balcony, went to the bed, removed my holster, and unsheathed my Mauser. I put the holster out of sight and I lay down, propping myself up with both pillows. I placed the Mauser on the bed beside me at precisely the place where my shooting hand would land at the first sound from outside my door.

In the meantime, I would read in German. Lunatic German, but it was all I could do at this point to anticipate my becoming Walter Brauer. The book would be for the man who didn't know Walter. The pistol would be for the man who did.

I laid the book in my lap. I put my palm on its cover and I did give Selene and the Armenians one thought: *If she was already doing a double—working for the Germans but actually passing on Enver's plans to the Armenians—then of course she would still be lying to me, at least by omission.* In this business you told as little as you strictly had to.

It was time to open Lagarde. He was known as an Orientalist and religious scholar. These "German writings" were his first plunge into political thought. Perhaps Walter saw some of himself in Lagarde.

I opened the book.

On the title page someone had written an inscription with a flexible-nibbed pen. The words were mostly English and the hand had an ornate, über-Spencerian style: *Mein Schnüffel, this is a first of a seminal—yes, a seminal—work. Read it closely.*

So Walter—the Orientalist, the Islam scholar—received this book as a gift. If his work for the Germans was a political act, then this would have been a logical book for one of his German handlers to have given him.

The German word at the beginning puzzled me. I didn't know it, though it sounded vaguely familiar. It was a nickname perhaps. Probably so. The *Mein* suggested a nickname. And the pure sound of *Schnüffel* suggested a nickname as well, in an almost childish way. I could hear a German parent call a child a *Schnüffel*; I could hear a young man use the word with his girlfriend.

This last thought made me think of Walter Brauer and what I knew him to be. And the little joke in the inscription suddenly came clear. Yes. A *seminal* work.

This was a gift from a male admirer.

I passed my hand over the words.

A man like Walter, in that covert culture: perhaps he'd had many lovers. Did such men treat each other the way normal men often treated women? No doubt. They were still men. And if they could not be openly legitimate in the world, then perhaps they accepted as their lot the fugitive physical connection that other men aspired to with easy girls before finding a virgin to settle down.

And yet. Passing my hand over these words, I saw Walter returning to his bachelor flat at number 70 Jermyn Street having just barely saved his own life from the sinking of a great steamship, a calamity that had taken the life of his lover. Perhaps a significant, enduring lover, the breakup on board trivial and deeply regretted now. And perhaps that lover had once given him a book and Walter felt driven to carry that book with him to Istanbul.

Yes. Cable the book dealer from Boston. I saw now the words "a first of a seminal . . . work." It sounded a bit awkward except if you heard it as professional shorthand: "a first" meant "a first edition." A first edition of a seminal work.

I'd wondered if that assignation with the late Cable had been prearranged. It had. Walter and this bookseller had known each other for a long time, had been connected for a long time. Walter was grieving more than I'd realized.

I could portray this man.

I understood him.

And I also felt stricken that I'd had to unceremoniously dump his body over the side of a ship into the North Sea in the middle of the night. There'd been no alternative. But I was sorry for Walter. Sorry for his friend Edward. I thought: *Too bad they could not have come to rest in the same sea.*

And a heavy knock came at my door.

45

My hand was on the Mauser. I rose and quickly put on my suit coat and placed the pistol in the right-hand flap pocket, tucking the flap inside. As I crossed to the door, I thought to touch the bandage on my left cheek. It was secure. I could never show my *Schmiss* as Brauer.

I slid the chain lock from its track and let it fall. I opened the door.

He was not Turkish.

That was good.

What struck me was this: he could have been Hansen's colleague at the embassy. He could have been Hansen's cousin from Topeka. He had the same sack suit and the same dirty gold hair and, from the first moment on, he had the same steady look of a professional in a trade that he didn't want to talk about.

But he spoke to me in German. "Good morning," he said.

"Good morning," I said in my best German.

He nodded.

And he waited.

But it took me only a brief moment to realize what for. "Gutenberg," I said. The password from the coded *Nuttall* instructions.

He smiled. "Mr. Brauer," he said.

I brought an empty hand from my Mauser pocket, with the option of a quick return.

He took my hand and pumped it as if the last time he'd been to this well it was dry. "Colonel Martin Ströder," he said.

He didn't look old enough to be a colonel, though I didn't doubt him. He started young, was well connected, had some special, dirty talent. He knew Brauer's name—*my* name—and I replied only with a nod.

He said, "Your room would be good for speaking. Perhaps the balcony."

I stepped to the side.

He came in and closed the door himself and slipped the security chain into place.

With seeming casualness I put my hand back in my pocket.

In the process of his turning around from the door, he gave the room a quick, efficient once-over.

This was either a precautionary reflex or a preparation for a bad intention. I slipped my hand around the grip and put my thumb on the safety.

He smiled at me. "They have put you in a nice place," he said.

"I am sure it is for the sake of the woman," I said.

He nodded an ain't-it-the-truth little nod.

"So," he said. "Let's talk briefly."

He led the way to the balcony.

Either that suggestion had to do with privacy or he planned to throw me over the railing.

I kept my hand in my pocket as we stepped outside.

There were two metal sidewalk café chairs. He sat in one and crossed his leg.

I pulled my hand out of my pocket and I sat on the other chair.

Ströder said, "I am an aide-de-camp of War Minister Enver Pasha."

Enver had spent time as the Ottoman Empire's military attaché in Berlin, and he spoke the language fluently. He was keeping his friends close even here. Ströder no doubt got a carefully stage-managed view of things. I understood the Germans' impulse: they could well use Selene's pillow talk.

"The plan has changed," he said. "Enver Pasha is preoccupied. The Italians are negotiating with our enemies to enter the war. This is an imminent thing, if in fact it has not been agreed to already."

He paused.

I said, "What does this mean for the woman?"

"The Pasha is very ardent about her."

I knew that when the Turk's feelings for Selene came up, I'd need to keep my face blank. I struggled now to do that.

The colonel went on, "But we must wait. Perhaps day after tomorrow."

"I see."

Though I did see that this was plausible, what I also saw was the more likely possibility that they were waiting for *Der Wolf*. The good Herr Gutenberg would perhaps hold off any suspicions about Brauer for the time being, but I didn't know for how long. If things were unsettled in this whole affair, *Der Wolf* might want to consult with their agent closest to the woman before going ahead.

"Why are you bandaged?" Ströder asked. Abruptly. As if he were trying to make me reveal something. But he had no reason to be suspicious of what might be beneath my bandage. And if he doubted me at all, this would certainly not be his opening shot.

"Didn't you know?" I said. "I was on the *Lusitania*."

He straightened in unfeigned surprise.

I said, "Our U-boat captains were too efficient in this case."

Ströder shook his head. "You saved the woman?"

I made a short, sharp laugh. "Have they told you about the man interfering with us?"

"Cobb?"

"Yes."

"They say he is an American agent."

"He saved her," I said.

"Cobb?"

"Yes."

"Was she compromised?"

"She left him at the first opportunity in Queenstown," I said. "To my knowledge they had little or no contact on board. He must have sought her out when it was clear the ship would sink. To try to take advantage."

Ströder, who had been sitting upright since his surprise, relaxed back into the chair. "This man," he said. "I have respect for him as a foe. For him to have the presence of mind to think of his mission in such a circumstance."

This was interesting to me, of course: the respect among the officer class of civilized fighting forces for their enemy counterparts. It was certain that Colonel Ströder himself had a spying mission. Cobb was his personal, respected foe.

I was.

"He's a killer," I said.

Ströder puffed faintly and nodded once. More respect. Of course he was a killer.

I said, "Is Cobb in Istanbul?"

"I do not know."

I was about to say, *Look, he could come after me.* These words shaped themselves in my mouth instantly. The Walter Brauer I was portraying would have this worry. But I stopped myself. I did not want Ströder to get it in his head to give me a guard.

But I wanted to know more about *Der Wolf.*

I said, "I understand we have someone on the way to take care of Mr. Cobb."

At this Ströder focused his eyes a bit more closely upon mine. He wasn't sure I was supposed to know this.

"Herr Horst gave me the alert in Berlin," I said.

Ströder let his eyes go casual as he nodded.

I said, "Have you met The Wolf?"

Ströder shrugged. "No one has," he said. And he laughed.

It was a joke he expected me to get. I had to be careful what I asked. I didn't know what exactly to make of the comment. Did it mean that *Der Wolf* was unlikely to have met Brauer or that he could have met him and Brauer didn't realize who he was?

I said, "I wonder if he and Cobb have tangled before."

Ströder shrugged. He didn't know. "It would be very interesting," he said.

"Very interesting," I said.

And now Ströder rose from his chair.

I did likewise, even as he turned and stepped through the French windows.

He was halfway across the room when he stopped and began abruptly to turn to me.

My right hand went instantly into my pocket, clutched the grip, thumbed the safety, put my forefinger onto the trigger, and Ströder was facing me, taking a step toward me. My right arm started to flex.

But he opened his palms to me.

"I almost forgot," Ströder said. "Enver Pasha said he was looking forward to seeing you again."

46

The door was shut and I leaned back against it.

Of course, in becoming Walter, I'd wondered what his role would be in all of this. Why him? I'd figured somehow he was a man both the Germans could trust and a bigwig Turk could feel comfortable with. I figured the role of go-between was a cultural nicety that didn't get widely broadcast. If the leader of the Turkish government wanted to take an American film-star lover by way of her German-director ex-lover, the protocol would be to have such a man as Walter bring her along to him and make the introduction. A formality for a Westerner to enter a Turkish goddamn harem. And maybe it was indeed something of the sort. But Walter had a history with Enver.

I had some planning to do.

And I had to get Selene to talk with me.

I went out of my room and stood before her door.

I put my ear to it.

There was only silence inside.

I knocked. There was no answer. I knocked again and I said, "Selene. It's Kit. Are you there?"

"What is it?" Her voice startled me. It came from inside but very near the door.

"I have some news," I said.

"I don't feel well," she said.

"About the meeting."

A few moments of silence. And then the doorknob turned.

I expected to enter, but she merely opened the door to the length of the chain lock. Her face appeared in the narrow gap.

"What is it?" she said.

"Are you all right?"

She looked pale. But perhaps no more than usual.

"I already told you I'm not feeling well."

"Can I help?"

"You can help by telling me what you have to say and letting me rest."

"Enver Pasha is preoccupied with matters of the war. We have to wait."

"Not tonight?"

"Not tonight."

"Good," she said. "Thank you."

She closed the door before I could reply.

I stood there for a while thinking what to do.

I had a hunch about her. The things still withheld from me might send her from this room.

I moved away.

I installed myself at a table in a corner of the Kubbeli Salon, my back to the wall, able to watch anyone emerge from the doors that led from the elevator and staircase. She would have to pass by me to leave the hotel, and unless she looked sharply over her right shoulder as soon as she entered the salon, she would never notice me.

I drank *raki,* a clear, fine Turkish brandy that reminded me in its clarity and burn of the *aguardiente* I'd come to like very much last year in Vera Cruz. I nursed a moderate sequence of *raki* all afternoon and into the early evening with an equally slow graze through a few orders of *meze,* small-portion plates, kashar cheese and mixed pickles and ripe melon and a paste of hot peppers with walnuts.

It was good to eat the local food, by turns hot and sharp and sour and sweet. The *raki* smoothed my mind and let me work at the challenges before me without an edge; though, to be honest, without the edge I could make no progress.

But I'd finished drinking before the evening and then I had a little more food and I was feeling good and collected and energized again and I'd been paying as I was served so as to be ready to leap up and follow Selene at once, but now I was beginning to think she wouldn't appear.

And then a figure in black floated before me, across the parquet floor, and I was the only one in Istanbul who could recognize her, because nothing of her showed. I'd seen the dress before and it fit her pretty close, but not an inch of flesh was visible, her hands in black gloves, her face shrouded in a black veil. This was the movie star *burqa*. But I knew who was inside.

I rose and I followed.

47

She went out the main doors and spoke to one of the brass-buttoned, pigeon-plumed boys, who led her to a taxi at the hotel's stand. I slipped past her as she was getting in and I got into the next taxi. I unsuccessfully rushed through English and German with the driver and found a mutual French just in time to have him follow.

We briefly descended the hill toward the Bosporus and then turned into the street the locals called İstiklal Caddesi—Independence Avenue—but which was known within Pera itself as the Grand Rue de Péra.

The taxis rushed way too fast for all the people and horses and carts and we slowed only for an electric tram. This was a car on the same line that this morning had been carrying the Turkish wounded to the German hospital in Pera, at one end crowded with Turkish men in suits and fezes and at the other with men in suits and Alpines—no doubt Germans—whose company included Western women dolled up and showing their faces and arms. How breathless with desire were those Turks on the tram, I wondered, at the public sight of these usually hidden female parts. And my driver drove more with his horn than his brake or his gearshift and I supposed Selene's taxi ahead was doing likewise.

We soon arrived near a brightly lit café and a darkened Bon Marché. I paid and delayed in my taxi and watched through the front window as Selene emerged.

I opened my taxi door and stepped out as she hurried directly across the sidewalk and disappeared beneath the arch of a marble building-front. I followed.

The Turks among the crowd of Western swells bumped past me in my crossing. The fezes never seemed to stop their forward hurtle in a crowded Istanbul street. A dance band was playing somewhere along the way. I passed through the arch, with two towering concrete Nubian maidens in diaphanous gowns posed at each side of the pier. A corridor led deep inside, bright with electric lights and lined with poster portraits of Chaplin and Fairbanks and Pickford and Gish.

I stopped beside the portrait of Bourgani, as Bourgani herself stopped a dozen yards ahead to buy a ticket from the cashier in a marble kiosk. She was in profile to me, though she had not lifted her veil. Beyond her were heavy swinging glass doors and above them, in thick, loopy, all-capitaled Art Nouveau style, looking like a stop on the Paris Metro, was the name of this place: CINÉMA DE PERA.

I was reconciled to her seeing me, but she did not look in my direction. She turned from the kiosk and moved toward the doors and I stepped forward and quickly bought a ticket.

Through those doors, the space opened up widely to the left and right, shaping an outer lobby. Along it were four archways opening to the auditorium's aisles: two at the far sides and two defining a large center section and two smaller side sections. I did not see Selene. I chose the left-center arch and stepped in and pulled up instantly. She was standing just a couple of paces before me, in the middle of the aisle, absolutely still.

The place was dim but I could clearly see its froufrou, its gilded cherubs and its rolling terra-cotta flowering vines and its theatrical masks as gaudy as any Belasco house on Broadway. The forward rows were mostly full; the high screen before us was not yet lit. From somewhere in the middle of the auditorium men's voices surged—in German—and broke into laughter. Perhaps they were some of the boys from the Pera Palace.

I took all this in but I kept Selene in the edge of my sight, and now I looked at her again. The back few rows were less populated, and just before her, the aisle seat in the left-hand section was empty. She took a step forward and sat in it. I sat on the aisle in the center section, one row behind her.

The house lights dimmed further and went out.

I realized I had not looked at the final poster, which announced tonight's film. Perhaps Selene hadn't either. I had a feeling she was here no matter what was playing. This was her house.

The screen lit up white and the clatter of the film projector began from above and behind us, and that soon faded with the sound of an accompanying piano—a strong, well-tuned piano—a grand, up front in the shadows beneath the screen.

The short subjects had already been played. The feature began and the first title card came up:

Max Reinhardt Präsentiert
DER LILIM

Selene's German movie.
And the next title:

Regie
Kurt Fehrenbach

I looked in her direction.
She was lifting her veil.

The light from the screen fell softly upon her face. I was a little behind her, but to see the screen she was looking across the center section of seats. She was almost in profile to me. She could see nothing of me—her angle put me just behind her periphery—but I had enough of her face in this darkened space for it to prickle my skin.

I looked back to the screen, even as the cinematographer credit—*Photographie*—faded away and the cast list came up, character and actor. *Personen.* And the star of this movie was at the top of the list, her name writ large:

Lilith Weiss . . . . . SELENE BOURGANI.

The second lead was somewhat smaller, Martin Beckenbach played by Emil Jannings. I did not read the list further. I looked again at Selene.

Her face was lifted slightly. The light flickered there but her face did not change for a long few moments, and then it did. Her eyes closed and I looked and she was there before us both, Selene Bourgani the film actress.

She was leaning against a bar in a nightclub and she was lit bright in the middle of dim bodies drinking and dancing and embracing all around her and the shadows were dark and sharp-edged and her splay of hair was a wild dark shadow of its own. We saw her face in close-up and her dark eyes were enormous—Selene's eyes seemed always to be the blackest thing on the screen—and she was burning. And we saw the object of her fire: a young man dancing with a woman across the room. But not dancing with the crazed self-absorption of all the other dancers. This couple was dancing with their eyes fixed on each other. This was a couple in love.

And the movie went on. She was good. Her performance seemed far more real to me, in that enormous image at the front of the auditorium, than I'd remembered from my previous encounters with her films. But from what I knew of her, what I knew of her body, what our two bodies knew of each other, perhaps from the fact that I had lately been the object of her fire, I could only see this woman on the screen as Selene.

In the next scene it was clear that this Lilith Weiss had come to possess the young man she'd desired in the nightclub. But she cast him off in the morning and ruined him with the woman he'd loved. And the movie went on, and she carried on in this same way. Selene played the modern succubus, seeking out men in the night and seducing them and then abandoning them and destroying them by exposing their deeds to their wives and to the world.

She had a long and sometimes delicate, sometimes horrific solitary scene in her own small room where she remembered her father and how he went out and destroyed women in just such a way and how he always came back home and beat her mother. And Selene rose after these memories and opened a drawer in her commode and took out a photograph of her mother and she looked at it and wept.

All of this was filmed in a severely stylized urban landscape, where nothing stood straight, where everything leaned and tilted as if to fall; where everything was stalked by or shrouded in shadow; where black and white abutted along razor-cut borders; where people appeared and vanished before your eyes.

And at last she saw a man in a park berating his wife and then slapping her across the cheek. And Selene—this Lilith—stalked this man, and she began the process of seduction, as she did the others, and she brought him back to her room. But this man she did not expose; this man she did not abandon. As he was eagerly stripping down to his union suit, she moved to her commode and opened the drawer, and for the first time we could see inside. There was her mother's picture. And there was a pistol. She took out the pistol. And she shot the man to death.

Several times I looked at Selene as she watched herself from an aisle seat of the *Cinéma De Pera*. Each time it had been the same: her face was lifted slightly, in precisely the same angle; her face flickered softly from the light of the screen; she showed no emotion whatsoever. And I looked a last time when the man she'd shot on screen doubled over and sank to his knees.

This time she closed her eyes, not to avoid seeing this act but softly, as if to meditate. And then she lowered her face and she opened her eyes. She turned her face directly to me. As if she'd known I was there all along.

I nodded to her.

She did not nod in return. But neither did she take her face from mine.

I raised my hands before me and I gave her a slow-motion, sound-less round of applause. When I finished, she turned her face away again. She lowered her veil and then she sat waiting, as did I, until the screen flickered dark, the piano fell silent, the house lights went up full, and the audience filed past us.

When the ushers rushed by, toward the front to prepare the theater for the next showing, Selene and I rose. I stepped into the aisle first and waited for her. She turned to me. She stopped. She even lifted her veil.

The face she presented felt recently familiar. It had a sense of an extinguished light, of a mind emptied of memory but full of its sad effects. It was the face of the solitary Lilith Weiss as she looked up from the picture of her mother in her hand.

"We have to talk now," I said.

And she said, "Not till we are sitting at your table in the hotel salon."

48

Selene Bourgani and I arrived at the corner table where I'd spent the afternoon. After four reels' worth of piano music at the cinema tonight, another piano was playing at the far end of the salon. We settled into our chairs and Selene lifted her veil, but the piano's slow, sad little waltz turned both our faces toward it.

Then she looked at me.

She shivered. Very faintly, but I saw it and I knew what it was about. I *sensed* it more than saw it, really. And I knew what it was because I felt a small, similar tremor myself.

"We both heard that," I said.

"Yes," she said.

On the *Lusitania* the night we met. "Songe d'Automne."

I laid my forearm on the tabletop, stretching halfway toward her, and she looked at it.

She slowly removed her black gloves, watching the process closely as she did so.

She sensed the incipient lift of my arm from the table, more intention than action.

"Wait," she said softly.

I stopped.

She put her bare right hand on top of mine for a moment. She squeezed. She withdrew.

"I haven't forgotten what you did," she said.

I wished I could omit the talk for this evening, could just drink with her and take her to her room and hope for *gentle please* on this night, as uncharacteristic as I'd always thought that was for me with a woman.

But it was I who had to get rough now, in another way.

I think she knew it.

She was reading my face. "Let's order some wine before we speak," she said.

"Yes."

"Something French," she said.

And so we decided upon a white, a chilled bottle of an oakey Pouilly-Fuissé.

We took our first sips without touching glasses. We weren't superstitious types. We both knew we had business to do.

"When did you see me tonight?" I asked.

"Before I stepped into the salon," she said.

"I'm glad you're taking precautions," I said. "Things will get difficult now."

She laughed softly. "As if they haven't already?"

"I prefer surprises to unknowns."

She nodded.

I said, "And there are too many unknowns ahead of us as it is. We can't have any between us now."

She looked at me. "I thought we had an agreement."

"That lapsed," I said.

She waited.

I had to play my possibilities as certainties.

"Why would an Armenian go to bed with a Turk?" I said. And even as her eyes flickered, telling me I was right, I added, "Especially a Turk with the blood of your people on his hands."

She made her eyes go dead and she took a sip of her wine.

"I told you I'm only doing this for myself," she said, though her voice was too soft, too much on the verge of a tremor.

"You need to hope the movies never start to talk," I said.

She knew what I meant.

"I'm not acting," she said.

"That's why I can tell you're lying," I said.

"Don't you think my people want to know his plans?"

That thought had continued to kick around in me and I figured it would stop kicking once she confessed it. It didn't.

"What's your name?" I said, moving away to the unexpected question for now, the easier question to answer. I would play this in that other persona, a role I found myself missing: Christopher Cobb, reporter. I missed simply getting a fragment of a fact here, another there, and then wedding them in my Corona, putting it on the street and moving on.

But my life was on the line. Hers too. I could do this like a reporter only if it worked.

"Selene Bourgani," she said, but she *played* the lie now. Her voice said to me: *Guess.*

Selene was the Greek goddess of the moon. "What's the Armenian word for the moon?" I asked.

She smiled. "My name," she said.

I waited.

She leaned to me across the table. Her voice went very soft. She said, "Can't we just go upstairs now and fuck?"

I am a man of words. Words and theatrics. King James for words. Shakespeare for theatrics. For both, actually. I love that forbidden word, to be honest. The possibility of that word. And at this moment her using that word felt as if she had just put her hands together at the center of her chest in this public place and ripped open her black bodice and exposed her naked breasts.

But I said, "No. We can't."

She didn't speak. She looked at me and I looked at her. Then she said, "Lucine."

I did not speak.

And she said, "My name is Lucine Bedrosian."

"Thank you," I said.

She did not speak.

"It's a beautiful name," I said.

Her eyes filled with tears. These were not sentimental tears. Her face had tightened; her jaw had clenched. I thought for a moment she was angry at me for forcing her to say her name.

But she said, "If we are ever alone again . . ." And she stopped. She worked to control her voice. "In the way that we *have* been alone." She was in control now. "I would like you to say that name."

"I will," I said.

"But never anywhere else," she said.

I nodded. I lifted my glass and held it between us. She lifted hers and she touched mine and we drank. And I wanted the curtain to come down on that. The chapter to end. But it couldn't.

Her glass was empty. I poured in three fingers. I did the same in mine.

I said this as gently as I could. "Did your father try to talk you out of coming here?"

There was a stopping in her.

I didn't mean to play upon her so ruthlessly. She had no idea I'd been there.

"Briefly," she said.

"I was at the pub on the docks in London."

This was a moment like the moment that eventually arrived in the sex between us. After she'd held her own, after she'd worked back at me, at some moment she would let go, she would let me carry us forward.

"You were there?"

"Yes."

She shook her head no, not to doubt what I said but to wonder at how she'd missed this.

"I was standing at the bar," I said.

"You followed me."

"Yes. Brauer did too. He was outside, waiting. I followed both of you."

She'd been sitting in the way women sit, dining or drinking in public: upright, nearly at the edge of the chair. But at this, her head and her shoulders did a slow slump, stopped by her elbows landing on the arms of the chair, and she turned her face away, looking off vaguely toward the far end of the salon, where the piano was playing a Chopin nocturne.

"That's why he came to me on the North Sea," she said.

Mostly to herself, explaining what she never quite understood.

When she let a few moments go by without speaking, I said, "And why you shot him."

She straightened a bit; she looked at me. "Yes," she said. "He didn't figure it out as completely as you did, and I guess that night at the bar he convinced himself this man was just some aging money bag who'd been keeping me. But some of the details kept working at him. And he finally came to my cabin and confronted me. He wasn't cut out for this work. He hadn't said anything to anyone else about his suspicions and he was stupid enough to tell me so. And he was starting to talk crazy. He was threatening to make trouble in Istanbul. What I did, it felt like self-defense. And he was going to hurt a lot more people than me."

This all came out in a quiet rush.

Then it stopped, and she took a slug of wine like it was whiskey. When her glass was down, she looked me hard in the eyes. "You would've done the same," she said.

And things began to fit together. The Armenians seemed to be, from all accounts, particularly inept at organizing and defending themselves. What good would a little bed talk from Enver Pasha do them? She wasn't giving herself to him for that. And then there was her question on the first night she and I made love. *Have you ever killed a man?*

And then tonight. As if I were picking a lock, the final tumbler lifted: she'd needed to see her German movie. The climactic scene. She'd played this role once before.

"You're going to kill him," I said.

49

And she fled.

She rose up instantly and walked away. I wasn't about to try to stop her. The Germans could be watching us from any of a dozen occupied tables around the salon.

Maybe that saved my life. She probably had her pistol in her little bag. Maybe she would have liked to shoot me dead there in the Kubbeli Salon for endangering her plan.

I could see how that plan would seem mortally important, once you'd committed to it. This was the manifesto of any band of nationalists whose numbers were small and whose people were unfocused and unorganized and accustomed to repression: one isolated act could change everything. And they figured this belief had been confirmed last June. An anonymous, undersized Bosnian teenager with a nationalist cause and a sandwich in his hand started the war with two bullets.

I gave her a few minutes to get to her room and then I rose and left the salon.

I was a bit unsteady on my feet. I'd had a lot to drink today. And I didn't know what to do next. This woman who had a hold on me had a new name and a deadly mission. I didn't give a good goddamn about Enver Pasha's life. But I was afraid for Selene.

No.

I was afraid for *Lucine*.

I was afraid she and her nationalist cohorts, whoever they might be, didn't have an adequate way out for her after the deed was done. How could they? This whole thing was full of unknowns.

I wobbled before my door.

I thought to knock on Lucine's.

But there was nothing to be done for now.

And so I went in and I lay down on the bed, and from the darkness coming upon me, I figured I would slip at once into asleep. But there was another darkness first. I thought: *She might even be in this alone. She might even be expecting to die.* Another thing she said that first night we touched, that goddamn first night: *An actress is a fallen woman.*

And I woke to her voice.

I opened my eyes. The sun was bright through my balcony doors.

I'd dreamed her voice, I thought. And I'd forgotten already what it was she'd said.

"Kit. It's me." Selene's voice. Lucine's voice.

I sat up.

She was outside the door.

A clear but restrained knock.

"Kit," she said. "Please."

I got up and crossed the room. I opened the door.

Admittedly I was groggy and my head was pounding from *raki* and wine, but I had trouble comprehending what was before me: an undersized teenage boy dressed in shirt and trousers of dark blue duck and wearing an oversized sunrain hat. A boy gone to sea. And then the pale face was familiar, and this was Lucine's little brother standing there. And then it was Lucine herself, as if playing some Shakespearean comedy heroine disguised as a boy. She was Viola or Julia or Rosaline, and she stepped into my room and closed the door.

She placed herself squarely before me and very near and she reached out and laid her palm in the center of my chest.

"Listen to me," she said. "I'm sorry for the way things ended last night. You are a very smart man. A very capable man. I'm not used to feeling that unprepared."

She took a minute breath and words were rushing to form in my mouth and she stayed them with a very soft push of that hand on my chest. "Especially about something so important," she said.

I insisted on speaking the words that had formed: "I wish I'd thought of some better way."

"No," she said. "None of this is easy. Will you come with me now, please? No questions?"

Without hesitating I said, "All right."

"I woke you up," she said.

"Yes."

"Make sure you're ready."

I seemed to be dressed except for my shoes. My Mauser was in place. I excused myself and I stepped into the bathroom and pushed the door mostly to and somehow this was not awkward with Lucine now. "Have you practiced doing this for your role?" I asked from where I stood.

"To hell with you and your Stanislavsky," she said.

I was ready.

I stepped out and she was standing in front of the door, facing me. She waited for me to cross to her.

She said, "I'll raise some eyebrows walking through the lobby. But it will be quick. Follow me at a distance. Just make sure no one is following *you*."

"Will we turn at the corner of the hotel?"

"Yes."

"Give me a few moments afterward," I said.

"I understand," she said.

Briskly now she spun and put her hand on the doorknob.

But she slowed herself; she paused.

She did not, however, look at me. She said, "Thank you."

"I've never kissed a boy," I said.

Now she turned.

"For good luck," she said.

I bent to her. She was no goddamn boy. We kissed, and in spite of her yet again withholding something important from me and in spite of her being in the midst of overtly portraying someone she was not, this felt like the first kiss between us in which our mouths truly, fully touched.

The kiss ended. Her eyes seemed bright as they opened to me. Our faces drew away slowly.

She said, "Have I changed you forever?"

"We'll see," I said.

And we went out.

I stayed four or five paces behind her as she moved across the salon with her hips fixed and her legs a little bowed—a boy from a ship at the quay—and a couple of faces turned to look at her but we were through the doors and into the foyer and past the bellhops without a word being said and she turned left and left again at the corner of the hotel and we were heading down the hill toward the Bosporus.

I took a few steps after the turn and I stopped and faced back the way I'd come. If a Hun was following, he'd come around that corner shortly.

I would wait. And I waited, and a couple of men in suits and fezes came round and went by talking intensely and seeming to utterly ignore me.

They continued on past the lingering Lucine fifteen yards or so farther along. She was standing a step or two into the street, smoking a cigarette.

After they were gone, I looked over my shoulder and a phaeton came around the corner at a gallop and rushed by, but there was no one coming on foot.

I looked back at Lucine and nodded, and she nodded, and she took off.

I followed her.

50

It was a Monday morning and the city was in high stir. Which felt, in some basic ways, not unlike Chicago or St. Louis or New York for a couple hundred yards, if you factored out the Frenchy flavor to the stores. But we crossed the Grand Rue de Péra and not long afterward we were heading downhill pretty severely and the street narrowed and the sidewalks filled with people and they were hurtling always and looking utterly through you and bumping your shoulders.

All the garbage and waste on this street and in every side street had been transformed by tramping feet and rolling cart wheels and dissolving rain into a Turkish carpet of unnameable waste, and you had to work hard to keep your balance with the angle of the hill and the broken cobbles and this slumgum of scum underfoot.

The buildings turned from stone to wood and smacked of the German expressionist cinema, with all the upper floors corbeled out to hang over one another and the street, and at all times they seemed about to tumble down upon you, and among these the Muslim residences identified themselves by the window latticework of the second and third stories, where the women sat to see the world without allowing themselves to be seen.

And still the bodies surged and bumped and went on and the air was full of the smell of rot and offal and mammal waste and the assertions of new food, as well, the stuff to keep you alive *now*, the roasting of a lamb, the cutting of a melon, the airing and cooking of pepper and garlic and onion, and of course the smell of coffee and the smell of tobacco.

Along the storefronts and along the rubble-strewn empty lots between buildings and along the ashlar walls were barbers and coffee servers and fruit sellers, and now I passed even a couple of scribes at tiny desks on the sidewalk hiring themselves out to the illiterate to write letters that dunned an acquaintance for repayment of a loan or begged a rich uncle for money or supplicated a woman's father to arrange a marriage or even wooed the woman herself.

With the lurch and surge of bodies it was always a struggle to keep the sailor boy in duck blue and the big hat in sight. But we made it to the bottom of the hill and entered the Place Karakeuï at the mouth of the Galata Bridge, and Lucine slowed and I didn't know if I was supposed to come closer.

She glanced over her shoulder and nodded and I came up. The welter around us was a great shrouding fog of humanity, though instantly we had to dodge aside as two *hamals*—men of the porter guild—bore down on us carrying their loads on their backs, one man lashed with three enormous gunnysacks, the other bent almost double with a four-foot-square wooden box strapped to him with leather, and they were screaming at each other in Kurdish and would have run us over if we had not looked for them and leaped away. And though their voices were near and were loud, they vanished at once in the great ocean roar of the voices and the languages of the drivers and porters and soldiers and boatmen and hawkers who all gabbled and cried and cursed in Turkish and Greek and Macedonian and Arabic and Albanian and Montenegrin and Corsican and a dozen more tongues, and these waves of human sounds crashed through the sounds of the steamer whistles and the auto engines and the snorting and panting of horses laboring by and now a camel brushing past grumbling and spitting.

Lucine plucked at my sleeve and we wove our way to the edge of the square and down stone steps smelling of fish long dead but also of the sea—the incongruously bright blue Bosporus was immediately before us—and we cut along the cobbles of the quayside.

"We're meeting the *Principesa Maria,*" she said.

She pointed along ahead. A ship was mooring off the quay, a one-stack steamer that looked to be a shipyard cousin to the *Dacia.*

"In from Constanța?" I asked.

"Yes," she said. "I'll go ahead now. Stay close. I'll find you." She nodded toward a loose gathering of people near the stand of phaetons and taxis at the quayside road.

I moved off in that direction, stopping short of the group, finding a place to stand alone and watch Lucine play the dockside boy, acting as if he were waiting at the bollard to tie off the incoming launch from the *Principesa Maria,* though hanging back enough from the actual dockhand so as not to be challenged.

It took a while, of course, the offloading of the first wave of passengers from the ship, the trip to the quay, the docking there, and Lucine playing her part, in the manner now of an apprentice to the work, watching intently, and then sliding away as the passengers came down the gangplank.

This was a bit of theater for me, with an actress I admired in a starring role, and it happened with a constant flow of people and carts around and before me, and for some time now—even in the descent from Pera—I'd more or less stopped closely observing things in specific. I'd begun taking things in as broader impressions, which was not my way as a newsman but which I'd lapsed into as I'd let go to Lucine directing the scene.

I'd stopped thinking. I'd stopped being fully, concretely aware. I simply waited to see what Lucine would do next.

It did not occur to me—distracted as I was by Lucine the young man—that *Der Wolf* might be on that ship. Not till later.

And so I waited. I stood there on the quay, a little apart from the others who were waiting, while passengers from Constanța and beyond flowed up the cobbled quay toward me and around me and past me.

And then there was a moment when Lucine fell out of character. I could see it in her body, its abrupt change from hovering apprenticeship to a motionless, upright focus directed at the gang-plank. I looked for who it might be in the present file of passengers emerging from the launch.

At the top of the gangplank, pausing briefly, scanning widely and quickly and then, starting to descend, was a broad-shouldered man in a suit, a man whose face was strikingly featured and came into recognizable clarity halfway down the plank. It was Lucine's father.

51

When he reached the bottom of the gangway, he fixed on the boy before him and I figured he recognized Lucine. After that one beat of a pause, she turned her back on him, faced in my direction, and started walking this way. He immediately followed.

She approached, a couple of arm lengths to my left, and I watched her face closely. Just before she drew near, she caught my eyes and did a careful turn of her head motioning me, as I understood it, to head along the quayside street in the direction away from Place Karakeuï. I had no choice but to trust that interpretation.

She passed, the father passed without looking at me, and I walked off, angling up to Rimtim Caddesi, and I began to follow it north. After about a hundred yards I was approaching the west end of the dry docks, near the nighttime rendezvous place Hansen had set up if we needed to exit Istanbul in a hurry. A short distance ahead was a sharp left turn at a warehouse. I stopped and turned to look back.

This was not a deserted stretch of road. Perhaps such a place as that did not exist within Istanbul during the daylight hours. Turks had been pressing past from the north heading south and a man on a bicycle had just brushed by me on the earthen shoulder of the road to my right, keeping off the cobbles, his bell clinging furiously. So when I turned, I found a Turk was striding toward me. He was close and I started a bit but I did not think for a moment he was follow-ing me; he was a Turk of the sort I'd seen dozens of times already along the streets, vending or getting a shave or drinking coffee on the edge of an empty lot. He already was adjusting his course to go around me but not by enough to avoid bumping me. I assessed his authenticity instantly.

But I saw a man following twenty yards or so farther behind, nattily dressed and carrying a kit bag, and this man was a Westerner—trim, moving light on his feet, heavily bewhiskered with muttonchops—and my suspicion sprung instantly into full flame. I made the immediate decision not to let him think he'd been recognized. As soon as I saw him I looked away, focusing without any pause on the Turk, who obliged by bumping me, letting me spin to his receding figure and curse him.

And then I continued to walk north.

If Muttonchops was following me still, I'd find a better place to confront him. And it was now that it struck me that the next ship from Constanţa could also have been bearing *Der Wolf* and there I'd been—standing in plain sight—and if he knew me I would have made his job very easy. I was aware of my Mauser in the small of my back.

Would he shoot me from behind in a busy Istanbul street?

I didn't think so.

The warehouse was approaching. I could make a last-moment dash for the building.

But this guy was a professional. A specialist with the knack. There were too many risks in public. And he didn't know I was portraying Brauer, so he didn't know where I was staying. For now, perhaps he'd just follow.

The warehouse was only a half dozen paces away.

I had to decide.

And then the plosive chatter of an automobile engine rushed up from behind and I saw the vehicle stopping in my periphery as I heard the goose honk of its horn.

I looked.

I stopped.

A Unic taxi was waiting beside me.

The door of the tonneau opened.

I could see inside. Lucine, her sunrain hat off, her hair piled beautifully on her faux-boy's head, and her father beyond her, his face brought forward and turned toward me.

I took the two quick strides to them and stepped into the tonneau and sat down facing father and daughter. Lucine closed the door and leaned across me—smelling only of herself this time, no perfume, just her own hot-morning musk—and she rapped on the front window.

As she retreated to her seat, I slid toward the center of mine and then rose up from it a little so I could see discreetly between her and her father and out the back window.

Muttonchops was continuing to walk in our direction and closing on us steadily. He was keeping his eyes forward with a disinterested air, but as the driver ground the taxi into gear, he turned his face to us.

In the morning sunlight, I didn't know if he could see through the back window and into the depths of the tonneau, but if he could, he and I were looking each other in the eyes.

I sat back down as we began to move, and he appeared again in the window, receding as we accelerated away. He had stopped. He was watching us. We made the turn west and he vanished from my sight. One thing seemed clear, and I strongly suspected another. This man was following me. And I bet he smelled of spirit gum.

52

As soon as I sat back in my seat, I felt the intense gaze of Lucine's father even before I fully saw it.

I turned to him, engaged the look, as Lucine was saying to me, "You already know this is my father. I've only had a brief time to explain our situation to him. Just since he and I got into the taxi."

"You're not Brauer," the man said.

"I'm not."

"You saved my daughter and you know too much and you're trustworthy."

"I did and I do and I am," I said.

And I waited for either Lucine or her father to carry things forward. Had this man just learned that her daughter shot a man to death? Or was that to come?

He turned to her. The intensity of his gaze had not diminished. "And so?" he said.

She had not told him.

This was a Lucine I had not seen before. Oddly, the illusion of her as a young man, barely out of adolescence, grew strong. She was a boy standing before a father, trying to confess a terrible thing, but a thing that directly touched on the boy's nascent manhood. And yet I believed the feelings I saw to be entirely hers, entirely Lucine Bedrosian's: the breathless thrum about her; her hand, faintly quaking, reaching for her father's without her taking her eyes from his. He was not aware of the gesture until she touched his wrist. He put his other hand over hers, also without moving his eyes away, but the intensity of his gaze faltered for a moment.

She said, "I killed him." This was soft and it was breathless but then I watched her rise up from herself, watched the actress in her assert itself, and she clarified her statement: "I had no choice but to kill him." And the voice was different and she had changed. She had returned to the Selene Bourgani I had known.

The father did not turn his face away, did not shift his eyes from her. I wondered if he too had heard a thing in her that he had not heard in a long time, that he had even forgotten was in her. If so, he also saw that thing vanish once more.

He showed nothing to me. Or to her. He simply kept his eyes on her.

She said, "He knew what we were going to do. He was a threat."
She said this quite convincingly.

Her father seemed, in his steady, neutral gaze, to be at least reconciled to, and maybe even satisfied with, maybe even admiring of what his daughter had done.

And as I watched this moment of silence passing calmly between them, the image returned: a father and a son, the father pleased with his boy who had just showed him he could be a man.

Then another obvious question came upon me: Did he know her intentions with Enver Pasha?

The moment between them ended with the father squeezing his daughter's hand. And Lucine moved her own from beneath her father's and squeezed his in return, but as a mood changer, as an encouragement. She simultaneously nodded toward me, saying, "I believe this man can play a plausible Walter Brauer. He is the son of Isabel Cobb."

The father's eyebrows jumped.

He squared around to look at me. Then he took a deep breath, his barrel chest rising, and he let go of my eyes, lifting his face and turning it slightly to the side. A beseeching furrow came upon his brow, and in a mellifluous baritone he began to speak what I now knew to be Armenian, the sounds rolling and plashing like breakers on an ocean's shore. There was no mistaking that he was or had once been an actor. It ran in the family.

His voice rose and fell and rose in wrenching emotion and then abruptly stopped. He fell out of character and returned his eyes to mine. "Do you know what I have said?" he asked, his English bent by his native inflection but bent intermittently by London as well.

"I do not," I said.

"To be or not to be," he said. "That is the question. Whether 'tis nobler in the mind to suffer the slings and arrows of outrageous fortune . . ."

And here his daughter chimed in and they finished in unison: ". . . or to take arms against a sea of troubles, and by opposing, end them."

He put his arm around her shoulders and gave her a little squeeze, and he let go just before her own hand fully rose to brush his away.

She angled her head toward her father, and she said to me, rather flatly, "I'm told he was a wonderful Hamlet."

He spread his hands before him, "Alas, only in my native language."

"This is the great Armenian theatrical star of Transcaucasia, Arshak Bedrosian," she said. I could not decide if she was sincere about his greatness or sarcastic, and so I decided she was both.

The father offered his hand to me at the belated mention of his name—which I grasped—but even as we shook, he continued his muted argument with his daughter, "I was with the Armenian Theater in Tiflis."

"My mother and I," Lucine said, "were three hundred and fifty miles away."

"On the bank of the Tigris. Where my wife had family ties and the only performers were donkeys cavorting for the moon."

"I never saw his Hamlet," Lucine said, and a faint but unmistakable wistfulness had slipped into her voice.

"You were merely a child," Arshak said, though he did not look at Lucine, keeping his eyes on mine. "And I did bring you to Tiflis."

"For a very brief time," she said.

"Do you know the greatest Hamlet I ever saw?" he said to me.

"Do you see how his mind works?" Lucine said.

"I'm talking strictly professionally," he said, arguing directly with her again. "To a man who knows the theater."

"This is the true reason he stayed in Tiflis," she said.

"To a man who knows what makes a great actress."

Lucine looked away from both of us, out the side window of the taxi.

I was watching all this in a sort of trance that these two were inducing in me. The scene they'd played together about the killing had segued into this quite different little drama with remarkable ease, with the two of them in instinctive cahoots even if this playlet was entitled "A Daughter's Lament for Fatherly Betrayals."

"The greatest Hamlet of all," Arshak said, "was a woman." He paused and lifted his chin. I glanced at Lucine, who had closed her eyes. "Siranush," he said grandly.

"His mistress," Lucine said.

"The greatest actress of the Armenian stage."

"I saw her perform only once," she said.

"The greatest of *any* stage," he said.

"She did not move me."

Arshak leaned in my direction. "Your mother is the exception, of course. I have heard how splendid she is. Has she ever played Hamlet?"

"She never has," I said.

I turned my face to Lucine, on stage even now as a man, her eyes tracking the street, perhaps inwardly soliloquizing about her failed parent. And she said to her father, "You fell for her britches."

"A lie," Arshak said. "It was her talent."

And I said to him in my head: *She's got you nailed. Didn't your daughter just prove her own britches to you? Didn't you fall for that? Isn't that why you were so quickly okay with what she did?*

Arshak drew back again into his seat. A moment went by. His daughter had stirred something in him.

I watched Lucine as she watched the street, and I listened to the silence coming from Arshak Bedrosian. And then he said, quite softly but clearly, "I hope she is still in Tiflis. They will kill her otherwise."

At this, Lucine turned once more to her father. I did too. He started a bit, at the attention. He looked to his daughter.

"I'm sorry," he said. "What is this talk we are making? We have lost our way."

"Yes," she said, though the inflection of criticism in her voice seemed directed inward, an acceptance of shared blame.

Arshak said, "'Tis nobler to take arms against a sea of troubles."

And they both looked at me.

They'd changed the play yet again.

I sought refuge out the window. I had not been keeping track of where we were going, though we were following the Bosporus north. A minaret flashed by and for a moment the water was visible beyond the mosque. Then it vanished with a run of trees and then a high stone wall that kept going on and on and contained within it, I suspected, the grounds of the Palace of Dolmabahçe.

Arshak began speaking Armenian.

I looked at him, thinking he and Lucine were saying things they didn't want me to hear.

But he was talking into the taxi's communication tube. The driver was Armenian. Of course he was. One of theirs.

I looked over my shoulder into the driver's compartment. He could have been the model for the character Lucine was playing. He was small and very young, a teenager still.

When I turned back to Arshak, he lifted his chin toward the driver. "They tell me his father was murdered a few weeks ago."

"Seems a tough kid," I said.

"This is what's left of his old man," he said, laying both his hands on the seat. Then, after a beat: "Which leads me to a request. May we have a little of your time to speak?"

"We already seem to be on the way."

"There's a safe place," Arshak said.

"We can speak," I said.

"Among some friends you'll find unlikely," he said.

"What your daughter has begun and I've gotten caught up in means nothing is safe."

He shrugged. "Of course. To be Armenian in the Ottoman Empire also means nothing is safe. But at least perhaps for the next hour we won't die. We do not intend to catch you up. Just to explain."

"I'm not afraid for myself."

Arshak laughed softly. "This much I could sense about you already."

Whatever he had to explain to me, I wanted it to be the straight dope. I figured—as I would if I were here getting an inside news story—that I needed to establish my savvy. I said, "When the two of you met at the Block and Tackle last week, you seemed estranged at first."

He turned sharply to Lucine.

"I didn't know," she said.

He turned sharply to me.

More or less the effect I'd hoped for. I'd cast them in my own little drama.

I stayed placid.

He smiled. He knew what was going on.

He shrugged. "Well, yes. I am her father. I did not like what she was planning."

"And you understand that to be what?"

"I'm not at liberty to say."

"Do you know she will try to kill Enver Pasha?"

Neither of them flinched.

So he did know. So the news of her killing Brauer had gone down easy because this man had already reconciled himself to his daughter taking lives. Brauer was a warm-up.

Only one point needed clarification. I said, with some heat, "You didn't like what *she* was planning? Wasn't this a request from the Armenian underground? An assignment?" I heard myself. It sounded as if I knew the answer to those questions was *Yes, this was an assignment* and I was furious about it in a personal way.

Though she said, "No. It was entirely my idea," and I believed this and it didn't surprise me.

As much in control of my own performance as I thought I was, I must have revealed something I was unaware of, because Arshak narrowed his gaze on me and then turned slowly to his daughter and looked at her. Something flashed into her face that she no doubt showed as a little girl when she was caught stealing a cookie or kicking the cat.

He looked back to me.

He was her father. He knew exactly what his daughter and I had been doing.

I watched for a flicker of jealousy.

"She fell for your britches," he said, with a little smile directed at her.

"It was my talent," I said.

"We'll see about that," he said.

I looked at Lucine and back to her father. I'd readily followed her this morning to the quay and into a taxi, but I had to slow down now. I understood that she needed me to deliver her to Enver Pasha. But my stake in this—my country's stake—was no longer a flow of high-level inside information. Hansen had figured that might be of interest to Trask and the boys stateside. But taking a hand in the assassination of the leader of the Ottoman Empire was a whole other thing. Even if it could stay covert.

"I have to be clear," I said. "I agreed to help a German spy in return for the same intelligence she gave them. I didn't agree to help her kill Enver Pasha."

"That's why we want to talk," Arshak said.

Talk? Perhaps. But when I leaned back in my seat, I was reassured by the heavy nuzzle of my Mauser.

53

But the talk—or whatever else they had in mind—was deferred. We rode in silence now as the taxi entered the outlying village of Ortakiöi and we turned at the green-domed mosque on the bank of the Bosporus and headed inland, up the hill and into the densely populated Jewish quarter. The taxi dropped us at the mouth of a narrow street and we walked into its compressed air, which was full of the stench of sewage and the din of street voices, speaking mostly Ladino, the special mix of Hebrew and Spanish that the Sephardim carried with them into exile from Iberia.

We passed between the rows of wooden buildings. Most of them followed the Turkish form of overhanging, corbeled stories, but we climbed on and finally approached a break in the attached houses, near the top of the hill. Here was a longer, flat-fronted, three-story building, with several entrances along it and with a street or an alley on each side, an architectural descendant of the *yahudihane* that filled this de facto Jewish ghetto a couple of centuries ago.

We turned in at the center of the three entrances to the *yahudihane*, its doorpost affixed with a mezuzah, its metal casing rubbed bright from the faithful passing through this door.

And inside, the sound from outside grew dim, and the stench faded with the smell of coffee and tobacco. The large central room of this coffeehouse could have been found in the coffeehouses in any part of Pera or Stamboul or Galata, with its divans and tapestry rugs and small tables for the coffee trays. The clientele, however, was special. The clearest sign was the group of half a dozen men sipping coffee together near the door. They were the most ardent *Sephardim* in their gaberdines and long beards. As for the rest of the men in the room, though they were dressed in Western suits and jackets like the coffee-shop Turks, the inner edge of their coats or vests showed the woolen fringe of their prayer shawls. Many of them wore skullcaps, the yarmulke, with their secular clothes, at least in this select company, and no doubt their shorter beards were managed by scissors and clippers only.

Among the suited, close-clipped contingent was the owner of the coffee shop, who greeted Arshak now with a *Merhabah* and then accepted his hand for a warm handshake. And immediately behind him was another man, a man with a boxer's build at the age when a boxer starts to think about retiring. He wore a dark gray fez that didn't taper to the top.

The owner stepped aside for him and he came forward to embrace Arshak, and the two men spoke quickly, intensely, in Armenian. Lucine and I stood waiting, and the owner, apart from us but watching us closely, waited too.

Then Arshak and the other man stopped and Arshak turned to us full of blustery goodwill. "Fine," he said. "Fine. Let's have some coffee." He was acting.

The Jew led the four of us through the room and out a back door into the courtyard, paved in field stone with a solitary fig tree growing in an earthen plot at the center. We sat at a horseshoe of iron benches: Arshak by himself on the bench at the apex, I on one of the sides, Lucine and the other man across from me, these two sitting at opposite ends of their bench. I sensed nothing between them.

The owner lingered briefly and bowed himself away and a young man in shirtsleeves, with yarmulke and ear locks, immediately whisked in with a low table, and another followed him with water pipes, and a third with coffee on trays.

In all of this, Lucine played the boy and kept her mouth shut.

After the young Jews left us and we were settled, Arshak said to me, "This is Tigran."

Tigran nodded at me while Arshak spoke to him in Armenian again, perhaps to explain my unexpected presence in their plans.

When Arshak finished, Tigran stood and stepped toward me and I stood too and we met in the middle and shook hands. He said something in Armenian.

Arshak translated, even as Tigran continued the handshake: "He said he appreciates your sympathy for our people in this dark time."

I said to Arshak, "Tell him with a grip like his, I'm glad we are on the same side."

Arshak laughed and translated and Tigran laughed and through Arshak complimented me on my own grip. And that was it with Tigran. He sat back down and more or less vanished. I'd seen this happen many times before, covering wars abroad. He and I were a couple of guys who might have gone on to talk about a lot of things in common, but instead we might as well have been a couple of fig trees in a field because of the one thing we didn't have in common. Words.

Then Arshak picked up his cup and saucer, and we all followed his lead and we took a sip of coffee, holding both saucer and cup, Turkish style.

Things suddenly felt oddly relaxed, given the situation. We seemed to be waiting for something.

I thought to keep my mouth shut and let them make the next move, even if it was in the conversation. But I said to Arshak, nodding toward the front of the coffee shop, "I don't find their friendship so unlikely." I knew enough about the situation to see past the classic schism of Christianity and Judaism.

"Then you know what binds us," Arshak said.

"Persecution."

"Good," he said. "I thought I'd have to explain that first. Ours is not so well known as theirs."

"You share the Turks," I said.

He grew expansive. "That's an odd thing," he said. "The Turks despise the Jews in the street, face to face. But formally, by government attitude and even decree, they've made them safe. The Muslims and the Jews share the Old Testament more directly, and I think that makes the Jews tolerable to them in the abstract. The Armenians, however. We're Christians. And worse, we are stained with the sin of having been a thriving nation in this land long before Turkey and the Ottoman Empire even existed, and by the fact that centuries ago the Turks stole everything from us. People and nations are the same: we preserve a special hatred for those we've already abused."

With this, he paused. Lucine had been watching him as if from the back row of the orchestra seats. But now she leaned a little in his direction.

"The matter at hand," she said to him with surprising gentleness.

He nodded in acknowledgment without looking at her. He said, "Three weeks ago, three hundred of the elite Armenian thinkers and leaders in Istanbul—writers and priests, politicians and publishers, teachers and artists, all of our best minds—were arrested by the government and deported overnight from the capital. They were imprisoned beyond Angora. Those that got that far. We've been told reliably that a group of them—twenty or so, ones with voices, writers like you—were murdered on the way to Ayaş."

"But they *all* will die," Lucine said. "Soon."

Her voice faltered ever so slightly. She paused. She was about to speak again when we all heard feet scuffling on the fieldstones from the direction of the courtyard door.

Two men stood there. They were suited up looking like Turks but I knew somehow they belonged. They could have been Tigran's sparring partners. One was a light heavyweight, one a welterweight. All three of them were swarthy and rough featured, of the same blood as the boys in the bar on the London Docks.

Part of me sensed trouble.

Tigran and Arshak stood up at once. Lucine looked to me and she rose. I rose with her. She stepped to me.

"I'm going back to the hotel now," she said.

"Who are these men?" I asked.

She looked in their direction.

"They're with Tigran," she said.

"Look me in the eyes," I said.

She did.

They were steady. But she was an actress.

"I thought you and your father had something to explain," I said.

"A thing has come up," she said. "They'd like to take you a little farther."

"Not you?"

"You can ride a horse?"

"Yes."

"Where you will go is out of the way. I need to get back to the hotel and prepare for Enver Pasha."

Her eyes lost their focus a little now, drifted. But not from lying. "First impressions," she said. "This one for him has to be distractingly good."

Arshak was beside me now. "Will you come with us?" he asked, as if I had a choice. But he was an actor.

"If I say no?" I said.

"Why would you?" he said. "You have come a very long way with us already."

I looked at Lucine.

I had.

But as far as I'd come, I didn't yet instinctively trust her. And why would I trust her father? Or these three Armenian toughs? She could have made her own arrangement with the Pasha, letting passion overrule protocol.

My only alternative was to walk away. Or if I couldn't simply walk away, then shoot my way out. But to go on with them now seemed more or less what I'd signed up for when I said yes to the secret service of my country. This was a rough-riding charge up a hill.

I looked at Arshak. "Let's go," I said.

54

The welterweight Armenian—he and the other had shaken my hand but no names were exchanged—led us farther up the hill, he and Arshak talking low and intensely up ahead. Soon the wooden warrens abruptly gave way to a several-acre market garden. We turned toward the center, moving through an orchard of apricots and peaches, and we came out of the trees in an open space with a central, span-roof greenhouse growing lemons and oranges. We circled the building and five horses awaited us, a boy tending them.

Arshak nodded me to a brindle and I stroked his nose and puffed in his nostrils and whispered in his ear and he nodded and gave me the eye like we could be pals for a few hours. I went up on him and the other boys mounted, and as they did, the sack suit coat of the welterweight fell open and I could see a pistol in a shoulder holster. I suspected the light-heavy and Tigran were armed too. Maybe even Arshak, all this time.

My little Mauser suddenly—reasonably—ceased being much of a comfort. If I needed it, I'd simply go down fighting. But I shrugged this off in my head. I'd made my decision some time ago.

And we rode away on a back path out of the gardens and we were soon beyond Ortakiöi, beyond greater Istanbul, beyond Turkey for all you could tell from the rising country and the upspringing of forests of sessile oak and oriental birch and hornbeam and chestnut.

This was a very good thing. I hadn't realized how full my lungs and my head had gotten with the stink and yowl of Istanbul. Of cities in general. We climbed a trail until the air grew cool in spite of the high sun and then we were plateaued for a short time and then began to descend, picking up a quick-running stream.

And we didn't talk. We had a clear enough way for much of the time to keep up a nice hand gallop, and my brindle was a good boy, very responsive to the lightest press of a calf, a heel, a shift of my center of gravity.

We rode till the stream gave way and the land grew flat again and we cut across an open stretch of meadow grass and onto dirt road. Arshak and the guy who was leading us were just ahead of me, and they exchanged a few words, the first words of this hour and a half we'd been riding.

The road was canopied in oak for a quarter mile or so and we rounded a bend and the trees fell away and we entered a village. A gathering of small houses, some of stone, some of mud and wattle, though these were nicely whitewashed. Then a fieldstone threshing floor. And some more houses on both sides, all stone. And the striking thing was the silence. And the emptiness. My first thought: *Everyone has run away.*

We were riding slowly now. The men around me turned to look from the waist, their shoulders swinging around; these guys had gone stiff, gone vaguely urgent, vaguely agitated. And there was something in the air. A battlefield smell when the ground was contested and lost and the action moved elsewhere and the dead had been dealt with but a faint afterstench remained.

The silence in this village changed its pitch.

I glanced at a passing house, and in the street before the door lay a single flower-brocade slipper. A fancy slipper, in a village like this, from some special time in a young woman's life. A wedding perhaps. She'd once slipped her foot into this shoe to wed. My eyes followed it as I passed. I turned my head to look at it lying there, unretrieved, in a muddy rut on the village street.

Something very bad had happened here.

A hundred yards ahead was a small village square.

Arshak raised his hand and we all stopped.

No one spoke. We just sat. And even though not a head cocked, not a head inclined even slightly to the side, I could sense these men listening.

The horses shook a little and nickered a little and also fell silent.

The treetops hissed with the movement of air. Someone's saddle creaked with the shift of a body. Nothing else in this moment. Or the next.

And I was struck by this: there was no sound of birds. Not in this street or in the stand of trees around us or in the fields beyond. The birds had fled.

Then a stronger leather sound: Arshak was turning in his saddle, throwing his leg over his horse to dismount. The others followed his lead. So did I.

"Mr. Cobb," Arshak said.

The light heavyweight took my reins, holding his own in his other hand.

I moved forward to Lucine's father.

"Will you walk with me?" he said.

I nodded.

We began to move toward the village square, a working square with a stone well in the center.

Arshak said, "One of the intellectuals escaped the net on the night of April 24. A playwright, as a matter of fact. He came here. A village of two hundred of us, including his uncle and aunt. They hid him in a root cellar."

He said no more.

We walked on. Straight for the well.

And a new smell began to break over me like an invisible wave from a polluted sea, another smell like a battlefield gone silent, a smell that came with a sharp, clinging burn in the nose. The smell of chlorinated lime.

Two paces more to the waist-high circle of stones, prosceniumed by a simple wood bucket frame. Arshak put his hand on my arm to stop me.

He looked at me.

I said, "I've seen war."

"Perhaps you haven't seen this," he said.

I made the smallest movement as if to begin to step forward and Arshak put his hand on my arm again.

"*I've* never seen it," he said, and his voice, his demeanor, which had been confident, purposeful since we'd left Ortakiöi, was suddenly something else.

Of course. He'd been raging at the situation from London. He'd heard accounts. He was an exile. So far this was all just imagination to him.

"You don't have to," I said.

He did not answer.

He took his hand from my arm.

I found myself backstage, quick-changed into another character. I had two roles in this drama. Not a spy in this scene. I was a reporter. A war correspondent. I was in a country at war, and words for later were already forming in my head. About the ride up here. The silence. The shoe. I thought I was another kind of professional now. Objective. In control of myself.

I thought wrong.

The bodies down the hole were children. The lime had been slaked by the well water and by rain and I could see only the limbs of the few immediately below the child on top but there were more beneath. Many more. Of the one I saw whole, I could not say if it was a girl or a boy. The body was on its side and curled into itself as if waiting in the womb of a corpse. My gut said girl because a girl seemed more innocent to me, a girl seemed more vulnerable, a girl made me hear myself gasp as if from a great distance and made the welling in me—in my chest and in my throat and in my eyes—seem like another wave breaking, but now the polluted sea was within me.

The lime had done its work. She had not bloated. She had not been devoured. She had not come apart. She had been sucked dry. She had begun to shrivel into a thing that you thought might last a thousand years and make a future man wonder what had happened here.

But I knew what had happened.

"Mother of God," Arshak whispered beside me.

I felt him draw away.

The Turks had thrown these children in here one at a time. Extorting the whereabouts of a man who wrote plays. Perhaps it took only a few of these children. Perhaps the rest—perhaps this little girl on the top of the pile—were simply the victims of the murderous inertia humans are capable of.

I stepped back. I turned away.

Arshak had moved off a few steps.

I could only take one.

He and I were both breathing hard.

The welterweight had come near, out of concern for us.

Arshak waved him off.

The man did not go past us to the well; he turned and moved away.

Arshak said, "There are fifty thousand dead since February in the eastern provinces."

I believed what he said. And I took the news with horror. But with an intellectual horror. Fifty thousand was too many. That one little girl was real.

Arshak said, "The Western world thrashes at a few hundred dead Belgians. And our legion of dead is hardly noted. There are more than a million of us in this country. It has begun now. By forced marches and by starvation and by outright mass killings they will try to wipe us all away. It has begun."

I had no words for him. But I moved up beside him.

He said, very softly, "They have rehearsed for years. Six years ago in Adana there were thirty thousand murdered. The women raped and murdered. My wife was one of them. Lucine's mother."

I felt I was looking down another well.

"She shouldn't have been there," Arshak said. "I took them both away from this country after Sasun in 1904. But Leniya's own mother was in Adana and was sick and she went to her."

His voice had grown husky. My mind kept wanting to move to Lucine, to fill in the answers to my remaining questions about her from all this. But Arshak was struggling. Before I could think what to say, he turned abruptly to me.

He roughed up his voice, played his righteous anger as a way out of his pain: "The rest of the village is in a mass grave in the middle of their spring wheat."

I had my own roughing up to do. I was a reporter. It wouldn't take long for me to confirm this story. "I should look," I said.

"All right."

They gave me a shovel, and none of these men could face this with me. I didn't blame them. As I moved off, they were each of them, one at a time, approaching the well and standing before it and making the sign of the cross: three fingers of the right hand joined for the Trinity and brought to the forehead and then to three points on the chest, the bottom first and then the left side and then the right. And finally the hand opened to a palm, in memory of a wound, and was pressed into the heart.

Amen.

I walked fifty yards into the wheat, following the cart ruts and drag rows, the spoor of the Turks covering this whole thing up to keep the rumor out of Istanbul until they could get their bigger plans underway.

I found the place. Fresh turned and refilled earth in a plot fifty feet square. I took only a few steps into it. I had little doubt now. And I felt uneasy standing upon the villagers. I felt uneasy disturbing them.

But I dug. I dug and sweated and dug and it didn't take many shovel strokes downward to open a seam into a miasma I knew quite well. I did not need eyes in this place to confirm the story.

I quickly restored the earth. I stepped off the grave.

And all around me was the growing wheat, the flag leaves unfurled, the wheat heads beginning to emerge.

55

Tigran had brought a bottle of *raki* in his saddle bag, figuring we'd need it. So before riding away from the village, we stood in a circle before our horses and passed the bottle, drinking it deep and slow, prolonging the burn.

When the bottle was empty, Tigran returned it to his saddle bag, which deeply struck me as the right thing to do. He didn't want to litter this place.

And as we rose to our saddles and settled in, Arshak looked to me and said, "Will you help us do this thing, Christopher Cobb?"

My answer to this had also been confirmed in the wheat field.

"I will," I said. "But we have to figure a way to get her out after the deed is done."

He stiffened and nodded and I knew he'd been wrestling with this himself.

And as well intentioned as I was, it took until the sun was verging into late afternoon and we had crested the mountain north of Ortakiöi before I realized how stupid I'd been for these past few hours. How self-absorbed.

I spurred my horse ahead and drew alongside Arshak.

"We need to talk," I said. "Not at a gallop."

He nodded and drew us all up.

He said something to the others in Armenian, no doubt announcing a piss break. We all dismounted and the other three moved away separately.

"Look," I said to Arshak. "I think I've been an idiot. On the ship from Constanța, did you meet a trim man, maybe forty or a little older, with muttonchop whiskers?"

His face instantly pinched tight in concern. "I did. What is it?"

"I saw a man like that when I got into the taxi with you at the quay. I think he was following me."

"Why?"

"What did he say to you?"

Arshak shook his head, like it was nothing, it was trivial. "Just small talk."

"What kind of small talk?"

"Why was he following you?" Arshak said.

I wanted his account first. But I said, "It's possible he's working for the Germans."

"We spoke English. He sounded like an American."

"Brauer sounded like an American," I said.

"Why was he following you?"

"To kill me. If it's who I think it is. Lucine probably didn't get around to telling you I'd done likewise to a German agent in a doorway in London."

"If she did, I might actually be liking you by now," Arshak said.

"Look," I said. "This could involve Lucine. Tell me what he said."

"Small talk."

"What about? Where you were from?"

"Yes."

"And you said?"

"London. He was from Philadelphia."

"Did he notice your accent?"

"Yes. Greek, I told him. I'm not stupid."

"Was he looking at you closely when he talked?"

"Yes."

"Brauer was also at the Block and Tackle when you met Lucine."

Arshak stiffened. No more trying to slough this off.

"He stayed outside," I said. "But he saw you leave. He had a good look at you. He knew you were doing something on the sly with Selene Bourgani. You went to a room around the corner."

"It's a safe place for us. It's clean."

"How long were you there?"

"I left by dawn."

"Long enough for them to put somebody outside to follow you."

Arshak looked away, his mouth pinched in a thin line. I'd felt like that a few minutes ago. Then he looked back to me. "Did he see us in the taxi?"

"He saw something," I said. "I'm not sure how much."

Arshak thought hard about this a moment.

"You're a theater man," I said. "Did you believe the muttonchops?"

This took him off guard. Arshak tried to figure this question out.

"The man's muttonchops," I said.

"I didn't look at them closely. Maybe not, now that you mention it."

"We need to ride," I said. "If he puts you and me together, even if he believed Lucine's disguise—and he'd be the one to see through it—she's still linked back to me through you."

He called out something in Armenian. Probably "Stop pissing, put your dicks away, and let's go."

And we all rode away at full gallop.

56

It was not easy to catch a taxi from the ghetto in Ortakiöi and so Arshak led me down the hill and we took the covertly Armenian Unic to get me back to the Pera Palace as fast as possible. Arshak drove, expecting trouble, leaving the young man with his mother. But I convinced Arshak to let me off before the hotel. For now it was best that he stay in the background. We were jumping to a lot of conclusions. And if the Germans were suspicious but had missed the direct connection between Arshak and me at the quay—which was quite possible—it was best not to give them a chance to see us together. They might still be playing this out slow. I'd drop out of the Unic in a side street a block or so from the hotel. We set up a time to meet later tonight after I'd been able to make sure Lucine was safe. We'd meet at the coffeehouse of the yellow dog.

We stopped a block down the hill and a block south of the Pera Palace.

I'd ridden beside him in the front and I opened the door.

We did not shake hands at the parting. Didn't even think to. But before I could step out, he said, "I trust you."

"Thanks," I said.

And then, with a slightly overplayed earnestness in his voice, he said something in Armenian that either meant "May God be with you" or "Don't fuck this up."

I simply nodded and I was out of the taxi and striding up the hill.

I entered the Pera Palace, crossing the lobby, heading for the marble steps up to the entryway of the Kubbeli Salon, keeping my eyes more or less forward but carefully noting everyone—not just forward but in my periphery as well—eliminating the locals and the uniformed Germans, though *Der Wolf* could have traded in his muttonchops for something else. But I saw no one I could take as particularly suspicious as I moved quickly into the Kubbeli and across the parquet floor.

The piano was playing ragtime and I looked at the drinkers and diners. A table near the doorway to the elevator had three German junior officers with pistols on their belts. They all three gave me a glance as I went by.

The elevator door was open and I went in and I told the operator in what was surely the new lingua franca of this hotel: "*Der fünfte Fußboden.*" He knew exactly what floor I meant. We started to rise.

There were tall, slender windows in the three walls of the elevator, side and rear. I stepped to the rear and craned my neck to focus on the fifth floor and I picked up the balustrade at once. But of course he wouldn't be cooling his heels outside my room, if he'd come for me. He'd have the key or he'd have picked the lock and he'd be inside, waiting.

I got off the elevator and I stepped quietly to the end of the passageway that led to my room. I let the elevator clank and grind its way back down to the bottom floor. I waited. I waited longer. If he were listening for me, he'd think I hadn't been the passenger this time. And while I waited, I played over the worst scenario, the one that ground inside me with the sharpest edges. The Germans were waiting for me but they'd already decided Lucine was a danger and they'd grabbed her.

It was time now. I started down the hall, treading lightly on the carpet. I reached Lucine's door and I stopped. I knocked. Softly.

There was no answer.

Behind me the elevator chains jangled into life.

I knocked again, louder, and I even put my hand into my coat to touch my lock-picking tools. I'd left them in my room.

Lucine wasn't answering.

I put my mouth near the door. "Selene," I said, loud enough to be heard inside.

Nothing.

She wasn't there.

The elevator was rattling its way upward.

I moved on down the passageway. Quickly now. Perhaps she'd left a note for me.

I arrived at my door. I put the key in the lock. I opened the door.

At the open French windows a man was standing with his back to me, wearing a *feldgrau* German officer uniform, blending into the darkening sky beyond him. The nightstand light was on. His peaked field cap lay on the foot of the bed. I restrained my hand from going to the Mauser, even as he was turning, even as I was beginning to recognize this man.

Colonel Martin Ströder, Enver Pasha's aide-de-camp.

"Hello, Mr. Brauer," he said. He had a Luger in a holster strapped around his waist. I didn't remember that from his first visit to me.

"Colonel," I said, closing the door behind me.

"I have come to take you to Enver Pasha."

He and I both kept standing where we were, he by the window, I by the door.

"I'm sorry to have kept you waiting," I said. "I thought you told me it would be tomorrow."

"So," he said. "The plan has changed once more."

I still didn't know how to deal with Enver Pasha, given that he was a friend of Brauer.

"Please come with me," Ströder said, taking a step in my direction.

I was thinking quick and hard about the room. He wasn't explaining why he was inside. Everything incriminating was in the false bottom of the valise. But things were already decided anyway, I suspected. He hadn't even asked where I'd been.

"I've been horseback riding," I said. "I'm not presentable."

He stopped.

"Can I have a few minutes?" I said.

He gave me a once-over look. "Time is more important to the Pasha," Ströder said. And then he smiled a little, flipping his chin slightly upward. "The Turks are not so scrupulous as we Germans in those matters."

"Do we need to get the woman?" I said.

He did not answer at once. He was reading me. The news was bad, I realized.

And he said, "We have taken her along already."

"Very well," I said. "At least may I wash the horse off my hands?"

He hesitated.

I nodded to the bathroom.

He nodded assent.

I stepped into the bathroom, switched on the light, stood at the basin, looked at my own face, the bandage gray from the ride, and I lowered my face to the basin. I let my hands do their task on their own. I had to think.

My mind was inclined to thrash now, but I held my thoughts steady. The Germans didn't simply come and shoot me. Perhaps the question of the man known at the Pera Palace as Walter Brauer was still open. Perhaps my knowing the password was still carrying me. Brauer's body was decomposing in the North Sea. If *Der Wolf* saw me at the quay and recognized me as Cobb, perhaps he still hadn't placed me at the Pera Palace posing as Brauer.

And perhaps, as well, Lucine had indeed arranged to do this thing on her own. With an insistent offer of her body, an expressed aversion to Brauer, she could have arranged to be taken personally and immediately to Enver Pasha. She didn't need her father and me to be meddling with this, trying to save her. An actress is a fallen woman, she'd said. Perhaps she was shooting the leader of the Ottoman Empire to death even as I rolled the bar of soap around and around in my palms. Perhaps she was herself being shot to death in this next moment, even as I placed the soap on the side of the basin and rubbed up the lather on my hands.

I was having a bad feeling about this whole thing now.

I had to assume they either knew or seriously suspected who I was.

If the Germans did know who I was, the fact remained: they didn't simply kill me, right here and now. Why the pretense?

And I understood. I'd been thinking in the old ways. The battle-field ways. They wanted to interrogate me before killing me. And it might suit them to begin the interrogation without tipping their hand. Perhaps even, for a time, to speak to me as if I were getting away with all this. And, of course, they feared me. They too knew I had the knack. They'd wait until I was in a much more controlled space before getting rough.

I could dry my hands, pull my Mauser and shoot Colonel Ströder to death.

I'd save myself but that would surely doom Lucine. I had to hope—and it would make sense—that they were taking me to the same place they were holding her. I had to let Ströder play this out so I could find out where that was.

All right.

I dried my hands and stepped from the bathroom.

Ströder was there, his field cap on his head. He had been watching me from the shadows, the bedroom light extinguished.

"I'm ready," I said.

"Good," he said.

I took a step toward the door.

He stopped me with a lifted hand.

"I'm sorry, Herr Brauer, but I must check for a weapon. Enver Pasha requires it."

I unbuttoned my coat, spread my arms.

For the possibility of his hands going around behind me, I readied my right leg, ever so slightly angling my knee toward his crotch.

He began to pat me down, his hands slipping inside my coat and traveling down my sides. The Mauser in the very center of my back wasn't even five inches wide. In my Chicago police beat days, I'd only ever heard of one man, a genteel grifter, who carried a weapon in the small of his back. I'd never known a military man to do this.

Ströder was feeling into my coat pockets.

I was ready to have it out with him hand to hand. But I still didn't know where Lucine was.

He pulled in closer to me.

I heard him stop his breath.

His arms went around me and he touched my back pockets, his two palms falling upon my backside. Gingerly.

It occurred to me I might still be Brauer to him and Brauer might actually have a reputation. Or Ströder had a reputation of his own.

Before he could lift or turn his hands I said, sweetly, coyly, "Careful there, Colonel."

His hands whipped off me and he stepped back.

"We shall go," he said.

The Mauser was still mine.

Ströder led me out the door and along the passageway and down in the elevator and across the salon and the lobby and through the front doors.

A closed-cabin Mercedes Torpedo sat at the curb, as gray as Ströder's uniform, its whole radiator arrowing forward into a point. The driver was a burly Hun in an enlisted man's uniform and a peakless field cap. As we emerged from the hotel he snapped to attention, saluted the colonel, and stepped to the back door and opened it.

Ströder led the way the few steps across the narrow sidewalk and he plunged on inside, which I was glad to see. The car was pointed north, to my right, and so following the colonel into the backseat, I would be traveling with him to my left and my shooting hand unencumbered and out of his sight.

I went in.

The driver slammed the door behind me.

The interior was pretty tight. But okay to maneuver.

The driver bounced heavily behind the wheel and shut his door firmly. There was no partition. The car smelled of leather and gun oil and garlic: the seats, their weapons, their breath.

None of us spoke.

We immediately went down the hill but then turned north and crawled for a while through the commencing nightlife of the Grand Rue de Péra, all three of us being, I sensed, from our eyes kept forward and our faces grimly set, sincerely of a single mind about this much at least: how ignorant and vapid were the bankers and diplomats and merchants and bureaucrats and ship captains and Western tourists and all their women who were dining and theatergoing and drinking and dancing while a war was going on from the Black Sea to the Irish Sea, from the North Sea to the Red Sea. And while three men were passing by, one or more of whom likely would be dead before the night was done.

57

We made our way toward the Bosporus, following the Grand Rue through the traffic circle at Taksim and then, just before the Palace of Dolmabahçe, we joined the road along the European shore. We turned north toward Ortakiöi and almost immediately we were running past the palace wall, the very ground I'd covered this morning with Arshak and Lucine.

I was itchy to do something. We were heading to her now. I was convinced she was in serious trouble. And I would be too, as soon as Enver Pasha took a look at me. I wanted badly to slip my hand into my coat and to the small of my back and get this started. But I had to wait. The Huns had to show me where she was.

Ströder lit a Turkish cigarette.

I watched out the window.

We passed through Ortakiöi, the dome and minarets of the big mosque at the quay barely visible in the gathering night. Outside of Pera on the hill, Istanbul was a dark city at night. A very dark city. Except for the handful of motorcars and their headlights, I caught only glimpses now of isolated candles and kerosene lamps: through a house window, before a sidewalk coffee shop, inside a café.

Then all at once the off-road light changed; the fleeting bursts were brighter, steadier. These were electric lights in upper-floor windows behind privacy walls as we entered the long run of waterside *yalis*, the villas of the wealthy that stretched on up the Bosporus a dozen more miles to Büyükdere and the edge of the Belgrad Forest. Enver Pasha had a *yali* along here. Of course. The roadside was lit now, a flash of electric lamp light rushed into our windows and away and then another and then darkness and then another.

I moved my head slowly, a small increment at a time, away from the window and toward Ströder. He was steadily lit at the moment from behind. He had taken off his field cap and the back of his head was bright, though his face was in shadow, and this I could discern: he was putting out a cigarette by squeezing the tip between the thumb and forefinger of his left hand.

The Hun behind the wheel made two small, simultaneous movements—a lean forward and a turn of his face to the right—small enough to suggest that the place he was looking for was still up ahead but he expected it soon.

I started slipping my right hand under my coat but careful not to shift my shoulders. I'd cut the flap off the holster in London and now I gently wedged it farther open and I slid my hand inside and took my Mauser into a shooting grip.

I was sure Ströder had seen no movement in me. His gaze was going forward with the driver's. I looked too. The road took a curve to the right, moved closer to the water, and then straightened, and a couple of hundred yards up ahead the street was lit bright.

Ströder leaned forward in his seat. "There it is," he said to the driver, who began abruptly to slow down.

I started to pull the Mauser from behind my back, still making as little stir as possible. Even as the pistol came free I was planning ahead. His weapon. Surely he wore it *Geladen*, loaded. As my right hand emerged and crossed before me, while Ströder was leaning back again into his seat, I switched the Mauser to my left hand just in case. This was the pistol he had to assume would go off at the slightest move, and I needed my right hand for his Luger to easily cover the driver down the road.

The Mercedes engine whined and the gears ground heavily as we slowed and the driver shifted down. The street lights approached.

I wrenched my torso around to face Ströder and I pressed the barrel of the Mauser against his head, into the soft space just above his cheekbone, between his ear and his temple, holding my arm high at the elbow and squaring the muzzle into his head even as I reached into his holster and removed his Luger.

This was all quick, the Mauser leading the way. Ströder was smart enough to go absolutely still at its first touch.

The Mercedes engine was noisy in its deceleration. I leaned toward Ströder and said, as low as I could for him still to clearly hear me, "We must drive on by."

We were going very slow, nearing the villa where no doubt there were armed guards that Ströder was thinking about.

I let only the briefest fraction of a second pass without him speaking and I nudged the Mauser muzzle into his head. "I will do this now," I said.

"Drive on," Ströder said, firmly, loudly.

The Mercedes didn't have a rearview mirror. The driver could not see the Mauser pointed at Ströder and his head bobbled a bit in the impulse to look back to us. He had his own pistol somewhere on or around him. I thumbed the Luger's safety forward into the off position, but I kept the pistol low behind the front seat for now. It would be unfortunate to have to shoot the driver in a moving car, though not as unfortunate as his shooting me.

At that moment another automobile passed us from behind, moving into the oncoming lane and going around and swinging back in front of us.

I saw all this peripherally with my main focus on the Hun behind the wheel. He didn't take his eyes off the road, settling for sliding his head sideways and angling his ear toward us. "Sir?"

I pushed with the Mauser.

"Do it now," Ströder said. "Drive on."

"Yessir," our driver said.

He sped up.

And we passed into the bright light.

I let myself take a quick glance.

A stone wall. A gate and two guards in uniform. The stone wall. And we were past and into the darkness. But I could find this villa again.

Now my plan was vague.

Incapacitate these two. That much was clear enough. I was not yet prepared to go back into the villa. The first audible gunshot would make their advantage in numbers impossible to get past. And it would instantly jeopardize Lucine inside. Metcalf gave me a good weapon for a shipboard murder. My pistol-shaped Winchester with a silencer. It was the right weapon for slipping into Enver Pasha's *yali* as well. But it was in the bottom of my valise, in the bottom of the wardrobe, in my room at the Pera Palace.

So these two had to be incapacitated for a good long while. But I kept rapidly playing that possible scene over and over in my head, staging it this way and that, and I was having trouble figuring out even how to safely get these two out of the automobile, much less effectively restrain them, and the only plan that seemed to have a chance of working was to preemptively shoot them both pretty much simultaneously in the head. Which was not what I wanted to do.

In the meantime we were driving north, accelerating again, and one of these two was still armed.

"Not too fast," I told Ströder.

And he repeated the order to the driver.

We stopped accelerating.

Ahead, just out of the range of our headlights, was the dim form of the automobile that had passed us at the villa.

We caravanned, the two of us, for maybe half a mile, and then the car ahead dropped back a little and came into the clarity of our lights.

I looked at it for the first time with my full attention.

It was a Unic taxi.

The Armenian model.

Arshak had hung around after he dropped me off and he'd followed us.

He was beginning to slow.

We slowed.

Arshak slowed even more, dropping back right in front of us.

The German driver honked his horn. He craned his neck to the left to see if the oncoming lane was clear for us to pass.

I nudged Ströder's head. "Let's stay behind this guy."

Ströder's face was in shadow so I didn't see him cut his eyes to me, but I felt the faintest push against the Mauser's barrel as he had the reflex to turn his head to look in my direction. He'd been making his own plans about how to handle this. All that just got overturned. He hadn't figured on an accomplice.

"Stay behind that vehicle," Ströder said loud and firm.

We were in a stretch of road either without a villa or in the owned and managed adjoining grounds of two villas. Arshak was going slower and slower.

We were going slower and slower.

Arshak was probably beginning to figure I'd gained some sort of control in the Mercedes.

The driver turned his head now, abruptly, as if to question these odd orders.

He had only a fragment of a moment to start to put things together before the muzzle of the Luger was pointed at the right eye of his half-turned face.

"Pull over," I said, straight to the driver.

"Sit very still, Colonel," I said, pushing lightly at Ströder's head. "Hair trigger." But I kept watching the driver, whose face was swinging away from me, going back to the road.

"Driver," I said sharply. "Both hands visible on the wheel."

Both the man's hands appeared at the top of the steering wheel.

He pulled to the side of the road.

The Unic rolled only a little farther and also pulled off.

I said to both my Germans, "It is very convenient to shoot both of you in the head now. So you need to sit very still. I will kill you at the smallest movement."

They complied.

"Cut off your engine," I said, and the driver moved the throttle lever on the steering wheel and the engine sputtered and went silent.

"Leave your lights on," I said.

He did.

And we waited, the three of us, with me sitting as still as these two, as if the pistols were pointed at me.

I figured Arshak was waiting for some sign from the car. But I couldn't step out or these two would do something stupid, especially the driver.

I could have asked for his weapon. But I had control of his empty hands. I didn't want to invite him to put a pistol in one of them, especially in this dim light and out of my sight.

So we waited some more. It felt like a long time, though it couldn't have been. But I knew the longer it went on, the more likely it was that one of these guys would try something stupid.

Finally the driver's door of the Unic opened. It stayed open for a moment and then Arshak appeared and drew back at once.

I was a lot braver when I was acting from my gut and quickly. This sitting was starting to get me steamed at Arshak. But he was only an actor, after all. He was used to being brave on a stage with fake whiskers. It was tougher to play the role you needed to play in the real dark by a real road along the goddamn Bosporus. So I wasn't upset. I was simply firm in thinking to this Armenian ham: *Jump out of your trench and charge.*

And he did.

He suddenly burst from the Unic with his pistol drawn and he hustled into our headlights and up to the driver's window.

"We're all taking it easy here," I said to him, having to will myself back to English. This whole incident was strictly German in my mind.

He looked in.

"Point your pistol at the driver and watch his hands," I said. "He's still armed."

And Arshak popped the muzzle of a Colt 1889 onto the driver's left temple hard enough that the guy's head jerked and his hands flew up.

"Hands!" I shouted.

They flew back down to the wheel.

I felt Ströder stir.

I kept my Luger pointed at the driver but twisted my torso and face to the colonel, tracking the little flinch of his head with the muzzle of the Mauser. Keeping him zeroed.

These kinds of things—small reflex twitches—could too easily escalate, take on a life of their own, get out of control.

"Settle down," I said to the colonel, flipping back to German. And then to Arshak in English, "Keep the driver covered."

"Got it," he said.

I opened my back door.

I swung the Luger to the left and aimed it at Ströder's chest. I eased the Mauser off his head.

"Careful now," I said to him. "Let me see your hands."

He held them up, framing his face.

"If one drops, you die," I said and I backed out onto the running board. "Follow me."

He did.

I put Ströder with his hands on the hood of the car, near the front passenger-side door, his legs stretched far out behind him and spread wide, leaving him on the verge of falling down. Then I opened that front door, and while Arshak kept his Colt on the driver's head from the other side, I reached in and relieved the man of his Luger.

Now we had two German soldiers—allies of the Turks and abettors of the massacre of the Armenians—pressed side by side against the hood of the car, the headlights starting to dim as they drew down the battery, Lucine sitting a mile up the road in mortal danger and me convinced that our only chance to get her out alive was to slip in silently, which meant going back to the Pera Palace before making a move. And time was ticking by.

My Mauser was tucked away again in its holster but my Luger was raised and pointing at the back of Ströder's head. I looked at Arshak and he was looking at me. His own new Luger was pointed at the back of the driver's head.

Here we were, Arshak and I: two men; two Lugers; two enemies who would do anything they could to reverse this situation; the opportunity of vengeance by proxy for the death of the innocents in the well; the shortness of time and the urgency of our mission; the sloppiness of any alternate plan. And a tidy, obvious solution before us. My trigger finger was prickling to do this.

But Arshak and I continued to look at each other.

"It's what *they* would do to *us*," he said.

"Exactly," I said.

A few accelerating pulse beats of silence later, I understood how I felt about that. I said, "You figure you've got tow-ropes in the back of that taxi?"

"Unics do get stuck," he said.

And it was decided.

58

Funny how this kind of thing sometimes works. We didn't kill our captive Huns, and as a direct result—while Arshak was off getting the ropes and I stared at the field-gray colonel blending into the shadows—my plan refined itself. I had Ströder remove his uniform, and after Arshak—who had learned some things in his working time at the London Docks—did some fancy knots on our two boys, I turned myself into a German army colonel.

The uniform fit pretty well. The hat was a bit small, but it squeezed on okay. The Luger in its holster and a magazine pouch were strapped to my waist. And just as the Mercedes headlights died, I carefully stripped off the gauze bandage from my left cheek.

"You're pretty frightening in that costume," Arshak said as I approached him.

I turned my face so he could see the scar in the starlight.

"Mother of God," he said. "Is that makeup?"

"No."

"Where'd you get it?"

"Long story," I said. "Let's go."

"The battery went dead."

"We'll catch a taxi," I said.

And I quickly explained where we had to go, what we had to do. To his credit, the ham took direction pretty well and we were off in the Unic.

We parked around the corner from the hotel, beside the iron fence along the public gardens. Arshak and I gave a wordless nod to each other and I got out and walked back down the street and approached the hotel. I ran an iron rod up my back and played my role, returning the salute of a major emerging from the front hotel doors, and I passed into the lobby and kept my eyes forward, looking at no one, walking briskly.

I approached the elevator, which had just arrived at the ground floor. The wooden and glass doors of the car opened and a man in a suit took the couple of steps to the outer cast-iron gate and pushed it open. I drew near.

It was the colonel from down the hall, the guy in uniform and *Pickelhaube* that Lucine and I followed into the hotel upon our arrival.

He took another step and still I wasn't registering on him and now we were about to pass and he focused on my face and then on my epaulet pips and then on my scar and then on my face—all in very rapid succession. And he stopped. The officers I'd encountered so far were of lesser rank. This guy was my equal and it was his business to know other full colonels in town. Maybe he thought he knew them all.

I brazened on by him with a little nod—he was in mufti, after all, and if he didn't know me, I didn't know him. I took another step beyond him and was about to pass through the art nouveau proscenium that led to the elevator carriage.

And the colonel said, "Colonel?"

I stopped and I turned and I said to the colonel, "Colonel."

I figured he had a strong hunch I wasn't a colonel.

I could see in his eyes that indeed he did think he knew all the colonels.

Maybe he was even in the process of placing my face as the man who'd followed him into the hotel thirty-six hours ago. He'd seemed to look past or through me in my couple of encounters with him, but he might simply have been cagily observant.

I kept my eyes on him but turned my face slightly to the right, thoughtfully, as if I were trying to figure out where I knew him from.

In the process, I reminded him of the *Schmiss* he'd noticed a few moments ago.

This drew him away from the broader face recognition he'd been attempting. It was a big thing to a man like him, this university fencing scar. It was a nobleman's badge of courage.

His eyes were still on it.

He had no such scar.

I smiled and chuckled patronizingly. "Heidelberg," I said.

He clicked his heels.

After all, even if he recognized me, what had he seen me do yesterday? I'd simply checked into the hotel dressed as he was now. And with a beautiful woman.

"I am sorry to be out of uniform," he said. "They've asked us to look like civilians when we are off duty. I am Colonel Conrad Lüdike."

I clicked my heels and flipped him a courtesy salute. He was flattered, giving an ardently crisp salute in return.

Then we shook hands with Germanic fervor.

"You are new to Constantinople," he said.

"I am. Let's soon have a drink together, Colonel," I said. "And we can speak of it."

"Yes," he said. "By all means."

And he continued the handshake.

"And now if you'll excuse me," I said, gently extracting my hand.

"Of course," he said, bowing at the waist.

"Perhaps tomorrow," I said.

"Of course."

And I turned my back on him and stepped through the iron door and across the carpet and into the elevator carriage, and I stopped in the center of the floor.

I turned.

Colonel Lüdike was already passing into the Kubbeli salon, and I let out a breath I hadn't even realized I'd been holding. "*Der fünfte Fußboden,*" I said to the operator.

And I was on the fifth floor.

I walked briskly, stifling the urge to run.

I passed Lucine's room.

I arrived at my door. I went in.

I would not be back, I realized. I'd be either dead or on the USS *Scorpion* before this night was through.

Too bad. I'd lose my third Corona Portable Number 3 in barely more than year.

I pulled my valise out of the wardrobe and set it on the bed.

I extracted the false bottom.

I pulled out the sawed-off and reshaped Winchester. I screwed the silencer into the muzzle. I laid the weapon on the bed and I put all the .22 Long heavies from the box into the two lower side pockets of my tunic.

I removed the remaining documents and stuffed them into the inner tunic pockets. No tracks left behind.

All that remained at the bottom of the valise were a few sets of whiskers and a bottle of spirit gum.

The German officer persona would help me in making progress through the villa. But it was possible *Der Wolf* was waiting with Enver Pasha. I figured I might find myself, in my improvisation, needing a little delay time before I was recognized. He'd seen my face. The revealed scar was not enough.

I removed a Kaiser Wilhelm uptwitched mustache—a good one, densely tied onto sheer lace in two parts—and the screw-stoppered bottle of spirit gum, and I stepped into the bathroom.

I turned the electrical switch and stood before the mirror.

I took one bracing glance into my own eyes, shaded beneath the brim of the peaked cap. I removed the cap and laid it aside. I gave myself one last look. My eyes again. And then the scar: that too was mine. It was *me*. Let anyone else interpret it as they would. I'd earned it.

I got to work. I brushed on spirit gum and applied the two parts of the mustache, leaving the central hollow of the lip appropriately naked. Done. I dropped the bottle into the basin.

I pressed my officer's cap onto my head.

I strode to the bed. I picked up my Winchester 1902, which had been mutilated and hushed into a deadly frame of mind. A one-handed weapon, all right, but not a small thing. I had to pass across the salon and lobby of this hotel.

I still had the leather portfolio Metcalf had given me in London. I retrieved it from the Gladstone in the wardrobe, and I stuck the Winchester inside, on the diagonal. I put the portfolio under my arm and went out of the room and down the staircase—hotfooting the steps—and through the salon, reining myself in now, making myself slow down. I should not draw attention, though the brain in my head and the heart in my chest were pounding at me to rush, to run, but I walked, briskly purposeful but controlled, across the lobby and out the door and to the left and to the corner and to the right and across the street and I was walking faster now and the Unic was ahead and I wrenched the passenger door open and slid in next to Arshak.

He reared back at my mustache. "Mother of God," he said.

"She's far away tonight," I said.

And we drove off.

59

We made the best time we could down the Grand Rue, quiet for now, Arshak concentrating on rushing without killing the oblivious pedestrians, me catching my breath.

The streets loosened up after Taksim.

And Arshak said, "So what's the plan?"

I said, "I only caught a glimpse of the place. Two guards at the front entrance. I don't know what's inside. But whatever it is, I need to get as far as I can without letting anyone know I'm coming. As soon as the audible shooting starts, Lucine's in immediate danger."

"As opposed to inaudible shooting?"

"Exactly. I've got a silencer."

I pulled out the Winchester now and dropped the portfolio beneath my feet.

Arshak whistled between his teeth.

"The problem," I said, "is that it's a single-shot."

"I want to go in with you," he said.

"The uniform is the best trick we have to make this silent. You're a walking red flag."

"What can I do?"

"Stay at the front gate after I get in. Take care of anyone arriving from outside. And when you hear a shot, come find me."

"All right."

"Not till then," I said.

"I understand," Arshak said. "Lucine first."

"Yes."

"If Lucine can't do what she came to do . . ." Arshak said, breaking off briefly. "I hope you won't let my daughter die in vain."

I knew what he meant. He wanted me to kill Enver Pasha.

"I intend to save her," I said. Indeed, that was the only intention I had at the moment. Whatever else might happen remained to be seen.

He did not reply. I wondered if he'd heard my own reply as a simple *no*. Wondered too, if it came to be a mutually exclusive proposition, whether he would prefer to lose his daughter if it meant killing Enver Pasha.

But that was all we said as we ran through Ortakiöi—I was getting to know this route quite well—and we headed up the shore.

And then, at last, the road took that curve to the right and moved closer to the water and then straightened.

Arshak and I glanced at each other. We both recognized the approach to Enver Pasha's villa.

And now we saw a bright flare of electric light up ahead.

"Drive past into the dark," I said.

We kept up our speed and approached the villa.

I watched carefully as we neared.

The villa's second story and peaked roof were visible in the spill of electricity, and I focused on the entrance to the grounds. Two Germans were standing with rifles slung over their shoulders, one on each side of an open iron double-wide gate. They were confident. They were still expecting Ströder.

We flashed by and they hardly glanced our way.

And now we were in the dark.

Arshak slowed immediately.

"This is good," I said, and we pulled off onto the side of the road in front of a stand of cypress.

Arshak shut down the engine and extinguished the lights.

We got out of the Unic and came around to the rear and stood shoulder to shoulder looking back at the villa, maybe seventy yards away.

I said, very low, "Hang back in the dark till I finish with the guards at the gate."

I took one big breath of air and puffed it out.

I crossed the road to the tree line and approached the villa low and quick. Just before the penumbra of streetlight I drew back into the trees and eased up and took a good look.

Thirty yards away two armed men flanked the entrance. In order to silently take them both out I had a single-shot Winchester with a minimum of seven or eight seconds between rounds. And the guy on the left was only partially visible from my present angle. I could go deeper into the woods and come forward from tree to tree till I had a hidden, straight shot at both of them. Play the sniper. While the second Hun figured out why his comrade just fell down, I might be able to reload and take him out before he knew how to react. But maybe not. Maybe he'd throw off some generalized field-of-fire shots right away. Or he could duck out of sight.

I thought of a better way; better for Lucine.

I had an open, direct look at the guard on the right. I retreated into the dark and then out to the verge of the road. I collected the three largest manageably throwable stones I could find, ranging in size from chicken egg to baseball. I crept back to my previous just-out-of-the-light position, which was about even with the near end of the villa wall, and I waited for the two men to have their faces turned away from my direction. Then I stood up straight and squared around to the wall and I threw the middle-sized stone over and into the grounds, hoping to hit something that would make a sound.

I watched the two men.

They lifted their heads, but it wasn't clear they'd heard anything.

I threw the egg-sized stone into the same general area. And then, immediately, the largest one.

This time I had their attention.

They looked back into the villa grounds.

They exchanged a quick word and the man on my left disappeared.

I pulled the hammer back on my Winchester and held my shooting arm straight down and I strode forward into the light, keeping the weapon out of sight.

I took two quick, long steps and a third before the remaining guard turned his face to me.

I was a German officer heading his way out of the night. The guard's rifle was coming off his shoulder, but slow. I was fast now, striding. The guard was crazy confused, trying to figure me out. Should he salute or should he raise his rifle and stop me?

Another stride.

This would be an easy shot now.

I drew my hand from behind me and lifted the Winchester and the guard's eyes went wide and he was rushing the rifle off his shoulder and I had the Winchester on him and I squeezed off a round and there was almost no kick at all and there was no recognizable sound, just a faint hiss and rush, and the center of the guard's chest bloomed and sprayed and he flew back and his rifle clattered into the gate and already I was dodging to the left out of immediate sight—the other guard must have heard, was surely turning now and would soon be looking for me—and I grabbed the lug and slid the bolt and popped the cartridge case and I stuck a fresh round into the breech and I could hear the other guard running, he was almost at the gate, and I took two steps into the street so I could have an angle on him, as I closed the bolt and pulled back the hammer, doing this with my back to the entrance, the Winchester hidden from view, relying on my uniform and my back to delay the guard, and I heard the Hun scuffle into the open behind me and I lifted my left arm and pointed to the woods.

"It came from over there, Sergeant," I said, looking at him over my shoulder, and he was hesitating, he was turning his face the way I was pointing and I kept my eyes on him and I was already swinging my right arm across my body and under my left arm and

I squeezed off a round that caught him in the left side of the chest, maybe straight into the heart because he went down heavy, like he was gone instantly.

I squared around to the entrance. But I didn't move. The two guards were very still. The two guards were dead. I breathed deep and I let it out. I reloaded the Winchester as if there was no one lying on the ground before me. As if I had nowhere to go. If I'd reloaded in seven seconds a few moments ago, this was a leisurely fifteen. And I wondered if other eyes had been watching the entrance, from inside the house.

Apparently not, as I waited there in the road. No sound whatsoever came from behind the wall.

I had to expect more resistance inside the villa, but I figured I could at least get to the front door without drawing fire.

I pulled my Winchester's hammer and cocked it. I liked this tough guy who nonetheless knew how to keep his mouth shut when he chewed.

And Arshak appeared beside me.

He must have followed me to the edge of the light.

He didn't say a word.

I didn't say a word.

He nodded.

I moved off quick, crossing to the entrance and stepping between the dead guards and through the open gate. The villa was done in a toned-down Italian style with no Renaissance frills. The basics but tasteful: two stories elevated on a terrace with a low-pitched, wide-eaved tile roof, a central court, and an arcaded, ground-floor loggia. The place was all white stucco tainted yellow in the electric light like dog piss in snow.

I went up the steps and across the courtyard, moving quietly and with my Winchester held low. I passed into the shadow of the loggia and approached the front door, which showed light within, and now it was time—since I'd not caught anyone's attention—for me to act a little suspicious.

I crouched and spanked past the first set of windows to the left of the door. I pressed back against the wall and then gave just enough of my face to the glass to see inside.

I was looking down a wide, central grand hall that stretched from the front door to a far set of veranda doors. The hall was lit by dim-burning electric faux-torches on sconces, and outside, at the far end, I could dimly see the columns and arches of a corresponding Bosporus-side loggia.

I looked to the right, closer to the door, and I flinched back.

But they did not see me and I needed to watch them: two more German guards, one tapping a cigarette halfway out of a pack and letting the other take it. The second soldier said something and headed for his post at the rear of the villa.

The first German began to turn in my direction and I pulled back. I waited a few moments. I peeked again. He was sitting on a stool, just inside the front door. I glanced the length of the hall. The second guard was outside, closing the veranda doors behind him.

I kept low and crept away from the window and moved a couple of paces out of the loggia. Then I turned and approached the house again, doing nothing to muffle my steps.

I was a German officer. And as far as these house guards knew, I'd been admitted by the entrance guards.

I stood before the door, and I lifted my left hand and knocked very lightly.

I heard a stirring inside.

Perhaps they knew to expect someone.

The door began to open and I backed two steps away and raised my right arm.

I told myself that if there were any way to reliably knock this man out and keep him out till I rescued Lucine, I would do that.

The door opened and the guard's face was shrouded in shadow and I was glad for that and he had not unshouldered his weapon—they were indeed expecting visitors and they were not expecting trouble—and I squeezed the Winchester's trigger and he flew back and landed hard on the floor, his body thumping and his rifle clattering.

I stepped out of the sight line of the door and reloaded the Winchester and cocked the hammer.

I did not put my body in front of the door but leaned and looked inside.

The guard was silent, though his feet were moving ever so slightly, as if he were having a dream about running. Perhaps he was. He would soon arrive.

The far veranda doors were shut.

No one was in the hall.

I moved forward, sidestepping the body, and I walked quickly along, vaguely aware of oil paintings and divans along the walls, but I kept my eyes forward and my Winchester behind my thigh.

I arrived at the veranda doors and opened one and stepped out, staying in the spill of electric light so I could clearly be seen and identified as an officer. As far as this last guard knew, I'd been certified by three of his comrades.

He was emerging now from the shadows to my left. He stopped and straightened and he clicked his heels and saluted.

I brought my right hand up and across my body and shot him in the center of his chest, and as he was going down I turned and strode back through the veranda doors and toward the front of the villa. I stopped in the middle of the grand hall.

To my right was an archway into the north end of the house, to my left an archway to the south end of the house. Either would do. I strongly suspected anyone else in the place was upstairs.

I lifted the Winchester. I looked at it for a moment. It seemed quite odd to my eye all of a sudden. Too long for a pistol, with the sawed-off rifle barrel and then the silencer. Quite long. But I did what I needed to do with it to prepare for whoever was next: bolt, breech, casing, shell, bolt, hammer. It was ready to fire.

And I found myself panting.

This also struck me as odd.

It wasn't fear. It wasn't about what I intended to do next.

Maybe not so odd: it was about what I'd been doing for the past few minutes.

It was about the knack.

It had been some months since I'd killed a man.

No, it hadn't.

I'd killed in London as well.

Before *that* it had been some months.

And before that not at all.

And now I could do it four times in rapid succession with very little thought and no remorse.

Unless this was remorse, what I was doing now.

But these were soldiers I'd killed. And I'd seen worse. I saw it in Nicaragua and I saw it in Macedonia and Greece. Sanctioned by nations and cheered by the victors' countrymen.

And I saw worse still: down a well in an empty village a few miles north of where I now stood.

Was I not killing for them, the slaughtered innocents? And for my own country? For Lucine? For her, of course. For Selene Bourgani. For that face ten feet high in a darkened auditorium. I was killing for the future of American cinema. For this odd and mostly remorseless thrill. What bullshit. Well, some of it wasn't bullshit. Some of it was true. Maybe all of it was true.

It made no difference. This was my role.

So I chose the archway on the north and stepped through it, and in the darkness to my right was a staircase that ascended to a landing and then—out of my sight—turned toward the front of the house and continued up to the second floor.

I moved to the stairs. I began to climb.

And I wondered if the next man I killed would be the leader of the Ottoman Empire.

I was treading very lightly, my Winchester raised before me.

But not lightly enough.

Near the top of the stairs another uniformed guard appeared. He was raising his rifle.

He saw my peaked hat and my epaulets and my tunic first and only a brief moment later did he see the Winchester, which clicked and hissed and blew him backward to thump against the wall and down to the floor and I was on the top step, and the dim hallway was empty to the left and to the right. I looked back to the left again, and down the way was a splash of light from an open door.

The house was quiet, so this click and hiss and thump might have been heard. I bent and laid the Winchester quietly on the floor and I drew the Luger, flipped off the safety, and I strode forward to the light and pressed against the wall beside the door and then looked quickly in. I pulled quickly back.

And what I'd seen made me say in German, "I'm Colonel Vogel from the embassy. Don't shoot. You're in danger from an American agent who is on the grounds."

I thought to holster the Luger, but I didn't. I kept it behind my right thigh and I stepped into the doorway.

Across the room, behind a desk, framed by open doors onto a second-floor veranda, stood Enver Pasha.

He was not lowering his pistol.

I gently let him see my pistol.

"Your Excellency," I said. "I have been tracking this man. Colonel Ströder, who asked me to come with him, has deployed your guards to search."

I kept my eyes fixed on his but I let my face move slightly to the right so he could see the scar.

I watched his eyes flit to it. He was working hard to figure me out.

And I was still studying him. Swarthy. Black Kaiser Wilhelm mustache. He was thinner in the face than I remembered in the news photos, though by no means did I have a clear image of him in my mind. I thought: *He's gaunt from stress in this war; he could be twitchy with that pistol.*

"This man Cobb could appear at any moment," I said. "He may have come in from the water."

I flipped my chin to the windows behind him.

He did not turn. But his head flinched just a little to the side and the muzzle of his own Luger dipped ever so slightly.

"I'm going to raise my pistol now," I said, while doing it.

He refreshed his own aim abruptly but I now had a chest-shot zeroed on him. And he had a chest-shot zeroed on me. The Luger P08 has a two-stage trigger. I had taken up the bit of slack and moved to the second stage and I was sure Enver Pasha had too.

Neither of us dared to shoot.

Besides, I didn't want to shoot him. Not yet. Gunshots still might imperil Lucine, if she was in the house. Which I was beginning to question.

I had to find her before anything else.

"Your Excellency," I said. "I'm very sorry to have raised my weapon. But I had to give your own hand pause. Shall we lower our arms now? I'm Colonel Gerhard Vogel. I am here at your service. This man Cobb is dangerous and we are afraid he is very near."

He did not move his pistol from his aim.

"Sergeant Schmidt," he said loudly.

"Your Excellency," I said. "We have been operating quietly for obvious reasons. Your excellent Sergeant Schmidt came downstairs at our small sounds. He is now helping to find Cobb. I'm here to protect you."

He did not move his pistol.

I did not move mine.

We looked at each other hard.

"Colonel Vogel," Enver Pasha said, "please step closer."

I did. Carefully. One small step. Another. Not letting my Luger waver at all. A third step and I stopped. We were no more than ten feet from each other.

We studied each other's face.

"I don't know a Colonel Gerhard Vogel," Enver Pasha said. His German was excellent.

Now that I'd heard a couple of full sentences from him, something odd was clicking in my head.

The tenor of his voice.

And there was something in his eyes.

Something familiar.

And then I felt like an idiot.

If Lucine was still in this house—and I was beginning again to think she was—and if they'd wanted to lure Christopher Cobb here to interrogate him and kill him, then Enver Pasha was not standing before me.

Der Wolf was.

He wanted to play the Pasha for me for a while. He liked dressing up, this guy.

Which was the familiar thing I'd sensed a few moments ago.

This was Squarebeard from the bookstore in London.

But I'd seen Squarebeard only from a distance. Now that I was close to him, his familiarity took an odd turn.

"Mr. Cobb, is it?" he said.

Our pistols both held very steady.

I didn't answer.

And he said, in English, a flat midwestern English, "How simple things would be if it weren't for the automatic reaction of the body's flexor muscles."

The words, the pedantry of them, were fitting into that familiar something. As was the sound of his voice.

He said, "It would then merely be a matter of who squeezes the trigger first. But alas, my bullet would reach you in what? Perhaps nine one-thousandths of a second, causing the eight flexor muscles in your forearm instantly to act on their own. Your bullet would reach me with a similar alacrity and we would both be dead."

And things were suddenly clear.

"So it wasn't simply personal after all, between you and Brauer," I said.

He smiled. "I meant what I said about admiring your work."

This he spoke in a Boston Back Bay accent.

This was Walter's shipboard lover.

This was Edward Cable.

He resumed the Midwest accent, which was, perhaps, his own. "I'd dramatically strip off my mustache for you now, Mr. Cobb, as if we were in one of Miss Bourgani's movies. But I'm afraid I'd abrade myself. I'll take it off properly when you're dead. Besides, I'd look a fright with my white upper lip in the midst of all this Turkish-tainted skin."

I stripped off mine.

It did hurt but I felt I had to make the point.

Given the fastidious lift of his right brow, the point seemed lost on him.

He was a different breed of cat.

"I'd hoped we might talk," he said.

"Is that why you're in costume?"

"I thought it would be interesting to hear your approach to the Pasha. I'm quite intrigued at America's involvement in all this."

"I think you mostly like dressing up."

Cable—if indeed that was his name—unfurled a smile that was part irony, part taffeta. "What else do we really have in this world but the small pleasures of a chosen and portrayed self?" he said. "The current of history runs far too deep. You and your Armenian friends and even the Enver Pasha. And yes, even I, as an individual. We are all ultimately helpless. We're all being borne along on the surface of things, moving our arms and our legs, giving the appearance of volition, but our course is set. Miss Bourgani will not stop the slaughter of her people. You will not preserve your country from this war. The Ottoman Empire will soon dissolve."

He paused. He seemed to have finished his point.

"And the German Empire?" I said.

"Ah," he said. "*That* is the deep-running current."

He was right, of course, about the flexor muscles. Still, I was tempted.

I think he saw it in my eyes.

He smiled again. No taffeta.

"I'm a good judge of people," he said, and he had resumed speaking German. "You're not a man who would sacrifice your own life simply to take mine."

"But as you pointed out," I said, shifting to German with him. "We neither of us count for that much."

"Except to ourselves," he said. "Don't mistake me. I admire you for that. And I will freely admit that I share the same attitude. But you understand why I can be so frank with you."

"Because you expect to win this standoff," I said.

We each glanced at the unwavering Luger muzzle of the other.

"Of course," he said.

"I have to ask," I said. "Have you been drawing this out in the expectation that one of your downstairs boys will appear behind me?"

"The thought had crossed my mind," he said.

"Given the silence of my arrival."

"I suppose there are alternate explanations for that."

"There's one," I said. "They're all dead."

He took this in without showing anything on his face.

"Well then," he said, "it's time to change the balance of power."

And in a voice pitched to the back row of the upper balcony, he called out, "Captain, if you please."

There was movement off to my left but nearer to Cable. A door was opening in the side wall.

I glanced.

Lucine emerged first, though a *feldgrau* arm was angled over her chest from left clavicle to right hip and she was dressed in a white nainsook chemise; attached to the uniformed arm was a bareheaded *Kapitän* with golden hair, and in his right hand he was holding the third Luger in the room, muzzled up against the same soft spot on Lucine that I'd threatened on Ströder, between the temple and the ear.

These two sidled into the room and ended up—with Cable saying "That's good"—freestanding an arm's length from the edge of the desk.

I could keep both my Luger and one eye focused on Cable—he knew I would not relinquish that relationship—but I could also clearly see Lucine's peril.

The Hun with the gun to her head was showing only his right shoulder and arm, his right side, his right leg; the corresponding left side of him was pressed against her from behind, his arm across her breasts.

She seemed impossibly small and impossibly fragile in every way but her eyes. Her vast eyes were burning hotly at me and, indeed, if it weren't for a German officer, a German spy, and two extra Lugers, I could have fancied from this look that she'd just stepped into the room to have rough sex with me.

"Selene," I said. "Have they hurt you?"

She said, "Besides throwing a coat around me and making me leave the hotel in my least interesting chemise, no."

"You might imagine from that," Cable said, "what a fruitlessly amusing time we've had in our conversations so far, Miss Bourgani and I. That will change quite dramatically now."

I said to her, "Do you know who this man is?"

"Not who I expected," she said.

"He's the man Brauer was with on the *Lusitania*," I said, glancing at her.

I saw her eyes cut sharply toward him.

But Cable wasn't taking his eyes off me.

I said, "One wouldn't expect the fussy little bookseller from Boston to be capable of saving himself from a sinking ship."

"Who knows?" Cable said. "He could have had a boyhood near a lake."

"But a wolf, on the other hand," I said.

Cable narrowed his gaze at this.

And I said in German, "The wolf is a good swimmer, I think."

He smiled at my knowing about *Der Wolf.*

He answered in German: "The wolf is quite a powerful swimmer, with strong, tight-muscled legs."

This he said with a complex little smirk. At his forcing an image of his body upon me, no doubt.

I have at times a freely associating mind, particularly when I am thrashing inside for a course of action.

And so I was led to a thought about what to do.

Even as Cable said, once again in English, "I'm getting tired of all this. The simplest thing would have been for me to shoot you dead as soon as you appeared in the doorway. But regrettably your own costume caused me too many moments of doubt. The dueling scar was a nice touch. Very realistic."

"This still feels like a standoff," I said.

"I think there was something very personal between you and Selene Bourgani," Cable said.

And I wondered: *Did he know Brauer was dead?* He might suspect it. But he could not know for sure. And he certainly didn't know how.

The thought I had was still working its way along, but it would help if I could get Cable to split his attention.

I moved my gaze to Lucine and she was instantly focused on me and then I quickly cut my eyes to Cable and back to her before returning slowly and fully to him.

"If she dies, so do you," I said.

"Then by reflex it would be all three of us," he said in English. "What an idiotic waste that would be. I am an admirer of the captain here, but what a shame if he were the only one of us left standing."

"I *bet* you're an admirer of the captain," Lucine said.

Cable ignored her. "I don't particularly care one way or the other about her. If you put your pistol down, I can arrange for her to walk away before you and I have a detailed chat. From which there would even be a possible safe exit for you as well."

Did he think I'd believe that?

"Selene," I said. "Our Mr. Cable may suspect something unpleasant has happened to Walter, but he can't know for sure."

"Oh, he asked," Lucine said. "I wouldn't give him the time of day."

Cable was staying calm. The gun was steady. His face was placid. But I could see his chest rise and hold and fall. He was trying to control his breathing.

"He's dead and decomposing in the North Sea," Lucine said.

He flinched ever so slightly at this.

She knew what I needed. If Cable really thought I would do anything to keep a bullet out of Lucine's brain—and he was right—he felt safe from me as long as the *Kapitän* had a gun to her head.

"And you disgusting bastard, Cobb," Lucine hissed. "What you let Brauer do to you to try to save his life."

Cable was breathing faster. His chest was moving; he was trying not to let it move his shoulders, move his hand. "Now that is certainly a lie," he said.

Selene said, "This is no lie. I shot him. It was me. With a pistol from my purse. I shot him in the heart."

Cable believed this. His eyes narrowed ever so slightly. He was thinking about this present balance of power. And I was talking to him in my head: *Go ahead, Eddie. If I shoot you, your Hun shoots my woman. So you can look at her. Just start to turn that pistol. I won't shoot you first because that would kill her too. Just start.*

My growing thought was as firmly rooted in the nature of our bodies as Cable's flexor observations: in the presence of great and sudden lower body pain, a man's dominant hand will automatically move in that direction.

And Cable's Luger started to turn—with the deliberateness of restrained fury—toward Lucine.

So I whipped my Luger downward and to the left, my eye fixing instantly on the target, my hand following my eye in thoughtlessly muscled ease, and I squeezed. And that target was the *Kapitän*'s exposed right knee. And the knee exploded with his shriek and his pistol hand was dropping and Lucine was slipping to her left and from beneath his loosened grasp and I was lifting my pistol, pulling it back toward Cable even as I urged my body to the right even as I leaned away at the hip and at the chest and as my right foot started to slide and my eyes swung toward this pistol that was recently pointing in my direction, the Luger in Cable's hand was in profile now rushing away from me like a bird breaking cover—he was smart, fast smart, he knew if he shot her I'd have him and he knew I was already coming back to him even as he was in those split seconds of figuring out what just happened and I'd have him anyway so he was getting the hell out—and I was coming around and he was already starting to duck and twist away to the side and I thought now of the *Kapitän* and how he might struggle through the pain for a shot and I wasn't ready but I squeezed a round at Cable and the veranda window to the left shattered outward and Cable was ducking low and lunging for the doors and I stopped my slide.

And Lucine cried, "Kit!" and I was swinging back left and the *Kapitän* was fighting his pain with rage even as he buckled downward on his shattered leg and he was pulling his pistol around toward me and I squeezed a round that went elsewhere beyond him and I was propelling right again and the *Kapitän* shot and I felt the whisk of his bullet past my left arm, glad that the pain had fogged his eyes and stiffened his shooting hand and he was falling fast now as the leg crumpled, and I stopped my slide and braced into the floor and I shot him in the right shoulder and then in the left chest and he spun away and backward.

And I was circling the desk and then easing out of the open doors, my pistol in both hands before me, expecting Cable to be waiting to try to gun me down as I came out. But he wasn't there and I figured he was permanently forgoing the gunfight. He was a pro. He was not a man who would seriously risk his own life simply to try to take mine, at least not with that sudden shift in the balance of power.

He would be content to track me later. So I needed to deal with this now.

I was falling behind and I dashed along the veranda and down the steps to the loggia below and he was nowhere before me in the arcade, but the light from the villa was spilling into the yard and I heard a distant panting thump going outward and I looked into the grounds at the back of the house and I saw him vanishing into the dark.

And I ran. Ran hard. Onto concrete and around a fountain and along the turf and into the same shadow where Cable had disappeared, my eyes adjusting to the night. The stars were very bright. I went down the back stairs of the terrace and onto a slope that fell toward the Bosporus, and maybe seventy-five yards away was a boat dock lit by a single electric lamp on a high post, and there was Cable jumping into a twenty-foot two-seat runabout.

I scrambled downward as fast as I could without pitching forward but the runabout's engine was beginning to spark into life and it was revving now and then fading and revving again and I stopped and I sat down on the slope at once and planted my elbows on my thighs and I held the Luger up before me in both hands and this was about a hundred-foot shot and he was lit just enough by stars and electric spill for me to see him as a dark shape and he was hunched forward working at the throttle and spark but he wasn't sitting down yet—he still had to cast off—and I sighted between him and the bollard on the dock and I waited, and he rose, crouching a little, but I had enough of his torso as he moved. I had him now, and I squeezed and the pistol barked and he rose up and backed away, toward the portside, and I shifted and sighted and squeezed again and his dark shape veered farther to port and over the gunwale and was gone.

The boat sat there, its engine idling, and I rose and I walked down the slope and along the dock, and the runabout's engine muttered and muttered and I arrived. And the boat was empty. I stepped in and switched the engine off, and it sputtered and fell silent.

The boat rocked a little.

The night was quiet.

The Bosporus was running past, and Edward Cable was gone. Dead. Carried away by the deep current of history that was bearing us all.

60

I walked back along the dock with the Luger still in my hand, feeling comfortable with it there, and a figure was running down the slope toward me. But before my shooting hand could rise, I heard Arshak's voice. "Cobb. Are you all right?"

I walked more briskly now. We'd made quite a lot of noise in the last few minutes.

Arshak and I met beneath the electric light at the front end of the dock.

"For the moment," I said to him. "Let's get out of here."

Arshak nodded and we jogged up the slope and across the courtyard and into the loggia.

Lucine was waiting just inside the doors of the grand hall. She was wearing a long, black velvet cape, which she held tightly closed over her chemise.

I stopped before her and we touched for a moment but only with our eyes, and then the three of us hustled across the floor and around the dead guard and out into the front courtyard and things were quiet still. Ahead the two entrance guards were gone, and then I saw them inside the wall, where Arshak had dragged them out of sight.

We paused at the front gate and looked. Things were quiet and we beat it back north to the Unic.

Here we paused a moment, huddled together on the off-road side of the taxi.

I said, "We are all three of us marked now to be hunted down. By the Germans and Turks both. But I've got a way out for us. There's a launch from my embassy waiting to take us to an American ship. We can leave Istanbul. We *have* to leave Istanbul. Without delay."

Arshak and Lucine looked at each other briefly. Arshak nodded a single, slow nod to her.

And Lucine took my hand.

I said to Arshak, "The foot of the street at the west end of the dry docks. Near where you picked me up yesterday."

He stepped away.

Lucine tugged on my hand and led me into the tonneau.

The Unic engine—familiar now, and comforting at last—muttered into life and we turned back toward the city and headed off.

Lucine held tightly to my hand.

We said nothing for a long while. My body was letting go from the clench and rush and thrash of the past hour. And I figured Lucine and I would have time for talk and time for our own rush and thrash when we were together upon the sea once again. I figured I would have a chance to speak her real name out loud.

After a while she leaned into me. And she said, "Thank you."

Only now did it strike me how little we'd actually said to each other through all this.

I figured how it maybe was a sign that a man and a woman were actually becoming something together when you could be comfortable in long silences.

So I said "You're welcome." and she kept her head on my shoulder and we fell silent again. As silent as her motion pictures. One of her good ones. No title cards necessary.

And then we were parked at the foot of Tophane Iskelesi Caddesi.

Lucine and I let go of our hands and we got out of the Unic into the moist dark and a muezzin's voice began its call to prayer somewhere to the north of us and we started down the cobbled quay toward the water and another cry began to the south. These songs came from the strongest voices of the most intensely faithful, but they were still very distant. They were small cries against a very large darkness. And the stars that were lighting our path away from this city, this country, were barely enough for us to see.

But soon I could make out the launch moored at the quay and a figure was coming out of the dark. And another behind it. Lucine and Arshak and I stopped.

A bright light bloomed in the middle of the nearest figure. A flashlight, which flared blindingly into my face and then scanned down my chest.

I was a German officer.

"Steve," the voice of the near figure said.

The rear shadow came forward, rattling a rifle.

"Ralph sent me," I said.

"Hold on," the first voice said to Steve. And then to me: "You are?"

"Christopher Cobb," I said. "I needed the disguise."

The man with the flashlight drew near, shining it now on Arshak and on Lucine.

"I told Hansen there might be one or two others who had to go with me."

"Just follow my light," the man said and the beam fell to the cobbles and he began to move away.

I turned to Lucine. Arshak had backed off a couple of paces.

Lucine came forward to me.

She stood very close, though we did not touch. She smelled of forest and of newly mown hay, of musk and of lavender. This was my first smell of her, from the *Lusitania,* the smell of her when we first lay down naked together. She'd put this on to kill Enver Pasha. And I knew what was coming. I figured this was the last time she would ever smell like this.

She said, "I can't go, my darling Kit. He might be right. I might simply be swept along and the world will have its way with all of us. But I can make no other choice. We'll stay and do what we can."

I took her into my arms. And I kissed her long enough and deep enough so she could know that I understood, and that I was riven with regret.

The kiss ended. We held each other a moment, our faces too dark to read.

"I'll write the news of what I've seen," I said.

As deep as the darkness was upon that quay in Istanbul, the stars let me see the tears that came now to her eyes.

And I let go of her and she turned and she walked past Arshak who had drawn near.

He nodded. I nodded. He did not offer his hand. Give the old ham this: he was content tonight to play a minor part; he knew that the final touch should be hers.

He turned and followed his daughter.

And I followed the flashlight onto the launch and the engine started up and I moved to the stern as we churned away from shore, Lucine and Arshak vanishing into the dark and the voices of the muezzins dying away.

Cable was wrong about the currents carrying us away. For all our insignificance and helplessness, we were actually like the passengers of the *Lusitania* going down. We couldn't save the ship. We couldn't prevent the consequences in the world. We couldn't save a thousand lives. But at least we could grab on to a deck chair and try to save the next life who floated past.

4